Violya

IN THE HEART OF THE MOUNTAINS
BOOK TWO

Rosalyn Kelly

Violya
by Rosalyn Kelly

This paperback edition (1) published by NValters Publishing
UK December 2019
Cover design © Damonza

Publisher's Note
This novel is entirely a work of fiction.
The names, characters and incidents portrayed in it are the work
of the author's imagination. Any resemblance to actual persons,
living or dead, events or localities is entirely coincidental.

For more information about this and other titles by this author,
please visit www.rosalynkelly.co.uk

ISBN 978-1-9998166-5-0

For my dad, Brian

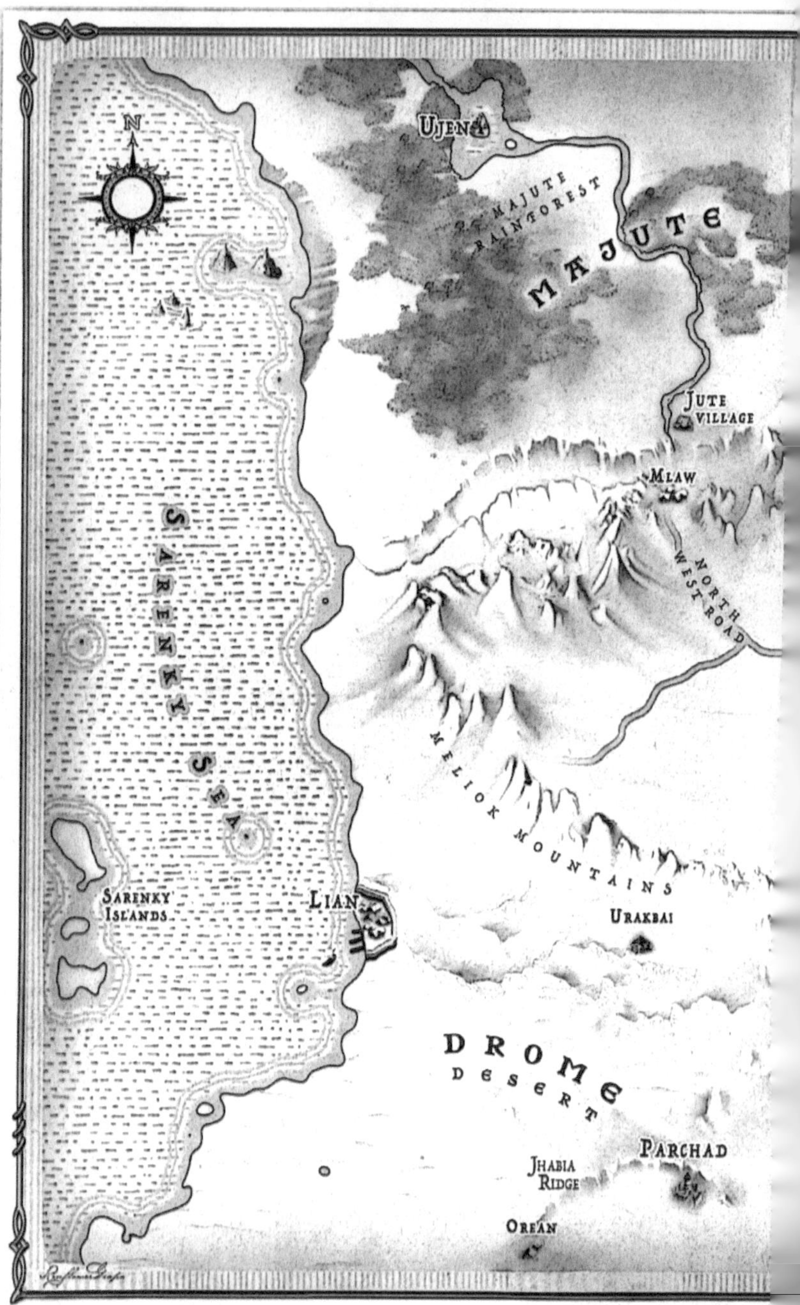

N
SARENKY SEA
SARENKY ISLANDS
LIAN
UJEN
MAJUTE RAINFOREST
MAJUTE
JUTE VILLAGE
MLAW
NORTH WEST ROAD
MELIOK MOUNTAINS
URAKBAI
DROME DESERT
JHABIA RIDGE
OREAN
PARCHAD

For my dad, Brian

N
UJENA
MAJUTE RAINFOREST
MAJUTE
JUTE VILLAGE
MLAW
NORTH WEST ROAD
SARENKY SEA
MELIOK MOUNTAINS
URAKBAI
SARENKY ISLANDS
LIAN
DROME
DESERT
JHABIA RIDGE
PARCHAD
OREAN

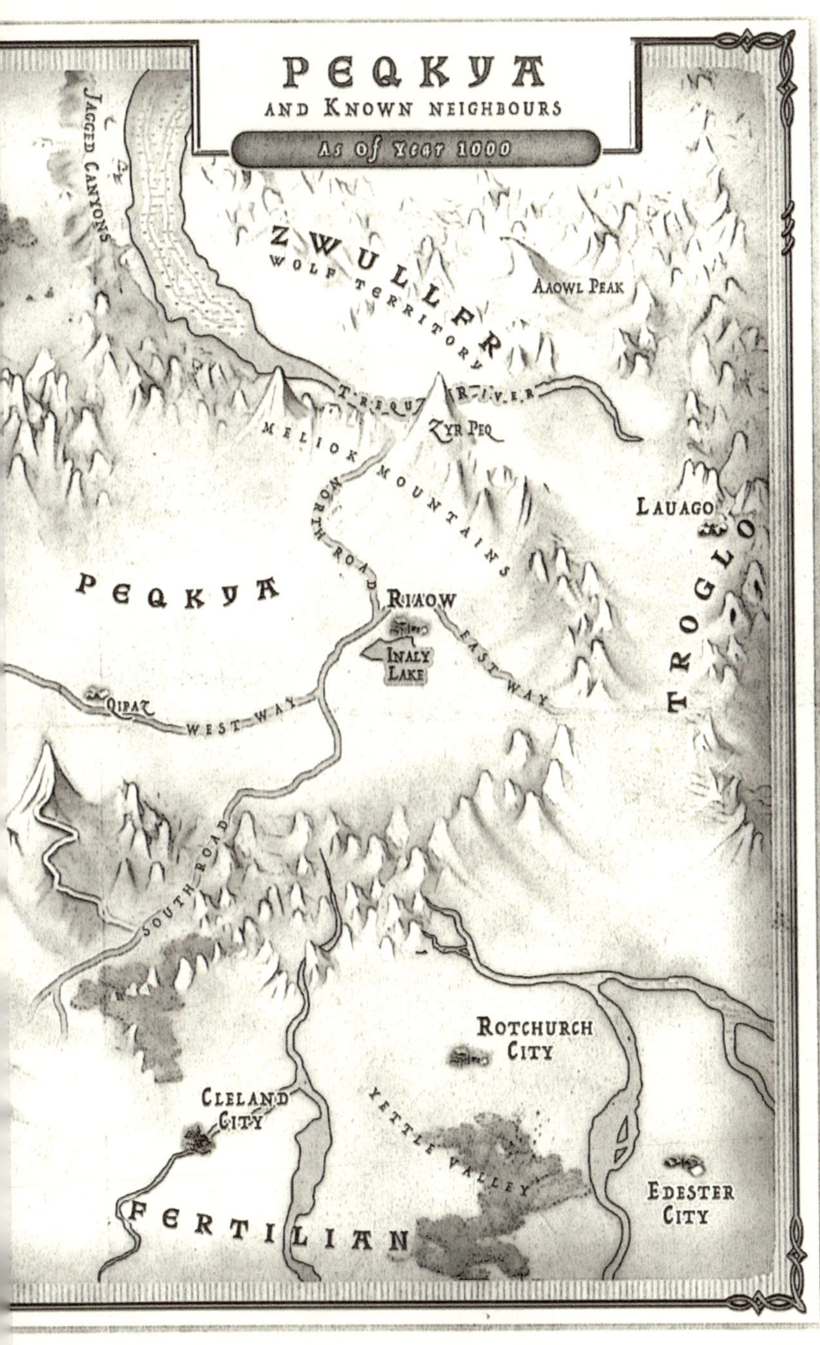

PEQKYA
AND KNOWN NEIGHBOURS
As of Year 1000
JAGGED CANYONS
ZWULLER
WOLF TERRITORY
AAOWL PEAK
TREQUZ RIVER
MELIOK MOUNTAINS
ZYR PEQ
LAUAGO
NORTH ROAD
PEQKYA
RIAOW
INALY LAKE
EAST WAY
TROGLO
QIPAZ
WEST WAY
SOUTH ROAD
ROTCHURCH CITY
CLELAND CITY
YETTLE VALLEY
EDESTER CITY
FERTILIAN

1

VIOLYA

808

"Cockfaces," the warrior Violya hissed as the enemy's ramshackle camp came into view.

In the dead of night, lit only by the camp's pathetic fires that spat and sizzled against the heavy snowfall, a small, deadly force of one hundred Peqkian warriors and one hundred Jute fighters silently climbed down the mountain slope.

The winding trail wasn't an option. Now plugged with deep snow, it was being watched by twitchy desert cammers, posted on the perimeter while their comrades slept. The soldiers huddled together, shivering violently. Misshapen, ugly humps poked out of thin, wretched uniforms not suitable for the cold weather.

The cammer soldiers eyed the rocky incline and the trail which they'd come from, surveying the dark, ominous hunks of jagged rock and looming boulders. The dwindling flames cast long shadows, and heads jerked at any hint of movement. Their white-knuckled, trembling hands gripped their swords. As if their weapons would save them.

Every now and then they glanced desperately at the start of the snaking path that led down the southern slopes and across the wastelands. A four-day trek away was the border to their own miserable sand-choked nation. But they hadn't made it to the dunes in time.

V had caught up to them. And now they would pay.

The Dromedars were crammed in the middle of a large, flat area of the mountains that jutted out with a sharp cliff below. In the shadows of the huge boulders, where this level expanse met the mountain slope, V eased herself gently from the rocks, meticulously placing one foot then the next in the snow.

Having left their bulky fur coats, gloves and movement-hindering wrappings back at their camp with the animals, the Peqkians and Jutes deftly landed around her.

"Tents," the warrior Lizya whispered to V. "First we've seen."

In the midst of the camp were seven small tents for the important cammers, the animal hide sagging under the settling snow. For three weeks V's small force had driven the hump-backed invaders out of the capital, out of the country, nipped and harried at their heels, and picked off the stragglers. These one thousand soldiers were the last dregs of the Dromedar army that remained in Peqkya.

"The male-child cammer has to be here," V said.

She itched to finish him. In a moment of uncharacteristic emotion back in Riaow, she'd had the chance to slice the zhaq Crown Prince of Drome in two but she'd toyed with him, wanted to torture him for what he'd done, for who he'd murdered. But he'd got away, minus his arms, and she was racked with guilt that gnawed at her. The regret strangled her every thought, like ivy twisting around a tree.

Foolish mistake, warrior, V berated herself again. But he was here. He had to be. And she'd have her vengeance.

The magic in V's blood pulsed in her ears.

Oh, use me, use me, use meee! We'll wreak devastation bigger than the world has ever seen… a rain of rocks to crush their cammer bodies… a flood of epic proportions to drown them all… a surge of wind to shove them over the edge of the cliff… a…

Be quiet, V snapped, *we have a plan.* The magic retreated, simmering in her veins. Her long-repressed power had erupted during the battle in Riaow but had been silent since. She would learn how to master it from the Stone Prophetess Sybilya, but until then, she couldn't risk using it and unleashing more harm than good.

The Jutes formed into tight rows, their copious weapons on show: blades of all sizes, throwing stars and axes. The pink-skinned, intricately inked creatures from the rainforest realm of Majute stood no taller than V's belly. Their small frames barely dented the calf-high snow.

V and her warriors shifted behind, soundlessly drawing their swords. The crackling fires and fitful hum of snoring cammers the only noise.

In the gloom, the Jute captain Brinjinqa bowed low to her, his blue hair fashioned into spikes just missing her hands.

"My dear, V," Brin said with a twinkle in his black beady eyes that always seemed to be looking everywhere at once, "we thank you for the opportunity to use this." He held up the vial of red liquid that hung around his neck and chuckled to himself.

Ridiculously strong pitfire juice, he'd called it. Pitfire was a crop grown in Majute. She'd first seen it when she'd ventured there leading a Peqkian trading party. When boiled and prepared as a drink it was as potent as wine or poppy.

It was a risk.

The Jutes hadn't requested to use it until now and she had no idea what it would do. She'd only seen people drunk and lethargic on it. But the deep snow was no obstacle for the light-footed Jutes and, as her force was outnumbered, the attack required speed. She trusted Brin. His ruler had sent him and his fighters with V. They had fought bravely beside the Peqkians since the invasion and were yet to take any casualties.

Brin whispered to V, "When we slow, it's safe to approach, as the pitfire will be wearing off. When we are in the high state, we cannot tell friend from foe, only others of our kind."

She nodded and Brin's large grin revealed front teeth that had been filed to sharp points.

He unstoppered the vial from around his neck and held it up to his face. One hundred Jutes did the same in complete unison. As one, each took the tiniest sip, carefully replaced the stopper, shuddered, and set off across the snow at such a speed that the Peqkians were momentarily left behind.

"Ack, ack, ack!" The Jutes' war cry increased in volume as they got closer to the camp.

"Love those crazy little freaks," the warrior Finya said.

Mangled shouts rose from the soldiers on guard as a sea of acking creatures smashed into them. The Jutes swirled like a tornado tossing cammers out of the way or trampling them flat to the ground. The Jute twister swept nearer and nearer to the tents on a random, jerky course, causing utter chaos.

Each individual Jute was going berserk. They slashed with knives, cleaved with claw-like hands, shredded with sharp teeth. But they moved as a whole. The mass crashed forward, a froth of frenzied fighters that blitzed a path to the tents for the Peqkians.

Throwing off sleep, cammer soldiers scrambled to their feet, unsheathed swords or jumped out of the way. All their attention focused on the progressing churn of pink bodies.

V signalled to her warriors and they charged. The snow hindered their momentum but the noisy Jutes masked the sound of their approach. They reached the edges of the camp and slew distracted cammers who fell in droves. Soldiers turned to face them and V and her warriors fought wave after wave of hump-backed Dromedars. She pushed forward to the tents, flattening anything that stood in her way, engaging without pause and storming through hastily-formed defensive lines as if they were mere blades of grass under her boots – she could not allow those under cover to escape.

This is your end Crown Prince!

Soldiers formed a muddled defence outside the tents, eyes on the Jutes who were rapidly advancing. Cammer swords came up to attack but the Jutes didn't engage. The whirlwind surrounded the tents and formed a circular wall of moving pink-skinned, blue-haired bodies.

The Jutes who faced the tents snarled and acked, trapping the soldiers and tent inhabitants and isolating them from the rest of the camp. Those who faced outward engaged any cammer that came near. The soldiers pressed in, attempting to find a way through the berserker Jutes to save those behind.

V and her warriors blazed their way through incompetent soldiers, no match for her seasoned warriors. Desert blood drenched the mountain rocks, doused fires, splashed up her arms and spurted across her face. The tang of iron clogged her nostrils and the wet gore slid past her lips to cover her tongue and teeth in a hot, sticky film. But there was only one whose blood she longed to spill and she was almost upon him.

As her company neared the tents, the Jutes' movements slowed. V directed her warriors to form a protective wall around the Jutes, whose chests heaved as they looked one another over checking for injuries and cuts. All were exalted, laughing, grinning and yammering to each other in their singsong language. They parted like water to allow V and twenty of her warriors through and then fluidly closed the gap.

Brin passed V as he and his Jutes continued to circle, sweeping his hand to the tents as if in offering.

"All yours, my dear," the Jute captain said.

She thumped her fist to her chest in thanks and beckoned to her warriors.

Soldiers protected those still in the tents, swords drawn and legs quaking. A few tent occupants had joined the fight, but the one she sought was injured. *He won't have left the tent.*

V whistled orders to her women and they struck the Dromedars down. When every cammer was on the ground, groaning in pain or crying out in their last moments before death, V sliced a deep gash in the side of the first tent and the warrior Daya ripped the cloth apart.

Empty.

The second contained an older cammer soldier, whimpering. The third, fourth and fifth were all empty. The sixth contained three soldiers in uniforms made of expensive cloth clutching each other.

The seventh…

Daya stared at V, and she knew.

The Crown Prince, the armless male-child Ammad, was not there. The worm had made it back to Drome.

Internally, V raged. Her magic screamed along with her, pummelled at her bones, sloshed about in her gut. She wanted to punch great holes into nearby boulders, thrash and kick. But she controlled her emotions. The expression on her face and stiffness of her stance betrayed nothing.

"Zhaq," the novice warrior, Monya, yelled, unable to master her emotions like the older warriors. In a frenzy, she slashed the tent to shreds with her sword.

The youngblood had expressed all of their frustrations, but once done, she studied her feet.

V took a long, slow breath.

The Jutes parted as she strode from the flattened tents, tailed by her warriors. Exhausted, half-frozen cammer faces gawped at her, but cowered as she passed. Her tall stature, glowing black skin, red hair and palms the colour of poppies marked her as different from her fellow warriors and sparked fear in the Dromedars.

The soldiers had no fight left in them. They lowered their swords, rooted to the spot. Most, she noticed, had metal cuffs around their wrists. Slaves. They followed orders. And now that the important cammers in the tents – their masters – were dead, these males posed no threat.

There is no glory in a needless slaughter. Most of the cammers wouldn't survive much longer without food and water. And she doubted the desert would be forthcoming.

In the east, the sun was starting to rise.

Her magic granted her the ability to speak in any tongue. In Dromedari, she said, "Drop your weapons."

The soldiers obeyed without hesitation and the thump and clang of falling steel echoed across the plain. She pointed with her sword to the path that led down the mountain. "Any soldier who is still here when the sun comes up will be executed. Run."

The soldiers nearest to her shambled towards the path, grabbing up packs and raggedy blankets as they went. Soon those further back understood what was happening and scurried behind them.

To the Jutes, V said, "Rest. You earned it."

To her warriors, she said, "We follow them to the border. Pick off any who lag behind. Let's get these cammer cockfaces out of our country once and for all."

***

A few days later, the last of the Drome soldiers slid, stumbled and fell down the loose rock of the earthquake landslide that had first opened an entrance for them at the Peqkian border.

Clouds of dust flew up behind them. They ran as fast as their cammer legs would take them across the wasteland the earthquake had torn apart and towards the desert.

Beyond the fleeing males were vast dunes, almost mountains in themselves, and undulating red sand for as far as the eye could see.

Somewhere out there was the one she sought. The Crown Prince of Drome. Ammad. He'd murdered Melokai Ramya. His army had invaded Peqkya to claim the country as his own. And he'd been responsible for her best friend's death. *Emmya.* She missed Emmya. He'd caused the deaths of so many Peqkians.

Was he alive? Until she saw him dead, she would believe it.

I will have my revenge.

After a while, Lizya touched her forearm and raised an eyebrow in question.

V turned to see her warriors poised and waiting for her order. They would follow her into Drome, into the vast desert without question. It still felt strange that she was their leader. Was responsible for her actions and the actions of many others.

She wanted to charge into the dunes, her quarry was that way. She'd hunt him down and finish him as she should've done when she'd had the chance.

But… There was something that needed V's attention now more than the armless worm.

"We return to Riaow," the red-haired warrior said. "Peqkya needs us."

2

VIOLYA

ໝ

V led her warriors and the Jutes toward Riaow, approaching from the South Road and following the path of destruction caused by the Drome army.

On the outskirts of the city they were greeted by warriors and one sent a clevercat ahead to find the warrior Laurya, who V had left in charge. They rode slowly down the wide, tree-lined road that ran directly to the Melokai's enclosure and army barracks at the centre of the city.

They passed destroyed dome-shaped wooden huts, the colourful facades now blackened with thick soot. Most of the woodcarvers' quarter was in ruins, the wooden buildings reduced to ash. Statues of past Melokais were mutilated beyond recognition, and trees that had stood for thousands of years had been scorched to stumps. The air was choked with a smoky, rotten tang. A smell that would linger stubbornly for a long time.

They passed the turning onto the circular Tatya Highway, the road in which V and her warriors had roused the Riats to fight back against the invaders. Large dents gouged the earth, no doubt from the galloping hooves of their ponies.

The heavy snowfall of weeks earlier had given way to light flurries, more typical of this time of year. The grey,

9

overcast day bore a sharp chill but the ground was still too warm for the snow to settle. Snowflakes fluttered, the bright white flecks a stark contrast against the charred city.

Six weeks had passed since the Drome invasion and the bloody aftermath of the battle. The corpses and gore had been cleared, and the city rang with the hammering of nails and the clanging of tools. The bustle of resolute activity. Riat women wrapped up in furs rebuilt huts gutted by fire, clearing away debris and putting their city back together. The women directed peons in goat-hair overcoats, who followed instructions with heads down and voices low.

Cats dashed from the maze of back alleyways and streets that sprawled off the main thoroughfare. They meowed as they jumped up at the animals. V's horse snorted as the felines weaved in and out of its legs, mewing up at V.

The Riats stared as the procession passed, eyeing with suspicion not only the Jutes riding their large shiny beetles, but V and her warriors too. The betrayal of Peqkians against their own was still raw. The once-trusting Riats now wary.

A woman walked alongside V. "What's your name?"

"Violya. V."

"I saw you and your warriors as you rode through the city calling us out to fight. And you chased the cammers out. You saved us. You saved Peqkya. We've all been talking about the red-haired warrior." The woman dipped her chin reverently.

She stepped back and shouted to all those around her, "V! V and her warriors and the pygmies have returned!"

Cheers rose from the women nearby and more Riats came from the backstreets to whoop and clap and wave at them.

"They're called Jutes," Fin told the woman as she passed.

"V and her warriors and the Jutes have returned!" the woman shouted again.

Soon the chant was taken up by the woman's companions and, as V and her procession moved deeper into the city, the noise brought residents forward.

Onlookers lined the street, all shouting V's name and cheering.

"I'm no hero," V said to Lizya, who rode alongside her.

"Well, I am," Lizya said with a huge grin. She waved back to the crowds, bowed and pumped her fist in the air.

"Isn't this remarkable," Brin said, riding his beetle behind them. "You Peqkians have some strange customs. Do you always welcome each other home from adventures as such?"

Lizya guffawed. "Not always."

Brin copied Lizya's movements and flourished his three-fingered, claw-like hand at the crowds.

V glanced over her shoulder. All her warriors smiled and waved, following Lizya's lead. The Jutes mirrored Brin's movements.

It felt odd to V that her actions should be celebrated, that she had become known to the Riats. *I am a warrior, I protected my country, I did my job.* But she raised her hand tentatively, smiling at those who caught her eye.

The noise of the cats and the crowds was overwhelming as they approached the Melokai's enclosure. The gates, that had remained open for as long as V could remember, were now closed. Being open had aided the attack on Melokai Ramya. The warriors standing guard identified them and the gates slowly opened. V and her procession rode into the courtyard. It had been cleansed of all signs of the battle.

The warriors within stood to attention and stable-peons ran out to tend to the horses. V dismounted and headed towards Laurya, who stood waiting for her. They clutched each other's hands, bumped their chests together and slapped each other on the back in welcome. V stepped aside to allow Lizya, Fin and Daya to each greet the warrior.

"Welcome back," Laurya said.

"The cammers are out of our country," V said. "We've left warriors at the border to guard the landslide road and the southern stretch, and replaced those who Ashya killed to ease the Drome army's entry."

Laurya nodded. "Riaow is secure, all fires tamed."

"Come, let us get some food, and discuss," V said as her stomach grumbled.

Laurya led them through to the warriors' mess hall, gave orders to the kitchen then returned to sit opposite V as the warriors and Jutes took their seats.

"The bodies of Ashya, her traitorous warriors and the cammers were dragged and dumped in a pit outside the city, covered with dirt to rot and feed the worms," Laurya said. "Our own dead were given a warrior's burial in the square. The pyre burned for many days, the ashes of those we loved scattered through the country that loved them. The huts we can rebuild, but the House of Knowledge was ravaged. The stone crumbled as the mortar melted." Laurya paused her report as crispbreads and pots of pickle chutney were brought out by serving peons and placed on the table.

V smiled. "My favourite."

"I know," Laurya replied with a wink.

Daya pulled a plate towards her. "Any food is my favourite, right now."

As V ate, Laurya continued. "A week or so ago we captured a group of Dromedars hiding in the forests by Inaly Lake. There were nearly one hundred of them. Incredible that they had evaded our notice until then. They made a stupid mistake and we captured them. They surrendered immediately, begged for mercy and we have them in our prison. There was one who led them."

"You should've butchered them all," Monya blurted and then looked intensely at a bowl of chutney.

"Laurya did the right thing, Monya," V said. "We could learn something from them, from this leader who kept them hidden. They could prove useful."

Bowls of steaming spicy chicken soup were placed on the table.

"Ah, now this is my favourite," Lizya exclaimed and leaned over the table to plant a smacking kiss on Laurya's forehead.

Laurya winked again.

"What is this?" Brin asked, holding up a brimming cup.

"Wine," Lizya said. "Probably like water to you after that pitfire juice."

Brin took a sip. Grimaced and then grinned. He glugged back the rest of the wine in one go. One hundred Jutes around the hall did the same. More wine was called for.

"What of the rebellious peons?" V asked.

"Most died in the battle. Some immediately after as an angry mob of Riat women hunted them down. Two hundred survived, including one of the leaders. They're in the prison too. It's pretty cramped down there."

Brin turned, vomited on the floor behind him and then continued to drink more wine. The Jutes were getting raucous and rowdy. Their unified movement fracturing as they became intoxicated.

"They love to drink," Fin laughed and clapped Brin on the shoulder who burped. "It's an honour for them to be drunk. You should've seen them go at it on pitfire juice in Majute."

"Speaking of Majute, the scholar and trader that you sent for arrived back from Mlaw yesterday. Safe and well."

"Good," V said, thankful for their safety.

"Amya," Laurya called.

A ginger clevercat came bounding from the back of the hall where other clevercat messengers idled and cleaned themselves. Amya was larger than average, about the size of a large goat, and she jumped onto the table in front of V, sending empty dishes flying.

The clatter woke her pet caterpillar with a start. The

size of a kitten and just as soft, Emmo had been fast asleep in her favourite spot around V's neck. She stuck out four of her ten berry-red feet and squeaked her annoyance at the clevercat.

V petted Emmo's orange head. "Now, now, girl." She pulled a crumpled pitfire leaf from a pocket and gave it to the caterpillar to munch on.

"This is your new clevercat, V," Laurya said. "Figured you were going to need one now that you're in charge of the army."

In charge of the Peqkian army? V's stomach lurched as it did every time she remembered her position. "Well, for now at least. Until they appoint a new Head Warrior." V turned to her messenger. "Amya, find apprentice scholar Robya and assistant trader Jozya and ask if they'll come to the warrior's mess hall."

The ginger cat mewed her understanding and jumped from the table to another hiss from Emmo.

Serving peons cleared away the plates and brought out baked apple with honey. Fin dove for the nearest bowl with a delighted gesture to Laurya.

"So, what happens now then?" Lizya said rolling her shoulder and grimacing at an old injury.

"Melokai Ramya's old councillors have been running the show, but everyone's waiting for blessed Sybilya to call a Melokai Choosing Ceremony," Laurya replied.

V could not feel Sybilya's presence; hadn't felt it now for many weeks. It worried her. As soon as time permitted, she would visit the Stone Prophetess' hut and check on the great lady.

"So, V, did you do the…" Laurya mimed shooting blasts from her hands, "again?"

Lizya laughed and slapped the table. "No, she didn't. And we're all bloody waiting for it. Starting to think we imagined it to be honest."

"V," a voice shouted from the doorway cutting through the rowdy Jutes and chitter of the cats.

There stood a tall, willowy woman, wilting under all the attention now directed at her. In front, was a short, slight woman with beautifully pronounced feline features.

"Oh, V!" Jozya, the assistant trader, shouted again and held up her arms. She attempted to wade through the writhing mass of cats to get to V.

V jogged towards the women, the cats parting for her and mewing as she passed. She pulled Joz and Robya into a tight embrace and led them to some chairs.

Robya sat and clutched her hands in her lap. Emmo crawled down V's arm and then jumped into the lap of the apprentice scholar. Robya smiled and stroked the caterpillar.

Joz was as animated as ever, her arms flying about as she babbled, "Oh, V. What on earth has happened? One minute we're venturing into Majute, the next I hear my profession leader and my fellow assistant trader are the instigators of a rebellion against our dear Melokai Ramya. Rivya and Toya! I honestly cannot believe it. I didn't suspect a thing."

"I don't think anyone did," V said.

"Riv had such a strong relationship with the Dromedars, but for trade," Joz said. "Not to make war. I mean, she was friendly with one of the ruler's many concubines, Jakira, and often stayed with her when we visited. And Jakira had a son, he was always sniffing around our trade delegations and leering at our warriors. Silly, vain boy. But he was someone important. Oh, wait…"

Joz's hand flew to her mouth and her eyes widened. "Riv was friends with Jakira and she's the Crown Prince of Drome's mother. They must've cooked up the plan." Joz's lips clenched shut and her entire body shook with anger. "How could she!"

"The Crown Prince of Drome is called Ammad el Wakrime," Robya said quietly.

V's magic bristled at the name. The knot in her chest

constricted. *I will have my revenge. But first, Peqkya.*

"Yes. That's it," Joz shuddered. "Are you well, V? There are rumours going around that you have The Sight! That you used magic."

V smiled and opened her mouth to reply but Sybilya's sudden, urgent voice filled her mind. *"Come now,"* the prophetess said, *"bring the councillors."*

V rode a pony ahead of Melokai Ramya's surviving councillors: Head Scholar Chaz, Head Speaker Zecky, Mother of Mothers Naomya and Head Teller Omya. Hanya, Ramya's Head Courtesan, had died in the battle. The warrior Lizya brought up the rear.

Gogo, the Head Warrior who V had loved, was noticeably, painfully absent – murdered as part of the traitorous Head Trader Riv's plot. *Where is Riv now? Hiding in Drome with that worm prince, I expect.*

No one in the party said a word. V had allowed herself and her returning warriors to relax in the mess hall, but the fresh wound of the invasion had yet to close. The pain of Melokai Ramya's death was still raw. Each was alone with their thoughts as they travelled through the city.

They reached the Mount of Pines and started to climb, passing under the blue arches that wove up the hill marking the path to the Stone Prophetess' simple wooden hut at the top. The paint was shearing off in clumps now, the wood of the arches cracked and rotting. The deterioration was stark compared to V's last visit, and she dreaded what she would find in the hut.

The cats were unusually silent, watchful, cautious. They kept their distance but tracked the group's progress. All knew Sybilya would call a Melokai Choosing Ceremony.

As was customary, the previous Melokai's councillors would have their tongues removed. The councillors she travelled with had made the oath; knew they would relinquish their titles at the end of their tenure and be muted. Sybilya cautioned that those who had tasted power were reluctant to surrender it, but without speech they could not corrupt the minds of others. To keep power distributed evenly and ensure no stagnation, new councillors were chosen with each new Melokai, usually every decade.

V's purpose was to keep the councillors safe whilst they attempted to rule the country until a new Melokai and council was chosen, and Lizya was here to ensure their protection.

At the summit, they dismounted. Lizya waited outside with Emmo as V followed the four councillors into the wooden hut. It stank of cat excrement and dirt. The air was stale, the pine scent from the trees bullied out by decay.

By a slow death.

Sybilya was now almost stone. She sat, as she had for the past three hundred years, on a wooden tree stump. Straight-backed, hands resting on knees. Her huge feet and legs had turned to stone many years ago, and it had been creeping to her hands when V last saw her.

Now, the only part of the prophetess that was not stone was her face, but it was edging past her hairline and along her jaw. Her once glorious, long red hair was now completely grey.

The councillors fanned out in a half circle in front of the prophetess. V positioned herself behind them and to one side. They looked respectfully up at Sybilya, eyes wet with tears, faces drawn and lips downturned at her obvious demise.

The great lady blinked slowly. Her face strained with the effort. Her little, wrinkled mouth creaked open and she attempted to form words. Instead she emitted a faint huff. She tried a second time but could not even muster a stirring of air.

Sybilya's presence filled V's mind, and as the councillors stood more upright, V understood it had also filled theirs. The Stone Prophetess could no longer form physical words.

"Welcome all," Sybilya said in V's mind. Her voice was frail, the words drawn out with long pauses. "It is time for a new Melokai."

The councillors nodded; they were all resigned to their fate. They'd known the end when they had taken on the title.

"Councillors, I release you from your oaths."

The councillors gasped, cast sideways glances at one another. This declaration meant they would keep their status and their tongues. Relief swept through the hut like the gust of wind that precedes a storm.

"You served Melokai Ramya well. You will serve the new Melokai as she sees fit."

The councillors lowered their heads in agreement.

"Now. We must have a new Melokai." Sybilya paused as if mustering the energy to continue. Eventually she said, "There will be no Choosing Ceremony. For I have chosen."

Shocked murmurs rippled between the councillors.

"Violya, come forward."

Faces turned towards V. The eunuch Chaz beckoned her forward.

Wide-eyed, she stepped in front of Sybilya. The councillors moved to either side to give her space; the weight of their gaze heavy upon her.

V stared at the prophetess and then down at her feet.

"Violya, do you accept the position of Melokai of Peqkya?"

Is this really happening? Could I refuse? "Yes," V mumbled.

"And you understand at the end of your reign your tongue will be taken, and you will be banished?"

"I understand."

"This oath is binding, Violya."

"I am bound, Stone Prophetess."

With a great effort, Sybilya purred, a soothing, contented sound. "Go," Sybilya said after a while. "I will speak now to the Melokai."

The councillors bowed low and exited the hut.

When they were alone, V spoke, "Sybilya, I am no Melokai, I am a warrior. I do not know how to rule a country."

"You will make the right decisions, V. Believe in yourself. Trust your instinct."

Sybilya's presence trickled away like water through fingers and V grasped at it desperately. She needed the great lady to soothe her self-doubt, to bolster her courage.

In a faint but firm voice, the Stone Prophetess said, "Peqkya will never be the same again. Customs must change if the nation is to survive. Customs must change…"

V waited for more, longed for another word, but Sybilya's presence had retreated into her stone body.

V stumbled from the hut in a daze. Outside, she took a long, deep breath of the crisp air.

Lizya was mounted and holding V's pony. The warrior waited for V to mount and then said, "What was that all about? The councillors look like they've seen a cat fly."

"Zhaq," V said. "I'm the new Melokai of Peqkya."

3

JESSIMA

୧୬୫୬

Air. Glorious, fresh air. Salty, fishy, but air nonetheless.

Queen Jessima Cleland of Fertilian sucked it down greedily. She felt giddy on it, as if she'd consumed one too many sweet plum wines.

Ahead lay the legendary walled city of Lian. A place she'd heard of her entire life, but never visited. She had finally arrived.

Although, not quite.

"Wait here," Lord Andrew Chattergoon's commanding voice travelled down the tunnel. "Get the Queen to her feet."

The donkey pulling Jessima's sand sled stopped, and promptly emptied its bowels in uncomfortably close proximity to her head. Had she still been moving, she would've gently bumped over it. Now still, the dung's pungent damp-weather smell threatened to overwhelm the fishiness. A few moments later two ladies-in-waiting hurried to her side. They carefully helped her up from the sled, led her away from the steaming pile and fussed about her. After many hours lying on the cushioned wooden slats, Jessima's legs wobbled like a new-born foal as she put weight on them. She smoothed the proud curve of her belly.

"Nearly there, sweetling," she whispered to her unborn child. "Nearly there."

Chattergoon strode toward her from the front of the group. "Your Grace, it is a gentle ascent now into Lian. However, I request you remain here, out of sight, until I can assess the situation at the tunnel exit. You are vulnerable at this point, and the fewer people who know you are here, the better. I'll organise a carriage to take you directly to Prince Ernest's residence."

She nodded her assent. Chattergoon bowed and jogged off towards the tunnel exit. She followed his progress into the pinprick of light. His asking her permission was simply a courtesy. He was in charge here, although she was quite sure she'd be able to work something out if she had to. Her recent visit to Peqkya had bolstered her confidence in her abilities. Chattergoon had remained perfectly courteous the entire journey, ensuring her comfort and never once neglecting his duty to protect her and deliver her safely, like a living package, into the care of her brothers-in-law.

For eight weeks they had traversed the tunnels under the desert of Drome from Fertilian proper to the outlying city state of Lian. According to Chattergoon, it had been an easy journey. He and his men had been constantly surprised by the lack of hostile Dromedars lying in wait to antagonise the Fert tunnel runners at airholes and at the notorious strike points they usually favoured. "The desert rats must be occupied elsewhere," Chattergoon had mused aloud to his men, precisely once, in Jessima's hearing.

She wondered what a hard journey through the tunnels might've involved and counted her blessings. Jessima wasn't entirely sure what day it was, or what time. They had stuck to a rigid six hours walking, six hours sleeping pattern in the tunnel and she had lost all track of time. As the pregnant Queen, she was afforded a ride on the back of a sand sled dragged along by a donkey trained to tolerate the enclosed space. Their only light had been from the torches Chattergoon's men carried and meticulously maintained. The only noise from their own movements. The oppressive silence in the tunnels had threatened to overwhelm but Chattergoon suggested, no, *ordered*, that they sing.

Some days the ladies-in-waiting warbled popular court ballads, some days Chattergoon's men belted out rather coarser ditties, no doubt learnt at taverns and brothels. And at other times, the twenty King's soldiers sang military marching refrains. Often Jessima and Princess Georgina would join in with the court songs, but Chattergoon didn't sing. He was preoccupied with what the tunnels were continually communicating to no one but him. He caressed their walls, cocked his head to listen for sounds Jessima couldn't hear and sniffed at the stale, heavy air like a hound latching onto a scent.

Now, just a few steps from freedom, she heard the faint hum of the hustling and bustling city drifting down from the exit on the clean, salty air. The sound penetrated the heavy silence that hung about her, that hung about them all. The city clatter lightened her being all the way to her bones. If it hadn't been for the hand of a lady-in-waiting on her elbow, Jessima thought she might've floated up and away into the daylight.

She patted her pregnant belly again. It had certainly swollen, but her short, doll-like frame had decreased, which perhaps made the bump more prominent. There was food and water, but it had been heavily rationed. Consume too much early on and there would be none left for the last days of the journey, or if there was a delay. Lord Chattergoon had calculated every detail, down to the number of daily nuts each person received. Not a handful, but seven. Counted out each time.

"I'm not waiting any longer," Princess Georgina declared and pitched forward. One of Chattergoon's men stepped in her way.

"Not yet, Princess," he said. "We wait for Lord

Chattergoon. That's his orders, and we follow 'em."

The princess swayed, transfixed by the light at the end of the tunnel and reached out a tremulous hand as if to touch it. But she obeyed. They all obeyed Chattergoon. Georgina muttered to herself, tugged her matted hair and itched the dirty skin at her neck. She turned from the light and stumbled in circles, rapping her knuckles on the tunnel walls as she passed, scraping her skin and leaving smears of blood. Her eyes glazed, oblivious to the pain she inflicted on herself. Jessima feared she had gone mad.

Georgina had been jolly at the start of the journey. Flirting outrageously with Chattergoon's men and the soldiers, and shamelessly taking a different one off into the tunnels to entertain whenever the party rested for any length of time. For a while she'd rotated the forty men and kept herself amused by taking more than one with her at a time. But the pleasures of the flesh could not keep the darkness at bay, and she'd started to fret. She'd attempted to run back the way they had come, or off into some random tunnel, shrieking uncontrollably that she needed air, air, air.

During the worst episodes, Chattergoon had ordered her to be sedated with poppy for her own safety. Her unconscious body had been squashed next to Jessima on the sand sled for a while until she awoke in a daze and was able to walk again.

Although Princess Georgina was Jessima's stepdaughter, they were of a similar age. Georgina was a pretty, buxom girl with a wicked penchant for gossip and an insatiable sexual appetite. Her husband, Lord Hadley Smyth, was blissfully unaware of her rampant infidelities, as was her father. No one dared break that news to the fearsome king.

King Hugo was a great bear of a man in his late sixties, dearly loved by his subjects and soldiers, lords and ladies. A popular king with military prowess, diplomacy and charm in equal measures. He was busy fighting back in

Fertilian proper. The Thorne Twins – Awful Arthur and Miserable Mary – had joined their armies after twenty-four years of quarrelling and marched on Cleland City, Hugo's seat of power.

The day Jessima had entered the tunnels heading west was the day King Hugo had led his army east to meet the Thornes at Yettle Valley. She worried about the dreadful pain he'd suffered in his heart before she'd left. His ill-health had shocked them all, but Jessima was certain he'd recovered, adamant his strength had returned in order to thrash the Thorne twins once and for all.

Jessima and Georgina had been sent to Lian as a precaution, but she'd be summoned back soon enough. Although, no doubt after the birth. *But will my sweetling cope with the tunnel? Perhaps we should rest here a while, until the baby is strong enough to return.*

Jessima shivered. Her body's attempt at shaking off the thoughts. The same had been repeated in her mind for the past two months. There wasn't much else to do when bumping along behind an incontinent donkey other than overthink everything.

Will I be a good mother? Will my child love me? It was her first and she didn't know how to care for a baby. As one of eleven children, she'd looked after her younger siblings before she was married, but they'd been toddlers. *I needn't worry, I'm the Queen.* This babe, if a boy, was the heir to the throne of Fertilian. There would be plenty of others around her with more experience to guide her.

Jessima was desperate for news from Fertilian proper. Had the battle been fought? In the eight weeks she'd been in the vacuous tunnels, she was sure it must have happened by now. Had the Cleland army thrashed the Thornes? She was certain they had. King Hugo's soldiers had been supported by one thousand formidable Peqkian warriors led by Captain Denya. An alliance Jessima had brokered with Melokai Ramya.

Her mind flitted to Toby, as it often did, and a warm

flush spread from between her legs up towards her cheeks. The gloomy tunnels always appeared brighter as she glowed with his memory. Prince Toby, Hugo's youngest brother and his army general.

And her love.

Hugo loved Georgina's mother, his long-dead second wife Jayne. That was no secret. But Jessima loved his brother. That *was* a big secret. They'd shared one night of passionate pleasure together and Jessima had conceived. She'd spent nine years with Hugo and nothing. She was certain Toby was her baby's father, but no one knew.

Well… one person knew. Ramya. Jessima's friend had guessed. *How is she? She must have had her baby by now. Is it a girl?* Jessima prayed the Dromedars hadn't tried anything stupid after Chattergoon had spied their army loitering at the base of the Meliok mountains. *Ramya will have put them quickly in their place. She's a ferocious warrior.*

A whistle sliced through the tunnel silence. Jessima startled at the noise and then chuckled to herself. *Jumpy little bird.*

"Let's go, my Queen," one of Chattergoon's men said. "We'll get you and the Princess out first and come back for the goods and animals."

The soldiers formed up around Jessima and Georgina. The two ladies-in-waiting positioned themselves either side of their queen, holding her elbows.

"Help the Princess," Jessima said, "I can manage." They dropped behind to assist Georgina, who, quite clearly, was not managing.

Jessima took a long pull of the fresh air, lifted her chin and walked forward. She knew she must look like a gutter woman; her knee-length blond hair was wild and unkempt, her clothes tattered and dirty, and her skin was hidden under an eight-week-thick layer of dust and grime, but she was the Queen and she had a regal manner to uphold.

The ground was smoother here, not as sandy, and the tunnel widened as it approached the exit. It was a gentle climb, but enough to make her breath quicken.

As she drew closer, she could make out the tall, lanky shadow of Lord Chattergoon.

"This way, Queen Jessima," Chattergoon said.

The tunnel spat her out into a bright, mild autumn day. Her eyes screamed as the daylight hit them. A shooting black pain danced through the sockets and pummelled at them. She clenched her eyes tight and brought her arm up as a shield from the assault.

"Oh," she exclaimed as her step faltered.

She felt Chattergoon's firm grip on her other arm as he led her on.

"There's a carriage in front of you, my Queen," the lord said, gently placing her hand on the side of it. "Open your eyes a little so you can see where you're going. Your sight will return in measures."

Jessima lowered her arm and raised one eyelid a crack. She stepped up into the plush carriage. The curtains were drawn and her eyes slackened in the gloom, opening to tiny slits. Princess Georgina and the two ladies-in-waiting joined her in the carriage. The door was closed, and the carriage pitched forward.

The two women wedged Georgina between them, propping up her slumping form and soothing her with soft words.

"I will never see again," Georgina wailed and attempted to claw at her face with blood-stained fingers. The two ladies-in-waiting held back her wrists.

Jessima listened to the clopping of the horses' hooves, the voices of the city folk and the hubbub of life. A wave of exhaustion crashed over her and her head lolled on her shoulder. She rested her hands on her bump in a protective hug.

In a fog, Jessima was ushered from the carriage by a flurry of women. They half-walked, half-carried her from an internal courtyard through a hallway, up a staircase and into a large room. She was undressed with little ceremony and plonked in a hot bath, scrubbed and washed, then dried and oiled, and put to bed.

She melted into the soft mattress and fluffy goose-down pillow, relished the touch of the finest bedclothes tucked around her after eight weeks of sleeping on the ground.

***

"Ahhh, Queen Jessima, it is an honour!" The man bowed low.

"Prince Ernest," Jessima said sweetly and gave him her hand to kiss. "Or should I address you as Lord Overseer of Lian?"

"Ernie, please." The man straightened and smiled broadly.

He was a taller, thinner version of her husband, and with a rounder belly. Ernie was in his late-fifties and had a slight hunch from age with a barely noticeable lean to the left. His clean-shaven face was jovial with ruddy cheeks. His grey hair had thinned on top but was perfectly coiffed nonetheless. He was not so rugged or chiselled as Hugo, not as handsome, but Jessima could see the resemblance.

Ernie turned and crooked his arm. "May I escort you to breakfast, my dear?"

"Why yes, Ernie." Jessima took his proffered arm and he led her down the hallway and into a modest morning room.

The two men in the room rose as she entered and bowed low.

Ernie guided her to a seat at the head of the table. She waited for her ladies-in-waiting to adjust her skirts and then she sat. "Please, gentleman, be seated."

"Oh, my dear, you must be exhausted," Ernie said before his bottom had even settled in his seat, "please eat your fill and then you must rest. I have handmaids primed and ready to assist your every whim. The only time I traversed the tunnels was to your wedding to Hugo, my dear, and the sand and dust found every possible crevice to penetrate and took days to scrub out—"

A sharp cough interrupted Ernest. It came from the second man sat at the table. He was dressed in full religious garb: a pristine white cassock stitched with gold thread. The collarless neck was edged in a deep purple and large pearl buttons fastened the robe from neck to floor. The same purple cloth lined his cuffs and across his shoulders was a cloak of the same material but embroidered with white and gold thread. Around his neck sat a heavy gold chain with the religious symbol of a star within a circle, hanging from it.

This man was short and thin, with child-sized hands. He was handsome, though, with prominent cheekbones and a dimple in his chin. He had a full head of well-oiled hair, which, even though he was coming up to fifty, hadn't started receding or greying. He didn't look like Hugo but had the same commanding presence. This was a man who was used to being listened to and having his orders followed.

"Do you remember Prince Charles?" Ernie said. "He is the Chief Cleric here in Lian. So, there's Hugo, the eldest, then me, then our dearest Edward, presumed dead, lost at sea you know. Then old Charlie here and the youngest Toby. Five boys, I'm sure our mother Olivia did despair… oh but I'm rambling…"

"Prince Charles," Jessima said with a broad smile.

"My Queen," Prince Charles replied.

He didn't bow or dip his head as was customary to the King and Queen. Instead, he raised his nose higher. Religious fellows in Fertilian proper showed their monarchs deference, but Hugo's brother clearly thought he was above all that. She wondered briefly if she should say something, assert her queenly right to the utmost respect, but decided to let it pass.

With her sweetest tone, she said, "Of course, I remember, you very graciously presided over my wedding to King Hugo."

She turned to Lord Chattergoon and greeted him with genuine warmth. He dipped his head in return. The men eyed the food and Jessima said, "Please, let us break our fast."

Jessima, tired of the tunnel diet of dried meat, stale bread and water, wanted to snatch at everything. Fruit, sweetcakes, tea. Instead, she controlled her urges and daintily indicated for a servant to ladle her some porridge. Jessima sprinkled a touch of cinnamon over it and stirred in a spoonful of honey and then waited until all three men were eating before she took a bite – a Queen seen to be gorging herself was not the done thing.

"Tell me, where is Princess Georgina this morning?" Jessima asked after swallowing her second mouthful of porridge to still her grumbling stomach.

She shifted in her dress. Ernie had commissioned it for her, but the seamstress had not appreciated just how pregnant she was. Some last-minute adjustments had let out the seams, but not quite enough. The design and cloth were not to Jessima's tastes but she'd had no other choice that morning. Her priority would be to ensure she was befitted in the finery seemly for a queen. She couldn't allow the Lianites to take their first glimpse of her in person in poorly fitted garments.

"Princess Georgina is still resting," Ernie said, "her handmaids took some breakfast up to her room."

"And what news from Fertilian, of the war?" Jessima blurted. Polite conventions dictated she shouldn't bring up such matters, or at the very least should've waited until after breakfast, but she was desperate to know.

The two princes stopped eating to gawp at her, surprised by her boldness. Chattergoon continued to fill his belly, listening but not looking.

"There has been none, my dear," Ernie finally said. "You are the first group that has arrived to us from Fertilian. All tunnel running has ceased." He blinked at her for a moment or two longer than was necessary, as if to say, *now eat your oats and be quiet like a good Queen.*

Jessima noted the admonition but ploughed on. "Is that to be expected, Lord Chattergoon?"

Chattergoon looked up, a fork with juicy gammon quivered in front of his open mouth. He dropped it to his plate, sat upright and addressed Jessima. "Yes, my Queen. All able-bodied men who usually work the tunnels would have been seconded to fight in the war against the Thorne Twins."

"Do not think on it, child," Prince Charles said with a stern tone. "God will send us a messenger with news when He wills it. Let the men manage those matters, and concern yourself with the prettier things in life. The division of the sexes is as God wills it."

Jessima's curiosity raged. Once her job had been to sit pretty and be silent, like an ornament. But since her journey to Peqkya, she felt capable, confident. She selected a sweetcake with pink icing and proceeded to nibble at it.

She'd forgotten Prince Charles was a religious fanatic, as addicted to religion as Princess Georgina was to sex. Charles had insisted on sermonising for hours at her wedding to Hugo. Jessima's sister, Geraldina, had joked afterwards that Grandfather Walter had snored throughout the entire speech, much to the amusement of those around him.

Her family. She'd not had news from the Walters in a long while. She wondered if Geraldina's letters were piling up back at Cleland Castle. She wouldn't be able to send a letter to her sister from Lian. *Are you all safe? I pray this war doesn't reach central Fertilian where you live.*

"So, my dear," Prince Ernest said with a mouthful of pancake, "has Lord Chattergoon filled you in on Lian?"

Chattergoon glanced at Jessima and continued to chew hungrily on his meat.

"Not as such, dear Ernie. Lord Chattergoon has been busy expertly guiding us through the tunnels," Jessima replied.

In eight weeks, Chattergoon had barely spoken to her about anything other than the job at hand. He wasn't one for informal small talk. All his communication had been entirely necessary and spoken with the utmost respect.

Ernie took a sip of his tea. "Oh, it is a unique place with an interesting history. One which I am well versed in. I shall be delighted to introduce you to our wonderful city."

"I'd be delighted to receive a tour, and to learn all about Lian. Perhaps later today?" Jessima said, clapping her hands together excitedly.

"Certainly not," Prince Charles said with a reprimanding squint at his brother. "You are delicate, and in your condition, you really should be resting."

"You are very kind to consider my health," Jessima said.

"Women are to be protected, it is as God commands," Prince Charles replied. He ran a hand through his lush head of hair.

"Of course," Jessima replied, "but I should like to—"

"After breakfast, the medics will check you over," Prince Charles cut her off.

Jessima acquiesced graciously, not wanting to disrespect her elder yet quietly fuming.

"Would you care for some tea, my dear," Ernie said and gestured for a servant to bring the pot.

"I would, Ernie, but I take it iced," Jessima said.

Ernie frowned. "Tea is at its finest hot and with a splash of milk. Here, let Mavis fill your cup. Iced," he chuckled, "who in all Fertilian takes it iced."

Prince Charles laughed. "What nonsense," he said, as he brushed crumbs from his lavish purple cloak. Abruptly he impaled Jessima with a stare. "What is it you want?"

Jessima, taken aback with the directness of his question and the rude nature of its asking, stumbled. "I... want... to be a good queen, to be a good mother..." She rested a hand on her belly.

"Indeed, I thought as much," Prince Charles retorted and fixed her with a glare that rooted her to the chair. "Then you'll do as we say. We are far more experienced in these things."

Jessima frowned.

"It's for the best," Ernie said brightly, lightening the atmosphere. He leaned towards her and patted her wrist like a child. He gestured towards the steaming hot cup of tea that the servant had placed in front of her.

She stared at it and, when Ernie wasn't looking, gently pushed it away.

***

"Here, Betsy Boo Boo," Prince Ernest called.

The small tan-and-black dog ran into the courtyard and jumped into Ernie's outstretched arms. He lifted the dog up in front of his face. Ernie puckered his lips in the shape of a fish's mouth and the dog sloppily licked them.

Jessima's breakfast curdled at the thought of dog slobber in her mouth. She much preferred cats, especially ones that purred so loud it thrummed through your body, and spoke, like Ramya's clevercat.

Ernest tucked the dog under his arm. "This is Betsy. She's very tame."

Princess Georgina, now completely recovered from her temporary tunnel madness, put her face in front of the dog's and it licked her nose. She giggled. "Oh, I love her, Uncle Ernie."

"Now we're all here, let's start our tour, shall we?"

"I simply cannot wait to see the Sarenky Sea," Georgina exclaimed as they settled themselves in the carriage.

It had been a week since they had arrived, and this was the first outing. Jessima was elated. She was starting to feel as contained and restricted in Ernie's residence as she had in the tunnel. She'd been desperate to explore Lian since she'd arrived, but Prince Charles had demanded they rest for at least a month before heading into the city. Jessima complied for a week and then insisted.

For their safety, Prince Ernest still hadn't announced the Queen and the Princess' arrival. It would be done at the proper time, he said. For this reason, the curtains in the carriage were partially drawn, allowing a small gap to peek through, and no chance of anyone looking in and recognising the occupants. Georgina gazed out one side and Jessima the other. Ernest sat travelling backwards, and facing them, with Betsy curled on his lap.

As they left the square interior courtyard, Jessima finally saw Ernie's residence from the outside. It was a grand stone building of three storeys. Not quite a castle, more a square fortress. It had a wall around the perimeter and then a moat, before the walls of the building rose up with turrets at each corner. There were a few windows around the outside, but most of them faced inwards to the courtyard, and many of these, like her own room, had small balconies. Along the top of the perimeter wall was a walkway. A handful of armed men – but mostly women – milled about there, seemingly unconcerned about any threats. The gate in the wall was left open with the portcullis raised and the drawbridge down.

The carriage made slow progress through the city.

"It's crowded," Jessima observed. There seemed to be more people, buildings, belongings and detritus crammed together in this small walled city than in the entirety of Cleland City, three times its size.

"Yes," Prince Ernest replied. "Lian is home to ten thousand people, although currently there's about seven thousand residents with the majority of able-bodied men at war in Fertilian. It is compact with mostly wooden buildings, but a few of stone. None of the original Dromedar mudbrick houses still stand from when Lian was Vaasar. There is absolutely no free space, every bit of land has a house, hut, stall or shack on it. I ensure that all space is used resourcefully and that the city, although crowded, runs proficiently. It is very different to Cleland

City."

Jessima watched from behind the curtain as animals were herded into the tiniest pens. Women scurried about, expertly weaving in and out of the other pedestrians, of the few carriages on the narrow roads, going about their business. There were a handful of children, the busy streets their only playground. All looked healthy and well-fed, the buildings and streets were well-maintained. It was clearly a wealthy city.

"So many women," Princess Georgina grumbled with a heavy dollop of disappointment. "All the men away at this damnable war." She hoiked up her breasts, as if having them closer to her face brought her comfort, and went back to staring out the window.

The war. In a week there had been no news, no tunnel runner had arrived. Lord Chattergoon had sent one of his men back to Fertilian but it would be weeks before he would return with any messages. And by then it would be old news.

The journey was excruciatingly slow. The women going about their business didn't move out of the way of the carriage, and Jessima soon understood, there was nowhere to step aside even if they could. Georgina's eyelids drooped with the rocking motion of the carriage and she rested her head against the padded interior.

"Wouldn't it be quicker for us to get out and walk?" Jessima asked.

"Quicker, yes. Safer, no. The city streets are like a maze. I couldn't risk losing one or both of you," Prince Ernest replied. "You two would stick out like a beacon on a dark night by not knowing your way, or keeping up with the rapid pace of us Lianites. There's no dawdling here. Furthermore, no one is yet aware you are in the city, and you'd draw unwanted attention to yourselves. There is a long history of assassination attempts on the city's overseers, and on Fertilian royalty. Sadly, there are still a few Thorne snakes in the grass."

Ernie indicated the two soldiers sat at the front of the carriage, either side of the driver. "Hence our need for them, and also for these." He tugged at a heavy curtain.

"Have there been many attempts on your life, Ernie?" Jessima asked

"No, thankfully. Security is much more robust."

"When was the last assassination?"

"Our dearest father, and your father-in-law, dearie. Lord Ernest Salmon Senior. Instrumental in building Hugo's army and Fertilian allies until his heart was pierced by an assassin's arrow in the street. After, our mother, Olivia, took over. The Thornes assumed that would be the end of it, but his death spurred mother – and Hugo – on." Ernie scooped up his dog. "A remarkable woman, my mother. Feisty. Isn't that right, Betsy?"

Feisty. Jessima rolled the word around her mouth like a boiled sweet. Until recently, she had been Hugo's trophy. Silent and shiny, representing his great wealth and achievement. But ever since she'd returned to Fertilian with one thousand Peqkian warriors, she received more notice, and from some – respect.

Ernie adjusted his rump on the cushioned seat and tapped Georgina's knee. She woke with a start.

"We are in the main square," Ernest said. "Can you hear the women crying their goods? It has been the main square since before Lian was Lian, when it was ancient Vaasar and belonged to Drome."

Both Jessima and Georgina looked out their respective windows. They were passing through a busy square with a river running through the centre. Three bridges crossed the river, all heaving with women and carts.

Jessima patted her swelling belly. "Tell me, Ernie, why so few children?"

"The wall around the city was built when Edgar, the first King of Fertilian, captured the city from Drome. The wall has been reinforced a few times, but it has never moved.

"In the two thousand years since, Lian has grown and been increasingly squashed inside these walls. That is why every useable bit of space has been claimed and built upon or used for farming or tending livestock.

"Perhaps one hundred years ago, a bumper harvest saw an influx of families from the mainland. Predicting catastrophic overcrowding, the Lord Overseer at the time tightened controls on new settlers, and decreed that only one child per woman was permitted. Those two laws have remained in place to this day."

"Only one child per woman?" Jessima exclaimed, thinking of her ten siblings. "How in all Fertilian is that managed?"

"Well, for a long while abstinence was the only way. But that soon led to a very uptight population." Ernie chuckled. "So, an ingenious butcher one day decided to use a cleaned-out sheep's bladder over his... er... manhood to... um... catch the seed. It worked and has become a thriving industry. We'll soon go through the pocket quarter, where you'll see them out to dry."

"I use them all the time when I'm not with Hadley," Princess Georgina said brazenly. "I do believe I kept Lian in business the amount I had brought through the tunnels to Cleland City, don't you think, Uncle?" She laughed.

"Well, I don't know about that, sweet niece," Ernie winked at Georgina. She leaned forward and squeezed his knee. Betsy yapped at her.

Jessima, a virgin before marrying Hugo and with no experience of using little pockets, said, "What happens if a woman has more than one baby?"

"There's limited space in Lian. Any family with more than one child pays quadruple taxes. If they can't pay, which most can't, they forfeit their Lian residency and are sent to Fertilian, where there's plenty of space for large families, but little opportunity and less wealth. Fertilian proper is not such a delightful place to live as Lian."

"From what I have seen, Lian is certainly a wonderful

place," Jessima said.

"And that, my dear, is why we have such a roaring trade in little pockets." Ernie guffawed and Georgina tittered. Betsy yowled with them.

Eventually their mirth cooled.

"Take a deep breath of that salt air, and look," he pointed out the window. "Welcome to one of the most majestic sights, the sea!"

"Incredible," Georgina said.

Betsy slid from Ernie's knees and jumped about the carriage floor.

"Yes, I know, Betsy Boo Boo, it's time to splash in the sea." Ernie banged on the roof of the carriage and a moment later, it stopped. He opened the carriage door and the dog launched itself onto the rocks and then bounded straight to the water's edge.

Jessima took in the endless blue and felt elated. Perhaps this place truly was paradise. She'd never seen the sea before, only great lakes and rivers.

"I'd like to get out and explore the pebble beach," Jessima said.

"Absolutely not, my dear, best to stay in the carriage." Ernie positioned himself to block the door.

"Do people swim in the sea?" Jessima asked, reminded of her swim with Ramya in the achingly beautiful Inaly Lake.

"Oh yes. It's a lovely experience. But, of course, you can't, my dear. You're the Queen! You can't be seen bathing in next to nothing. I'm certain Hugo and his court would deem that most improper, and heaven knows what Charlie would make of it," Ernie replied.

For the sake of decorum, Jessima swallowed back the urge to shove him aside and fling herself at the beach in the same manner as Betsy. She believed Ernie and Charles had her best interests at heart, but they were suffocating her.

***

Jessima waited in a private, windowless hut behind the stage. Three weeks had passed since her arrival, and the princes had decided it was time she was presented to the people of Lian. Ernie assured her the Lianites were respectful and honoured their royals. And besides, rumours had spread of her presence in the city. So, rather than deny it, Ernie felt it would bolster their spirits. It was an excellent distraction, he'd said, as no news had arrived from the mainland about the war with the Thornes.

Lord Chattergoon, although he resided at Ernie's fortress, spent most days occupied with business at the tunnels. There had not been one tunnel runner as yet with a message. A fact he found *discouraging*, as he'd told Jessima at breakfast that morning when she'd asked.

The women of Lian were getting impatient for news of their loved ones, just as Jessima was growing impatient of news of the King… and Toby.

Prince Charles had just finished a long and rather dull sermon and Prince Ernest was now on stage doing the honours to introduce her.

She swirled in her new dress and savoured the delectable swish. She had commissioned the garment for the occasion to show off her growing bump and she knew she looked spectacular. Her long blond hair had been teased into an elaborate design with curls, plaits and pearl combs. It had plenty of height, all the better to offset her tiny frame. Her face had been powdered and painted, and her neck and wrists heaved with fine jewels.

Hugo had always conducted all public speaking, and although this was her first speech as Queen, Jessima wasn't nervous. Ernie and Prince Charles had written a speech for her, and she had rehearsed it until every word tripped off her tongue with little effort.

"Oh, I am so excited," she said to one of the handmaids bustling about her in the hut. "This will be just like my performances as a child. My father had a stage built in our home for his eleven children's little shows. He used to invite families from all the neighbouring estates to watch. It was the only time he paid me any attention."

The woman smiled but didn't answer. Jessima desperately missed her handmaids Marcy and Tina back at Cleland Castle. They had become like friends.

A knock on the hut indicated the stage was set for her grand entrance.

She waited for the handmaids to gather up her skirts and shimmering train and a steward helped her from the hut and up the few steps to the stage.

"May I present your Queen. Queen Jessima!" Prince Ernest announced.

It was mid-morning, the best time according to the princes as the marketplace was at its busiest. Briefly, after waiting in the dark hut, the sunlight blinded her as it had done when she had emerged from the tunnel. She beamed brightly until her eyes adjusted and lifted her hand in a royal wave to the crowd.

She was expecting a resounding ovation in return, but there was none.

There was no applause, because there was no crowd. No faces eagerly turned to the stage to see and venerate their Queen.

That was not precisely true. There was a crowd, but none of them paid her any attention. The women were buying and selling, shopping for goods, packing and unpacking fruit, haggling over the best cuts of meat. They wore practical, working clothes. Many were dressed in typically male garb. They had taken on their men's jobs, when they had gone off to war.

Her handmaids fussed about her person, organising her train. She gestured for them to leave her, suddenly feeling overdone and out of place in her finery.

But this was a show, and the show must go on.

"Ladies and children of Lian," she began, projecting her voice as her childhood acting master had coached her. When no one turned, she repeated herself, louder, more enunciated.

"Ladies and children of Lian, it is a pleasure to be here in this wondrous city. As your Queen, as the Queen of Fertilian, I am proud to stand here before you—"

A loud cough at the side of the stage distracted Jessima. She glanced down. A lone woman stood there. She folded her arms as she peered up, and Jessima smiled brightly at the woman.

Work the crowd, the voice of her master reminded her. And since Jessima's crowd consisted of only this one lady, she walked towards her and crouched, offering the woman her hand to kiss.

"I am proud to stand here before you—" Jessima continued.

The woman looked at her outstretched hand, confused, and then brought her own out and offered it to Jessima. The queen faltered as blackened, filthy fingernails hovered in front of her face.

The woman slapped Jessima's hand away. She laughed wildly, and hiccoughed.

Shocked, Jessima clutched her stinging hand to her chest. *Drunk, the woman's drunk.* That was a male habit. It was not the proper thing for respectable women to be drunk in Fertilian. Perhaps the Lianite women had taken on more than just their men's work. They'd taken on their manly habits too.

Two of the King's soldiers came forward to accost the woman, grabbing her aggressively. The woman yelped.

"No," Jessima said, upset by the notion that this woman might suffer violent punishment in the soldiers' hands. "Leave her be. Let her speak."

The soldiers stepped back and the woman stuck out her tongue at them.

"My Queen, my pretty Queen," the woman slurred. "The only thing me and my friends here want to know, is when our menfolk are coming home. Do you know?"

"My husband and family are also fighting in the war,

and I eagerly await news from them. When it comes, I will be sure to share it with you," Jessima said and smiled.

The drunk snorted. She pointed a finger at Jessima. "You don't know anything, do you? Beneath that beauty, you're stupid. Spineless. You're speaking words someone else told you to and don't even know the meaning of them. Can't think for yourself, can you? Your job is to sit pretty, to do as you're told. A puppet! Look around. No one cares what a toy has to say…"

A steward came on stage and gestured urgently for Jessima to leave. At the side of the stage, Jessima spotted Ernie desperately waving at her to exit. The soldiers closest to the ranting woman put their hands on their swords and edged forward, but the drunk woman wouldn't be deterred.

Spittle flew from her lips as she continued, "Bet you didn't even dress yourself. Can't even take care of your own body. Bet that babe will go straight to suckle on the breast of another woman. Can't even feed your offspring."

Embarrassment bit at Jessima's cheeks as she hurried from the stage. *Is this really what the people think of me? Are they that disinterested in what I have to say?*

"Go on," the woman jeered, "run away. Go and hide from your problems, your inadequacies, from ever taking any responsibility for anything important."

The queen was bundled into a waiting carriage, the handmaids stuffing her skirts and long train in after her. As she was taken away, the drunk woman's final words rang in her ears.

"We don't need a doll, we don't need *you!* We need a queen, a leader – *someone* – who gives a shit."

4

AMMAD

ઉ૪ૈૺ

Ammad was aware of screaming. High-pitched, pained, halted occasionally by wracking sobs. Even through his fug, it hurt his ears.

Sounds like Mama. A little voice cut through the swirling dust to pierce his consciousness. *Mama.*

Peeling an eyelid open, the Crown Prince of Drome glimpsed a flash of turmeric yellow material, a hint of sheeny, honey-coloured skin, a streak of lustrous, dark-brown hair. He struggled to keep his eyelid open, but it was too heavy and closed again. He focused on his nose. Smelling required no exertion. He simply let his body continue to breathe in and out. Mama's scent of aniseed and nutmeg tickled his nostrils.

I want my mama.

The screaming subsided, to be replaced by rapid conversation. One voice, two, three, perhaps four? They floated over him, through him, under him. Ammad couldn't feel his body. He was breathing, that was enough. He embraced a sensation like endless falling. To fight it was pointless, to welcome it was pure bliss. He knew he was dosed up on poppy, he'd embraced the feeling numerous times before now. But this was a euphoria bigger than any he'd experienced. If only everyone would just be quiet, then he could enjoy it.

He pushed out a sound from a mouth that he hoped was still there – he couldn't feel it – and a short groan emerged.

His conscious mind grasped at something, a memory. *Pain. Blood.* But it was chased away as his eyes were rudely drawn open. A face peered at him.

Mama, he tried to say, but it came out as 'urgghh'.

Jakira leaned in and, Ammad guessed, kissed his forehead. But his skin was numb to the touch.

"Oh, flesh of my flesh, oh my son, my son."

His mother's soothing voice felt like water seeking out and settling into any worrisome cracks. He tried to smile, wasn't sure if his lips had moved.

"Medi, bring in a brazier and make a fire, right there. Send for the healer to take these dirty bandages off and burn them. Bring fresh wrappings, more poppy."

Ammad's heart leapt. *More poppy!*

His eyes registered movement as his mother's head slave dashed from the room. *His room.* He was in his bedroom, at his mother's craterside villa in Parchad. *Of course, where else would I be? I've been on a poppy binge and they've found me in some seedy den in a stupor.* But something niggled in his mind, an image of mountains.

"Tell me, Whaled, what happened to my son?" Jakira's voice was firm. She was finished with her screaming and sobbing. Ammad's shrewd, composed, formidable Mama was back.

Ammad saw Whaled step forward, his head down. *What is the Minister of War doing in my bedroom? Slightly awkward and inappropriate.* The hairy beast of a man was filthy, covered in blood, dried and crusty. Sadly, he didn't seem injured. *Someone else's blood…*

"The Crown Prince fought valiantly with Melokai Ramya of Peqkya. He killed her. It was a proud moment. Never forget that, Jakira," Whaled said.

I killed the Peqkian Melokai? A memory flitted onto the edge of Ammad's consciousness. He attempted to grab at it, but it evaporated faster than a drop of water on scorching sand.

His mother waved her hand impatiently for Whaled to continue.

"A red-haired warrior challenged him. She was furious at the Melokai's death. Fast. Faster than I've ever seen before. She…" Whaled indicated Ammad and Jakira nodded.

She what? Ammad tried to ask. He puffed instead.

Whaled continued, "I pulled him away before she could finish him and we ran through the city, to the camp we'd set up and straight to the healers' tent. The blood was staunched, the wounds cauterised and poppy administered. Then we took horses, supplies and rode as fast as we could away from Riaow, to the border. I left all my army in the city…" His voice choked and he shook his head. The hairy man's eyes glistened. Ammad waited for the blubbering fool to start sobbing and screaming, but he took a deep breath to steady himself.

"We travelled over the mountains and to the camp we had left in the wastelands. Swapped horses for camels and crossed the border into Drome. It's been a hard ride, but six weeks later, here we are. Your son survived, the little bastard. I can't say the same for my men. I left them in Peqkya."

Whaled dipped his head and covered his face with his furry-backed hands. He screwed his palms into his eyes.

Jakira walked to the hairy man, leaving Ammad's side. Without his mother's support Ammad's eyelids drooped. He forced them open and witnessed his mother tenderly kissing the Minister of War. She stroked Whaled's cheek and looked lovingly into his eyes.

That isn't right.

With a monumental effort, Ammad grunted to draw Jakira's attention, to get her away from that hairy beast of a man.

She turned back to Ammad just as Medi entered with

the brazier and two healers. Jakira exchanged hasty words with the healers, too fast for Ammad to comprehend. They nodded. Ammad watched as the broad-shouldered slave positioned the brazier by the window. He expertly lit it and stoked it.

The healers fussed around Ammad. He couldn't feel their touch but could see their shadows shifting in his periphery. A healer handed bloody, sand-yellowed bandages to Medi over his chest.

The head slave threw them on the fire.

Jakira moved to the door and ordered another slave to fetch Riv.

My Peqkian Aunty, Riv. Ammad attempted to smile.

A few moments later, Riv entered with another Peqkian woman. Ammad couldn't recall her name. He knew, though, that she had bad teeth, and the fact that he remembered this made him chuckle. It left his mouth as a pathetic groan.

His odd noise disturbed Riv and she wailed. She waved her hands at Ammad, rambling in Dromedari about "how they never should have done it" and "such a mistake" and "what were they thinking".

Jakira walked to her and planted a slap smartly across the woman's fat cheeks.

"What's done is done. This is not over, Rivya. I will destroy that vile little country of yours for what they have done to the flesh of my flesh."

Riv curbed her tears, looked at her feet and nodded to his mother.

Jakira stared intently at something Ammad couldn't quite see. She dropped to her knees, the top of her head level with his gaze.

"What of this child?" Jakira said.

"That is the son of one of the peons who assisted us," Riv said. "He wanted the boy to be taken out of Peqkya, and I agreed. We should've just dumped him somewhere on the road, but Toya here has become quite attached to the little brat."

A few words passed between the two Peqkian women in the Shella language.

"His name is Artaz," Riv said to Jakira.

"Hello, Artaz, you are a curious little boy," Jakira said.

"Mistress," a healer said from over Ammad's head.

Jakira turned and a look of such horror came over her face that Ammad felt ashamed, although he had no idea why. Riv and Toya gasped. Whaled grimaced.

Jakira's eyes narrowed. "Get out. All of you, get out!"

Ammad heard the shuffling as the room cleared. A pinprick of pain jolted through him, through his arms. *No, not through my arms, through my chest.*

"We've administered poppy," a healer said.

"Artaz," Toya yelled as the boy dashed towards the fire.

Ammad could see him now. A small Peqkian boy with black skin and reddish hair. *The same red hair as…* Ammad clutched at the memory, at the knowledge but it slipped from his grasp.

From the doorway, Toya repeated the boy's name and said something in Shella, no doubt beckoning for the child to return to her.

"No," Jakira said. She watched the boy intently. In fluent Shella she continued, "He can stay. Close the door."

Artaz hovered open-mouthed by the brazier, completely mesmerised by the fire within. The reflection flickered in his pupils.

"We are done, mistress," an unseen healer said. "The bandages will require changing in the morning."

Jakira dismissed them with a flick of her hand. Ammad heard the door latch quietly close. He couldn't understand why his mother showed so much interest in that child and not him, her son. He tried to grunt, but nothing came out. He could feel himself sinking into a poppy-induced daze. Usually he would welcome it, but not now. Ammad wanted answers.

He fought the ecstasy and forced his eyelids to remain

open. Jakira knelt next to Artaz and put one arm around his little shoulders. She put her other hand up and into the fire.

Ammad attempted to shout, "Mama, no! You'll hurt yourself!" But the words curdled in his throat.

She didn't flinch and her flesh showed no sign of burning. She smiled to the boy.

He reached out and thrust his little hand into the flames. A big grin spread across his face. As with Ammad's mother, the boy's flesh didn't burn, he seemed completely unperturbed by the flames that licked up his wrist.

Jakira gasped. "Well, aren't you the surprise. I think I'll keep you."

A poppy-addled delusion, that's all.

The fug crept forward and fogged Ammad's eyes. He succumbed to the weightlessness and allowed it to envelop him completely.

Ammad choked and desperately tried to claw at his throat but he was buried deep in the desert sand. Each movement sifted sand into his face and although he clenched his mouth shut, the fine grains filled his nostrils, poured into his ears and pushed into the corners of his eyes. A worm. He was a worm.

It was at this point in the nightmare that Ammad always woke, and he immediately recognised the desperate thirst. The first sign the poppy was wearing off. It was also always at this point he wished he was from the poor Eqmadeh desert nomad clan and had a huge, misshapen hump on his back from which he could draw water.

But then, as always, he'd remember he was terribly vain. And the Crown Prince. And he would rather have the small, smooth hump on his back that drained of water far too quickly, than the ugly, misshapen monstrosities that could hold thirty days' worth. He was the Crown Prince, after all. There would be a servant nearby to fetch him a drink.

He opened his eyes. Daylight streamed through a window and he squinted with a grimace. *What den allows daylight in? I must remember not to frequent this disgraceful place again.*

After the thirst always came the inevitable cramping, debilitating headache. The light would bring it on quicker.

"Fuck," Ammad grumbled.

His eyes slowly adjusted and he scanned the room searching out some minion to fetch him a glass of sugared lime juice. He wasn't in a poppy den. He was in his old bedroom at his mother's craterside villa in Parchad.

In flashes, the night before returned to him. His mother screaming. Whaled close to tears. A Peqkian boy.

Peqkya.

Ammad thought hard. *How did I get here?* He had no recollection.

His body juddered as a memory hit him, smacked him across the cheeks as viciously as one of his guard Qabull's famed punches.

I was in Peqkya fighting the hisspits and invading that stinky little country. And now I'm home. And Qabull is dead.

Then the memory of the invasion, the battle in Riaow, the fight with Melokai Ramya ran through his mind as if sped up.

He had thrust his sword through Melokai Ramya's chest. So what was he doing back in Drome? Why was he not revelling in his victory in the mountain country?

Then he recalled the tall, red-haired warrior.

His face itched, just under his chin, like it always did when the poppy wore off. He moved his hand to scratch it. Found that he couldn't. The itch intensified.

Ammad tilted his head and looked down at his body.

He screamed.

Screamed and screamed.

The hisspit bitch had hacked off his arms.

5

VIOLYA
ⱷ

V sat quietly on a stool in the council room. Her back straight, one hand resting on the hilt of her sword, the other flat on her thigh. She had asked Lizya to come in with her, and the warrior now stood just behind V's left shoulder. Ramya's old councillors, who had witnessed Sybilya's proclamation shuffled into the room, unsure as to whether to sit on their old stools or not.

Everything was in disarray.

No Melokai Choosing Ceremony, none of the usual customs. They weren't following procedure and nobody, V included, knew what to do next. Clevercats and assistants came and went delivering messages.

V studied the table in front of her, carved in the shape of Peqkya's natural form. Mountains, rivers, lakes and settlements. *This country is now mine to rule.* V's nerves spun in her chest. *And I must rule. And rule well. Think, V, think. What do I need to do first?*

"Amya," V said quietly.

The ginger clevercat bounded towards her, jumped on the table and leaned in close. V spoke a message in the cat's ear and the large feline hurtled down the table, leapt from it and darted out the door.

V took Emmo off her shoulder and placed her on the

table. The caterpillar immediately flopped on her side and stretched out. V caught a glimpse of red. She put her hands in her lap and turned them palm up. *Believe in yourself, V.*

She blocked out the chatter and the bustle and focused on an image in her mind of the Sarenky Sea. The view from Chaos Cliffs in Majute, where one of the leaders, Potenqi Utuli, had been blown off his little feet. The endless blue, the jumping fish, the crashing waves.

"V?"

Joz's voice startled her from her reverie. V smiled at her. The little trader stood beside her, open-mouthed and lost for words.

"Councillors," V said. "Please, take a seat. Lizya, Joz, Brin, please take a seat. Everyone else, please leave us."

The councillors shot each other confused looks but then took their places. Lizya hustled people out of the room and gave orders for two novices to stand guard before closing the door. She took a seat and gave V a wink.

"One of the Stone Prophetess' sayings, that our great nation is founded upon, is, 'Embrace change, for when it comes you cannot stop it'," V said, looking at each of the councillors in turn. "We are experiencing great change. So rather than fight it, let us embrace it. I was not expecting this. I am as shocked as you that there was no Melokai Choosing Ceremony."

Head Scholar Chaz cleared his throat. "I believe that perhaps the people would not have made the best decision as to what Peqkya needs at this moment in time, my Melokai," he said. His arm was in a sling due to a shoulder injury inflicted by traitorous pleasure giver, Ferraz.

"And what does Peqkya need?" the Head Teller Omya asked. She sat bolt upright, squinting at them.

"A warrior with a heart," Joz said, beaming at V.

Lizya clapped V on the back. "Sybilya's picked the wrong woman here then." And laughed heartily.

Brin and Joz laughed along, but the old councillors remained mute, still shocked. V smiled, but any light-heartedness snagged behind the weight of new responsibility.

Chaz cleared his throat once more. "My Melokai, you must receive a new council. Each of the council professions will vote for their next leader and that person shall be your councillor. We will organise a vote, but it will take some time, and then of course they'll need time to settle in and learn everything…"

Sybilya's words rung in V's mind: *customs must change.* V considered her options, reached down into her gut, into the fibre of her being, to see what it told her. *Evolution*, she heard, *for the survival of Peqkya.*

"There will be no need," V said. "We do not have the luxury of time. Chaz, Omya, Naomya and Zecky, you all know how to rule this country in your honoured professions, and I'd like for you to continue. Melokai Ramya trusted you, and I trust you. Will you serve me as you served Melokai Ramya?"

There were surprised mumbles and gasps as the councillors digested this.

Naomya, the small, acne-scarred Mother of Mothers replied first, "It would be an honour, my Melokai."

Three more voices echoed that sentiment.

"Thank you," V said, relieved. "Please call me Violya, or V. The 'my Melokai' formality makes me uncomfortable."

"Ah, yes of course, V," Chaz answered.

Zecky pulled out a stack of parchment and a pencil and scribbled a note to herself. When she noticed V looking, she explained, "Just making notes as to what to tell the people, my Mel… er, V."

"And I would like to ask you, Jozya, if you would be my Head Trader?" V said.

"Issee!" Joz exclaimed and then clapped excitedly. "I'd love to."

"Lizya, you will be my Head Warrior."

Joz clapped even more excitedly. "Oh, Lizzy, well done you!"

A short intake of breath betrayed Lizya's surprise but then she grinned. "I thought you'd never ask."

"I believe the seventh councillor is of the Melokai's choosing, often a courtesan? Well, I have no friends who are courtesans, but I do have you, Brin. Brinjinqa of Majute, will you be my honoured advisor, when I call upon you?"

"I am yours to command, V," Brin said with a flourish and kissed the vial of red liquid that hung from a chain around his neck. Joz clapped again.

Zecky frowned and scribbled. "Well, I suppose Ramya brought a man," she flicked her eyes pointedly at Chaz, "and then a Trogr to this council, so what's a pygmie?"

"He's a Jute," Joz told her sweetly and Zecky made a show of crossing out a word and rewriting another next to it.

V's councillors turned to her, waiting for her to speak. *What usually happens at these meetings?* V considered what she wanted to say, as all in the room stared at her expectantly. Apart from Lizya who rolled and stretched her shoulder, accustomed to V taking her time to think before speaking.

"Melokai Ramya did much to improve the city and the country, the wellbeing of the people and for that she will always be remembered," V said after a while. "Melokai Ramya ruled over a peaceful and prosperous Peqkya. But Peqkya is no longer at peace with its neighbours.

"Much happened whilst we were in Majute and much is unknown. The warriors who came with us to flush out the Dromedars told us of events in the north-east, where Sybilya's Strongcats forced back the wolves. In the east, where five of our women were kidnapped by Trogrs and a violent, deadly clash with our warriors proved unsuccessful. And in the south-west, the Dromedars lick their wounds after an attempted invasion."

It felt good for V to say these thoughts out loud. Those in the room listened intently.

She continued, "It seems to me we have two allies left. Majute and the Ferts. One of our skilled captains is in Fertilian with one thousand of our warriors fighting an internal war in that country."

V placed her palm on the table, carved in the likeness of Peqkya. "My priority is to protect our country from its enemies. To keep our people safe, fed and watered. There will be no more grand social schemes. These were important and appropriate for a country at peace. But not now."

V raised her voice and slapped the table once for emphasis. "We are at war."

She paused to allow the words to penetrate. "We must channel funds and effort into necessary food, homes, healing centres. Into rebuilding an army with weapons, cloth, armour. Stockpile. Prepare. Get the medicinal quarter functioning again. Train more steelmakers to make swords and more carpenters to make tent frameworks and carts to transport everything an army could need."

"'Food is bountiful if we all share,'" Joz said, repeating one of Sybilya's Sayings. "Well, I've been chatting to my fellow traders. It's no surprise that trade with Troglo and Drome has come to a halt. Trade with Fertilian has also stopped, I'm guessing the internal conflict is holding things up there. But trading with Majute is picking up. They love our vegetables and clevercat messengers and we've been getting nuts in return. They last forever, taste delicious and sustain you for hours. Be good for the warrior's diet, I should suppose."

Brin reached into his pocket, and then put his fist, knuckles down, on the table. He unfolded his three fingers to reveal a nut. "This is my last one. I'll be glad to eat them again. We call them…" And he proceeded to speak an unpronounceable word in his singsong language.

"And we shall call them Jute nuts," Joz said with a

bright smile.

"We have plenty of money," Omya said squinting in V's direction.

"Omya, where are your eyeglasses?" V said.

"They came from Drome and I smashed them. I would rather be near blind than see through something made by those cockfaces." She sneered and slapped her hand on the table. Naomya jumped at the rare show of emotion from the Head Teller. Omya collected herself. "The Ferts paid us in advance for a year's supply of birds' nests. The money arrived before the Dromedars, thankfully. Along with five hundred of the one thousand Fert horses Queen Jessima Cleland of Fertilian promised Melokai Ramya."

"I will leave it to you, Omya, to allocate the funds as you see fit."

Omya nodded curtly and folded her arms.

Chaz leaned forward, careful not to knock his sling. "V, the House of Knowledge was destroyed. All our history records, all our library. I understand we cannot rebuild at this time, but we cannot simply neglect to record that which is around us. And attempt to salvage and reproduce some of the most important tomes."

"Find somewhere suitable, Chaz, to accommodate the House of Knowledge for the time being," V said.

"Why not that traitorous warrior Ashya's apartment? I've heard it's going spare," Lizya said.

V nodded and Chaz dipped his head in agreement.

Zecky looked up from her notes. "I'll organise the burial of Melokai Ramya, and the announcement of her successor Melokai Violya, who also has The Sight. The people will want to celebrate after so long with no new magic."

"I entrust that fully to your care, Zecky," V said. She was pleased at how this meeting was progressing.

"Well, if everyone else is saying their bit, then so will I," Lizya said. "The Dromedar invasion exposed vulnerabilities at the border. It's the first time a foreign army has ever crossed into our land, and it will be the last. I will make some changes."

"Thank you, Lizya," V said.

"And you'll need a guard. I'll assign you Monya. She might be a youngblood, but she'll keep you in order."

V smiled.

"And we need to talk about you know what," Lizya said.

V's smile faded. "We have a new threat. One from the inside."

As her councillors crunched their foreheads, she gestured to Lizya.

The new Head Warrior said, "The stone army, for one thousand years rooted to the ground, is coming alive. As Sybilya's power wanes, the stone males are starting to move. We witnessed it on our return from Mlaw."

"Coming *alive?*" Chaz repeated, "Remarkable. I should like to study this occurrence… these… stone creatures…"

"Oh my," Naomya uttered.

"Zhaq," Zecky blurted and scrawled a note on her parchment.

"We'll send Daya with some fresh warriors to assess and report back," Lizya said. She rolled her shoulder and a dark cloud passed across her features. "Our warrior numbers are diminished and stretched thin. We suffered many losses with the wolf war and the invasion. We need to bolster our force, and rapidly. Any bright ideas?"

The question hung in the air as all considered this.

V collected her thoughts. *Customs must change if the nation is to survive.* This was a matter of survival, of life and death. What custom had served Peqkya up until now but was now redundant?

"The peons," Sybilya's voice blurted in V's mind and then was silent.

The peons. When Sybilya created Peqkya, from the ashes of the country of Xayy, she punished the surviving males for their atrocities, renamed the male children as peens and adults as peons. She set quotas on the number permitted to live from peen to peon, devised strict usefulness tests that must be passed at fifteen. *Life and death. Life* or *death. Life.* V had to be bold. Had to choose life to continue living.

'There is no use for useless peons', the saying went. But what if they could be valuable? Peons were not permitted to become warriors, but the peon rebellion had proved that they could – and would – fight for a cause.

The red-haired warrior cleared her throat. "I appreciate many Peqkian customs have changed this day. But I have one more. All peons are to pass into peonhood. Those who would've been ended at fifteen will be trained to fight. Both girls and peens will learn basic combat training from childhood."

A stunned silence greeted this pronouncement.

Zecky's pencil paused in mid scrawl. She squeezed it so tight in her fist it snapped. "Ramya gave the peons a sniff of power and they turned against her, sided with the Dromedars and traitorous Peqkians. They should be treated with more severity not more leniency. Allowing useless peens to live goes against everything Peqkya stands for. This cannot be allowed to happen."

"Here, here," Omya said.

"Scrap the usefulness tests…" Naomya, the Mother of Mothers who ran the pens and the peen usefulness tests, said, and stared out the window, bewildered.

"Issee," Joz uttered and her hands flew to her cheeks.

Chaz, a eunuch by his own hand to demonstrate his devotion to Peqkya and his scholarly profession, grinned. The white patch over his right eye, in the exact shape of the country, flushed red.

Head Warrior Lizya frowned, but realisation slowly dawned on her face.

"They will not be useless," V insisted. "They will fight for their country. Their purpose will be the protection of Peqkya. How many peens are ended each year at fifteen?"

"Perhaps a thousand," Zecky replied reluctantly.

"That is one thousand more to protect our nation," V said.

Lizya bobbed her head, slowly at first and then enthusiastically.

Zecky flicked her long rope-like braids from one side of her head to the other. "They will rebel again and this time they'll know how to fight."

Will the peons rise against me as they did against Ramya? She had to believe they would not, had to trust her gut.

"We'll whip them into shape. They won't blink unless a woman says so," the Head Warrior said.

"Customs must change if Peqkya is to survive," V repeated the words Sybilya had spoken earlier that day.

Zecky raised her eyebrows and stared down at her parchment. She picked up one half of the pencil and furiously scribbled. "The people won't like it," she muttered, "how to tell them…"

"I will see to this, V," Naomya said.

"Thank you."

"Truly, a momentous day in Peqkya's history," Chaz exclaimed raising his hands in the air. "I will be delighted to record this in the new histories."

"That is all. I appreciate your counsel," V said.

Lizya stood abruptly. "About time. My arse has gone numb."

***

Gwrlain wailed from inside what had been Melokai Ramya's apartment.

It was the same sound he had made when V had burst through into the assembly hall and had seen her Melokai slain by that cammer prince. When that cockface's sword had thrust through Ramya and out through the baby tied to her back. In one horrific moment Gwrlain had seen his soulmatch and his daughter murdered.

V understood his desperate sadness; felt the same deep within, an eternal ache for lost loved ones. She had a hollow space in her chest where her friend Emmya's death echoed. V did not need a personal guard, but Lizya had assigned Monya. The young novice warrior reminded her of Emmya with her thin braids often piled up in a bow atop her head. Her slightly chubby face but short and sturdy body, her inquisitive and friendly brown eyes and her exceptional skill with a sword. V liked to remember Emmya when she looked at Monya.

"It has been too long now," Zecky, the Head Speaker was saying. *My Head Speaker.* It still felt weird.

"We need a public send off for Melokai Ramya. Everything is ready. People are expecting one, asking when it'll happen. And then we can announce your appointment to the people officially. But no one can get near the cave creature and no one is certain what to do, as he was Ramya's companion and was therefore afforded certain… *privileges.*" Zecky spat the last word in disdain.

"Why will no one go near him?" V asked.

"We've tried but he lets out a low hum. It rattles the room and if a person gets too close it stops them in their tracks and shakes them right to the bones. They retreat. I tried to take Terya from him," Zecky glowered at the memory, "but he let out this death-rattle. I thought I might shake apart."

"And the state of the bodies?"

"Both decomposing, of course. He has hugged them both to him since their death. If he's not making his racket, he talks to them. Coos over the baby, sings. He hasn't eaten since their death, he has become like a sleepwalker, not communicating with anyone. Enough's enough. We need those bodies from him."

V put a hand on Zecky's shoulder. "I will do my best." She handed Emmo to Monya and as the caterpillar scampered up the youngblood's arm, said to her guard, "Stay here."

V opened the door and entered the room cautiously.

Gwrlain was huddled by the fire, on his knees, rocking

back and forth hugging the dead bodies of Ramya and the baby Terya to his chest. The corpses flopped over his arms, as if the insides had turned to liquid. Terya looked like the ragdoll V had played with as a child in the pen. Ramya was missing her teeth and nails, and her hair was matted.

The organs had putrefied, the stench overwhelming. Both had gone through the bloat stage and were now in the shrinking phase. Ramya's once strong physique now thin and saggy. Gwrlain sang a haunting lament to them, kissing Ramya's shriveled, rotting cheek every now and then.

V moved closer to the Trogr. His skin was almost translucent. She could see his sinewy muscle, veins and organs. His body was covered in fine, downy hair and in place of eyes he had two pink mounds. He was taller than V by a head and had a powerful, sculpted body with long limbs.

"Gwrlain, do you remember me? I was once your personal guard."

The white giant turned his face to her. His shoulders stiffened and he clutched at the bodies with one hand, pulling them away from V. His nostrils flared as he took in a deep breath. He held his free hand out, palm up as he let out a throaty hum. He paused, cocked his head to listen and then emitted hums in short pulses, shifting his head at different angles to hear the responding echoes. He stuck out his tongue for a moment to taste the air. This humming and smelling was the blind Trogr's way of seeing, his race having evolved in the deep, black caves and having no need for eyes.

"Violya. Warrior," he said.

"Yes, and I am now the Melokai. Life has moved on. Ramya is gone but she will never be forgotten. Her people need to say goodbye, and she would want to say goodbye to them. You know this. She loved Peqkya, and you are keeping her from her people."

"My… soulmatch," Gwrlain choked. "My… daughter. You cannot take them from me."

"Gwrlain, it's time for Peqkya to say goodbye to Ramya and Terya. It's time for you to say goodbye to their bodies. They're not coming back. They must be burned."

Gwrlain's shoulders slumped.

"Ramya wanted to rescue the women taken by the Trogrs, by your people, did she not?"

"Yes."

"She is no longer here to rescue them, but you are. You can rescue them. You can do this for Ramya."

Gwrlain turned his face from V and clutched the ragdolls to his chest again. "I miss them, Violya."

V's breath hitched in her chest. "My best friend Emmya died, Gwrlain. My mentor, Ramya's Head Warrior, Gogo, has died. I've also lost my Melokai. I miss them. But I carry them here," she tapped her heart, "and here," she tapped her forehead. "Grief will consume us if we let it. For our loved ones we must go on. You must go on, for Ramya."

Gwrlain's body convulsed in great heaving sobs. Her own sorrow scratched at the corners of her eyes, but she blinked it back.

"What would Ramya have wanted, Gwrlain? For you to sit here wasting away clutching her rotting body? Or would she have wanted you to finish what she had started? She loved her people, she'd want to be remembered. She'd want her passing to be marked and commemorated in the customary way."

Gwrlain's sobs slowly eased.

"She must say goodbye to her people," V said.

He mumbled in the throaty, harsh, guttural language of Troglo.

"You can honour her memory by finding a way to get the kidnapped Peqkian women back from Troglo."

He paused, and then nodded.

"You have important work to do. Ramya would be

proud to know you are helping her people."

V moved forward. "Let go of the bodies, Gwrlain."

Gwrlain jumped to his feet. "No!" He hummed a low, staccato sound, the death-rattle as Zecky had called it. V's body vibrated violently, her teeth chattered, and it took all her will to stop her quivering legs from collapsing. The danger woke her magic.

Shake him back! It said.

I can do that?

Of course! You can do anything.

I do not want to harm him.

The magic sighed, a whisper that tickled across her skin. *Then don't. Mimic the vibrations, control the air that surrounds him, just as he is controlling the air that surrounds you. A simple trick.*

V focused on the shaking, pinpointed the air and copied it. Gwrlain jerked back, his translucent skin flushing red. His body tremored as hers was.

He fought against the shakes, his face taut, his skin turning a deep purple. With a yell his fingers uncurled from the bodies and slowly they slid from his grip to the floor.

His death-rattle ceased. And V ended hers in return. They both rubbed their arms and legs, the rattle's aftermath feeling as if it had dislodged skin from bone. Gwrlain stared at her for a long time, a pink flush on his cheeks.

"Take them," he said eventually. "Ramya deserves to say goodbye."

He took one last look at the bodies on the floor, carefully stepped over them and stopped next to V, his head hung low. "I go to my bird nesting tower," Gwrlain whispered. "I do not belong here."

***

Melokai Ramya and her baby Terya were burned the following night in the square in front of the ruined House of Knowledge.

The pyre was lit and all held their breath as the fire licked at the wood under the bodies, and then caught with a sudden whoosh of heat and light. The blaze enveloped the honoured dead with a roar and burned bright, casting shadows on the huts around the square and shrouding those who stood nearest in a golden glow, the blazing pyre reflected in their eyes.

Everyone who was able had turned out to watch the celebration of her life and legacy. The peons in attendance wailed and keened, or were silent. These were the peons who had loved Ramya, not joining the rebellion.

Cats crawled through feet and legs to get close to the fire, encircling it, mewing. Head Speaker Zecky gave a rousing speech, Ramya's favourite pipe player and dancers performed, wine was drunk in great quantities and people feasted.

V stood at the head of her warriors. The councillors each headed those from their professions.

The noise and commotion of the funeral unfolded around V, and as she watched the fire in silence, an image flashed in the flickering flames. *Ammad plunging his sword through Ramya's chest.* Sparks spat and flew. *Terya's tiny head slumping.* An abrupt shift in burning wood and the fire flared. *V slicing off his arms when she should've killed him.* Smouldering embers crackled. *Ammad, still alive, evading her grasp...* Again and again it repeated until V wanted to smack her forehead with the heel of her hand to get the thought out.

"V?" Monya's voice sounded far off.

A squeeze of V's wrist brought her to attention and Monya's face was close to hers.

"V, one of Denya's warriors has arrived from Fertilian. What she has to say cannot wait. She is injured."

V ran towards the barracks, Monya at her heels. A warrior was slumped between two novices as medics dressed her wounds. Lizya was gently giving her water from a cup. V did not recognise the warrior.

"Marshya, your message," the Head Warrior said and dismissed the novices and medics with a hand gesture. Lizya wrapped one of the warrior's arms around her neck and tucked her shoulder under Marshya's to take her weight.

Marshya glanced around, to ensure no one stood nearby and thumped a weak fist to her chest. "Melokai Violya."

"Marshya." V thumped a fist to her chest in return. "You can speak in front of Lizya."

Marshya nodded and said, "Captain Denya betrayed Melokai Ramya's orders to help the Clelands. She deserted them and switched sides to the Thornes. Her warriors followed her, as we are trained to do. But I defied her, I could not abandon Melokai Ramya's command. I broke the code. I, too, deserted, to return.

"Denya sent warriors after me, to catch me. I took an arrow to the gut, but I evaded them. I have travelled here to tell of her disloyalty. And I arrive, to hear of an even greater treachery, to hear of the Drome invasion and of the warrior Ashya's treason with Head Trader Rivya. It is too much."

Marshya coughed up blood. V took the cup from Lizya and helped the warrior to drink a few sips. Marshya stood a little straighter and looked V in the eyes, "Once the Thornes take Fertilian, they mean to conquer Peqkya and put Denya on the throne. Fertilian is hostile. It can no longer be counted on as an ally."

The warrior's knees gave way and she drooped against Lizya.

"I've told my message to the Melokai… it is time for me to die," Marshya slurred.

"Medics," V shouted as she slapped Marshya's cheek to keep the warrior conscious, but it was too late.

6

DARRIO

"Let's hunt," Warrio announced, standing to all fours.

He stretched out his back by reaching with his front legs, keeping his muzzle close to the ground and sticking his tail in the air. He reversed the move by dropping his backside, pushing out his back legs and standing up on his front ones, sticking his nose in the air. He emitted a low, satisfied groan. He popped up to stand on two legs, bent his head to each side and flexed his muscles. His glossy brown fur rippled.

He has grown tall and strong, Darrio thought, *my son the warrior.*

Darrio's daughter, Sarrya, did not stir. She rested on her belly, front legs outstretched and her head placed on top of them. Her tail straight out behind her. The patch of dirt where she lay was at the crest of a hill, in the space under a huge, fallen tree. The exposed, gnarly roots framed her in a spiky, twisted half-circle. The grey, sun-bleached tangle kept off the snow and protected them from the bitter northerly wind.

Darrio was curled up with his eldest pup, Harro, grooming the yearling's fur. Harro had not grown in the same way as his brother and sister. *He looks more wolf, more like me.*

"Come on," Warrio insisted, nudging Sarry's neck with his nose. "We lie here all day."

"Visitors," Sarry mumbled, ignoring his pestering.

"Where?" Warrio made a show of sniffing the air and scanning the forest. "Pappy," he bounded over to Darrio and put his front paws on his father's ribs, tail wagging, "let's hunt."

"Wait. We go when visitors have come," Darrio replied.

Warrio sighed. He rolled his shoulders and, after a moment's consideration, leapt onto Sarry, who barked in surprise. They tussled and yipped, each attempting to take the other's muzzle in their mouths, nipping at ears and striving to pin the other to the ground.

"Always the same," Harro said.

Darrio snorted. *Harro, his serious boy.*

Harro watched his siblings scrap then launched himself at them, joining in the game. Sarry and Warrio were not as rough with their smaller sibling as they were with each other. The trio yapped and snapped, kicking up dirt as they twisted and folded around one another.

It had been two moon cycles since the tigers had pushed the wolf army north across the river and out of the Lost Lands. Since Sarry had saved Harro and negotiated a truce with the tigers and, by association, the Peqkians the beasts fought for.

"I command the wolf army," Sarry had declared, on that day, and not one wolf had objected. They had returned to their dens to lick their wounds and mourn their dead. And life in Zwullfr had returned to relative normality. Old packs reformed, newly single alphas paired up and new dominant breeding pairs split off to form new packs. The wolves hunted, staked claims on their territory, watched juvenile wolves and pups grow.

But life wasn't the same. The battle with the Peqkians loomed over them like the blackest of clouds, and all in

Zwullfr knew it wasn't done.

Darrio and his three pups had returned to the Wulhor-Aaen den. The alpha, Arro, had welcomed them back but it no longer felt like home. Darrio and his pups were now outsiders, because of Sarry. The first standing female in Zwullfr and now the wolf who tamed the tigers and claimed control of the army.

Arro, devastated at the loss of his mated female, Lurra, in the war, understood he must rebalance the pack. He took a new alpha female, who had lost her mate and most of her pack. She brought to the Wulhor-Aaen den three newborns and two yearlings, and Arro adopted them readily. His remaining packmates accepting them without question.

But Darrio recognised the signs: the not sharing of hunt meat, the backs turned against him and his pups at rest, the alpha male barely speaking to them.

It was Harro's idea to find their own den. "We our own pack now," he had said. Harro the Wise.

Arro had gracefully and gratefully let them leave. They had gone to the secret thicket, which became their rest area, and this mound of dirt under the fallen tree had become their daytime space. Their lives had forever changed.

A scent on the wind. Two wolves from a distant pack. Darrio grunted at his pups, sniffing the air. The tussle ceased as the pups caught the scent. Warrio moved down the hill to stand on all fours, in front of his sister. Darrio moved next to Warrio while Harro stayed back, to one side of his sister.

Sarry sat at the top of the small hill with the tangle of roots fanned out behind her.

Two light-grey wolves slunk into view, low to the ground and tails down. Submissive. They paused to ensure they had been seen, and then continued creeping forward until they crouched on their bellies at the bottom of the small hill. Eyes down, ears lowered, fur flat. One carried a hunk of meat on a bone, the other a freshly caught rabbit.

"Welcome," Sarry said.

She had become better at receiving wolves. At first, they had found it odd that so many came to pay their respects. But soon it was accepted as a near-daily occurrence, one which they embraced.

One lone wolf had attempted to take Sarry down, howling that she was an abomination who cavorted with tigers. That attack had prompted the current formation. Although Darrio knew Sarry could fight – she was the strongest of all of them and had decisively stopped the lone wolf in his tracks with one swipe of her paw – they did not want to take that risk again.

The larger of the grey wolves dropped her hunk of meat. "Tiger tamer, Sarrya, Darrio's daughter, I am Zerra of the Arracht-Aaen and this is my son Navrro."

Sarry nodded and the smaller of the two dropped the rabbit.

"We travelled many nights across Zwullfr to honour you. Our pack not in war, did not hear in time to come. But we have heard now of your bravery. Will be ready to fight when you call us. Will not be late again."

"Thank you, Zerra of Arracht-Aaen."

"My son of age to form pack. Is yours to mate with."

Darrio had lost count of how many wolves had been presented to Sarry to mate with, to form a pack as the alpha pair. Sarry had rejected them all.

"This my pack. Father and brothers. All I need. But thank you for offer. Navrro, you will form a great pack. First mated female will die in whelping. Don't despair. You find another who is stronger within a moon."

Navrro's eyes widened and the older wolf crouched lower.

"Appreciate gift. Will send word when you are needed," Sarry said and she turned her back to them to show they were dismissed.

The two grey wolves backed away, keeping shoulders

low and head to the ground. When they had reached a respectable distance to show Sarry their backs, they turned and ran into the woods. Darrio watched them with his one eye until he could no longer see or smell them.

Warrio dove on the hunk of meat and devoured it. Sarry grabbed for the rabbit. Harro shrugged. His appetite was not as big as his siblings, but Sarry tossed a rabbit leg to him and he ate. She nudged the other leg toward her father.

Warrio licked his lips. "Now, we hunt. Only made me hungrier."

Sarry chewed down her meat in one go and sprinted into the forest, Warrio on her heels. Darrio and Harro picked up their rabbit legs and followed.

"Pappy and I go to Peqkya tomorrow," Sarry announced as they settled down for the night in the centre of the secret thicket, bellies full of elk from a successful hunt.

Darrio's shoulders tensed and fur prickled. His head shot up and he turned his one eye to stare at his daughter.

"Peqkya!" Warrio spat the word and scrambled up to sitting. "Murderers. Thousands of wolves dead. Twice took the Lost Lands from us. You tame tigers, but tigers follow Peqkian orders. You go to take revenge?"

"No. Friends. Need our help."

Warrio stood to all fours, his hackles raised and tail high. His lip curled back to show sharp fangs. "Not friends, Sarry. Enemies," he snarled. "You fight them not long past."

"Because then did not know. Now, understand," Sarry said. She lay on her side, completely at ease.

"Know what?" Warrio shouted in his sister's ear.

Sarry's ear twitched but she did not rise to the challenge. "The enemy comes. From east. Must fight with Peqkians if we are to prevail. Not against."

"Enough, sister." Warrio swiped Sarry across the jaw. She yelped at the viciousness and sat up.

Darrio sprung up and bundled into Warrio, clamping his son's muzzle in his jaw. Darrio was now smaller than his son, but Warrio submitted to his father out of respect. Darrio eased the pressure on Warrio's muzzle and snapped his jaws in warning.

"Family. No violence."

Warrio's eyes narrowed and his nose crinkled as he showed Darrio his teeth.

"Should not go Peqkya," Warrio said as he shrunk away into a corner of the thicket. "Wolves need you here. Their new pack leader. Pappy united the packs, you lead them."

"Yes," Sarry replied. "To lead, we go to Peqkya."

Warrio huffed and turned his back, lying down in a tight coil, his nose a hair's breadth from the sharp thorns of the undergrowth that sheltered them.

Darrio rolled onto his side, back against Warrio to give him a small comfort.

"Sarry," he said gently. "Peqkya dangerous. Wolves not welcome."

"Wolves welcome," Sarry replied as she sniffed at the ground and pawed it before lying down again.

"Warrio stronger, take him," Darrio said.

Sarry raised her voice to ensure her brothers heard. "Warrio and Harro stay. Greet wolves that come. Keep order. Rule for me."

Darrio felt Warrio's back stiffen against his own. Harro, silent until now, licked his lips noisily to indicate he'd understood.

"Sarry, cannot simply enter Peqkya," Darrio insisted.

"Can. And will, Pappy."

"Sarry—"

"Pa," Sarry cut him short, "You do not want to come, but you must. I need you. You are wise, you guide me. You are my father."

"As you are my daughter."

***

Harro saw Darrio and Sarry off from the thicket. They

touched noses and rubbed against each other, snuffling fur to take in their scents. Warrio had disappeared before they had awoken, and had not returned. Sarry shrugged it off, but Darrio was desperate to see his son before they left. He did not think they would return.

As Darrio and Sarry jogged south towards the bank of the Great River, Darrio said, "Sarry, do not know way."

"We find a way," Sarry replied.

"How so certain about these things?"

Before she could answer Warrio jumped into their path, hackles raised, teeth bared and snarling viciously. "Do not go to Peqkya. Will not let you. Enemies do not deserve help."

"Warrio, son…" Darrio started but Sarry surprised him and lunged at Warrio.

She clamped her jaw around Warrio's neck, shook it violently and then rolled back and over so that Warrio spun in the air and slammed down on his side. He scrambled to his feet and rammed into her, snapping at her neck. Both wolves emitted a high-pitched whine.

Darrio shouldered into them, forcing both off their feet. "Family! No violence!"

He grabbed at the scruffs around their necks, stood to his two back legs and yanked them apart. Holding them to either side of him. Both attempted to wriggle free of his grip, but he held them tight.

"Pups," he rumbled in the same tone he used when they were scrabbling newborns. "Behave."

Warrio shook himself free of Darrio's grip and licked at a slash on his leg that Sarry had inflicted.

Darrio dropped Sarry and stood between them. She clamped her jaw together and refused to look at either of them.

"We go to Peqkya. You and Harro stay," Darrio said.

Sarry trotted away towards the riverbank.

Darrio watched her back and turned to Warrio. His son's chest heaved, and his brow was scrunched tight in anger.

"Sister is unique. Must trust her." Darrio licked Warrio's wound and nuzzled his neck.

"She is strong," Warrio muttered. He head-bumped Darrio and turned his eyes down in respect and submission. "Be safe, Pappy. Come home."

Darrio snorted a goodbye in his son's ear, and then took off after his daughter.

Sarry was waiting for him nearby and they fell in line, padding through the snow.

She kept her head lowered and bumped her body against Darrio. "Sorry, Pappy."

He continued to run and did not look at her.

"Warrio will betray us," Sarry said in a small voice.

Darrio stopped, turned to her. She could not meet his eyes.

"Have sense of what to come," she explained.

"Do not believe it. Cannot believe it," Darrio replied.

Sarry kept her head low. "Don't know when or what form future takes, but know... Just like knew tigers would not harm me."

Darrio remained silent. Sarry had not mentioned how she had negotiated with the tigers for Harro's release and return. How she had not been slaughtered herself. He wanted to know, had asked her, but until now, she had not been ready to tell.

Sarry continued, "Tigers answer to her, Pappy, the stone female from my dreams. She summoned me to them. I... I spoke feline. They said I was The One the stone female, Sybilya her name, had been seeking."

"The One?"

Sarry shrugged.

"Spoke feline?"

Sarry shrugged again. Darrio nudged her cheek with his own and she met his gaze.

"Say something in feline."

"No, Pappy," Sarry laughed, suddenly shy. "Come on."

They set off running once again. Soon they reached the river and ran out on the ice along the bank, skidding here and there. When they came to the edge of the ice, Darrio hesitated but Sarry sploshed straight into the freezing water. Darrio took a deep breath and followed. The chill hit him like a heavy tiger swipe and for a while he struggled to exhale the breath stuck in his frozen lungs.

He chased after his daughter, and they swam together for the other side, breaking through ice until they heaved themselves up onto the southern bank.

Both shook out their fur and rubbed themselves together for warmth.

Darrio looked up at the mountains that loomed before them and marked the border of Peqkya.

"Where now?" he said to Sarry.

A strange, purring voice answered. "This way."

Darrio yapped in surprise and wheeled about to see a pack of one hundred tigers, fangs bared, creeping out from the darkness of the forest, surrounding them. Darrio moved close to Sarry and crouched into a fighting stance.

The tigers hissed and Darrio snarled in return. Sarry was silent, flicking her eyes from one beast to the next. Their slathering jaws came at them.

"Sarry," Darrio said, for the last time, as he prepared to attack.

He knew he and his daughter had no chance of survival. They would meet their end here in the Lost Lands, just a few paces from their home.

Sarry stood to her full height and produced her roaring howl. It echoed throughout the trees and was thrown back at them by the mountains. It silenced the tigers; it stunned him. He shook with the power of it and glanced at his daughter, awaiting her instruction as to their plan of attack.

She was powerful, more so than he realised. Perhaps… perhaps they had a chance.

But the howl was not a declaration of her strength, it was a greeting.

Her eyes brightened and as the howl tailed off, a smile played across her lips. She dropped to four legs and bounced up and down, hind legs to forelegs in a display of joy, wagging her tail and allowing her tongue to loll happily from her mouth.

Astonished, Darrio flicked his attention from her to the beasts.

The tigers roared in delight. And then they kneeled.

7

JESSIMA

ೞ

With the Meliok mountains behind her in the north, Queen Jessima looked south across the endless dunes. Some were as high as the wall on which she now stood, some giants the size of the mountains behind her.

Prince Ernest was taking her on a tour of Lian's famed walls. Built when Edgar, the first King of Fertilian, took the city from the country of Drome two thousand years ago, and reinforced since.

They paused to take in the view of red sand that stretched for as far as Jessima could see. These dunes belonged to Drome. King Edgar had no use for them, had only wanted the harbour town the Dromedars had called Vaasar. A heat haze shimmered across the horizon with dust and fine sand swirling up, caught in the wind.

At first, Ernie had been reluctant to bring her to the great wall. Prince Charles had adamantly voiced his opinion that it was no place for a woman, and that the staircase climb would not be beneficial for Jessima, in her condition.

But, finally, she was here, almost two months since she had arrived in Lian from Fertilian proper through the tunnels, and five weeks since her failed debut in the marketplace.

Ernie had told her not to concern herself with the drunk's outburst, and when Jessima had suggested she try again, Ernie had said, "The people know now that their Queen is in Lian and that is enough. You should remain on a pedestal, lofty and inaccessible. You are not one of the people, and never will be."

As much as that had rankled Jessima, she had remained in Ernie's residence, her insistence on going out into the city continually ignored. Instead she had reluctantly prayed – a rather ridiculous amount – with Prince Charles. She was convinced God now found her prayers tiresome, the number of times she had repeated them to Him.

Jessima was only on the walls because Princess Georgina, not one to shy away from doing and saying precisely what she wanted, no matter the vulgarity or uncustomary nature, had joined her voice to Jessima's and nagged her uncles incessantly about the trip.

The princes relented and an outing was arranged. Jessima delighted in the news, giddy to venture out of the fortress and further explore Lian.

The day had arrived and, at the last moment, Princess Georgina had taken her leave. She was otherwise engaged, she'd said. Working her way through the few male soldiers and staff that Ernest kept at his residence, Jessima knew. Prince Charles had a congregation to sermonise to and so could not attend, much to Jessima's relief.

So, Prince Ernest, Betsy the dog and Jessima headed out to the walls, accompanied by a number of female soldiers.

Betsy darted back and forth along the narrow pathway, circling Ernie's feet while he strolled.

"There are no doors or openings in this entire wall. It contains the city, and keeps the Dromedars firmly out," Ernie said. He relished his role as historian and had a bottomless well of knowledge about Lian.

Jessima soaked up the detail, intrigued. She had never

been taught history, other than the most basic of events. She had no idea about politics or the law. Her mind, like so many other noble women, had been filled with fripperies. Destined to be pretty, decorative wives, and nothing more.

Ernie continued, "The city is impenetrable. There is no way down from the mountains to the north. No one ever attempts this as the peaks are vicious and a pathway has never been discovered. There are two ways into the city. First, by water," Ernest pointed west towards the endless blue sea, "but we have watchtowers on either side of the harbour, and a small, easily defendable opening into the bay. We've never been attacked by sea, the only ships coming and going are ours or that of the Sarenky islanders, descended from Ferts."

He paused to take in the sea for a few moments, losing his train of thought.

"And the second way?" Jessima prompted.

"Ah, yes, well you know it intimately, my dear. Through the tunnels."

"Has anyone attempted to get in from out there?" Jessima asked and pointed to the vast desert.

"Oh yes, dear, come here." Ernie beckoned her forward, and with one hand clutching her arm to prevent a fall, he pointed down.

Jessima shifted her pregnant belly to one side and peered over the lip of the wall. "Oh!" She moved back, a hand to her heart. Her baby flipped inside her as if sensing her surprise.

Piles of skeletons were amassed against the bottom of the wall, some fresher than others. The mound stretched around the wall in both directions.

"These are all cammer skeletons, from two thousand years' worth of attempts by Drome to get into the city and take it back. They couldn't get past the wall."

"So, some of those skeletons are thousands of years old?"

"Oh, I expect those ones are all dust now. Dromedar sand dwellers, either individually or in their clan groups, have tried for many years to get in. Not as an attack, but desperate for water, food and shelter. To live here."

"And?"

"Well, they can't get in. Unless we throw down ladders, which we are not about to do. About one hundred and fifty years ago now, some Lianites took pity on these desperate souls and tossed down food and lowered water. But then a camp grew against the walls as more and more emerged from the dunes. And the Lord Overseer at the time, quite rightly, didn't want to feed more mouths, so Lianites were firmly forbidden to help."

"But there are Dromedars in Cleland City, they do not pose a problem, they work for us, as spies," Jessima said, repeating what she'd learned from sitting in on many of King Hugo's council meetings.

"Yes, my dear, and they are very strategically chosen by Lord Chattergoon and his men. We can't take care of every destitute man, woman and child with a hump. There is simply no space in the city."

Jessima waved for a handmaid to bring her some water, and she took a long draught. Sweetling had been restless all morning, squirming and kicking. She stroked her bump, attempting to soothe her baby's agitation. She looked east, in the direction of Fertilian proper.

"What if we were attacked from the tunnels?" she asked.

"We can collapse the entrance to the tunnels and we have the sea and all the food in it, and clean water from the river. We are self-sufficient," Ernie replied.

There was a commotion at the head of the steps as Ernie's female soldiers blocked the path of a few men. Jessima recognised the imposing figure of Lord Chattergoon, and with him two scrawny men. The pair squinted at the light. *They've come from the tunnels. The war is over.* Her buzz of excitement stirred the baby again, who jerked indignantly.

Ernie's soldiers stepped aside as they identified Chattergoon. The lord loped towards her and the prince, the two bedraggled men lagged behind, clearly exhausted. Two further soldiers followed, eyes on the pair from the tunnels, alert to any sign of danger.

The lord gave a small bow as he reached them. "Queen Jessima, these men bring news from Fertilian."

The smaller of the pair cleared his throat. "Your Grace, we were sent here by Prince Toby to deliver you, and only you, this message."

A message from my Toby! "Go on," Jessima urged.

"It's a hard message to tell…" The man choked up and Chattergoon slapped his back.

"Get on with it," the lord said.

At the man's glaring distress, Jessima's delight turned to dust faster than one of the thousand-years-old skeletons.

His eyes welled with tears and he swallowed, wiping his grimy brow with a dusty hand. "The Cleland army has fallen, Queen Jessima. King Hugo is… dead. The Thornes march on Cleland City."

"And Toby?" Jessima blurted. "Prince Toby, is he alive?"

"Unknown, your Grace."

Jessima reached out and clutched the nearest thing to her, which happened to be Ernie, whose shock had also made his knees weak. Together they fumbled but he found his feet faster than her and, clutching Betsy under one arm, managed to prop Jessima up with the other.

Jessima looked at Chattergoon. The lord's face was emotionless. He looked precisely as he always did: serious and astute.

The smaller man, aware of the affect he'd had on those around him, swallowed again and coughed. "There's more."

Chattergoon gestured for him to continue.

"The Peqkian Captain Denya and her warriors deserted

King Hugo and are now fighting for the Thornes."

Jessima collapsed to her knees, Ernie letting her slide down as carefully as he could.

"Does Melokai Ramya of Peqkya know?" Jessima asked. Her friend would be outraged.

The smaller man looked from Jessima to Chattergoon. "You… you do not know?"

"Know what, precisely?" Chattergoon said.

"Then it seems I have more news, your Grace. Peqkya was invaded by the Dromedars and Melokai Ramya and her child died. The situation in the mountain country is unclear, my Queen. All spies were pulled back to fight and trade has stopped."

Jessima wailed, her hands over her face.

"There, there, dear," Ernie soothed. "It is a terrible shock, but we must now consider what to—"

Jessima's screech cut him off rudely, her hands flying to her belly.

"The baby," she screamed. "I think the baby is coming!"

***

The boy gurgled in her arms. She'd given birth in a blur, her pain eased with poppy. But she'd done it and he was perfect in every way.

One week after the birth, she'd felt strong enough to leave her bed. She'd been made comfortable on a sofa and the nurses had placed him in her arms.

She was still drowsy from the poppy, but the mist was clearing and although she had watched and held her baby numerous times, up until now he hadn't seemed real. She took him in slowly, admiring this new life that she had created.

He had his father's green eyes. *I pray no one remembers that King Hugo's eyes had been blue, or notes that my eyes are also blue.*

There was a knock on the door. This was the first time after the birth that she'd received visitors. Jessima gestured for the door to be opened by whoever was nearest. Her living quarters teemed with handmaids and nurses.

Prince Ernest entered with a huge grin. He came to stand over her on the sofa, his round belly unpleasantly close to her face.

"Well, isn't he a looker," Ernie said, "Hugo was always the handsome one. And Toby, of course, although he was always so much younger than the rest of us, and that naturally made him the looker." The prince chuckled.

"King Hugo," Jessima mumbled. Her voice was rusty from little use.

"What's that, my dear?" Ernie said.

Jessima cleared her throat. "King Hugo," she repeated, louder this time, "we must organise a mourning period, some kind of celebration of his life and commemoration of his passing. We must mark this devastating occasion."

Ernie frowned. He pulled over a nearby chair, sat down and clasped his hands across his gut. "Yes, of course, my dear. However, don't fret as it has all been taken care of while you've been recovering. We gave him a good send off, no need to concern yourself."

Jessima felt crushed in a vice as the air was forced from her lungs. Tears prickled her eyelids as she fought to draw a breath. She might not have loved Hugo romantically, but she loved him as her King. He had always been kind and generous to her. She wanted to mourn him with his people. "I… I should have been there… He was my husband… I was his Queen…"

Ernie dismissed her with a flap of his hand. "Nonsense, dearie."

Through the pain of loss, Jessima filled her aching lungs and composed herself.

"I have decided on a name," she said, changing the subject before the floodgates burst.

"Ah," Ernie said.

Jessima parted her lips to speak but Ernie held up a palm.

"Let me stop you there. That has also been taken care of," Ernie said with a smile.

"Wha… what?" Jessima managed.

"We announced the birth and the baby's name at Hugo's commemoration. We wanted to end on a joyous note."

Jessima, stunned, gawped at Ernie. They had mourned her husband and named her baby without her, without any input from her, the queen.

Ernie took her silence as excitement. He tapped a drumroll on his thigh. "Your baby is called… Edward Hugo Cleland."

Jessima remained mute, staring at her brother-in-law. Her baby's name, the one she had chosen, died on her lips.

"Charlie and I deliberated for a while but settled on Edward Hugo. It's after his great grandfather, the great King Edward, of course. And also for his uncle Edward, lost at sea for all these years. That was a splendid day when he set off, I can tell you…"

Her baby began to bawl. His little face scrunched and reddened.

"Sorry, you'll have to tell me that story another time. The baby needs feeding," Jessima said, in no mood to hear one of the prince's rambling tales, and shifted her son's position in her arms.

"Right, certainly, I'll fetch a wet nurse," Ernie said. He hurried to apprehend one of the many servants in the room.

Jessima gazed at her baby before he was peeled from her arms.

Edward. His name is Edward.

Jessima tossed and turned. She flung back the bedcovers.

I need some air.

She donned her bedgown, went to the open door and stepped out onto the balcony. The courtyard was dark and still. The entire household was sleeping. She looked across to the balcony of the next room where Eddie slept with his night-time wet nurse. The window was ajar, like most of the windows in the fortress.

Although it was autumn, the air was still and stifling. It was warmer in Lian than Fertilian, due to its proximity to the desert. She needed to move, to create her own breeze, and headed out on one of her night-time wanderings.

Ever since she had married Hugo, nearly ten years before, she had wandered around Cleland Castle at night. It was her time for reflection. All day she was ushered here and there and had a full schedule that she had no say in. She was expected to attend engagements and reside over ceremonies and be at her husband's – and his advisors' – disposal.

But now her husband was no more. King Hugo was dead. Eddie, a mere babe, was the King. She gently pushed her door open and glided silently down the corridor, past Princess Georgina's room. It was quiet, for a change.

Jessima walked in a loop around the square fortress, staying on the first floor. She paused at a large hallway window that overlooked the internal courtyard. The small pond in the centre reflected the moon, the still water a molten silver. Eddie had been conceived on a night like this, in the pool at Cleland Castle.

She missed Toby. *Is he even alive?*

A chill settled over her. It was time to return to the luxury of her bed. To fluff the goose-down pillows and attempt to sleep again. But first, she wanted to look in on Eddie sleeping. His peaceful, beautiful chest rising and falling was a calming tonic to Jessima's overactive mind.

Not wanting to wake her baby, or his nurse, Jessima silently opened the door to Eddie's room, deftly slipped inside and pushed the door to with no noise. Years of moving silently at night having made her skilful in the art of slinking like a cat.

Eddie's cot was in front of the window. As usual, the curtains were open and moonlight streamed through. In front of the cot stood a dark figure.

The nurse?

She flicked her eyes over to the bed and saw Eddie's nurse. Her eyes were open and her hand was stretched towards Eddie. The bedsheets were tangled around her legs, one of which slumped off the bed. Her bare, white foot touched the carpet. In the centre of her chest a blooming red mark seeped into her nightgown.

Jessima's eyes jerked back to the figure. A broad-shouldered man, for it was definitely a man, dressed in a black overcoat, leaned over Eddie's cot. He slowly raised a bloody dagger up and over the wooden frame.

An assassin.

Jessima grabbed the large, ceramic jug from the baby's washstand and ran forward. She raised the jug up and smashed it down on the man's head.

Pieces of pottery flew at Eddie and in her face. She prayed none had hurt her baby. Eddie woke at the noise and grumbled. The man grunted and stumbled backward. He turned to face her, swiping his dagger in the same movement.

The knock on the head had momentarily rendered him unsteady and his jab missed its mark. She grabbed his wrist and pulled, using the momentum of his thrust to carry him forward.

She stuck out her foot and he tripped, falling face first onto the floorboards. His hand slapped down and the dagger skittered from his grasp.

She lunged for it, but a heavy grip tightened around her ankle and she fell too. She kicked out at him and stretched for the dagger, touching the handle with her fingertip, but he yanked her back.

She screamed viciously and with a momentous effort grabbed the dagger. She twisted and sliced at the arm that clasped her ankle.

The man hissed and let go. He stared at her. His face was covered with a black cloth, only his eyes bare. She saw death there. He'd come to kill. To kill Eddie.

She sprung forward with a snarl and plunged the dagger into the man's shoulder, retreating hastily before he could grab her. He groped for the dagger's hilt, found purchase and pulled it out with a huff.

Jessima scrambled to her feet. She picked up the ceramic washbowl from the washstand, stepped forward and slammed it down on the man's head with a roar.

It shattered noisily. In a daze the man yanked Jessima off her feet. She slammed down on her back, her feet towards the man. He grabbed her nightdress and pulled her forward with one hand, with the other he stabbed the dagger in her thigh. She screamed again.

He straddled her, rammed a knee in her belly and held her neck between thick, calloused fingers. She clawed at his arm that pinned her down. He slid the dagger from her flesh and raised it for a second strike. Jessima squirmed. With all her strength she punched him between the legs. He buckled, but kept a firm hold on her and his blade.

A second dagger glinted in the moonlight, tucked in his waistband. His head was close to hers and his grip around her neck had loosened. She bit his nose at the same time as reaching for the second blade.

He moved to stab her in the neck just as she stabbed him in the gut.

"Queen Jessima," a guard's voice shouted.

The man was hauled off her before his strike could land. Hands under her armpits dragged her away.

The assassin fought back against the guard, and the second guard dropped Jessima to join the skirmish. Jessima pressed a hand to her blood-dampened thigh, and realised she still clenched the dagger.

She clambered to her feet, took a step forward on her unharmed leg and watched the three-man tussle. She waited until the assassin showed her his back and punched the blade between his shoulders.

"Queen Jessima!" Lord Chattergoon shouted. She

could hear the thunderous footsteps of more guards in the corridor.

The assassin's ferocity slackened and he slumped to his knees. She put a hand on his back and pulled out the blade. With an ungodly roar that shocked even her, she thrust it into the side of the man's neck. Blood spurted from the wound and covered her hands.

The guards edged back as the assassin collapsed face-first on the floorboards.

"Is he dead?" Jessima asked.

"Queen Jessima, move back. Let's get you out of here," a guard said.

She swatted away his hand. "Is he *dead?*" she demanded.

The guard dropped to his knees to feel for a pulse. He looked up at her. "Yes, my Queen."

She nodded.

It was only then that she heard Eddie's screams. She flew towards his cot, and saw him in Prince Ernest's arms.

"Give him to me," Jessima said, wiping her bloody hands on her bedgown but Ernie backed away.

"You're injured and in shock, my dear," Ernie said. "We need to get you to a medic, you're bleeding."

"Give him to me," Jessima yelled. "Now!"

Ernie gasped. He held the baby out to her, and she whipped the boy from his arms.

"There, there, Eddie," Jessima soothed, checking him over for any scratches or signs of injury from the sharp, broken ceramic. "No one will ever harm you," she whispered to her son, "not so long as I'm here to protect you."

Holding Eddie close, she slumped in a nearby chair.

"We need to take the baby now," the medic said.

She was an efficient, no-nonsense woman with greying blond hair pulled into an orderly bun on top of her head. Her hands, although always busy, were cold. Ernie had sent for the best, and the most discreet, medic in the city to tend to Jessima's stab wound. Ernie had introduced her with a comment about how all the male medics had left the city to fight in Fertilian proper for Hugo, and that she was the best of the female medics who remained.

In a fog of pain and headiness from blood loss, Jessima hadn't caught her surname, but her name was Martha. Jessima remembered that vividly. Her mother's name was Martha.

A wet nurse hovered nearby as Martha attempted for the third time to prise Eddie from Jessima's arms. She hadn't let him go since taking him from Ernie, perhaps an hour earlier.

"I've examined the wound and you're going to need stitches," Martha said patiently. Her voice calm and steady. Trustworthy.

"I will hold Eddie while you stitch me up," Jessima said. The pain in her thigh throbbed so loud that she scrunched up her forehead.

"I'll need to administer poppy. You'll fall asleep and you'll drop the baby. Do you want that to happen?" Martha said.

Jessima noticed she'd forgotten the royal niceties, not addressing Jessima as 'your Grace' or 'my Queen'. Jessima found she didn't care. All that mattered was keeping Eddie close to her, protected from all other would-be assassins lurking out there.

"Do it without poppy then," Jessima said. "I'm not letting him go."

"It will be painful," Martha said, already reaching for her bag filled with her healing tools.

Jessima was already in excruciating pain, but she'd not cried or whimpered. Eddie was sleeping soundly on her chest; she didn't want to wake him. "Do it," she muttered. "Quickly."

Martha shrugged and held a needle in a nearby candle and then up to a thread.

"You're not going to convince me otherwise?" Jessima said.

"You're an adult. If you've made a decision then you've made a decision. Why say it if you don't mean it?" Martha said. "Have you changed your mind?"

Jessima looked away. Could she really bear this pain? She studied her son. She wasn't ready to let him go, not yet. Perhaps, not ever.

"Ready?" Martha said.

"Yes," Jessima replied.

Martha's cold, steady hands rested on Jessima's exposed flesh. She winced and clenched her teeth.

As the needle pierced her skin, she gazed at Eddie and did not make a sound, although inside she screamed and screamed.

"What are you going to do?" Martha said, while her cool hands continued to stitch Jessima's flesh back together.

"What?" Jessima pushed out the word through clamped teeth.

"What are you going to do, about this assassination attempt?" Martha said. When Jessima didn't reply, Martha continued, "Talking will help distract you from the pain. Any ideas?"

"I… I don't know," Jessima uttered.

"Don't know?"

Jessima shook her head, gasping from the pain.

"I know what I'd do," Martha said.

"What?"

"Find out who the bastard was, how he got in and who sent him," Martha said.

Jessima bit back a scream. "Got… in?"

"To Lian. All the men are gone, pretty much."

"The Gruesome Twosome sent him," Jessima hissed.

"The who?"

"The Thorne twins!"

"You know that for certain, do you? Sometimes things

aren't so obvious."

"Hmm," Jessima managed.

"And once you find out, then what are you going to do?" Martha continued.

"Ah, I… ah… I don't know."

"You don't know much, do you," Martha replied. It wasn't a malicious comment, she was simply stating fact.

Before Jessima could reply, Martha said, "All done."

Jessima let out a long breath.

Martha packed up her bag. Eddie's face furrowed and he cried. Jessima shushed him but the babe was relentless. A wet nurse came forward but Jessima waved her away.

"He's hungry," Martha said.

She had a kindly face. Open and caring, like her mother. In that moment, Jessima wanted to know how to nourish her son, she wouldn't let him be taken and fed by another. He was her responsibility. Jessima said, "Will you help me? I've… I've not fed him yet."

Patiently, and with no judgement, the medic showed Jessima what to do: expose a breast, hold the baby like so, latch the mouth on.

When Eddie was successfully feeding, after a painful latch that paled in comparison to her stab wound and a sense of relief that her swollen breasts were finally releasing milk, Jessima said, "Thank you, Martha."

Martha nodded and stood from her stool. Her knees creaked. "I can tell you how to change his nappy and bathe him too, if you're interested."

"Yes, please."

Martha told her precisely what to do in an efficient, straightforward manner.

At the end of the lesson, Martha turned to leave. "I'll be back tomorrow to check on you and see how the babe's doing on your milk."

Jessima watched Martha go and turned to the servants milling about her room.

"Leave me," she said.

They exchanged glances and bowed to Jessima as they left.

She stroked Eddie's cheek as he guzzled contentedly. "You will grow strong off my milk. You will grow into the finest king that Fertilian has ever seen."

A new cot had been placed by the window in Jessima's room. While holding Eddie carefully in one arm, she lifted herself off the sofa, wincing as she put pressure on her injured leg and hobbled to the cot. She dragged it across the floor until it was next to her bed then placed Eddie gently down to sleep, tucking the covers around him.

Jessima limped back to the window and shut it. Then headed to the door and turned the key in the lock. She edged herself into bed, keeping her bandaged leg straight and moved the pillow and covers so that she could reach Eddie's cot.

She fell asleep with her hand resting on the cot's wooden frame and her fingers splayed between the slats.

A few hours later, after Jessima had successfully fed, bathed, dressed and changed Eddie's nappy following Martha's instructions, she held him to her and left the room. The nurses, handmaids and soldiers loitering outside snapped to attention.

She gestured to them not to follow and limped along the corridor and down the stairs to the first floor.

It was a clear, dry day and she quietly let herself out into the courtyard. She tarried by the door, in the cool shadows and welcomed the crisp draught on her hot cheeks. The air soothed Eddie too.

Opposite, a door slammed. Prince Ernest and Prince Charles stepped out, deep in conversation. Ernie was holding a wriggling Betsy. They did not see Jessima.

"For safety, we need to hide her and the child away until he's sixteen and ready to take the throne," Ernie said.

"Indeed. She's insisting on feeding him herself. Whoever heard of a queen doing such a thing? As soon as he's weaned, we take charge of the boy and grant her one short visit per week. He needs to be around men," Prince Charles replied as he funnelled his fingers through his thick hair.

"Agreed," Ernie said. "And the finest tutors will train him to be a king."

Prince Charles snorted, "Where will he rule? Fertilian is likely lost to us now. Will he be the King of Lian? What a farce."

"His father, dear Hugo, clung on to Fertilian rule for twenty-four years and once again the Clelands have been ousted by the damn Thornes," Ernie said.

"Young Edward will ride forth and reclaim it in years to come," Prince Charles said.

"With what army? There are no men left in Lian."

"It's doubtful he'll be strong enough until he's at least sixteen anyway, so we've got a while to strategize."

"I fear the Thornes will be so entrenched in the country in sixteen years' time that any endeavour by young Edward would be disastrous."

Betsy barked and squirmed in Ernie's arms. The prince put the dog down and she ran straight to where Jessima stood eavesdropping and barked at the queen's feet.

Jessima slipped back inside unseen.

Once in her room, Jessima put Eddie in his cot. She paced, each step on her wounded leg shot a stabbing pain in circles around her thigh. A stinging reminder of her strength, of her determination. She'd saved Eddie.

A farce. Disastrous. One visit per week!

She would not do what the princes told her. No. She'd make her own decisions about the wellbeing of *her* son.

She caught a glimpse of herself in the full-length mirror. She was wearing a simple, loose dress, to ensure the bandages on her thigh stayed put and were easily accessible. Her long blond hair was tied in a simple braid, she wore no jewellery and her face was clean.

She pulled up her dress to expose her thigh. Some

blood had seeped through the bandage and the bright red made Jessima's stomach lurch. She tutted at herself.

I killed a man.

The memory of the fight came flooding back. Bursting through the blockade she had erected in her mind. She'd stabbed a man three times until he'd died. No one had told her what to do. She had successfully protected her son, when a fortress full of soldiers could not.

She would prepare Eddie for leadership, and she'd look after his throne until he turned sixteen. She wanted to give him a country he was proud to rule, one that he was proud to inherit from his mother. One that was safe and peaceful. She needed to teach him by example. She needed to rule, to lead, to take charge.

I will be fierce. For Eddie.

"Who sent the assassin?" Jessima said that afternoon. She had called an urgent meeting and dismissed Prince Charles' reply, that insisted she rest.

Jessima had chosen the room designated as the throne room at Ernie's fortress. She'd been shown it briefly when she'd arrived on a tour of the building but hadn't been back.

Before the others had arrived, she had sat herself in the grand chair raised on a platform. This would have been Hugo's chair. She held Eddie.

The two princes had arrived and frowned at her overt assertion of her royal position. She ignored them. Lord Chattergoon came next and simply stood to one side.

Prince Charles stepped forward. "Really, child, what is all this—"

"Take your seats," Jessima had said, her voice sharp and impatient.

The two princes sat in comfortable chairs in front of her, forced to look up at her from the lower level.

"Who?" Jessima insisted when no one answered. Charles pursed his lips and Ernie's brow knitted. Eddie grumbled in her arms at her raised voice.

"We've discussed all of this," Prince Charles said with a dismissive flick of his hand.

"Well, you'll have to discuss it all again then, won't you," Jessima said, her tone barbed.

Charles bristled in his seat and Ernie ogled him.

"Don't make me repeat myself!" Jessima shouted.

Ernie replied in a rush. "We haven't had an assassination attempt in this residence for generations. Our father was murdered on the streets. This… is a safe place."

"*Was* a safe place," Jessima retorted.

Ernie flinched.

"Are you responsible?" Jessima pointed at the eldest prince who baulked. "Is that why you won't answer me? And you," she pointed at Prince Charles, and his sour expression curdled all the more.

"Us? Your Grace, why would we want dear Edward dead?" Ernie replied.

"Because you, Ernest, were second in line to the throne and you, Charles, were third. Then Eddie was born, a male, and altered the order of succession."

"No, no, Queen Jessima, you're mistaken about the royal succession," Ernie rambled at a faster pace than usual, "Charlie and I both abdicated formally decades ago. Charlie dedicated his life to the church and I, well, I am happy here in Lian as overseer. I had no desire to leave here and head to Fertilian, to be forced to marry someone I didn't love…" Ernie glanced at the door where an older male steward waited, holding Betsy under his arm. The steward blushed at the attention.

It was Jessima's turn to be surprised – and a little impressed – that Ernie relinquished his monarchical position for love.

She softened. "Who was next in line to the throne?"

"Well, the closest male heir was Prince John. Hugo's eldest daughter Matilda's eldest son," Ernie said, his pace returning to usual.

"*Was?*" Jessima said.

"Yes, Johnny died a year or so ago in mysterious circumstances. An accident out on the salt flats in south Fertilian. He somehow became separated from his companions and was never seen again. It was a terrible mess."

"In what way?"

"Well, Matilda believed it was Prince Toby, her own uncle, who had orchestrated it. He was the last to see the boy alive. She declared that Toby wanted to strengthen his claim to the throne. Because, you see, with Charlie and I out of the running, Edward lost at sea, you still childless, and no Johnny, Toby would then be Hugo's male heir. Matilda's claims were ridiculous, of course, and it caused a huge rift between Hugo and his daughter. Their relationship had always been strained, but this was ruinous." Ernie shook his head sadly.

"Why was I not told of this?" Jessima asked.

"Why in all Fertilian would you be told?" Prince Charles scoffed.

"It was a terrible business, my dear, Hugo likely decided you were best off not knowing," Ernie said.

"Toby would not send an assassin to murder my child," Jessima said.

"Enough with all this nonsense," Prince Charles threw his hands in the air. "It was the Thornes, of course."

Jessima shot Charles her most withering look, before beckoning a steward. "I want scholars here this afternoon to tell me of the Thornes. I want to know everything about them, about their history, about why they suddenly joined forces. I want to know it all. I will know my enemy."

"Child," Charles said, "that really is not something you need to concern yourself with."

"Thank you for your counsel thus far, Prince Charles. However, from herein, if I want your opinion, I shall ask for it. Eddie has no one to reign in his stead. You and Ernie renounced your positions of power, and Toby is in

Fertilian. As there is no suitable male, we are breaking with tradition. I am the Queen Regent until Eddie comes of age. As with the rest of Lian, there are no males to do the job, so I am doing it."

"You are clearly still in shock, you are not fit to—" Prince Charles said.

"Prince Charles, you are *clearly* going deaf, for you are not listening," Jessima said, her ears burning hotter than a fire poker. "I am the Queen. You follow my rule, and unless the Thorne army conquers Lian, this city follows my rule. And I have ruled that you do not speak to me unless spoken to."

Jessima signalled to the soldiers. The two nearest Prince Charles shifted their feet and put their hands on their sword hilts in warning. She had positioned the twenty King's soldiers she had arrived with from Fertilian around the outside of the room. They followed the King's orders, and now, hers. Although she had never commanded them to do anything until earlier that day.

Prince Charles glared at the soldiers. He stood, touched one hand to the gold pendant that hung around his chest, raised his nose and strutted out of the room.

"Ernie, who was this assassin?" Jessima said.

Ernie, still staring at the door his chastised brother had just exited, spun back to face the throne. "My Queen, he arrived many years ago from the mainland and had a menial job at the dock. He was registered blind, which is why he was not sent to Fertilian to fight. He fooled my assessors."

"What do you make of all this, Lord Chattergoon?" Jessima asked.

The lord stepped forward. "I suspect he was a sleeper," he replied, completely unconcerned by her sudden elevation in status to someone now questioning him, "planted in Lian by the Thornes to remain undercover until a specific event meant he could carry out his order. His order must have been to kill King Hugo's male heir, whoever that might be, if he had the opportunity." He paused. "I have a suggestion, my Queen." He waited for her permission.

Jessima gestured for him to continue.

"That all able-bodied men still in Lian who were not sent to war for one reason or another be reassessed. This will help root out any more Thorne supporters," Chattergoon said.

Jessima considered this for a moment. Eventually, she nodded. Eddie's cry cut through the room. "That is all, gentlemen."

Ernie retreated as quickly as he could, Lord Chattergoon, however, hung back.

Jessima stepped down from the platform. "Is there something else, Lord Chattergoon?"

"Yes, your stand against the assassin was highly commendable, Queen Jessima," the tall lord said.

"I had to protect Eddie."

Chattergoon didn't reply, his face showed no emotion. But she had an overwhelming sense that he was encouraging her on silently.

"I remember watching the Peqkian warriors training on my return journey from Riaow. They instructed Prince Toby's soldiers in hand-to-hand combat, among other things. Perhaps that came to me in the moment."

"It might be prudent to recall more of that time, my Queen," Chattergoon replied. "Should you need to protect yourself, or our King, again in the future."

"I can't possibly do what they do, Lord Chattergoon. Those women are warriors."

"You already did, Queen Jessima, you fought off an assassin with your bare hands."

"Yes." The enormity of that was still settling. "Go on," Jessima said, discerning he wasn't finished.

"If I may be as bold as to say, your Grace, you are stronger than you think."

8

TOBY

❧

They'd been rumbling along for weeks, and Prince Toby Cleland knew precisely where those damn Thorne twins and their revolting mother were heading. Cleland City. To take the castle and claim Fertilian as their own.

He'd been captured, beaten and, when they had realised who he was, flung in a covered cart, arms and feet bound, lying on his side.

Canvas was tied tightly across the top of the cart but a sliver of daylight broke through where the two met. He pushed himself up and touched his nose to the canvas in an attempt to widen the gap to see out, but with his hands bound behind his back, his shoulders screamed in pain and he lay on his side once again.

Each morning a male servant brought him a weak broth, stale bread and water. A Peqkian warrior would pull down the back of the cart, heave Toby out and onto the ground, and stand, watchful and hard-faced as the servant pulled Toby into a sitting position and fed him. Then the warrior would heave Toby to his feet so the servant could pull down his breeches and spread out his legs. The warrior grabbed him under the arms and held him just off the ground so he could piss and shit right there.

The first time this happened, Toby couldn't go. Couldn't do his business in front of an audience, but by day five, all dignity and embarrassment had passed. He counted the days by this little ritual.

When he was finished, the breeches were pulled up and he was forced back into the cart. On the first day he had struggled, using his bound feet to push against the cart. The warrior had dropped him on the ground, punched him expertly so as not to do any lasting damage but enough so he passed out. He woke up in the cart and in agony, and decided after that it was best to comply.

The Thornes hadn't called for him. Although he was, without a doubt, their most prized captive. He'd seen Hugo die in the battle. His brother, his King, dead. Many others had seen it, and if the Cleland soldiers weren't already close to giving up, when they saw Hugo fall to a Peqkian warrior, they caved. They charged about stupidly, broke formation, ran and fled. The warrior had looked thoroughly bored, not even aware of the significance of who she had felled, just another body to chop down. And once Hugo was down, she moved on to the next man in turn.

The battle had been a disaster for the Cleland army, as Hugo and Toby had known it would be the moment Captain Denya and her company of one thousand warriors had deserted them. The Thorne twins' army was lumbering, ponderous. But the Peqkians, who hours earlier had been on the side of the Clelands, moved like magic, dispersing and reforming, communicating effortlessly with whistles down the line, instinctively knowing where to put their horses, when to dismount and engage.

The Cleland army had been forced back by the sheer momentum of the Peqkian's charge and the Cleland cavalry ended up trampling its own infantry. A disaster that saw the Cleland force dissolve into chaos.

Toby sighed. It would be another long day in the back of the cart. The morning ritual had been and gone and he had the entire day and night to lay on his side, attempt to ignore his burning arms and attempt even harder to not dwell on the battle. He had accepted his current circumstance, but he hadn't accepted the defeat. The betrayal of Denya. He was desperate to know what the Thornes had offered her to make her switch sides, to desert her Melokai's orders, to go rogue. What had they given her that he couldn't? *It should've been a Cleland victory.* The bitter statement throbbed behind his eyes ceaselessly.

After the cavalry trampling, the Cleland soldiers had retreated. Toby with them. They ran and ran until the Peqkians had picked off most at the back, but then darkness fell and the Peqkians returned to the Thorne camp. The Cleland soldiers formed up and made a hasty camp, exhausted. Toby had attempted to rally them, ordered them to pick up arms, to be ready for anything. But they all thought the unspoken code would be honoured. Battles happened during the day.

A mistake. The Peqkians didn't follow that code, probably didn't even know it. They knew victory and nothing else. In the middle of the night, they had surrounded the camp and attacked with no mercy. Some men got away, some were captured, most were murdered where they slept, not even having the chance to pick up a weapon. The cats were that fast.

Toby had been awake, and he'd fought. He'd been recognised by a Peqkian who disarmed him and bound him faster than he could comprehend and then taken him to Denya. It was that Peqkian's bindings that were still around his wrists and feet. Damn, he had to admire the skills of the mountain warriors. Everything so precise. Even a knot made in haste, in the middle of a skirmish, had held true for weeks. It hadn't budged. In fact, Toby was certain it was getting tighter.

But today was different. He was heaved out of the cart, blindfolded and dragged through mud, through men talking, through the camp to a building. The air changed and dark filled in the blindfold's edges. He was lugged down a set of stairs, the air getting danker, cooler. A hinge creaked and he was flung onto a cold, stone floor.

But then, a kindness, the Peqkian warrior unbound his hands and feet and pulled off his blindfold. She shoved him into the little cell so hard he landed on his knees and then shut the iron gate behind him, locking it with a big, extravagant key.

I'm in Horfe Castle. They've taken the town. It was the only castle on route to Cleland City, and the timing was right. The Cleland army had stopped in on the way to Yettle Valley to demand, politely of course, food and supplies. The Nithercotts, the family who resided at the castle, had invited Hugo and Toby to sleep in their guest rooms, but Hugo had refused, insisting they be close to their men.

Toby had heard no sounds of a battle, but then his cart had no doubt been at the back of the army line with the supply wagons. And perhaps Lord Nithercott had surrendered gracefully, agreed terms, willingly opened their castle dungeons for the Thorne's captives.

Footsteps sounded on the stairs and Thorne soldiers trudged in more captives. Toby recognised some of his men, but there were some in Nithercott colours. So, the Lord of Horfe Castle hadn't given in so easily.

Cells to Toby's right and left were packed with men, but Toby was kept on his own. Three walls of his cell were stone, the iron gate and a line of bars looking out on a corridor. He crawled to the bars and leaned against them watching as men were marched past his cell. Desperate to catch someone's eye, to learn what he could without the Thorne men noticing, he gestured subtly with his finger. But the captives stared at their feet.

An argument broke out along the corridor over the groans of the crammed in men.

One Thorne soldier said, "There's no more room in this last one."

The second said, "Shove him in that cell."

"I've tried, and that cell and that one. There's no more room. I say we just kill him. No one's going to know."

A third soldier, "Can't kill any of these ones, the cat wants to question them."

"Look at the state of him, the fucking cripple isn't going anywhere, shove him in with the prince. What's he going to do, help him break free?"

They laughed at that and Toby heard them approaching his cell. He carefully stood, wobbled on legs that hadn't been used for days and felt weak. Toby had a few moments to decide if he would charge and attempt escape. But when the soldiers came in front of his cell, there were five of them.

I need to bide my time. There will be better opportunities than this.

He hobbled away from the bars to stand against the back wall of the cell as the gate creaked open and a bedraggled man was pushed in, back first. The man fell on his rump, curled up into a small ball covering his head with his arms, and was silent. The soldiers pulled shut the gate, locked it and then stomped up the stairs.

From the other cells, men groaned, begged for air and space to sit, shouted that another was standing on a foot, or that an elbow in their chest was stopping their breathing.

Toby took a few tentative steps, eyes fixed on the man on the floor.

The man swung up, pushed himself to standing, went to the gates and looked along the corridor, then up the stairs. Satisfied there was no one other than the prisoners in the vicinity, he turned and with one revolting look, the lipless soldier spy Elmgard grinned at Toby.

"Lippy," whispered Toby, and a huge grin spread across his own face. He resisted the urge to hug the man, having never done it before, but then thought, *sod it*, and embraced his old spy.

"Prince Toby," Lippy said in his strange numbed voice

over Toby's shoulder. He'd lost his lips for mocking a Peqkian soldier on their journey from Riaow to Cleland City.

Toby let the man go and they took each other in. *Awkward.* Shaking off the impromptu embrace, they huddled in one corner of the cell, with eyes on the bottom of the stairs should anyone come.

Lippy, not hesitating for any pleasantries, appreciating their time together might be short, filled Toby in.

"The last time we met, you asked me to find out that Peqkian bitch captain's payment. Well," the lipless soldier chuckled, "I did. She didn't want money, she didn't want horses, or power, or land, or nothing that anyone else would want. False Queen Charlotte Thorne haggled and haggled but Denya said no to it all. It infuriated the old bird, she's got seventy-odd years of scheming behind her and couldn't sway this one cat. It's said that the old bird bit down her pride, creaked to her knees and begged, pleading with Denya to know what it would take to make her switch sides and..." Lippy chuckled again, "that wily cat captain said, 'You.'"

"Denya asked for Charlotte? For what?"

"Denya likes women, we all know that, right? Well, according to my sources, she's known for frequently falling in love with unsuitable, hard to get, powerful, *older* women. Had a long relationship with an older warrior back in Peqkya, Ashya, the turncoat who helped the Dromedars invade, so I heard. And rumour has it that back in Cleland City she seduced Lady Cynthia Sumner right under her husband Alon's nose. Cynthia's notable all right, and she ain't no spring lamb."

"Denya betrayed her Melokai's orders to bed that crusty old hag, Charlotte?" Toby's eyebrows nearly shot off his face.

Lippy laughed silently. Chest heaving in great mirth, but not wanting to draw any attention. Laughter carried on the air and neither wanted it to float up the stairs and into the ears of a Thorne soldier, or worse, a Peqkian.

"How did Charlotte speak to Denya? They must've met face to face."

Lippy's laughter subsided. "Ah, so you won't be pleased about this. Charlotte dressed up as an old hag – totally fitting if you ask me – and snuck into our camp as a follower serving broth and food to the men."

"Shit," Toby muttered, angry that his camp guards hadn't spotted the intruder.

"The first time she came to negotiate, Denya nearly killed her. It was on the eve before the first battle. But then the cat became infatuated, let the old hag live and listened to her piece. Denya refused everything that Charlotte offered. Then said she wanted Charlotte in her bed, as her woman. Charlotte stomped off in a huff, so I heard. Blathering how much she was insulted, had never heard of such a thing blah blah. But then she must've thought on it whilst the Thorne army were battered and we won that first battle. She returned the next night and agreed. Denya left that same night. The following morning's when I last saw you.

"Rumour has it, Charlotte's been moaning in pleasure every night since. And Denya looks like the cat that's got the cream."

Toby grimaced.

"But, if you ask me, that Denya's a sneaky cat. She wants power all right. She wants to rule Peqkya. Charlotte thinks she's holding the reins of that relationship, thinks the cat's besotted with her, the arrogant fool, but Denya's scheming and playing the long game. Wouldn't surprise me if Denya aids Charlotte to take Fertilian, then uses the Thorne army to destroy Peqkya. Just an inkling."

"You are an excellent spy," Toby said, "with excellent inklings."

"I haven't learnt much else. Other than we're on our way to Cleland City, and we're at Horfe Castle, but I think you know that."

A slight movement caught Toby's eye and he looked up to see a Peqkian warrior at the gate. She had come down the stairs silently and so fast that Toby and Lippy hadn't noticed. They both jumped. They'd been caught in the act.

She left in the same manner as she'd arrived and Lippy looked at Toby, then clambered over to the other side of the cell and curled up in a ball. Toby drew his knees up to his chest and put his head on them. This was the position they had wanted to be found in, as if they hadn't spoken, didn't know each other.

The same five Thorne soldiers who had deposited Lippy in Toby's cell came down the stairs, followed by three Peqkian warriors. Using hand gestures and movement, the warriors herded the men and lined them up in front of the gates.

The Peqkian warrior who had caught Toby and Lippy in conversation pointed at Toby, indicated the cell and held up one finger as if to say, 'Only that one man in this cell.' She then pointed to Lippy and slowly shook her head.

The soldiers were terrified. They shot desperate looks at one another and then the blame tumbled from lips, each accusing the other of disobeying orders.

In a heartbeat, two Thorne soldiers were dead, throats slashed by the two warriors behind them. They slumped to the stone flagstones, leaking blood into the cracks. The warriors' bloody daggers were then held to the next throats.

The warrior who had gestured pulled a dagger strapped to her arm and held it to the nearest soldier's throat. He tried to move, to go for his sword but he was slow, as if he moved through mud rather than air. With her other hand, the Peqkian tapped a finger to her ear. The meaning clear, 'Next time, listen and obey.'

She nodded at the other warriors and the daggers were withdrawn. The remaining three soldiers gulped and clutched their still-whole necks. She dismissed them with a glance and they scarpered up the stairs, not looking once at their fallen comrades.

Somehow, although she speaks their language, her silence is even more menacing. I will have to remember that.

She turned to look at Toby and shook her head. She handed the key to one of the warriors and jogged up the stairs, leaving the other two watching Toby and Lippy. The women held the same pose, feet slightly apart, one hand on sword, one resting on thigh. *Poised and ready. Elegant but lethal.*

A whistle rung down the stairs. The warrior with the key opened the gate, the second entered and grabbed Lippy. She hauled him up, as if he weighed no more than a child, and pulled him out. He turned to give a last glance at Toby. Toby dipped his chin in recognition of the man's outstanding service.

Both knew this was unlikely to end well. He'd be tortured for information. *Denya can't know he is a spy, can she? She'll think he's just another camp follower. I kept him secret from her. Or will she remember when he caused trouble and one of her warriors sliced off his lips?*

Hours later, Toby got his answer.

A Peqkian warrior shoved Lippy – barely alive, bloody, with no fingers, eyelids or teeth – against the bars for Toby to see.

Toby scrambled to his feet and reached for his spy, his friend. "No!"

She drew her dagger and sliced it across the front of Lippy's neck. Hot blood spurted on Toby's outstretched hand and he watched the life drain from Lippy's eyes.

"Elmgard," Toby whispered, "I'm so sorry."

The warrior dropped the lifeless body on top of the two dead Thorne soldiers and walked away.

Lippy's blood gushed to mix with the soldiers' blood. The tide pooled in cracks and spread further into Toby's cell. Toby huddled in the furthest corner and watched as the blood river crept ever nearer.

He glanced up. Lippy's lidless, dead eyes bored into him.

9

TOBY

 C8⊰⊱⊃

The sack was whipped off his head and the shunt from dark to light struck him forcefully with a sickening dizziness. He blinked to steady the swaying, and his vision adjusted to see green. The outline of hills sharpened, and a stunning view down into a valley came into focus. Beyond, fields for as far as the eye could see.

He knew precisely where he was – Forty Marshes. Only a week's march from Cleland Castle, he realised, and his heart grew heavy.

The Thorne army had rested at Horfe Castle for five days and then were on the move again. He'd been shoved back in the covered cart and the morning broth and shit ritual had been reinstated.

That morning, after his breeches had been pulled up again, a sack had been pulled over his head. He'd been carried over someone's shoulder to a horse, slung over its back so his belly rested on the beast's shoulders, and then continuously pounded in the ribs as the horse plodded, following whoever led it.

With the sack removed, Toby was forced to turn and kneel on a blanket, his arms still bound behind him and his ankles tied. The blanket was laid out for a picnic, food in parcels, wine, cushions. He shook his head in bewilderment.

A horse whinnied and he looked to the crest of the hill to see his brother's majestic white stallion tethered to a tree next to the bareback horse he'd arrived on. The guilt at Hugo's death was a dead weight around Toby's neck and it tugged savagely at the sight of the stallion. A few paces away, the Peqkian traitor Captain Denya – who had clearly commandeered King Hugo's horse for her own – held her arms up to nothingness, as if helping someone down.

Then the horse materialised, and an old woman was in Denya's arms. She was dressed in the finest linen, sumptuous leather riding boots and with a delicate silk shawl around her shoulders. Gently the warrior placed her feet on the grass. The old woman looked up and smiled. Toby gasped, his eyes widening. *They have a Flame!*

The Flame horse snorted and meandered under the shade of a tree and grazed on the grass. It wasn't tethered and it didn't stand close to the other horses, instead showing them its rear. The horse's coarse hair shimmered as if a fire blazed beneath it and its eyes glowed a deep red. Fertilian Flames granted their rider complete invisibility. Sight, sound and smell were masked. Although if you were to walk into one, you'd still feel it. The breed had supposedly died out, but Toby had heard rumours a few still lived. He'd never seen one before and was mesmerised.

The two women strolled downhill, arm in arm towards him. Only when they reached the blanket did he tear his eyes from the Flame to consider them.

"Ah, Toby Cleland. Once a Prince, now a pauper," the old woman said.

"Ah, Charlotte Thorne. Once a false queen, always a false queen," Toby croaked. He hadn't spoken a word since his doomed conversation with Lippy.

Denya stepped forward and slapped him viciously. He

slumped to the side like a tree felled. Denya grabbed his hair and pulled him up to kneeling again.

He eyed her and then looked back to Charlotte. "And her pet cat."

Denya slapped him again. She held his hair this time so that he wouldn't topple.

"Speak again without leave and I'll break your teeth," the Peqkian captain said.

He glared back at the woman who had once been on his side, who he'd vehemently vouched for, and who had lost him his brother. Guilt and anger coursed through his veins.

"That's enough, Denya, my dear. I simply can't abide to see blood at lunch." Charlotte beckoned for the warrior to help her sit. Denya obliged, helping the old woman to get comfortable on the cushions in front of Toby.

Denya, a hulking warrior, the fiercest fighter Toby had ever seen, then lay down on the blanket, on her back with arms folded over her hard stomach and head in the old woman's lap. Charlotte stroked the warrior's cheek and Toby was certain the mountain cat purred with pleasure. *She melts like butter under the False Queen's attention.* If Denya was faking it to play the long game, as Lippy suspected, she was doing a commendable job.

Toby stifled a frown and hid his contempt by turning his attention to his knees. Already they ached, and his arse cheeks were digging into his heels.

Charlotte took in her surroundings. "This is such a beautiful spot. My Benjamin used to bring me here when we first moved to Cleland City."

"You didn't *move* to Cleland City, you took it by force, you bitch."

Denya growled and made to sit up but Charlotte rested a hand on her collarbone and Denya settled to gladly receive the old woman's fuss.

"I did think you'd be better company than this, Toby. I was certain your mother, dear Olivia, would've brought you up to be polite and respect your elders.”

Toby sneered. This woman had no idea about his mother.

At his silence, Charlotte continued, gazing into the distance as old people did when they thought of the past. “It was such a fabulous change to the bleak and dreary Froggerton where Benjamin and I holed up with the twins until he was ready to reclaim the throne from your grandfather. Such a dreadful place, overrun with damn croaking frogs.”

She leaned forward and surveyed the picnic spread. She picked up and examined each morsel of food before either delicately adding it to one of two plates or replacing it with a tut.

“We ruled happily as King and Queen for fifteen joyous years. And then your nasty brother came and took the throne back, killed my darling husband and banished me and the twins. Hugo should’ve killed us, the fool. It may have taken twenty-four years to exact revenge, but the throne will soon be in Thorne hands again.”

She popped a cherry tomato into Denya’s mouth and then put one in her own. Toby’s stomach grumbled. He’d eaten a watery gruel that tasted of old underclothes and stale bread since his capture. It was growing tiresome.

Charlotte looked at him expectantly.

“Oh, come now, you must have something to say?”

Joyous my arse! he wanted to shout, *for fifteen years you persecuted the Fertilian people, raised taxes and ruled with torture and intimidation.* But the only sound that came from Toby was a low grumble from the pit of his hollow belly.

Charlotte sighed. “Arthur and Clement are off pretending to work out a strategy to lay siege to the city and take the castle. But we already have a plan, don’t we, my darling.” Charlotte patted Denya’s head and the warrior stretched out her toes in apparent bliss. “And my sickly daughter is resting with a headache, as usual, and I desired conversation. And I thought, we have a guest who

I should meet."

Toby snorted. His knees were in agony. They certainly *weren't* being treated like a guest's knees ought to be.

"Well, yes, I admit, Denya wanted to torture you for information, but I did insist on conversation first. Food is ready, sweetling."

Denya turned on her side, hitched herself up on one elbow and ate the food Charlotte had put on her plate without question, without even glancing at what other delicious fare was on offer in front of her. The warrior gazed dreamily at the view as she chewed, unfocused, and openly at peace on this late autumn's day. Toby watched her shamelessly. He was still having trouble connecting this soft woman with the hardened warrior captain he knew. It was as if she had a twin with a starkly opposite nature.

Charlotte brought her plate up to her chest and ate from it. She swallowed and said, "It took me years of bargaining, of nagging, of cajoling to make Arthur and Mary see sense. To join their forces. The fools both take after their father in that respect – stubborn and self-obsessed. Although Mary was simply following her husband's orders. Particularly headstrong that man. But of course, their mother was right."

Charlotte looked at Toby to ensure he was still listening. He tore his eyes away from Denya's soppy double and looked back, forcing himself to focus. *The old bat wants to boast. Listen carefully, she might reveal a titbit of information I can use to bring down this bastard Thorne family once and for all.* Toby lowered his gaze and nodded, to encourage her to continue.

She did so willingly. "And then I had to get Princess Matilda on side. Oh, that did take some doing. She was fiercely loyal to her daddy, although Hugo had married her off at a young age to get rid of her. She still loved him dearly and she was a proud Cleland. But I got to her through her family, as is usually the way of these things."

The old hag laughed haughtily and a soggy, saliva-saturated crumb of pie flew from her mouth and landed on Denya's forehead. Denya let it sit there, apparently too in love with the woman whose lips it had sprung from to mind.

"It took oh so many spies, and oh so many years, but we turned Matilda against her family. My infiltrators twittered in her ear and she became convinced that you had killed her boy Johnny on that salt flat excursion. As Hugo's grandson, Johnny was heir to the throne and she believed you wanted him out the way to claim that position for yourself."

Toby gritted his teeth as anger sizzled up his throat. The Thornes had been responsible for that unexplained disappearance. He should've known. They had searched for weeks for the boy. It had been a horrific mess. He caught himself from shouting, from attempting some kind of launch across the picnic blanket. But what could he do bound and trussed? Nibble at her shawl? Headbutt her knee?

Seeing the effect of her revelation on Toby, the False Queen Charlotte continued with glee.

"That was my opening and, naturally, I exploited it to full effect. How? You might wonder. I targeted the husband. According to my little moles, Lord John Iddenkinge had a stallion Flame, the last in Fertilian. And we had the last female Flame. He wanted to continue their race, as did we, so I negotiated with him to breed them."

She selected a small sweetcake and held it up, as if offering it to Toby, and then slowly tongued the icing off the top in an odd sensual movement that turned the bile in Toby's empty stomach.

Charlotte licked her lips. "And, next, the icing on the cake. I arranged for Princess Grace, Matilda's eldest, to be betrothed to Arthur's eldest boy Jeremy. So, Iddenkinge and Matilda would still have a royal child. A Queen though, rather than a King, but better than nothing. Well, that sealed the deal of course – and the fate of that bastard Hugo."

Suddenly, headbutting her knee felt like a solid option. Toby wanted to cause even the smallest amount of pain to this vile old woman.

Charlotte swatted at a wasp that was bothering her plate. Toby urged it to bite her. But in a flash, Denya's hand shot forward, caught the wasp, crushed it and threw it into the grass with a snarl. She continued to eat.

The False Queen put down her plate, poured wine and handed a glass to Denya. The warrior refused and Charlotte held it out to Toby. Before he could catch himself, his entire body leaned forward, his buttocks lifting off his heels, led by his gaping mouth that was yearning for the taste of wine. Spittle gathered under his tongue.

Charlotte smirked and then tipped the wine into the dirt at the side of the blanket.

Old hag.

The Flame plodded down the hill and stood behind Charlotte whickering. She picked up a juicy apple and held it up to the horse. "Here you go, Ruby." The horse took the apple from over her shoulder and then stalked away munching it.

Charlotte watched as the Flame retreated.

"Such a good old girl," she mused. "She was Benjamin's pride and joy. Carried him into battle against your grandfather Edward. She just keeps going. Flames are blessed with long life if treated well, and I treat her very well."

Denya sat up and stretched her head from side to side. "It is time."

Charlotte squeezed the warrior's arm. "War is such a drain. No time to yourself to enjoy simple pleasures. I'm delighted to be able to picnic, however briefly, in this beautiful place that reminds me so much of my late, great husband. But there is a throne to reclaim."

Denya leaned in and kissed the old woman passionately

on her wrinkled lips.

Goodness, no, they can't… they won't… not in front of me… Toby scrutinised the blanket below his knees and attempted to shut off his ears to the wet smacking noises.

To his relief, Charlotte gently pushed the warrior away. "Less of that, ha!" She stroked Denya's face tenderly. "And of course, once we secure Fertilian for ourselves, then, just for you my dear, we'll take Peqkya."

Toby let rip a snort as he recalled Lippy's hunch and Charlotte looked at him, mistaking his reaction for disbelief.

"Don't you believe we can? Denya knows all the country's weaknesses, just like she knows all the weaknesses of Cleland City and its castle. I do hope you'll join us to watch its defeat, should be quite a show. Then we'll take Lian and wipe out all the repugnant Clelands once and for all. I don't imagine Hugo's pathetic wife will put up much of a fight."

The smirk on Toby's face faltered and slid away. *Jessima. His love. God help her, for I have failed and cannot.*

Denya sprung to her feet. She helped Charlotte to stand and to mount the Flame horse. The old hag and the horse turned invisible as soon as she was settled in the saddle.

Denya turned to Toby. All softness had evaporated from the woman and the scowling, coiled tension was back.

The False Queen's voice came from nothingness. "It was a success, you know," she said. "Well, of course it was, because I managed it."

Toby rolled his eyes. *What is the old bat boasting about now?*

As if she'd heard his thoughts, she said, "The Flame breeding. Turned out Iddenkinge didn't just have one stallion, he had four. And we discovered an old farmer in the west had hidden two female Flames. So, now we have quite the herd. We were all ready to use them in the battle at Yettle Valley, but then Denya dearest crushed the doleful Cleland army so completely it was unnecessary."

Charlotte cackled like the old hag she was, as Denya pulled the sack back over his head, heaved him up and flung him over her shoulder.

10

AMMAD

ભેઠળ

"**I**'ve got no fucking arms, give me more poppy," Ammad yelled at the three healers who lingered around his bed.

The poppy was poor quality, disgusting even, but it gave him a high, however short-lived and tainted. His poppy supply had come from Peqkya. But, irritatingly, that had dried up after the failed invasion. They'd had to start cultivating it in the palace garden, but it was dire in comparison.

The healers looked to Jakira, ignoring his instruction, and he exploded. "I'm the Crown Prince, do as I say or face a violent punishment. Guards!"

The healers didn't move. And neither did the two guards stood by the door. They were new. Watchful and silent. Not like old, trusty Qabull. He would've followed orders.

Ammad felt even more impotent than his broken cock. Now, he was an invalid in his mother's villa with no say anymore.

He kicked his feet, thumped his torso onto the bed, writhed from side to side.

Jakira watched him with pursed lips. He thrashed and kicked, became aware that he was drooling, that his entire

"

body itched like a nest of ants crawling over his skin.

He yelled and with a final effort at jerking his body, managed to roll off his bed. He landed on the floor with a heavy, mortifying thud. The healers rushed forward to help but Jakira held out a halting palm then gestured for them to leave.

Ammad realised her motherly patience had finally worn thin as he cowered from her scowl. He knew that face from his childhood, knew what was coming.

"Flesh of my flesh. You are no longer in pain. Your injuries have healed and you do not need the poppy. This," she waved her hand at his sorry body slumped on the ground, tangled in sheets and with his tunic wound up around his waist, "is the result of poppy withdrawal. I want my son back. This," she indicated him again, "is not my son. This is a poppy-addled fool."

"I have no arms, Mama," Ammad whimpered into the cool stone tiles.

"No, you have no arms." She pulled off a slipper, leaned over him and slapped his forehead with it. "But you still have a brain." Then she bashed the slipper on his chest, "And lungs, and a heart and all your internal organs." She hit his thigh. "And you still have legs."

She hit him with her slipper until her breath quickened, then she took his chin in her other hand and squeezed her gold-painted fingernails into the flesh of his cheeks. "Ammad, you are the Crown Prince. Arms or no. Act like it."

She replaced her slipper, and left him on the floor, slamming the door behind her.

Ammad screamed, attempted to get off the floor but the effort of manoeuvring without his arms was too much and he slumped back again, yelling in frustration.

***

Days later Jakira's head slave Medi came into the room, pulled Ammad to his feet and walked him to the washing area outside the villa. Ammad sat on a stool whilst several male slaves washed him gently. He was pleased it wasn't the female slaves, even his mother's eldest female slave would've looked at him in pity, whereas before they always admired his beautiful body.

But had it changed that much? He looked down at his honed chest, the ripples in his stomach, the lean muscles of his legs. They had softened in the time he'd been lying in bed, but they were still defined. But what could he do? He couldn't wield a weapon, ride a camel, or hold a polo mallet. Polo, the beautiful game. He'd never play it again.

The slaves oiled his skin and hair, massaged his feet, shaved and sculpted his beard and trimmed his eyebrows. He did not resist, he had always enjoyed the preening and pampering that enhanced his beauty. They dressed him in fine lounge clothes that had been adjusted, he noted, so that there were no sleeves. They fit him perfectly. His mother's doing.

He knew he would look dashing, and he did, in fact, feel somewhat better. But the mirrors had been removed from the dressing area. And Ammad realised he hadn't seen himself since his return from Peqkya.

Since that red-haired hisspit had taken his arms.

Medi, who had been standing discreetly to one side keeping an eye on proceedings, stepped forward and beckoned for Ammad to follow.

"Your mother," the head slave said.

Ammad followed Medi to one of the lower floor rooms which had once been Ammad and Selmi's playroom. It was at the back of the house, out of the sun and cooler. Ammad hadn't been back to this particular room since he was about seven and had become obsessed with polo.

It was exactly as he remembered. Toys and playthings scattered about, the wall painted with bright motifs, intricate coloured glass depicting an orchid in the window. Two slaves monotonously fanned the room with large palm fronds.

Jakira sat in the centre of the room on plush cushions

playing with a child. The Peqkian boy with red hair and black skin. Ammad had snatches of memories of the boy. His mother laughed as she handed a camel figurine to the boy and he galloped it along the thick carpet. A carpet from Peqkya, no less. *How fitting.*

Ammad frowned at his mother and she looked up at him.

"Ah, flesh of my flesh. Do you remember Artaz?"

Ammad shrugged.

"He arrived with Riv and Toya and I have taken him in as my own. He is a *special* boy."

She said special in such a way that a pang of jealousy chimed in Ammad's mind. He raised an eyebrow. She kissed the boy on the cheek and stood effortlessly from the cushions.

"I have business at the palace and will be away for most of the day. You will watch over your little brother."

"I am no woman to mind a child," Ammad said. If he'd had his arms, he would've crossed them.

Jakira's tone turned sharp. "You have something better to be doing with your time? Somewhere else to go?"

Ammad remained silent and Jakira pointed at the cushions. "Make yourself comfortable. Medi will be here in case there is anything you need."

To observe and report back on my conduct.

The child sensed that Jakira was leaving. He leapt up and started to cry, clutching at her exquisite silk dress with grubby hands.

"No, no, no," he wailed.

She knelt so her face was in line with his. "I shall not be gone long, Artaz. Look, your big brother is here to play with you. Why don't you show him your camels? He loves camels. Where are they? You'd better find them."

Distracted, the boy scampered away and started lifting piles of toys and cushions to dig out his camel figurines. She shot a glance at Ammad and then nodded at Medi.

Both men watched Jakira leave. The slaves, trained

impeccably to blend into the background, continued their fanning with neutral, unseeing faces. Medi took his place standing by the door.

Jakira's scent of aniseed and nutmeg lingered in the room, and when Ammad thought he could no longer smell it he moved to some cushions piled in the corner and reclined, leaning his shoulders against the wall.

The child – with an armful of playthings, not all of which were camels – waddled over to Ammad, spilling toys. He dumped them on Ammad's lap and looked up at him eagerly.

The boy had piercing blue eyes. He was attractive, bound to grow up to be a handsome man. Ammad glowered at him.

Artaz pointed at the toys. "Play," he said with a huge grin.

"Get away from me, brat," Ammad hissed.

Artaz's face dropped at the tone. "Brat?" he repeated and continued to look up at Ammad. His expectant gaze turned Ammad's stomach and the Crown Prince shoved the child away with a foot in his chest.

Artaz stumbled back and plopped down on his rump. He wailed, only pausing so his breath could catch up with his wailing.

"Shut him up, Medi," Ammad said. But Jakira's head slave ignored him and gazed at nothing as expertly as the fan slaves.

"Shut up," Ammad shouted at the boy, but the child's screams only intensified and gouged great caverns out of Ammad's ears.

Ammad went to stand, to leave the room. Medi would have to move aside, no slave was permitted to touch a master unless granted permission, and even Jakira's orders couldn't cross that code.

But Ammad was wedged in such a position on the cushions that he couldn't get his legs in the right position to heave himself up. "Fuck," he shouted.

After a number of futile attempts, he gave up.

The child had stopped it's bawling and was watching him with wide-eyed curiosity, mouth gaping, head to one side.

"That's right, brat, I have no arms," Ammad said and glared at the child. "I can't stand up."

Artaz shrugged and turned to play with the nearest toys.

Ammad gritted his teeth and closed his eyes. But his eyelids refused to remain shut and kept opening so he could seek out the child and watch him.

In truth, Ammad was fascinated by this red-haired boy with the same hair colour as the warrior who had maimed him. He had only ever seen Peqkians with black hair, never red.

His mind, unfettered from poppy, functioned for the first time in months.

Was this child related to that warrior? Can I use him to hurt her somehow? How can I destroy Peqkya? We failed once, but not again. A minor setback. We now know our way in to the country, know the layout of Riaow. I can rebuild the army, find some way to overcome the hisspits. A weapon. I need a new kind of weapon. Swords won't work because the Peqkians are skilled at swordplay.

His musing was interrupted by slaves bringing in lunch. The same old house slave propped Ammad upright and fed him, bringing a spoon from bowl to mouth. This had mortified Ammad previously, but he found today he didn't much care. He was thinking. He was planning. He felt more like himself.

The child watched the slave feeding Ammad and then put down his spoon and pointed. The young slave who was holding his bowl glanced quickly and started to feed Artaz exactly as Ammad was being fed. After each mouthful, Artaz beamed with pride at Ammad.

The food was finished and taken away and Artaz yawned. Ammad slouched against the wall, all his thoughts on digesting. The child edged his way around Ammad's legs, remembering the kick from earlier, and came closer to Ammad from the side.

Ammad, longing for his arms to swat the brat away, tensed as the child leaned in and rested his head on Ammad's chest. The boy's breathing slowed and as it did, his head slipped down to rest in Ammad's lap.

Satiated by the food, Ammad too fell asleep.

Ammad woke to raised voices. Artaz was no longer in the room. Medi was also gone. And there was only the one fan slave now, different from earlier. The Crown Prince must have slept for hours.

It was his younger brother, Selmi, doing the shouting. *Unusual.*

"Those in power shouldn't lie to their people," Sel yelled.

"Oh, not this again, flesh of my flesh. Those in power should *always* lie to their people," Jakira replied, her normally smooth, controlled voice sharp. Ammad knew from experience that she was reaching tipping point.

"I've had enough, I will not go to another polo match," Sel retorted, and Ammad imagined him stomping a foot. "I told you, I do not agree with Mastiq's rule, with the corruption of religion, with slaves, with how this country is so unfairly run. Father has the power to change this country for the better, not to continue to run it as it has always been run – as an oppressive regime where the rich get richer while the poor starve. He should be ashamed—"

A sharp crack sounded. Jakira no doubt slapped him, for his insolence.

"You, fan slave, get someone to help me up. Now," Ammad said.

The slave, a teenage boy, jumped at being spoken to by a master and almost dropped his fan.

"Now," Ammad bellowed and the boy threw down his palm frond and ran from the room.

How dare Selmi speak that way about our father! He'd

reprimand the little runt.

"Mastiq must know by now that I'm not Ammad," Sel continued in a lower tone that held a hint of a snivel. "It's so obvious, I know we look similar but I'm taller than him. He must have heard by now about Ammad's injuries. I refuse to pretend to be him anymore, it's a stupid farce and I won't lie to the people any longer. They deserve to know. I will say something!"

Pretend to be me? Taller?

A house slave arrived to help Ammad to his feet. He stomped out of the room in search of his mother and brother. When he reached the main lounge, which opened out onto the terrace overlooking the city, Sel had gone. Jakira was stood in the small breeze, her back to Ammad.

"Mama, what is all this about Sel pretending to be me?" Ammad said but Artaz ran past him and straight into Jakira's legs.

"Mama," Artaz sang.

Jakira turned and swept up the boy in a twirling embrace.

"Ah, Ammad, we have a polo match to attend in two weeks' time. Sel has taken your place while you have been recuperating, but you're ready. Mastiq expects you to play, but we will be spectators. Mastiq is not aware of the *extent* of your injuries. And neither is the public." She skewered him with a meaningful glare. "And they shall *never* know."

"Enter," Ammad said as a knock sounded on his door much later that evening.

His mother's head slave, Medi, entered.

"What do you want? It's late." Ammad puffed on a shisha pipe that had been rigged into position so he didn't need to hold the hose. He blew smoke in long, fragrant streams.

"A gift from your mother," Medi said and ushered in two women. Ammad knew immediately who, and what, they were. Expensive whores dressed in belly dancer outfits.

Medi left the room and closed the door as the two women grinded against one another seductively. One singing sweetly. Ammad watched the show. His mother had often sent him whores when he had pleased her or had a job to do and was about to please her by following her explicit instructions. He knew this gift was to appease him for Sel's pretence, for doing as told during the upcoming polo match. Jakira no doubt had a plan for the event, she always did.

The singing ceased as the two women kissed and undressed one another, making their way slowly to Ammad. He shifted on the cushions. Looked down at his trousers. Nothing. Not even a tingle.

"Fuck," he growled and the whores took this as a sign to straddle him and seek out his cock.

"Oh," one giggled as she rubbed her palm between his legs, "We'll need to work harder on this royal appendage."

The second whore pulled Ammad's tunic from over his head. "Perhaps he needs our tongues tickling his skin," she said.

The first whore found the waistband of his trousers and hitched them down.

"Get the fuck off me!" Ammad hollered.

These two beauties did nothing for him. His cock was dead. Had been dead since taking that hisspit warrior by force. He was starting to believe that he had been cursed by the Peqkian stone witch.

"Playing hard to get, are we," one of the women said and nibbled at his neck, all the while continuing to rub his penis through his trousers.

"Get the fuck off me," Ammad repeated, this time with more force. "Leave this room before I have you both beheaded. Medi!"

The two women screamed and retreated to the centre of the room, gathering up their garments.

"Never again," Ammad said as the head slave burst

through the door.

Medi blinked twice at the Crown Prince in surprise, after all, women had been Ammad's second favourite sport after polo, but then nodded. He grabbed both women and threw them out of the room.

Ammad yelled in frustration. Kicking his heels into the cushions.

***

"Your mother," Medi said as he collected Ammad from his room and took him to the wash area the next morning.

Slaves carefully dressed Ammad in clothes that he used to wear to train in, which he found odd. They had been altered, and now had no sleeves. Once attired, Medi led him down the craterside to the camel stables and sand pit where Ammad had learnt how to sword fight. *Is this another doomed gift from my mother after last night's whore debacle?*

There was no one else around and Medi indicated for Ammad to sit on a bench in the shade.

Medi whistled and a young man came out of the stable and stood next to him.

"What is this? More rotten entertainment?" Ammad said.

The man was from the Affarah clan, evident by the large back hump and wide nose. His baggy yellow trousers marked him as a street fighter, his bare chest inked with line tattoos for every fight he had won. He was muscular, with thick legs and a torso that Ammad hated to admit that he coveted. Every defined muscle bulged, and his shoulders sloped up to his ears with a bulk of muscle around the neck.

The most ripped man Ammad had ever seen had no arms.

"This is Samark, otherwise known by his fighter name as Street Sam," Medi said.

Ammad rolled his eyes. "Where's Mama?"

"Jakira wanted you to meet Street Sam," Medi replied.

"Because he has no arms? I want nothing to do with

this Affarah street scum. He might be spreading diseases to me as we speak."

"Not because he has no arms, but because of what he can do. What *you* could do," Medi said.

Ammad let out a long, bored breath and pursed his lips.

Medi continued, "Sam was born with no arms—"

"My heart weeps with sorrow."

"… his father was a street fighter," Medi continued, ignoring Ammad's interruption, "and his only son would also be a street fighter, there was no other choice. He adapted his training and strength equipment to accommodate Samark. And Samark is now one of the top fighters."

"What a delightfully dull story." Ammad made to get up off the bench.

Medi nodded to the lowly man who ran across the sand, turned and then ran back at them flipping his legs up and around and landing back on his feet.

Ammad sat back on the bench. The street scum had just performed a perfect tumble. Something Ammad had spent years perfecting as a young boy. Something he hadn't dared attempt in a long time – even when he still had his arms.

"Can you do that?" Medi asked Ammad, a smirk on his face. "Are you telling me that this Affarah man is stronger, more powerful, *better* than *you*? Royalty no less?"

"A cheap trick," Ammad said.

"As far as I'm aware, there are two men in this city with no arms. Samark and you. Samark is number one. How does that make you feel, Crown Prince?"

Ammad squirmed on the bench. He hated to be second best. "Those he fights take pity on him and let him win."

Medi whistled again and Ammad's weapons instructor came out. Gad was a large man who towered over Samark. Gad was also a man who would not take pity on an opponent. He had never taken pity on Ammad, often leaving him bruised and bloodied. But that was how Ammad had learnt to be the best.

Gad nodded at Ammad. The Crown Prince returned the gesture, he had nothing but respect for the man. The instructor lived comfortably in his own apartment in the servants' quarters with his wife and two sons. He had taught Ammad everything he knew about fighting.

"These two men have never fought before," Medi said. "Neither knows the strengths or weaknesses of the other. Your mother has offered a one hundred drimar payment to the winner of this fight, and a job here training you. Either Gad will win and continue to train you, or Samark will take his place. Gad and his family will be thrown out of the villa's household. May the best man win."

Medi came to stand next to Ammad as Samark and Gad squared up.

"Begin," Ammad said.

Samark let fly a high kick that caught Gad in the jaw, dislocating it. Ammad couldn't believe the diseased Affarah scum had reached so high with his foot, his legs scissoring so that his torso was parallel to the ground. Gad stumbled, threw a punch. Samark dodged it effortlessly and swung a low kick, taking Gad's legs out. Once the weapons instructor was down, the street fighter was on him, wrapping his thick legs around Gad's neck and squeezing his bulging thighs.

Gad's face went red as he choked. He held out until Ammad thought he was seconds away from suffocating, but the man tapped out. Samark released him and stood to one side. Gad turned onto all fours, coughing and spluttering and gasping for air.

Ammad had the greatest urge to clap, and cursed when he realised he couldn't. "Fine entertainment," Ammad said. "I never thought I'd see you bettered, Gad, and by that scum."

Crestfallen, Gad hobbled away.

Samark, not even out of breath, spoke for the first

time. His voice was high-pitched, and not what Ammad was expecting from such a beast, but the Crown Prince was not about to mock him for it.

Street Sam said, "Your training begins now. Get up, you useless piece of camel shit."

Ammad got to his feet.

11

AMMAD

Ammad felt fucking ridiculous. And fucking angry. Here he was in the royal box at the polo stadium *watching* the match. He gritted his teeth as the Parchad Prowlers turned their camels the wrong way, stumbled into one another, lost possession of the ball time and again. The team from Orean in their tatty, mismatched attire and on their shabby, inferior camels was thrashing them.

It was because he wasn't there to carry the Prowlers. Of course, it had nothing to do with the fact that Jakira no longer had to fix the games always in his favour. He had been the best player in scorch seasons. Ever, in all likelihood.

And now, here he stood next to his father and in front of his mother as a mere spectator.

Ammad wore an elaborate tunic in the Wakrime royal colours of silver and gold. His mother had outdone herself in choosing the fabric and design. It truly was a resplendent outfit, but she had been careful not to outdo that of his father. Our Ruler Mastiq's ensemble was gaudier, but entirely shapeless. His large gut was hard to dress, even by the most skilled tailor. Ammad imagined his father's tunic could double as a tent for a family of six or so back in the slums.

Mastiq wore his revolting headdress, which he cherished and Ammad privately derided. Made of a wire frame in the shape of a hand, fingers spread with palm facing forward, it was covered with exquisitely expensive material – mostly from Peqkya, as Ammad recalled with revulsion – gold nuggets, jewels, bells, and small bones from Mastiq's father and Ammad's grandfather, Our Ruler Shaan. These trinkets knocked together in an inane jangle that set Ammad's teeth on edge.

Ammad certainly looked the part of Crown Prince, apart from one humiliating detail. The arms of his fine tunic had been stuffed with straw and cloth and shaped. The hands, however, were real. They had once belonged to some insignificant slave or another, punished for stealing. They had been stitched into his long sleeves. One was overly tanned with wiry black hair. The other, Ammad was certain, was a woman's hand.

"What happened to 'the people need a hero' and that being a 'heroic brave prince' will endear me to the people?" Ammad had demanded of Jakira earlier when she had presented him with his stuffed arm tunic to wear to the match. "I'm a war hero, I shouldn't have to humiliate myself with this farce."

"Your father needs some time to adjust to the idea that you've lost your arms. No one has officially told him yet. I will tell him when the time is right, flesh of my flesh," Jakira had replied.

And the public, they too needed some time to adjust to Ammad's evolved form. Rumours had spread from the men who had returned from the war in Peqkya about the red-haired warrior and the injuries the Crown Prince sustained.

But anger had spread quicker.

The lowly scum women had rebelled when fathers, husbands, sons hadn't returned. The furious scum had instigated an uprising, rioting outside the palace, vandalising the palace walls. The ruler's elite guard, the Cuttarrs, had been called in when the city's guard had failed to contain the violence after days. The cutthroats, as everyone called them but never to their faces, had quashed the unrest with especially brutal tactics involving plenty of cut throats and bodies left to rot in the streets to serve as a warning to anyone else considering speaking out against the ruler or his decisions.

Ammad, never usually bothered with *the mood of the people*, as his mother called it, today had a strong sense that they were seriously pissed off.

His mother had ordered more guards to accompany his litter as it travelled from her villa to the stadium, with the strictest instructions to keep the curtains firmly closed so his identity remained unknown.

The stadium was half full, and there was no cheering or clapping when a goal was scored. Ammad wondered if Ruler Mastiq's advisors hadn't told the cutthroats to round up the street scum and force them to come and watch. Not one person there looked as if they wanted to be.

Mastiq stood at the front of the royal box, hands on rail, ridiculous headdress balanced precariously on his head. He seemed to be the only one enjoying the game. But he kept glancing back to Ammad, sneaking glances at the fake arms, looking confused as if there was something not altogether right that he couldn't quite put his fat finger on.

Ammad was also stood. There was a seat for him, next to but slightly behind Mastiq's own. The Crown Prince couldn't sit though, even if he had wanted to. His hanging fake arms only looked natural when standing. When sitting, they looked fucking ridiculous. He pretended to be passionately involved in watching the dire game that was unfolding before him. So immersed, that he couldn't possibly sit.

He had been intensively training with Samark and already felt stronger. The man was a beast. And although

Ammad hadn't attempted to get back up on a camel just yet, he would. He had spent years training his camel Yoyo to be the best, and his heart had broken when the loyal animal had dropped dead in that hole, Urakbai.

Two days ago, Medi had surprised him with the news Jakira had purchased a new camel for Ammad and had hired the best in the business to train it to respond to foot and voice commands. It had cost one thousand drimars. Yoyo had only cost eight hundred. He couldn't wait to get back on that pitch, his camel kicking up sand as it hurtled towards the goal.

His reverie was distracted by Advisor Farack whispering in his father's ear and nodding in Ammad's direction, specifically at his arms. Mastiq looked concerned. A cough burst forth from Our Ruler's lips followed by a chunk of phlegm. Automatically, Farack held out a cloth to Mastiq to hawk in.

Ammad sneered. *He must've pocketed thousands of those lump-filled cloths in his time.* Farack was one of Mastiq's most trusted advisors, with him from the start of his tenure. Jakira had never succeeded in buying him. He'd always remained loyal to the ruler.

Advisor Farack glided away and Mastiq abruptly sat, as if following direction. He patted the seat next to him.

"My son, come and sit with your father," Mastiq said, his other hand resting on the top of his gut.

Shit. "Ah, but Dada, the game," he said in a whine and didn't move, "it's reached a critical point, the prowlers are staging a comeback…"

If Ammad had been anyone other than the Crown Prince, he would've been reprimanded in a less than pleasant way for not doing precisely what Our Ruler Mastiq had requested.

"Ah, yes, son, you carry on," Mastiq said jovially and turned his eyes to the pitch.

A cough from Advisor Farack reminded him of his purpose.

"Come and sit, Ammad," Mastiq said more firmly and clenched his lips together.

Ammad glanced at Jakira, she subtly tilted her head in warning. He took a step towards the chair but didn't sit.

A scream pierced the glum, silent mood of the stadium. It echoed around the stalls. All eyes in the royal box looked out into the crowd.

With a thud, a projectile hit the cloth draped over the top of the royal box that kept out the sun.

"Oh!" Mastiq exclaimed.

Then more came. Rotten food, dead rats, lumps of camel dung and other unidentified detritus was pelted at the royal box. It slapped into the wall of Cuttarrs who fanned out to surround those in the box, their perfect uniforms smeared with dead animal innards and ichor, and their fierce faces splattered with stinking gunge. The cutthroats pulled their swords and snarled at the crowd. The mob was gaining in confidence and pressing closer as spectators piled from their seats.

Two guards rushed to Mastiq and bundled him away from the rail and towards the secure royal tunnel that led from the box to the street.

The silence in the stadium erupted into boos and jeers. Shouts of "Mastiq killed our men!" and "Mastiq is a fool!" gained in pitch and boisterous repetition, soon to be shortened to "Fool! Fool! Fool!"

Ammad, shocked by the palpable threat that roiled off the lowly mob, looked for his mother. She had already been ushered into the tunnel. The crowd was closing in but staying just out of reach of the cutthroats' precision sword swinging. He knew the guards would be remembering faces. Would take revenge for the rotten shit that now soiled their resplendent uniforms as soon as the royal group was safely away.

The royal box entourage, now Mastiq and his immediate family was safely out of the way, were pushing their way into the two-person wide tunnel, cursing and screaming at those in front to hurry up.

Ammad, momentarily frozen in place by this unexpected turn of events, came to his senses, and realised he was still stood by the railing. He hurried towards the tunnel.

"It's armless Ammad," an old woman with a gravelly voice jeered. "Give us a wave, Crown Prince!"

Ammad's cheeks burned but he refused to look. His entire body twitched for a throwing knife, for the ability to throw it. He could kick the haggard old bitch to death, choke the life out of her with his thighs. Samark had shown him how, but that didn't help at this precise moment. Ammad pushed his torso into the royal hangers-on blocking the tunnel.

"Move," Ammad shouted. "Your Crown Prince demands you stand aside and let him pass!"

The bodies in front didn't budge, the women screaming and men shouting orders. Ammad shoved harder.

The old hag kept on and, like the wind kicking up fine sand across the dunes, the chant caught on with those around her, and soon, the entire stadium.

"Ammad give us a wave!" rolled around the stadium followed by "Ammad scratch your arse!" and "Ammad pick your nose!" and everything else their little minds could think up.

He made it into the tunnel, disgusted that he was the last of the party, and a line of cutthroats formed up behind him, blocking the way to any in the crowd stupid enough to attempt to follow.

As he scurried down the steps towards his waiting litter, he heard screams and the trampling of feet on the boards above. The cutthroats had no doubt fanned out into the crowd, merrily cutting into flesh. He knew they would show no mercy for the hecklers.

He especially hoped the old hag received a slow, painful death.

Back at the palace, in one of his father's formal audience rooms that Ammad had never stepped foot in before, Mastiq paced and wrung his hands.

Ammad stood, agonisingly aware that one of the fake arms had slipped and the woman's hand now hung near his knee. He gritted his teeth against the overwhelming desire to wrench it off.

The ruler, distressed by the events at the stadium, had gone straight to his private quarters to compose himself, but had given orders for the Crown Prince, Jakira and the Minister of War, Whaled, to attend him.

Now the three of them stood in the ruler's receiving room, flanked by Cuttarrs. They watched as the ruler blundered back and forth muttering to himself. It was obvious he was plucking up enough courage to say what was on his mind.

Jakira eyed Ammad's arm and then gazed at him venomously, as if it was *his* fault that *her* fake arm had been shoddily sown in and was now slipping nearer and nearer to the floor.

Whaled stood still, stolid and patient. The only thing that moved on his body was his mass of hair sprouting from face, nose, brows, ears… that swayed in the gentle breeze from a nearby slave's palm-frond fan.

Mastiq stopped and faced them, gesturing to the plump floor cushions arranged in a half circle around a low table set with dates and mint tea. "Let's sit."

As Mastiq arranged his unwieldly self on the cushions, Ammad squatted and sat, as Samark had taught him, with little effort. His arms splayed out. Jakira watched him closely and then sat strategically between him and Mastiq, arranging her svelte self to hide Ammad's arms from Mastiq's view. Whaled sat to Mastiq's other side. His finger worried briefly at his cavernous nostril, before he folded his arms.

Mastiq turned towards Whaled, the ruler hefting his

great gut to get more comfortable. While his back was turned Jakira discreetly arranged Ammad's arms as best she could, refusing to touch the hands, which weren't quite as fresh looking as at the beginning of the day.

The Ruler of Drome sighed heavily and then reached out a hand to Whaled and rested it on the great hairy man's thigh.

"My dear friend, we have known each other since boyhood. And I am so…" Mastiq circled his other hand as if he couldn't find the right word. He continued on without one, "that you didn't disclose the extent of my son's injuries."

Whaled opened his mouth to reply but a sharp head shake from Mastiq stopped him.

Mastiq took his hand from the Minister of War's thigh and turned to Jakira. "And you, my dearest, my favourite concubine, the mother of the Crown Prince. You too…"

The ruler was at a loss for words again and waved his hands about in a fluster.

Jakira dipped her head and looked up through her eyelashes at Mastiq. "Oh, my darling, we so wanted to tell you sooner, but Ammad nearly died and has been gravely ill. We knew it would be too much for you to bear, we couldn't put you through that trauma."

She shifted closer to Mastiq, sweeping her luscious brown hair over one shoulder. His eyes glazed and his entire body softened as he was sucked in by her beauty.

But he shook himself out of it, putting up a palm to stop Jakira's seductive advance. Jakira's shoulders tensed momentarily in disbelief. Her charms had never been denied before.

Mastiq addressed Ammad, but couldn't look at him, staring instead at the dates on the table. "And you son… those are…" and then in a hot, spewing rush, "not your hands!"

If he could, Ammad would've clapped at the old fool's superior deduction skills. "Oh, Dada, Dada," he said in his most childish, pathetic voice.

But Mastiq wasn't swayed. Bolstered by his first-ever rebuff of Jakira, he ignored Ammad and turned back to Whaled.

"I've thought long and hard about this and venturing into Peqkya was a mistake. The army needs new leadership, you will step down," Mastiq said with a nod.

Whaled's eyes narrowed and his fists tensed. Carefully controlling his tone, he said, "Ruler Mastiq, I argued *against* invading."

Mastiq waved Whaled's retort away and turned to Jakira. "And I'm sorry, my dear, but Ammad can no longer be Crown Prince."

A sound like a great glass window shattering and falling to the ground crashed in Ammad's ears.

"Oh, my darling, you must reconsider!" Jakira slid gracefully into Mastiq's lap, wrapping her arms around his neck and nuzzling into it so he had a full view of her chest.

"Do you remember the first time we met?" She whispered sweetly in his ear, in between nibbling it. "The moment you set eyes on me? I'd fallen in your lap..."

Mastiq ogled her cleavage for a moment. Took a great breath in, as if smelling her scent for the last time, and shoved her inelegantly off his lap. Jakira landed on the floor by his feet, her hand on her heart. A hurt look spread across her features and tears welled in the corners of her eyes. As fake as Ammad's arms. He knew his mother would be furious.

"He is a war hero," Whaled said, to Ammad's surprise.

Mastiq shook his head.

"People respect a man with military prowess," Whaled insisted, and Ammad didn't think he could get any more surprised.

"Yes, and also one who is whole," Mastiq retorted, refusing to be persuaded.

Jakira, debasing herself and with a hint of distaste across her lips, leaned forward and planted little kisses over Mastiq's feet.

"You must see it from your son's point of view," she begged, hugging Mastiq's lower legs and looking up desperately at the ruler. "He is the same man, with the same intelligence. He is the perfect Crown Prince and will be an exceptional ruler when you care to grant him that honour. He—"

"Is no longer whole, my dear."

Jakira continued, "Grant him a scorch season and the people will love him again. He is learning to fight again, he will play polo again. It just will take some time…"

Mastiq shook his head. "No."

Jakira's tone turned icy and she used his legs to hoist herself up. She loomed in front of him. "But who will you pick? Not your firstborn Hallid, he is a drunken embarrassment. Who? *Who?*"

Mastiq, flummoxed, shrunk back. He waved his hands in front of his face as if trying to swat the question away. He clearly hadn't thought that far ahead. Ammad knew it would've taken all his father's wits to have used Whaled as a scapegoat for the Peqkya invasion to deflect the people's anger away from him.

"Guards," Mastiq shouted and two Cuttarrs stepped forward, "escort my guests out."

The three men stood. Ammad as quickly as Whaled, he was proud to note. Mastiq took some amount of time, and eventually a Cuttarr came to help him up.

Enraged, Jakira's cool veneer crumbled and she made a grab for Mastiq, as if to shake some sense into him. "He is your son!"

Whaled, Ammad and the two guards all lunged for Jakira. Whaled got there first, grabbing her and pulling her away before she could strike the ruler.

Ammad took his mother's place in front of the ruler and, so they had something to do, the Cuttarrs grabbed Ammad's fake arms.

Shocked by Jakira's venom, Mastiq said, "I know, I

know, and I pity him, the poor, poor boy. Now a cripple."

Pity! A cripple! I'll show that old piece of camel shit.

Ammad sprung forward. The guards who held his arms reacted in precisely the way that he wanted them to – they pulled them backwards. He squatted and kneeled forward and his tunic, complete with fake arms, was pulled straight off over his head.

With a naked chest and just his trousers, Ammad jumped to his feet, bent his knee and kicked Mastiq in the face. It was a swinging kick Samark had taught him, and one that Ammad was proud to admit he'd mastered quickly and was pretty fucking good at.

"Oh!" Mastiq exclaimed as he fell on the cushions, clutching his jaw.

"I'm not a fucking cripple. I don't want your pity. You owe me your *respect*," Ammad shouted at his father.

The guards, recovering from the shock of holding a tunic with arms and no person within, came at Ammad with their hands. *Ha!* The other reaction he was hoping for. Samark hadn't yet taught him how to deal with men bearing swords.

He kicked out at one, connecting with the guard's chin. Not as high as before, Ammad noted with annoyance. The other barrelled into his torso, slamming him against the wall and pinning him there.

That wasn't expected and Ammad had no idea how to get out of it. He wriggled and struggled but to no avail. He needed more time to train.

Whaled, the second time that day protecting Ammad, said gently to Mastiq, "He is upset, my friend. I understand your actions, but he is still young. Forgive him for striking you. Forgive him."

"Ammad," Jakira hissed.

Ammad stilled his squirming, allowing his body to slump into the cutthroat's grip. "Dada, oh Dada, forgive me, forgive me," he grovelled, adding a sniff and a whimper for effect.

"Forgive him, my love, please," Jakira said.

Mastiq's decision-making that day was well and truly spent and he immediately agreed with their suggestion. "I forgive you, my son. You must be distraught. Jakira, I am releasing you from concubinage so you can focus fully on caring for him. He needs you more than I do. Whaled, my friend, you will be well compensated. Take them away."

And with that, Jakira, Ammad and Whaled were all relieved from their positions of power and conducted unceremoniously out of the palace. The message clear – never return.

12

VIOLYA
ᏣᎦᏅ

V sat on a wooden bench on a raised platform in the great hall. Her councillors sat to her left and right, and warriors lined the edges. It was teeming with women, come to see the new Melokai for themselves. Had the weather been better, this official ceremony would've happened in the square, but days of heavy winter snowfall and a blizzard that had whipped up in the night had put paid to that idea.

Everyone was wrapped up in thick fur cloaks and woollen clothes, waxed leather and animal hide boots. Those who had arrived early were sat on wooden benches, but most stood, squeezing into any space available.

The hall was cold. The last time V had been here it had been full of Dromedars. And she had failed to kill Ammad. She shuddered and Emmo squawked. The caterpillar was in her usual position around the back of V's neck, her little feet clinging to V's collar.

Head Speaker Zecky was doing what she did best: speaking. V admired her easy confidence when it came to talking in front of a crowd. V's stomach fluttered and she wanted to duck and hide from all the eyes pinned on her. But she couldn't. She was the new Melokai and she needed to be seen. To be appraised, to be judged.

Her mouth went dry as memories of her childhood came back. The bullying for being different, for standing out. Well, she was different now. She had bright red hair instead of black and red-stained palms, was taller than most Peqkians and her skin glowed with a visible aura. There was no blending into the background now.

"Our beloved Stone Prophetess has spoken, and we have heard. There will be no Melokai Choosing Ceremony. Sybilya has chosen our Melokai."

Murmurs and grumbles around the room as women discussed this with their neighbours. These public assemblies were always open and casual. V had attended them when she was the personal guard of Ramya, and debate was encouraged. But now they were discussing her, and V's bubbling stomach launched bile up her throat.

"The people should have a say," one woman shouted from the back. "We've always had a say in who rules us. I understand the Stone Prophetess has spoken, but we don't know anything about this woman. We haven't seen her fight or take part in the aptitude tests and ruling trials. How do we know she can lead?"

Voices rose as women agreed and disagreed. V's cheeks burned. Why had Sybilya chosen her? She didn't even know if she could lead.

Zecky flicked her thick rope braids out of her face. "From peace, Peqkya has now entered a period of turmoil. Sybilya created this nation, Sybilya protects this nation. She would not do this if it wasn't for the good of Peqkya."

The Head Speaker beckoned V forward, and put a hand on V's shoulder. "Violya is a skilled warrior. She led the army to victory against the Dromedars, the traitorous warriors and peons. She drove the cammers out of our country. She was trusted by Melokai Ramya. She is trusted by the Stone Prophetess."

"Is it true she has magic?" A woman at the front shouted.

Ripples of excitement spread across the hall.

"It is true," Zecky said. Cheers went up. "For many long years we have sought another with The Sight. And this warrior, our new Melokai, is that one!"

Chants of 'Melokai Violya' drowned out the women still in disagreement. Zecky bowed low to her then shuffled away leaving V stood on her own in front of the crowd.

V swallowed down her trepidation. She was a warrior, not an orator. As the cheering and excitement simmered down, V raised her hands and heard gasps at the sight of her red palms. Her voice wobbled as she said, "I promise to do my best."

There was a pause as people waited for her to say more and she had to force herself to continue. "I promise to rule fairly and always with the best interests of Peqkya at heart. I will use my power for the good of the nation, for the good of all of you."

V stopped and an awkward silence filled the hall. *I'm no orator.*

An excited clapping started up and the new Head Trader, Joz, exclaimed, "Melokai Violya, I believe in you. I believe you will rule us well. Melokai Violya!"

Lizya repeated, "Melokai Violya!" and warriors echoed the chant.

The women in the room looked at one another and then joined with their voices. The clapping and cheering intensified as V bowed low to her people and felt elated as they bowed back. Then she swiftly exited the stage and left the hall. Monya following closely behind.

***

Melokai Ramya had visited Sybilya every week during her tenure, and although V could sense the Stone Prophetess' presence and hear the great lady speak in her own mind, V continued the custom.

Two weeks after V had been announced as Melokai, she sat cross-legged in front of the great stone lady and allowed her mind to calm. Sybilya didn't always communicate but V could sense the prophetess was grateful for her presence.

"Do not be scared of your magic," Sybilya said laboriously in V's mind. Her voice was low and breathy. Faint and unsteady.

V waited as the Stone Prophetess gathered her energy to speak again.

"It will control you if you let it. You must learn to master it. Do not let it fool you, your ability is not limitless, but it can be staggeringly powerful."

"How can I master it?" V said.

"Practice and meditation," Sybilya finally replied. "Meditate every day, listen to its chatter, become at peace with it. And then practise. In the time of Xayy, thousands of years ago, there were schools for magic. I went to one." Sybilya's laugh was more of a huff. "I'm so old."

V smiled.

"Practise with each element. Earth, fire, water, air. Practise with your body, and with the bodies of others. Practise using the magic as a weapon, and for the everyday mundane."

"I will."

"Be careful, don't push yourself too far. Magic will drain your body of its strength if you use too much in one go. I wish… I wish I still had the strength to train you, V." Sybilya's voice trailed off to silence.

V remained seated, closing her eyes and listening to her breathing. She blocked out the stench of the place, the howling wind outside, the cold, hard ground on which she sat. Removed those things from her consciousness and listened.

Turn her into a woman again! Drive back the stone curse, fight with the old, poisonous magic that binds her body.

We could fly over mountains and desert and straight to that worm's hiding place in Parchad. We could blast him to little pieces.

What are you waiting for?

We could do anything.

We could rule the world.

How long she listened to the magic, she didn't know but when Monya touched V's shoulder she snapped alert, her hand drawing her dagger instinctively.

"It's getting dark, V. We should return before we can't see the path."

Monya helped V to her feet. Her entire body felt stiff, her feet numb, but it was a small price to pay for Sybilya's instruction.

***

V woke when the novices did. She had refused Ramya's old apartments to stay in the barracks in her old bunk, preferring the noise and bustle of the army sleeping quarters. Above her was no longer Emmya, but a novice who crept around not wanting to wake or disturb the Melokai who slept beneath her.

After the announcement ceremony, V had attended a few of the court dinners and traditional ceremonies to "show her face", as Zecky had called it, but she favoured the boisterousness of the warriors' mess hall. Brin and his Jute fighters were invariably drunk and rowdy, there was good banter to be had and people forgot she was anything different to them.

She left Emmo curled on her pillow and dressed with the novices, not waking Monya who slept nearby. V followed them out into the training ground, pulling up the hood of her cloak to mask her face and grateful for the gloves that hid her red palms. No one paid her any attention as she ran through the daylight dances with them, the series of moves and postures to keep their bodies supple, and listened to the orders from the captain.

They filed out into the streets, grabbing shovels as they went. They were on snow duty. The peons whose job it was to clear the roads of snow were struggling. Their numbers lessened by the peon rebellion. The city needed to function, and the warriors always needed the physical exercise so Lizya had allotted the task to the novices. The blizzard of a month past had blown over but a heavy snowfall in the night had deposited a layer of snow over the city up to V's elbow.

It felt good to listen to orders and follow them. To not have to think. The snow had made it impossible to venture into the bamboo forest and V needed to feel anonymous for a while. Yearned for it. Being close to others but not having to communicate was a welcome respite.

She and the novices worked tirelessly to shovel snow from the busiest of Riaow's thoroughfares, from the marketplace and main square. When no one was looking she lifted chunks of snow from the ground and onto the cart using her magic.

This is so boring, it moaned at her.

This is practice, she replied.

She shovelled and cleared an area, moved on to the next. Her breath formed little clouds in front of her face, her body warmed with the exertion under layers of fur and wool.

Daya had not yet returned from Ashen Valley with news of the stone army. V knew the warrior would be gathering as much information as possible, watching the stone men, testing them to understand any weaknesses. And the winter snows would make travel back along the West Way treacherous. *Be patient.*

The snow had also prevented them from taking action in Drome, but taking their full army into the desert was a mistake. V knew she had to try another way. But what? It had been a topic of discussion with Lizya for many nights in the mess hall.

As she continued to clear the road, her thoughts turned to Fertilian. Captain Denya had disobeyed a direct order from Melokai Ramya. She'd broken the warrior code, she'd deserted.

Cats surrounded V, dashing under her shovel to circle her feet. They jumped up at her legs and pawed at her in a frenzy, all the time mewing and yowling. The other novices stopped their work to look at the spectacle.

It was a sign, V understood, but for what?

A warrior headed down the half-cleared street, crunching through the snow until she reached their group. She spotted the captain in charge and headed towards her at a run, relieved to no longer be wading through thick snow. She didn't notice V.

"Sybilya's Strongcats have been spotted on the North Road, heading into the city," the warrior announced. "The Melokai and Head Warrior must know. Our clevercat is entranced by the tigers so I'm carrying this message. Send others, we must find them quickly."

The warrior continued to run towards the Melokai's enclosure, and the captain turned to the two novices nearest her and ordered them to take the same message to Head Warrior Lizya. Then she shouted at the remaining warriors, including V, to hurry up and clear the rest of the road for the tigers.

V knew she should run back to the barracks, knew they would be searching for her, that Monya would be desperate with worry at losing sight of her, but she remained.

She had never seen Sybilya's Strongcats. The tigers were legendary, once used in battle, they were loyal to the Stone Prophetess. They had come to the aid of Peqkians when called up by Sybilya and had helped them win the battle against the wolves just months before.

V reached out in her mind to Sybilya. The Stone Prophetess' presence was still, calm. Perhaps a hint of excitement danced around the edges. V couldn't be certain. But the great lady was in no danger.

They shovelled quickly, clearing the road to the edge of the city where it joined the country pathway. V and the novices waited, catching their breath. They watched in hushed awe as a group of what had to be one hundred tigers came towards them.

They were majestic creatures. Their striped black and

orange fur was dotted with snowflakes. Their huge paws padded over the snow effortlessly and their sleek forms were elegant yet deadly, lithe yet coiled with explosive power.

As they neared, V caught glimpses of brown fur through the moving orange. They surrounded two animals also moving on all fours.

Wolves!

V saw a flash of the face of one and her heart leapt into her chest.

Darrio.

13

VIOLYA

ᥬᥬᥬ

Two years earlier…

V had been moving for days. North-east, Sybilya had told her, and that was precisely what V had done. She had left Riaow on her eighteenth birthday and taken the North Road, trekking over the Meliok mountains and pausing to camp beneath the looming, snow-capped peak of Zyr Peq. It jutted into the sky like a spear, framed by swirling clouds. She debated whether to attempt to scale the highest mountain in Peqkya, but decided to press on.

At the Trequ Valley, V avoided the border warriors; this was her time, her chance to be alone, to adventure. She didn't want to talk to anyone.

The great Trequ River marked the edge of Peqkya's boundary. It flowed down from the mountains to the east and away west towards the Jagged Canyons. She looked out at the great expanse of dense forests, snowy tundra and mountains higher than Zyr Peq.

"Keep going," Sybilya's voice urged.

V had never ventured out of Peqkya, and her curiosity drove her on. It was a gloriously sunny, late autumn day, and the crystal-clear river looked crisp and refreshing after hours of jogging. The land beyond beckoned. The wolf lands, she knew, but she had her sword and daggers. She saw no sign of wolves on the other side.

She tracked upriver and stopped where it narrowed. The pace of the water was lazy, and she could see the stones of the riverbed. She tossed a twig into the water and watched it drift away.

Satisfied there weren't any dangerous currents, V stripped off, bundled her clothes and boots into her pack and tied her weapons to the top. She slipped into the water, the chill making her feel more alive than ever. Holding her pack high, she waded across, her feet searching out solid footing on the slimy pebbles. At its deepest the water lapped at her chin.

V threw her pack onto the northern bank and hauled herself out. It was grassy and soft underfoot. She found a clearing in the trees and sprawled in the sun, head on her pack, to dry off. She noticed steam rising from behind some trees. V shouldered her pack and crept towards the source.

There, a rapid flowing tributary hurtled down over rocks towards the river she had just crossed. The steam wafted off a natural pool that had formed in the rocks, in the bend of the river. A hot spring.

Fantails darted back and forth into the rising steam catching the fat midges that drifted languidly above the water. The birds' acrobatics were mesmerising. After twisting and turning to fill their beaks with a squash of insects, they would fly to a nearby nest to feed their squawking brood. When their cache was gone, they returned to the ripe hunting ground in the midst of the steam.

V edged closer. The air above the pool was not only steaming, it sizzled. The surface was still, the rapids rushing past it but not disturbing the water that gathered within the circle of rocks. She dropped her pack on the bank, and stepped onto a smooth rock, crouching so that she could lower herself in.

Movement in the trees. V froze.

A large brown wolf emerged from the shadows. It stood on its two back legs, its head low, eyes downcast. Its entire body seemed weighted down, and V was surprised at how human-like it appeared. It didn't look around, didn't see V as it stepped into the pool.

The wolf submerged itself, then popped up and sat against the rock V was crouched atop. The wolf sighed and soaked up the heat, watching the flying insects and the birds that swept down to pick them off.

"He is significant," Sybilya's voice sounded in her mind.

V hesitated. *Significant?*

But she trusted the great lady implicitly and silently eased herself into the pool with the wolf, cautiously circling around him to sit opposite. She dipped her hair back in the hot water but kept her eyes firmly on the animal.

He watched her with little interest. She splashed her face and felt all the aches and tension in her muscles unwind with the heat. She rubbed at her feet, massaged her calf muscles and thighs, enjoying the bath.

The wolf rubbed a paw across his nose. "A vision. Madness disease. I succumb, finally."

V's breath caught in her chest. She had understood his words, spoken in a language of growls and barks. The wolf blinked a few times at her and then looked back to the birds.

"My name is Violya," she said in the wolf tongue, enunciating every word. She was convinced he wouldn't comprehend, that she had imagined hearing him speak.

But the wolf's head snapped back to her. "A furless vision that speaks. Truly going mad. But no fear of water yet." He scrunched up his brow, brought his nose to the pool's surface, sniffed and then lapped at it.

"What is your name?" V asked.

His dark eyes narrowed at her. Then he sighed again. "Darrio. Do not have pack. All dead from madness disease. Am last. But you here to claim me, too."

"You are alone?"

"Yes, packless. Watched family die. Tried to help. Was only one who did not get sick. But, pointless. They all died, no matter what I did. Have been waiting for days to succumb. Must be my time. Seeing things that don't exist." Darrio slapped his paws on the surface of the water.

"Not a vision. Peqkian. Human."

She touched his leg with her foot under the water. Darrio yelped, jumped out of the pool onto the grassy bank. Shook out his fur on all fours and snarled.

V jumped out too, beads of water rolling down her skin.

The wolf growled, lowered his head, hunched shoulders and crouched in an attack position.

He launched himself at her and they both fell to the ground. His jaws went for V's neck but she fought him off, yanking his maw apart and ripping her hands to shreds on his teeth. His sharp claws scraped at her skin and her blood smeared onto his brown fur.

She kneed him in the genitals, and he whimpered, loosening his grip. V released his jaw and jabbed her fingers in his eyes. The wolf rolled off her with a high-pitched yap and she punched his face before finding her feet and kicking him in the ribs.

He turned and sank his teeth around her ankle, pulling her off balance and to the ground.

Her fingers scrambled in the dirt before finding a rock. She bashed it into his head, and he stumbled away, stunned. V clambered on top of him and raised the rock to bash him again, and he struck out with his back legs, forcing her backwards.

He leapt on top of her, snapping at her face then clamped his jaws on her shoulder. She screamed. The pressure slackened, and he let go, rolled off and sprawled next to her on the grass. Both were panting and bleeding.

"Want to live but should die. Have no one now. Take

me, will not resist. Everyone else dead. No one to live for."

V could've snapped his neck, found her daggers in her pack and sliced the creature to shreds. But she didn't. Curiosity won out again; she wanted to learn more about him, his kind, his world. She'd discover why he was significant.

They lay side by side. The fantails swooped and dove overhead. Their breath gradually returned to normal. He turned and licked at the deep gash on her shoulder.

"You will bleed to death before I die. Cannot bear to see more death."

V tried to raise her shoulder to inspect the wound, found that she couldn't. He was right, she was bleeding heavily.

"Will you help me clean and wrap it?" she said.

Darrio huffed. "Why not. Nothing else to do, nowhere to go, no wolf to go to."

So V told him what to do. And he did it.

***

"For you," Darrio said and dropped three rabbits at her feet.

She grinned. "I'll cook them for breakfast. But first, our daylight dances," she said in the Shella language.

Darrio stood opposite and mirrored her movements, groaning as his body twisted in unusual postures or when he stretched out a tight muscle.

"Talk to me in Shella," V said. She had been teaching him for months and the wolf understood her speech but struggled to form the words in return.

"Let us go back to den before breakfast," he said in his own language falling onto all fours and attempting to nudge her towards their little cosy sleeping area in a small cave.

She had only just emerged, but Darrio had been up and hunting for hours. He liked to bring her breakfast. It was usually meat, but one day he had dragged back a fallen branch full of ripe berries. Another day he had taken her empty pack and returned with it brimming with mushrooms.

V laughed. "No." She pushed him away. "Dances and Shella."

Darrio rolled his eyes and stood upright again, copying her movements. "I am Darrio. You are V," he said in stunted Shella as he flowed through the movements she had taught him.

"And where do you live, Darrio?"

But Darrio didn't reply, instead he said in heavily accented Shella. "How many moons?"

V continued with her poses in silence for a while. Darrio counted the nights rather than the days. She had told him when they first met, how many days she had before she must return to Riaow.

"Two hundred and seventy-five days," V said eventually. "I've been here for three months. I have another nine to go."

"Stay here, stay with me. Don't return to Riaow," Darrio said in Shella.

V took his head in her hands. "I can't, Darrio. This, us, it cannot last. You know this. I must return. I cannot disobey an order; it is warrior code. If I don't return when I'm meant to then I can never go back."

Darrio's eyes dropped and he walked away from her on all fours towards the steaming stream. V followed him at a distance. He sat on the bank, lowering his head between his front paws.

She sat beside him, resting her head against his shoulders.

"Lost everyone. Cannot lose you," Darrio said in his language.

She replied in Shella, knowing he would understand. "Sybilya sent me out to explore for a year, to see what I have never seen before. And I met you and have stayed here. I have let her down. I haven't heard her voice since the day we met. I cannot bring myself to leave you. I do not want to see anywhere else, be anywhere else but here. But when the day comes that I must return to Riaow, I will go, Darrio. Know this, I *will* go. I have to."

"I know. I understand. We enjoy what we can together. We enjoy each day until the day." He nuzzled at her neck. "Now, can we go back to the den and start this day again?"

***

V gently woke Darrio, careful not to disturb the three babies that snuggled into his warm fur. She had fed them one by one, kissed them tenderly and then placed them next to their father. They slept contentedly; days old, still blind.

Darrio opened his eyes but didn't move. Didn't want to disturb the babies. He looked up at her. Tears streamed down V's face. She gently kissed his forehead, on the smooth fur just above his eyes.

"Today is the day," she whispered, her voice choked with emotion.

She had delayed her journey by a few days already, but she was out of time. She toyed with the idea of staying here with her love and her new family, but she was a Peqkian warrior and this pulled at her, wrenching her back to Riaow. She had an order to return on her nineteenth birthday. And she had never disobeyed an order.

"I'll care for them. And when you can, come back," Darrio whispered.

She backed out of the den, heart ready to burst. She shouldered her pack and ran. Ran all the way back to Riaow. Her breasts heavy with milk and her heart heavy with loss.

And shame.

Every step further away from Darrio, from the idyllic year she had spent with him, from the three children she had left behind, her shame grew heavier. How could she ever explain a relationship with a wolf? How could she tell Sybilya she hadn't explored? By the time she had returned to the city, her soulmatch and her babies were buried deep. A secret she would never reveal.

She was a Peqkian, a warrior. Not a lover, not a mother.

14

VIOLYA

ೞ

arrio.

V threw down her shovel and ran up the freshly cleared street to the Melokai's enclosure. She dodged her way through warriors running towards the tiger procession. In the courtyard, Head Warrior Lizya was giving orders and then ran after her warriors.

"Lizya," V shouted, and the Head Warrior turned on her heel.

"Where the zhaq have you been? Wait here. Warriors! Protect your Melokai. And you, find Monya and the Melokai's clevercat." Lizya turned and ran off, leaving V stood with a group of warriors forming up around her. V did not believe the Strongcats posed any threat, but Lizya was taking no chances.

Cats dashed from the courtyard and towards the procession. Others swarmed around her legs. Amya came bounding up and put her front paws on V's waist before dropping down behind her. Monya sprinted from the building to stand next to her, relief etched across the youngblood guard's features.

The procession came slowly up the street. Riats moved to each side and watched as they passed. The cats were yowling, hissing, meowing, and when the procession passed, they dipped their heads in respect, and then joined the trail of cats that were following behind.

At the head of the procession was Head Warrior Lizya. Behind her the tigers enclosed the two wolves. Lizya's warriors formed a line either side and behind the tigers, in a typical protective barrier.

Lizya gestured and the warriors parted. The Head Warrior walked up to V, thumped her chest and stood closely by her side.

The head Strongcat approached. V could not see the wolves through the wall of tigers behind their leader. The tiger spoke in a language that V had never heard before.

V's clevercat Amya said, "I can transsssslate feline into Sssshella."

"There's no need," V said. She understood the tiger's words and replied in the same language. "Strongcat Otiss, welcome to Riaow. I am the Melokai of Peqkya. Melokai Violya. The Melokai before me, Ramya, was murdered. It is an honour to meet you." V dipped her head and then showed the tiger her red palms.

"Sybilya has chosen you," Strongcat Otiss said in his feline language of chuffs. "The honour is mine." The tiger considered her, then said, "We bring the leader of the wolves to you, the Melokai of Peqkya, in peace."

The leader *of the wolves? Darrio was once a lone wolf.*

V's excitement bristled in her chest, but she remained passive, her face and body neutral. She watched closely as Otiss moved to one side, his tigers behind parting to show the two wolves.

Both unfurled to full height and walked a few steps closer to V. Her breath caught in her chest as she saw him. It had been more than a year since she had left him with their babies. *Darrio.*

He walked with a limp and had only one eye. *So many more scars than when I last saw him. So many battles he must have fought.*

Her eyes caught his. His eyebrows twitched and he

blinked rapidly. He didn't give anything away. Remained as impassive as her. He was following her lead here, and for that she loved him even more.

The second wolf caught her gaze. Taller than Darrio, and a head above V. Younger, certainly a female and with more human features than her father. She was the same rich brown as Darrio but with creamy fur around her head and shoulders. Her eyes were stunning: a glowing orange. She looked around her in wonder, obviously curious about everything those radiant eyes fell upon.

Sarrya? V thought abruptly.

"Yes?" came a reply. The female wolf's head snapped to attention.

Both V and Sarry jerked, stood taller, stared more intently at one another.

"Are you speaking in my mind?" the female wolf said.

"Yes…" This was new to V. She had never heard another's voice in her mind apart from Sybilya's. *"How are your brothers?"* V asked suddenly.

"How do you know I have brothers?" Sarry replied, confused. Then she barked in surprise and the tigers around her prickled and scanned for danger.

Sarry's mouth dropped open. *"Are you my mother?"*

"V," Lizya said quietly in her ear, "this isn't the best time for one of your reflective moments."

V smiled broadly, wrenching her focus from the female wolf. "Welcome, I am the Melokai of Peqkya. Melokai Violya." V repeated the greeting in the wolf language, in feline, and then in Shella.

Slowly Sarry raised her paws. The pads were a bright red. V's eyes widened, and she heard Monya gasp. V raised her own poppy-red palms and Sarry looked sharply at her father, who nodded encouragement.

Sarry turned back to V, and in fluent Shella, said, "Melokai of Peqkya. I am Sarrya, daughter of Darrio, leader of the wolves. I come with my father to offer assistance. The Stone Prophetess has led me here."

My daughter, just over a year old, is the leader of the wolves?

"Sarrya," V said, "I am…" *your mother?* V looked at Darrio and he made the tiniest gesture: 'She does not know. I haven't told her'.

V regained her composure. "I am honoured to meet you and your father. What brings you to Peqkya? Not so long ago our peoples were fighting in Trequ Valley."

"We have come to broker a truce between our peoples. We have come to offer our assistance," Sarry said, still staring at V.

"Assistance for *what*, exactly?" Lizya said.

The Head Warrior was suspicious. The Strongcats were Sybilya's, and all in Peqkya trusted the Stone Prophetess. So, all in Peqkya should trust the Strongcats. But they were known to be wild and unpredictable. Why had they brought the wolves here? What was their purpose? V knew Lizya wouldn't rest until she had answers.

Sarry glanced again at Darrio and he encouraged her with a dip of his nose.

"There is trouble coming from the east," she said. "We must unite the nations to fight it. Otherwise we fail. Peqkya is at the heart of these mountains, the centre of our known world. The enemies will pick off the limbs and then come for the heart. But if we all work together, we might succeed in driving them back. This the Stone Prophetess Sybilya has told me. Trouble will come from the east. And it comes for us all."

She is far wiser than her years, V thought.

"We have more pressing trouble in the south right now," Lizya said. "And the northern border with your kind is not exactly stable."

"What is this truce you speak of?" V asked.

Sarry pressed her red pads together, and then dropped them to her sides. "Your kind killed our kind. And our kind has killed yours. Enough unnecessary bloodshed. We are neighbours. Let us live together peacefully. Let us share. There is enough land, water and prey to satisfy wolf and human bellies in the place you call Trequ Valley. Wolves once roamed that place south of the river, and they want to roam it again."

"We can't just forget the past," Monya blurted. "Hundreds of Peqkians have died because of the wolves."

Sarry considered Monya and swept her orange eyes across all of them one by one. "Why are we so ruled by our ancient pasts? Bloodshed and fighting has failed. Hundreds of wolves have died at Peqkian hands. Let us think to our future. We must fight together to survive the coming evil. So, let us live together. The wolves are bitter at losing the south Wul-Onr Valley. Give it back to them and keep it for yourself. We both win."

"She sounds sensible. A bit like you," Lizya said in a hushed tone in V's ear.

V beamed inwardly at the intelligence and reasoning of her daughter. Coolly, she said, "I will think on it, Sarrya, leader of the wolves. Come, we should go and see the Stone Prophetess Sybilya."

"The Strongcats will accompany you," Otiss said in his feline language. "We have been too long away from Sybilya."

V beckoned the wolves to walk with her in the direction of Inaly Lake as the tigers and warriors formed up around them. Otiss and Lizya headed the procession, talking amiably using Amya as a translator. Lizya's hearty guffaws peppered their conversation.

They trudged through the deep snow as cats swarmed around their feet, getting in the way. The wolves snarled at them, swatting them away when they got too close.

"You'll get used to them," V said with a smile. "Cats are sacred in Peqkya."

Darrio kept a few steps behind Sarry. V could see him out of the corner of her eye and knew precisely where he was. She wanted to talk to him, to embrace him, to learn of what had happened to him, and how Sarry had come to be in this position of power.

Sarry was quiet, glancing at V every now and then.

From behind, Darrio blurted, in fractured Shella, "Melokai Violya, how did you become Melokai?"

Sarry looked over her shoulder at her father, her face scrunched and in wolf speak said, "You know their language?"

Darrio shrugged off the question and V answered before Sarry pushed the point further. "I was chosen by the Stone Prophetess. A neighbouring country and some of our own traitorous people joined forces to attempt to overthrow our nation."

"An enemy we must turn to our cause," Sarry said, looking once more at the road ahead.

Darrio huffed behind V and she turned to look at him. A corner of his mouth twitched up in a grin. Her heart raced and she turned away, watching the road as her daughter did.

Otiss slowed to allow Sarry to catch him up. "Shall I tell you about Sybilya?"

Sarry nodded, and V slowed her pace to walk alongside Darrio. She longed to reach out to him. A strip of air crackled between them as her heart quickened. She was certain he felt the same.

She whispered in Shella, "I will tell them when the time is right. It is to protect you and Sarry. There is some hostility towards foreigners and the wolf war is not long finished."

"I understand," Darrio replied. "I will wait."

V brushed her fingertips lightly past his paw.

"I've been thinking," he whispered. "Have you considered that finding me was what you were meant to do? And having your babies was what Sybilya desired all along?" He nodded at Sarry who was raptly listening to Otiss.

V said nothing for a while. The shame of not exploring as Sybilya had bid her, eased. And an awareness dawned like a new morning. *Was bringing Sarry and her brothers into the world my purpose all along?* "I think you could be right," she said in an undertone.

Sarry sniffed at the air as they paused at the foot of the Mount of Pines for Otiss and Lizya to give orders. The wolf glanced over her shoulder at her father. "Place from my dreams," she said in the wolf language and gazed back at the path that snaked up the hill.

As they ascended, passing under the arches that led up to Sybilya's hut, the tigers peeled away and disappeared into the pines, leaving only Otiss with them. Lizya had ordered all the warriors to wait at the bottom, including Monya. And so, two Peqkians, two wolves and a tiger made the journey up the hill.

"You are my mother, aren't you?" Sarry's voice sounded in V's mind. She was walking in front of V with Darrio at her side. *"I can feel it. I know it. I just seem to know things now. Pappy lied, he said you'd died."*

"Your father did what he believed was best for you. Forgive him."

Sarry huffed in amusement in V's mind. *"There's nothing to forgive. Would've been pretty hard to explain that one."*

In front, V watched as Sarry leaned in to lick the fluff around Darrio's cheek. He snuffled her forehead tenderly.

"I'm thinking you've not told anyone either, huh?" Sarry said.

"No. That… is something I will need to do at the appropriate time."

"A Peqkian mammy. I can't quite believe it." Sarry snorted out loud. *"When will that time be?"*

"We will tell them when the time is right. You must prove yourself on your own merit. Make the people love you. Respect is not down to bloodlines in Peqkya."

V could sense Sarry angering.

The wolf's shoulders tensed. *"Prove myself?"* Sarry's voice was loud in V's mind. *"Sybilya chose me, I did not choose this! I don't want to have to prove myself. I don't want to be here. I want to be running around with my friend Ricarro and my brothers, playing with pine cones and catching rabbits."*

V's voice was soothing, patient. *'I did not want this either, daughter. I must prove myself to my people, to Sybilya. You must prove yourself worthy of Sybilya's favour. I know you can do it, Sarry."*

But Sarry shut off the link between them and they climbed the hill in silence.

"Our great Sybilya is near the end," Otiss said sadly from behind V.

It was too painful to reply but she could feel it. The Stone Prophetess' presence that had filled them all with kindness and happiness, was shrinking. Retreating from their minds, their bodies, their world and curling into a tight ball.

In her mind's eye, V saw this ball – now about the size of her fist – glowing bright. But it was shrivelling until finally it would be a mere pinprick in the world. And then…

Darrio and Lizya waited outside the hut whilst Otiss led V and Sarry inside, followed by a squall of cats.

Sarry was in awe, dropping down to her four paws and dipping her head low. V stood in front of the great lady and bowed. Otiss went up to Sybilya, put his paws on her stone knees and gazed intently into her eyes. Otiss smoothed his head around her neck, chuffing deeply. He licked her stone cheek once before jumping down and running from the hut with a keening roar.

Sybilya's eyes, the only part of her not yet stone, looked at them.

"Sit, my children. There is little time. And I have much to tell you." Sybilya's frail voice echoed in V's head, and she sat cross-legged on the hut floor. Sarry also sat, her back legs hunched, belly on the floor and front paws outstretched.

"Magic is found in the blood. When the right blood mixes, the magic comes alive. Not for many years has there been any mages with The Sight. One thousand years ago, mages were forced to fight by the warring Xayan tribe rulers at the Battle of Ashen. I turned both armies to stone so the mages' blood, and the magic in it, was frozen in time.

"I knew the risks, and I took them. To end the cruel reign of *men*," Sybilya hissed as she said the forbidden word, "magic had to be sacrificed. I saw a glimpse of the future when I looked out over that battle. The vision told me I would die when magic was reborn. I did not know when that would be, but I knew I would die. And I conjured the magic to turn all those thousands of males to stone anyway.

"The vision also showed me the consequences of my death. I have held the stone army for one thousand years in place by my magic. They are tied to my life. When I am gone, they will no longer be rooted to the ground. I do not know what they will do. I have had no sight on that. V, you must stop them, for they will endure forever and destroy everything in Peqkya if left unchecked."

Sarry awkwardly cleared her throat to speak, but Sybilya's voice continued.

"Your question, my child, is an important one, which I regret every moment of every day. Why did I turn them to stone and not kill them? I was young then. Foolish and reckless. I wanted to make those evil males suffer for all the suffering they had inflicted on the country of Xayy and its people. On women. I wanted to demonstrate my power, for so long mocked and shunned by the rulers of those very men.

"I should've killed them all. Instead I turned them to stone. But not completely."

Sybilya's voice paused. In V's mind she said, "Yes, you did the same, V."

V replied directly to Sybilya, keeping Sarry from hearing. "With Ammad. I toyed with him, wanted to punish him. But I should've ended him swiftly. I was young and foolish too."

Sybilya blinked slowly. "Yes."

She continued to them both, "There is still a flicker of life in the stone soldiers. An awareness of what they have become. For one thousand years they have stood as still as statues, but their minds have been active. They do not remember what or who they were, have no memory of their lives before the battle. It has been a slow, awful torture. But I tied my fate to theirs."

"Is that why you're stone too?" Sarry said.

"Yes. The magic I mustered to turn them to stone and to keep them that way has slowly infected my own body. For the glory of Peqkya, for a new way of life ruled by women, I sacrificed myself."

A wave of sadness washed over V.

"You are both young. The magic takes years of mastery. You have it in you, but neither of you are aware of what you are capable of. The power varies, the visions of the future, the awareness of what is to come and who to trust."

Sybilya's voice faltered and the ball of light contracted to the size of V's thumbnail.

"No," Sarry shouted and stood to all fours.

"I saw a vision of my death. My time would end when the three discovered their magic. That time has come. The third has awakened."

"Three?" V said. "Who is the third?"

Faintly, rasping, grasping for every word, Sybilya said, "A peen. You must save him from corruption, V... hurry... hurry."

The Stone Prophetess' voice trailed off and her eyes glazed. Sarry fell into V's arms and they held each other as they watched the grey stone creep inwards, across Sybilya's pupils and meet with a faint clunk at the bridge of her nose.

A desperate, but emphatic *"Go!"* sounded in their minds.

V and Sarry bounded from the hut.

"Move," V shouted to Darrio and Lizya.

The group ran down the hill, under the arches and came to a halt at the foot of the hill. With their sudden arrival, Lizya's warriors pulled their swords, alert to danger. They looked around and up the path to see what might be chasing them, ready to engage.

A cracking, hissing sound met their ears and the arches ignited, each sizzling and spitting as fire consumed them. A snake of flames wound up the hill as the fire jumped from arch to arch.

It danced towards Sybilya's hut and then consumed it fully. The hut burned brighter than the rest.

Cats came dashing down the hill, away from the fire and towards the city, their fur on end. The sound of their wailing choked the air, mingling with the smoke.

A huge emptiness swept through V and she fell to her knees in the snow, clutching her chest, her belly, her head. Something was missing. A part of her was gone. She felt hollow.

Lizya and the warriors dropped to the ground, grasping and clenching at their bodies in the same manner as V. Sarry let out a painful howl and collapsed.

Darrio stared, baffled. He was the only one not affected by the loss of the great lady. He looked desperately from V to his daughter, one writhing in agony, the other still on the ground. He went to his daughter, nibbled at her fur, attempted to rouse her.

Cats gathered around the fallen wolf, mithering at her fur and mewing. They surrounded V, desperately scuffing away the snow to rub their bodies against hers for comfort.

***

Even in the furthest corners of the country, every Peqkian felt the death of Sybilya. A huge hole wrenched open in their hearts. A part of themselves lost forever.

For seven days the fire blazed up the hill, consuming the arches and the hut. It jumped to nearby trees and scorched the earth.

No one spoke, barely were they able to move or to eat. The city was still, the people in a daze.

When the fire finally died away, a charred path led up the Mount of Pines to a blackened area where the hut once stood. The heavy winter snow did not settle on this scorched earth. It would forever burn, like the charred earth in the Ashen Valley. Snowflakes sputtered and steamed to nothing before they could touch down.

In the centre was Sybilya the Stone Prophetess. Now an unliving, stone statue, looking out over Inaly Lake and the city of Riaow. And when the clouds cleared, the sun illuminated the breathtakingly beautiful snow-capped mountains.

15

GWRLAIN

The warrior Finya was suspicious. Gwrlain felt her stare gouging deep holes in his back. An elevated heat sizzled off her in rapid waves. But he didn't turn around.

"I thought you'd been banished," she snapped. "Why did they just let you in?"

What could he say? He was tired of lying. So Gwrlain said nothing.

He stuck out his tongue to taste the air and listened. The movement told him Fin was giving hand signals to the four warriors who trailed behind. He heard the scholar Robya mumble, but he didn't pick up the words.

When the air had stilled, and Fin's thumping heart had steadied, Gwrlain continued. He weaved down the dark tunnels effortlessly, knowing the maze like his own mind.

They had arrived at the trading point days ago. But rather than enter the cave, Gwrlain insisted they turn north. He led them to a cave opening in the mountain unknown to the Peqkians. It led directly to the Troglo capital Lauago. Outside the cave entrance they had left the donkeys and a clevercat messenger in the care of one warrior and three serving peons, shouldered their provisions, lit torches and tramped into the dark.

In the twilight zone, where the sunlight from the entrance only just penetrated, lounged five singing Trogrs. Their spears propped against the rock. They were guards but hadn't stirred as the group came upon them. They would've heard the echoes of their steps and the movement of their breathing from the moment the group had stepped foot on the rocky platform outside the opening. They would've identified Gwrlain long ago from his scent.

When they had come upon them, the Trogr guards had stopped singing and hummed continuously, their way of seeing their surroundings, and simply nodded at Gwrlain to pass, making no sign they'd even noticed the five Peqkian warriors, one scholar and three serving peons that followed in his wake.

So, now the warrior Fin was alert and suspicious. And the scholar Robya's mind was working hard to put the pieces together.

Before the small party had set off, they had both been briefed by the Head Scholar Chaz as to Gwrlain's history, the story he had told Ramya. That Gwrlain had been banished from the eastern cave country of Troglo for killing his father who had tried to rape his sister. That his mother was dead and the species was dying as no females had been born and only five remained. The reason Gwrlain survived was that his friend Bance had taken pity on him and left him near the Peqkian border in the hope the mountain women would show mercy and help him.

Lies.

Melokai Violya had told them to go to Troglo to negotiate and bring back the five kidnapped Peqkian women. For Gwrlain to lead the way. It was a dangerous mission and V put her trusted warrior captain, Finya, in charge. V also sent her friend, who she had ventured into Majute with, the scholar Robya. Her purpose was to record and converse, being exceptional at languages and fluent in the Trogr tongue.

Fin had protested, of course, insisting on violence. To take revenge for the dead warriors at the hands of Trogrs; to mount another attack to save the kidnapped women. But V, in her wisdom, had insisted on negotiating verbally, peacefully. A wise choice. They would've all died.

The warrior's fury simmered near the surface for the entire journey from Riaow. But, in respect of her Melokai's orders, Fin would not use force unless absolutely required. Before they left, in front of Gwrlain, V had told the captain to trust him. The Melokai's innate power had told her Gwrlain was not the enemy. V had given him a loaded look. But what did she know? What could she know? Perhaps everything, perhaps nothing. No matter.

Gwrlain avoided Fin. He avoided all of them. Remained aloof. He mourned the loss of Ramya and his baby, Terya. Their deaths like a gash across his heart that would never heal.

But the fear he displayed, of returning to his country that had cast him off, that… that was a lie. In truth, he could not wait to return. To be swathed in the blackness, to drink up the water in the air through his skin, to be at one among his people. To sing a lament to his dead link and to their daughter. To sing, sing, sing.

Now, though, Fin wanted answers. A little way past the guards, she grabbed his shoulder and pulled him to a stop, spinning him to face her. With her torch in one hand, she brought her face close. Her breath was warm beneath his chin, the heat of the flame dancing against his cheek.

Fin was short and squat, a similar build to Ramya. He towered over the captain, but in a fist fight, if it came to it, she would be a difficult opponent. Perhaps even a match for him. But it wouldn't come to it. His weapon would flatten her and her companions before her fingertips could even brush her sword.

"What the zhaq is going on, Gwrlain?" she growled.

Gwrlain's face remained blank, impassive. His stance meek. *I lied,* he wanted to declare, *I lied to Ramya and I'll never be able to tell her the truth, to set things straight. And now the guilt eats at me, but life continues. Trogrs must go on.*

Robya came forward, he heard her steps. In a softer voice, with a distinct undercurrent of concern, she said, "Gwrlain, please, we need to know what we are walking into. Did those guards not recognise you? Why would they allow Peqkians to enter without so much as a conversation?"

"Lauago is this way," he said and dipped his shoulder down out of Fin's grip and backed up before turning and continuing down the cave tunnels.

After a brief pause, the Peqkians followed.

They came across no other Trogr on the journey into the deepest, darkest caves, into the roots of the mountains. Down, down they trundled until they emerged on a ledge in a great cavern. It was in complete blackness, the Peqkian torches would only light a few paces around them and they could not see what lay in front.

But they could hear it, smell it, sense it in the vibrations that would tickle up from the soles of their feet. A city, as the Peqkians called these big settlements. *His* city. Lauago.

It was just the same as when he had left it and a rush of love swelled through his organs, bringing a heat to his skin that any Trogr would sense, but not these Peqkians, they were too reliant on their eyes.

Gwrlain took in a great breath, let it out with a deep throaty hum and listened to the echoes. He stuck his tongue out to taste the city, to assess what had changed, if anything, before they ventured down.

It was small in comparison to Riaow. There were no huts or dwellings, the few thousand Trogrs who lived there slept together, ate together. There were no set pathways or roads, the Trogrs lounged where they pleased. The only walls were those of the cavern. The air was deliciously hot and humid, the temperature always steady, none of these shifting seasons he had experienced outside the cave.

Gwrlain stripped off the Peqkian cloth they had

insisted he be wrapped in. He threw it to one side of the tunnel. There it would remain until he ever had need to pick it up again. The dampness in the air clung to the clay that covered his translucent skin and he smeared it off. Ramya had insisted he be covered in thick clay if he was outside to stop the sun's rays from scorching his skin. He had also worn huge hooded cloaks in the winter and held above his head a wooden contraption covered in a heavy cloth in the summer.

The clay slid down his skin and clumped around his feet. He drank in the moisture through his skin. Once he was naked and his thirst quenched, he felt whole again. He lifted his arms in delight. The restriction of clothes and contraptions gone.

"This is Lauago," he said.

Fin glared at Gwrlain. She controlled her wonder and repressed all emotion, as warriors did. Instead she assessed for threats, holding out her torch in an attempt to see what lay ahead and around them.

The scholar Robya, however, gaped at the cavern. She could not see far, but she could hear the Trogrs singing, the endless trickle and drip of water. She could smell the sulphuric tang in the air. She could sense the scale below her.

"Issee, Fin, we are the first Peqkians to witness this. Just as we were the first in Majute," Robya said in wonder.

The captain didn't reply. Gwrlain sensed her shrugging, clearly not as impressed as the scholar.

"Follow me," Gwrlain said and pointed to some stairs.

They descended slowly, the steps had been carved into the rock and were damp and slimy. No problem for Gwrlain's large feet that sucked up the moisture beneath them, but slippery for the Peqkians.

As they reached the bottom, Robya gasped audibly as she saw the first of the Trogrs. They glowed a bright white in the Peqkian torchlight. Their veins and sinewy muscle showed through their skin and the fine fur that covered them glinted in the flickering light. They hummed and sniffed at the passersby, curious but not eager to get close or investigate.

"All men, as expected," the scholar said, as if to herself. To note the detail to record in her journals later. "A few children. They all seem to be… resting. And singing. Exquisite. Not all in unison, not all the same song, but beautiful… utterly beautiful."

They picked their way over and around reclining Trogrs, every step eliciting a crisp crunch.

"What is on the ground, Gwrlain?" Robya asked.

"Birds' nests. Of the swifts," he replied.

"But I thought you ate those?"

"We eat as many as we please, the rest are dropped to the floor, used as bedding."

The scholar nodded. "Are there any other settlements like this in Troglo?"

"No, only Lauago."

"And what do you all do here?"

"Lounge about and sing mostly. Singing is our religion. It's how we tell our tales and pass them down to the next generation. We have a slow metabolism and we live for many years. There is no rush in our lives. We sing our histories and add to the songs. Some songs can take hundreds of years to sing and, once started, a Trogr will sing the same song for a lifetime. When not resting we grow and harvest swift nests in the near dark. And every now and then we hunt fish, salamanders, spiders and insects."

Gwrlain paused as two children, both male, meandered past him laughing and squealing in between pulsing hums to see their surroundings. They edged in and out of the Peqkians with ease, missing them by a hair's breadth, their assessment of the echoes working perfectly to detect the objects in their way.

The smell was intensifying as they stepped over Trogrs towards the centre of the cavern. Gwrlain had never noticed it before, but now he realised it stank of shit and piss, rotting flesh and semen.

Robya had also noticed. She brought her hand to her nose and said, "Where do you, er, get rid of your own waste?"

"We leave it where it falls," Gwrlain said, suddenly conscious that this would no doubt horrify the Peqkians who were obsessed with keeping their skin and their dwellings clean. "It attracts the animals and insects that we eat. To us it is not waste. It is precious. It is what feeds the animals which feed us."

"Oh," Robya said and crinkled her nose. She tripped and stumbled forward, Fin reaching out a hand to steady her. The scholar was clumsy. Tall and long-limbed, her feet would often get away from her.

"What was that?" Robya exclaimed. "It looked like bones… a ribcage…"

"A skeleton. We leave our dead where they fall too," Gwrlain said.

He heard the bile rise from Robya's stomach and into her mouth. She swallowed it down with an effort and a faint smell of sick reached his nostrils. The Peqkians burned their dead, allowed fire to scorch the bodies of loved ones. He'd watched Ramya and Terya burn. That custom was abhorrent to him.

"You will get used to the smell. Soon you'll no longer notice it," Gwrlain said.

"How soon?" Fin said.

"Perhaps in a few years," Gwrlain said.

"We do not plan to be here a few years," Fin said, her voice sharp and impatient.

Gwrlain shrugged. "So get used to it quicker, because it is how it is."

As the party neared the centre of the cavern they started to walk uphill. There was a small hump of rock. The Trogrs didn't lounge up the sides, preferring the flat rock around the outside.

At the top of this mound of rock reclined the only two female Trogrs left in the entire world as Gwrlain knew it. As well as a decrepit old male.

The females were at rest. The younger of the two had a male baby suckling from a breast.

"Living Goddesses, I return," Gwrlain said.

The two females slowly turned their bodies to face him and hummed in pulses. He waited for the Peqkians to gather behind him. And then beckoned the captain and scholar forward.

"This is Finya and Robya," he said to the eldest of the two women in his language.

She lounged on a pile of birds' nests, naked. Her body betrayed her age. The skin hung from her bones and her breasts sagged low, the huge nipples a sign she had suckled hundreds of babies. Her muscles had shrunk and deep wrinkles cragged her face.

"This is Gruack," he said to Robya.

"Gruack?" Robya said, confusion tinged her voice, and then louder in the Troglo tongue. "Hello Gruack."

Gruack ignored Robya, and said, "Gwrlain, my son, you return. Daneil, your son has returned from his mission."

Daneil, the old male, didn't move or make a sound. He didn't hum either, a clear sign he was close to death and his body was shutting down.

He heard Robya choke and stifle a cough. She whispered a translation to Fin. Once again, the warrior's anger bristled off her in waves. It struck against Gwrlain's exposed skin and he was impressed by its force.

"Your parents are meant to be dead," Fin snarled. Her hand went to her sword and she hissed.

Gwrlain ignored her. "Hello, Mother. Hello, Father."

16

GWRLAIN

ᎧᏋᏜᎧ

Finya pulled her sword, and her four warriors behind did the same. She positioned herself ready to fight.

But there was no one to fight. The Trogrs remained at ease. It was a time of rest – it was almost always a time of rest. They conserved their energy. Gwrlain's body had forgotten how it felt to shut down after expending energy. He ate more with the Peqkians, had adapted to their being awake and moving for longer periods.

Gruack ignored Fin's drawn weapon. She sung. The melody swept over Gwrlain and heightened his senses, as if a great gush of ice-cold water had been splashed over him. He swayed at the words that cut to his core. It was pure and it elated his being. The fine fur shivered and tickled his skin as it stood on end.

When Gruack had finished, Gwrlain could sense the Peqkians bristling next to him. They were unsure what to do, impatient for something to happen. But Trogrs didn't rush their lives. Greetings, in the Peqkian's concept of time, were lengthy. He would explain later.

Gwrlain sung and his mother swayed happily as he had done. Then his old father, with effort, propped himself up on an elbow, and faintly sang the same song as his mother had. Gwrlain welcomed it in his being once again. He replied with a song that affected his father in the same way. Daneil lowered himself back onto the birds' nests and sprawled contentedly. The same was repeated with the second female on the rock platform.

When the greetings were complete, Gwrlain turned back to the Peqkians. Fin still had her sword drawn, but it was pointed down.

Gwrlain stuck out his tongue and could taste utter bafflement in Robya's odour.

"When we are born, we are given two names," Gwrlain explained to the scholar. "One is a spoken name, such as Gwrlain, and the other is a song. The song is unique to each individual and is created by the mother at birth. We sing our own name-songs whenever we please and greet each other by singing theirs."

"Interesting," Robya said.

"When Terya was born, I gave her a name-song because Ramya couldn't."

"I see."

Fin scowled. "We are getting distracted. Why are your parents alive, Gwrlain? Where are our Peqkian women?"

Before Gwrlain could answer, Gruack spoke. "Your mission was a success, son. You bring us more women to mate with. But so few. Where are the rest?"

Robya, who understood, jerked away from Gwrlain and moved closer to Fin to translate in her ear. The warrior raised her sword again.

"Mission? What mission, Gwrlain? We are not here to mate!" Fin sprung forward and pointed the sword at Gwrlain's neck. "V told us to trust you, but everything you've told us has been lies."

He sighed. He raised his arm and gently moved the sword away. Any show of aggression now would see every Peqkian dead. That was not what he wanted.

The second female stirred and slapped the rock she reclined on. Around her, on the flat rock beneath the mound, Trogrs roused. One climbed onto the rock platform and took the baby from her. A second came up behind her rubbing his erect penis. She manoeuvred her body onto all fours and he entered her from behind.

Whilst he thrust, she turned to Gwrlain. "Brother, I need to get pregnant again. I've only had male babies. I must have a female. Time is running out. Mother is pregnant again. She has not born a female since me. There have been no more female babies since yours. We sent a swift. The other females have all died in the time you have been away, their wombs spent."

"Brother?" Robya said.

"That is Lulac," Gwrlain said to the scholar.

The Trogr grunted as he ejaculated and pulled out. He made way for a second Trogr, who entered Lulac. Behind him stood a line of males, waiting to have sex with her. She would receive male after male until her womb quickened again with child.

"I am getting old and tired, son," Gruack said. "I fear this will be my last pregnancy."

"Let it be female," Gwrlain said in unison with his mother and sister and every Trogr nearby.

"But we have hope, Mother. One of the Peqkians is with child," Lulac said as a third Trogr thrust away.

"Let it be female," Gwrlain chanted again with those around him.

A line of Trogrs had formed up next to his mother. But not to procreate. She lifted a finger and they started forward. One by one they placed gifts at her feet such as nests, a few drops of salamander blood in birds' skulls, rock carvings of babies and birds. They sung her name-song before walking away and joined the queue to mate with Lulac.

"What is going on?" Robya, exasperated, grabbed Gwrlain's arm.

He reacted harshly and regretted it immediately. He emitted a deep hum that shook Robya off her feet. She collapsed on the birds' nests that covered the floor in a crackling heap. Her body convulsed.

Fin raised her sword and lunged at Gwrlain. Her warriors positioned themselves to attack at her command behind her. From deep in his chest, Gwrlain produced the same hum that had floored Robya, what Zecky had called his death-rattle. Within seconds all the Peqkians were flattened, convulsing on the floor. The noise having no effect on the Trogrs.

Fin gritted her teeth and fought against the force, attempting with all her might to come at him on her knees. He was impressed by her strength and persistence. He upped his vibration by the tiniest fraction and she fell back, her body rattling and her sword falling from her fingers.

"Are there any matches?" Gruack said. She hadn't moved from her position, and was in no way alarmed by the proceedings. Trogrs continued to drop offerings at her feet. Lulac continued to receive seed.

Gwrlain stopped his vibration and the Peqkians groaned on the floor. Fin attempted to stand, but her entire body wobbled. Gwrlain knew it would be a while before they recovered.

"Did you not get my swifts?" Gwrlain said.

"Perhaps," Gruack said with a languid turn of her head. "I do not recall."

Gwrlain's skin flushed momentarily. He had sent a swift ahead with a message: 'Treat me as if you hate me. Resist my entry, do not allow us easy passage. The Peqkians are clever. Our plan must change.' But Gruack either hadn't received that message, had forgotten its contents, or – most likely – had ignored it altogether. What did Trogrs care about Peqkian cleverness? Peqkian strong wombs, however, those they cared about.

"We have been expecting your return with many Peqkian women to link with and breed. When you did not return, our situation became desperate and we sent males to the trading point to attempt to link with Peqkian women there. It worked. Five linked," Gruack said.

Gwrlain nodded. kneeled next to Fin and Robya. Both Peqkians still writhed on the floor, attempting to regain control of their bodies after the vigorous shake. He could sense Fin's intense anger.

In Shella, he said, "Listen. Be calm. I was sent to link with a Peqkian woman. The woman I linked with happened to be your ruler. I loved Ramya. That is true. When a Trogr finds a mate, we mate for life. We made a baby, a female baby. Our species joined. The Peqkian women were not kidnapped, they came willingly. They linked with Trogr males. It happens instantly. We do not force ourselves on females, that is not our way, we honour them, they are precious in our culture."

"What... is... link?" Robya stuttered as the aftermath of the vibrations surged through her body.

"Every being has a unique vibration. When your vibration is perfectly in tune with another's, they sing together. Ramya and I shared this connection. You will only ever find one other with a matching hum. I will never love another again," Gwrlain said.

His head dipped as he remembered his soulmatch and his baby. Terya's name-song came to his mind and he longed to sing it. But later, he would remember his daughter later.

He continued, "Many Trogr males would've sung out their songs to the Peqkian women at the trading point in the hope that they would link."

Fin gritted her teeth and pushed herself up to sitting. "So this is a trap?" She spat out at Gwrlain as she slowly got to her feet. "You've lured us here to use our wombs?"

"No. You came here of your own free will. Your ruler sent you."

"If any male cave creature so much as comes near me I'll spill the cockface's innards," Fin replied, her fingers finding the hilt of her sword.

Robya coughed and spoke in his language, so that Fin wouldn't understand. The scholar's voice still quivered. "So, from the moment we stepped foot in Lauago the Trogrs would've been attempting to link with us, to see if one of us shared their vibration?"

She was clever, this one. "Yes. Clearly none have been successful," Gwrlain replied, sadly. He had hoped that one of these females might've linked with a Trogr, but it wasn't to be.

Robya's eyes widened. She reached a shaking hand out to the captain. "They will not touch us, Fin," she said in Shella.

Fin considered the scholar and Gwrlain sensed her rage shrinking to sit beneath the surface of her skin, still hot but not molten.

The captain turned to Gwrlain. "Where are our women? Take us to them. Now."

The other Peqkians were also recovering and starting to stand once again.

Fin picked up her sword and sheathed it. She glared at him. "Don't ever do that rattle thing again, understand?"

He didn't reply, and silently led the wobbly Peqkians away from the main cavern of Lauago and along a tunnel with a gradual incline.

"We're heading back towards a cave entrance," Robya said. "The air is getting fresher."

"Thank Sybilya. Your city stinks, Gwrlain," Fin said.

Gwrlain ignored the warrior. "Correct, Robya. The Peqkians and their mates live in the near-dark where there is enough light for the women to see by."

It wasn't long before they came upon a small cave hollowed out in the mountain.

Gwrlain hummed to picture the scene. Fin and Robya gawped.

Leading off this hollow was another tunnel that was lit by daylight. A few steps and it opened to the outside. And surrounding the hollow were small openings that had been carved out of the rock to house a place to sleep and a small area to sit. Within the hollow was a small fire, the smoke lazily drifting out the entrance tunnel. Bustling around this fire were five Peqkian women and five Trogr males.

Some were cooking, some were sewing, some were learning songs and teaching each other their language. Some were coming and going from the tunnel carrying wood or water in buckets. It was a happy, bustling, lively setting.

As the residents of this little hollow noticed they had guests, and Peqkian guests at that, they jumped up and came forward.

"Welcome, welcome!" one small and smiley Peqkian woman said. Her face glowed and she bloomed with joyful good health. "What news from Peqkya, of Melokai Ramya?"

"You are *truly* here of your own free will?" Fin asked.

"Yes, of course. We fell in love with Trogrs whilst working at the trading point," the woman said.

"What is your name?" Fin demanded.

"Freya," she said frowning at the warrior's venom.

"Freya, warriors died trying to save you and these women. It was understood you were kidnapped."

"Kidnapped? Died?" Freya repeated, scrunching her forehead.

Fin leaned in close to the woman and stared closely at her eyes. "Are you under some spell? In some kind of trance?"

"No," Freya said. "I'm blissfully happy. This is my soulmatch." She beckoned forward a Trogr who came to her side, put his arm around her shoulders and rested a hand on her belly. Freya kissed him sweetly on the cheek. "I am pregnant," she said to Fin.

"Zhaq," the warrior captain swore and spat on the ground. "Warriors are dead. Peqkians, your own kind, died coming after you."

"I did not know this." Freya turned to her Trogr and,

in basic Troglo language, said, "Is this true? Why would you kill these warriors? We came willingly."

The male dipped his head and replied in heavily accented Shella, "We did not want to lose you, we were protecting our bond. Those who have not experienced the link, cannot comprehend it. They wanted to take you away from us."

"We would have explained that we were happy, told them we wanted to stay," Freya replied.

The male simply shook his head.

Freya turned her attention back to Fin. "I'm sorry that women died," she said in Shella, dipping her head.

"We are here to take you home," Fin said. "To rescue you."

Robya put a hand on Fin's arm and gently shook her head. With the other hand she indicated the little cavern. "They are home."

Freya nodded and the Peqkian women around her clutched at their Trogr partners.

"It is a beautiful thing," Freya said. "Not every one of us will link with a Trogr. I didn't realise, but thousands of males sung to me before one melody thrummed in my entire being. Spoke directly to my core. There were hundreds of females working in the trading point. Only us five linked. We all just thought that the Trogrs liked to sing, we didn't realise it was a love chorus. They were singing for love."

Fin tutted, but Freya persevered.

"Once I heard the song, I stopped what I was doing and walked towards it. Towards him. There was an instant attraction. We made love that night, and every night since."

Fin rolled her eyes.

"Is this what happened with Melokai Ramya, Gwrlain?" Robya said.

"It is." Gwrlain's white skin tinged a sallow yellow with sadness.

"We believed that if our Melokai could take a Trogr for a soulmatch, so could we. We didn't think it would be perceived as kidnapping," Freya continued. She rested a hand on her swelling belly.

The captain hissed, still disbelieving of the power of the link.

"We have much to tell you, Freya. Ramya is no longer the Melokai," Robya said.

Freya's hand went to her mouth and her Trogr male caught her as she staggered. "Oh, Sybilya save us. Come, sit. Let us bring you food, and we shall talk."

"And we thought *you* were the trouble from the east," Fin laughed a few hours later.

She lounged on a smooth rock in the area that had been named 'Peqklo' for the Peqkians who lived here with their Trogr soulmatches.

In the warrior's hands was an empty bowl, once brimming with birds' nest soup prepared by Gwrlain. He had given the same soup to everyone in attendance, it was his famed recipe. But for the warrior, he had added a little something else. A few sprinkles of the mildly euphoric, and immediately relaxing, blood of a rare spotted salamander.

Gwrlain wasn't proud of his actions, but her aggression would get her killed. She needed to calm down, to accept the situation. The Peqkians had no idea just how powerful Trogrs were. Fin had experienced just a small taste back in Lauago.

She had sniffed at the soup, seen everyone else eating it and tucked in. Robya sat straight-backed and knees crossed furiously writing in her bound parchment journal. Fin's four warriors crouched strategically around the outside of the cave. They, too, ate the soup, but would not strike unless their captain ordered it, or their captain herself was threatened.

Fin was lounging in much the same way as a Trogr. She

even attempted to sing when the Trogr males started up their melodies. The five Peqkian women had helped Gwrlain to serve the soup, until Fin ordered the three serving peons that had come with them to do that job.

"We like to serve our soulmatches," Freya had said, lovingly stroking her linked male's face. "We are treated as goddesses; they do everything for us. But we like to care for them too. It was strange at first. But they're not lowly peons, they're more like equals."

"Do not insult us," Fin had seethed, and the peons had been ordered to distribute food, tidy and clean.

Gwrlain replied to Fin in Shella, "We could still be the trouble."

"No, you're no danger. I mean, you can do that hummy thing, but there's only a few thousand of you. If you came face to face with a Peqkian army, outside these caves, you'd quickly be overrun."

Doubtful. His death-rattle, at its weakest, had stunned her. At its strongest, and joined with the hums of other Trogrs, it would flatten an army. But they'd need to be stood quite close, perhaps a few hundred paces away for the vibrations to reach. And Trogrs could only produce the death-rattle for a limited time before having to refill their lungs. And then, usually, the spears were used.

The Trogr hunters had perfected their attack when prey was located. They hunted in packs of three or four, depending on the size of their quarry. They would hum together in a continual blast that stunned the target. At the point the prey was wracked with the shakes and frozen in place, the hunters came in with spears to kill. If they continued to hum, the prey would simply burst apart. No good for eating. And picking scraps off the rock was tedious work. *Would that happen with a human? They are larger than our usual prey...*

"Let us hope that will never happen, Fin," Gwrlain said to appease her.

Fin snorted. "If only we had some of that pitfire juice,

eh, Robya?"

The scholar blushed, heat rising from her cheeks. "That was one time, Fin, one time. The only occasion I've ever been drunk. I don't wish to ever repeat it."

The warrior laughed and fought against her drooping eyelids and the sleep that Gwrlain knew would now be clawing at her.

She looked around the cave drowsily, taking in the hazy scene. Her eyes flicked open with urgency and she sprang to her feet, surprising Gwrlain. Her warriors threw down soup bowls and stood to attention behind her.

"Where are the peons?" she said and eyed Gwrlain.

He sensed the suspicious tinge back in the warrior's scent. He was amazed she had got to her feet so quickly. The strength of this woman continued to surprise him. But then, Ramya's force and determination had always impressed him too.

Gwrlain hummed to picture the cavern. Robya also looked for the peons.

"Silence," Fin shouted, and the Peqkian women nudged their Trogr soulmatches to stop their singing.

As the noise settled, a faint grunting could be heard from along the tunnel that led back to Lauago.

Fin gestured to her warriors, grabbed a lantern and took off down the tunnel with three in tow, leaving one to keep watch over Peqklo. Robya set down her pencil and parchment and ran after Fin. Gwrlain close at her heels.

"Zhaq." Gwrlain heard Fin swear up ahead as he caught up with her.

She stood at the opening to a small cave off the tunnel pathway. Her arms were folded. Robya's eyes almost popped out of her head.

"Lulac," Gwrlain said with surprise.

His sister sat astride one of the serving peons, rutting him hard. In her hand she rubbed another peon's erect penis. The third peon was lying to one side, catching his breath, his penis flaccid.

The peon on the ground grunted as he ejaculated. The one whose penis Lulac held stared at Fin, attempting to wriggle out of Lulac's grip. But she held him firm.

"Brother, your presence here has lessened their erections. Please leave," Lulac said, shifting to allow the peon underneath her to move away.

"What are you doing?" Gwrlain said.

"It works both ways, brother, you males can breed with female Peqkians, and I can breed with Peqkian males. We must save our species. No Trogr male is capable of planting a female in my belly, so I am harvesting the seed of these males in the hope that they can. They were willing." Lulac guided the peon to stand in front of her by pulling at his manhood. Seeing that his penis was now soft, she took it in her mouth to work it back to life, gripping his buttocks so he couldn't move.

The peon stared at the group in the doorway, pushing at Lulac's shoulders, attempting to get free. The other two huddled together, eyes downcast, in the furthest corner of the little cave.

Robya translated Lulac's words for Fin. The warrior glared and her hand twitched toward her sword.

Gwrlain filled his lungs. Lulac was a Living Goddess. He would hum and hum until Fin burst if she tried to touch his sister.

Fin laughed, slicing through the tension.

Doubled over, she clutched at her belly and guffawed so intensely that she almost lost her footing. "Your sister should wait to meet our Pleasure Givers. These are the runtiest runts. Peqkian women would not touch these peons. Of course they are willing. I doubt they've ever had a woman. If all she's after is their seed, and no pleasure, then she can carry on. Look at their little faces, this is the happiest they've ever been." Fin pointed at the peons. "Pleasure this female Trogr for as long as she requires, as often as she requires."

The peons vigorously nodded.

"If I hear any complaints from her, the usual punishment will apply. Well, what are you waiting for? Get yourselves ready again. Gwrlain, tell your sister that we gift her these peons to pleasure her and service her until she has no more need of them." Fin headed back to the cavern, a smirk on her face.

"They are yours, Lulac, may their seed bring forth a daughter for the Trogr people," Gwrlain said.

Lulac didn't reply, she was too busy pulling the peon whose cock had been in her mouth to the ground so she could straddle him. She flicked a hand at Gwrlain as she grinded. Behind, the two peons rubbed at their penises, ready to service Lulac again.

17

JESSIMA

⚘

"**S**weet dreams, my love," Jessima whispered to Eddie and stepped silently away from his cot.

The boy had grown in the past few weeks and his face had filled out. He was looking more like the Cleland side, but she was certain he had her dainty nose.

She had woken with him at dawn and breakfasted in her room while feeding him. It was his first nap of the morning and she knew he would sleep for an hour.

Now, she would dance. She changed into some old, thin cotton leggings and a loose-fitting bedshirt that she knotted at her stomach. Jessima pulled her hair into a high clasp then opened the window a crack to allow the mild winter breeze to circulate the room. Lian winters were warm, Ernie had informed her, and had laughed when she'd asked if there was ever snow.

Positioning herself in front of her full-length mirror, she found her starting position and ran through a series of movements, focusing on doing them in the correct order, pushing herself to hold a pose until her muscles ached.

Two weeks ago, when Martha had given her approval for activity, Jessima had forced herself to remember the Peqkian routine and each pose. Every morning on her journey back from Riaow to Cleland City, she had watched the Peqkian warrior Denya and her thousand-strong host flow through these movements fluidly and in unison. A stunning dance, that led on to Denya directing drills and training skirmishes, and all before breakfast. Then the warriors would jog alongside the Ferts on their horses for the rest of the day, never falling behind.

Jessima had watched as Captain Denya taught Toby every move, had seen him contort his body into strange positions and listened as Denya corrected his form or berated his posture. Jessima imagined Ramya guiding her, thought of her friend's voice instructing and encouraging. It was her way of keeping Ramya alive.

I am strong for Eddie, in mind and in body, Jessima repeated as she twisted into a move.

This mantra bolstered her, and by the time she had finished her Peqkian dances she was drenched in sweat and determined to be a good mother for Eddie. And to be a good mother, she must be a good queen.

But how?

After her unsuccessful attempt to engage her subjects with a speech in the main square, she'd determined that if the commoners were not interested in her, then the wealthy and noble families would be. She'd receive them formally, offer refreshments and entertainment, learn more about them and their lives.

So, having not socialised at all since she'd arrived due to the princes' restrictions, Jessima had ordered a banquet that evening to meet the Lian noble families. In Cleland she had attended numerous feasts and parties with Hugo, it was part of her queenly duties.

As she wiped away her sweat with the crumpled, dry end of the unknotted bedshirt, a knock sounded at the door, precisely on time.

"Come," she said.

Three handmaids entered; two to help her bathe and one to take care of the room. Princess Georgina followed, fresh and awake. She ignored Jessima and went straight to

Eddie.

"Hello, little brother," Georgina said and gently tickled his chest to wake him. She had become inexplicably attached to the baby, and had helped Jessima with him every day for the past week.

At first, Jessima had watched her stepdaughter vigilantly, suspicious of her intentions. But there was nothing dubious in Georgina's manner. She was his half-sister, after all. She had no reason to harm him.

"I've had every man in this place," Georgina said, "and this little man is the only one who continues to amuse me." She kissed the baby's forehead as he grizzled. "I've had my years of fun, but now I'm ready to start a family."

"With Hadley?" Jessima asked before she could check herself.

"Of course," Georgina smirked and then sighed. "But Hadley would've been with dear Daddy on the battlefield. Dear Daddy didn't make it… perhaps Hadley… the Cleland army…" Georgina's voice trailed off. She rallied herself and draped Eddie over her shoulder.

"Your bath is drawn, my Queen," one of the handmaids said.

Jessima kissed the back of Eddie's head on her way to the washroom.

Georgina muttered, "Who is there to help them, Jessima, who?" before lifting the baby in the air and making him smile with delight.

"To be a good queen I must meet my people," Jessima said.

"Not these people," Prince Charles muttered under his breath.

She was waiting for her guests to arrive in the room next to the receiving area. It was the first time she'd seen Prince Charles since her rather curt banishment of him from the throne room.

"Did you say something, Prince Charles?" Jessima said.

The prince pursed his lips, still reeling from her reprimand.

His brother stepped in. "As I previously mentioned, my dear, we do not have nobility here as we do in Cleland. Wealth is distributed more evenly in Lian. The wealthy families are mostly merchants."

"And, as I've previously said, Ernie, I will meet the heads of these families," Jessima said.

"You do realise they are all women," Prince Charles said, "all the men are in Fertilian."

"Then I imagine I'll find it easier to converse with them," Jessima said.

Prince Charles snorted.

"They are… well… quite demanding, my dear," Ernie said. "They are not high-class women of leisure and luxury."

Jessima waved his pessimism away, and turned to a steward. "Are all the preparations ready?"

"Yes, my Queen," she replied. "The first guests have arrived."

"When the room is full then you can announce me," Jessima said.

She'd commissioned a new dress for the occasion and had found handmaids who were adept at applying bone powder and stain to her lips and cheeks. She'd spent most of the day getting ready for the evening. Her jewel-decorated hair had taken hours to tease into place.

A grand feast had been planned, with musicians and the finest wine from Ernie's cellars. She'd introduce herself to the important families in a magnificent, memorable fashion. Be the queen she was expected to be – regal and ornamental, as she had been in Fertilian.

The princes spoke to each other in hushed tones in the corner of the room as Georgina sashayed in and took a seat. Betsy bounded up to her and she petted the little dog, while holding her skirts away from the eager paws.

Jessima waited impatiently, resisting the urge to pick at

a thread on her dress. When she could stand it no longer, she beckoned to a steward.

"Have all the guests arrived?"

"Perhaps ten," the steward replied.

"Ten?" Jessima said. "Did the invite not go out to two hundred households?"

The steward nodded. "Addressed to the head of the household, as requested, your Grace."

Prince Charles, cutting off his discussion with his brother, projected his voice across the room to infringe on her conversation. "Most women still believe the head of the household to be the male, as is God's decree. And all the males are in Fertilian proper."

Jessima clenched her jaw, realising her mistake. She should've specified the current, *female* heads of the household. "We'd better go and meet our guests who are here."

The steward gesticulated at various servants and moments later the musicians started up a fanfare. The two princes entered the receiving room first, followed by Princess Georgina. Jessima heard their names announced.

She followed and the fanfare reached a crescendo as she entered the room. She swept in with a huge beam on her face as the steward announced her.

"Welcome, dear friends," Jessima said, mimicking the words Hugo had used on many a majestic occasion.

Instead of the clapping and cheering Hugo inspired, Jessima was met with blank, stony faces. A handful of women stood before her. They were dressed in simple, functional dresses or in men's trousers. Their hair was tied simply away from their faces, their appearance fraying around the edges with fatigue.

She waited for the steward to introduce her to each of the women. One stepped forward and Jessima gave this first woman her hand to kiss. As she did, an image flashed across her mind – of her hand holding the assassin's dagger, a great rush of ferocity engulfed her as she remembered stabbing the man and hot blood spurting from his neck. She shook it off and turned her mind to entertaining, widened her smile and held her hand out firmer, but the woman didn't take it, instead she nodded curtly.

"Lady Jane Fletchling," the steward said.

"Lady Fletchling," Jessima said.

She dropped her hand and looked the woman in the eye, fixing a kind expression on her over-powdered face.

"I think, Queen Jessima, I speak for all gathered here when I say that we are honoured by your invitation to dine," Lady Fletchling replied, putting an immediate stop to Jessima's rounds. "And we wanted to come to express our gratitude at your kindly thinking of us. However, we will not be able to attend the meal. With our men gone, we find ourselves to be running households, running businesses, raising children and keeping our families afloat. Sadly, we have no time to attend feasts, even those hosted by royalty. My sincerest apologies."

"I see," Jessima said.

She looked at the other women gathered. All nodded at Lady Fletchling's words, and subtly shifted their positions so that they stood behind her.

"We have just one question, which we are hopeful that you will grant us permission to ask," Lady Fletchling said.

"Of course," Jessima said. "Please speak."

"When will our men be coming home?"

Once, the lady's direct question would've alarmed Jessima. Polite custom dictating those subjects were not to be broached at a grand dinner, and especially not to be answered by the Queen. But times had changed. She had changed.

Jessima cleared her throat. "I am not certain, Lady Fletchling. The situation in Fertilian is yet unknown. We await news."

Mumbling fluttered across the women gathered behind the lady. They shared loaded glances at one another.

"There is no update whatsoever? We do not know if the Cleland army still holds the country?" Lady Fletchling said, unable to hide a tinge of desperation in her voice. "How… how can you not know? My husband and son are in Fertilian, your Grace. I just want to know they are safe, that they will come home."

Jessima opened her mouth but she had nothing. Her heart sank.

Another woman said, "My husband is there and my father. I just want to know if they are alive. That's all I ask."

The voices of ten women launched into similar laments, all taking a step forward, beseeching Jessima for news of their loved ones that she could not give.

She shook her head and glanced at the two princes who stood to her side. Prince Charles had a look that said, 'I told you so'. Ernie was distraught, these being women he had to keep on side, and wrung his hands. He launched himself forward.

"Ladies, please, Queen Jessima does not have an answer for you. If you are not planning to stay for refreshment and entertainment, then I would kindly ask you to be on your way. I will be in touch with regards to business matters as I very much value your contributions to the way Lian is run."

Lady Fletchling dipped her chin. Her face, a few moments ago so hopeful, drooped and Jessima realised just how weary she looked. She bowed to Jessima. The women behind her bowed in turn and left the room, following an usher who directed them to the gate.

"Well," Princess Georgina said into the stunned silence, "can we eat now?"

***

In the afternoon of the following day, after a morning of Peqkian daylight dances and history lessons, Jessima took Eddie from Princess Georgina.

Worry sliced through her. "He feels very hot."

"He's not been himself all day. Lots of tears," Georgina replied.

Jessima held Eddie up so his little face was at the same height as hers. His cheeks were pale and his body was listless. She sniffed at his nappy and took him over to the changing table. She undressed him and gasped. His body was covered in purple splotches. She undid his nappy and gasped again at the fouler-than-usual contents.

Georgina joined her at the table. "Oh!"

"Get Ernie to call for Martha," Jessima said.

As Georgina hurried from the room Eddie began to cry. The sound pierced Jessima's heart in its profound unhappiness. It wasn't a hungry cry or a full-nappy cry but one of pain. Jessima fastened on a clean nappy and held Eddie to her, his skin scorching her own.

Georgina returned. "A messenger has been sent to find Martha. I've asked for some cool water to be brought up."

Jessima nodded. Eddie's face scrunched up tight and his mouth turned down at the corners with a quivering bottom lip. Servants arrived and Jessima placed a cool compress across Eddie's forehead in an attempt to bring down his heat. It only made him scream more. She bathed him in cool water, to no avail.

After a little while, Ernie entered the room. "My dear, the messenger has returned. Martha cannot attend Eddie here. She cannot leave her hospital. It seems there is a crisis with many sick babies."

"We shall go there. Martha will know what to do."

"I'll get the carriage," Ernie said.

"No," Jessima said. "It's faster on foot."

Jessima handed Eddie to Georgina. "Hold him while I change out of this dress."

A few moments later, Jessima hurried through the streets in a shirt and men's breeches holding a screaming Eddie in her arms and surrounded by soldiers.

Thankfully it was early afternoon and the streets were relatively quiet as Lianites took their midday meal. When

Eddie's screams picked up and he felt like a burning coal in her arms, she ran.

At the hospital, Jessima demanded to see Martha. She was pointed in the direction of the children's ward.

It was overflowing when Jessima arrived. Screaming babies, panicked mothers holding them, nurses running here and there. And in the midst of the chaos stood Martha directing her team, seeing each child in turn.

Jessima bundled her way towards her.

"Martha, Eddie is sick," Jessima said, her voice a pitch higher than usual.

Martha glanced at her and continued her administrations. Checking over a baby and then telling a nearby nurse what medicine to administer and in what dose, depending on the severity.

"So are all these babies," Martha replied.

She held her hands out to the next baby in the line, rather than Eddie.

"Martha, you need to help Eddie," Jessima insisted. "He is your king!"

"Do you want to tell all these mothers that your baby is more important than their own? Because he happens to have a title?" Martha gestured behind her.

Jessima turned to the line of frightened mothers who clasped their screaming babies as tightly as Jessima held Eddie. They all stared at her. She glanced at Martha and retraced her steps to join the end. Martha gestured the next baby forward.

"Get those soldiers out of here," Martha said after examining the baby and giving an order to a nurse, who struggled to get close to her. "They are taking up space and preventing my nurses from doing their jobs by getting in the way."

"Wait outside," Jessima said.

The soldiers shuffled out as the line shuffled forward. More mothers clutching squalling babies joined behind Jessima.

Finally, it was her turn in front of Martha. The medic touched the back of her hand to Eddie's forehead, pulled back his eyelids to look at the whites of his eyes, checked the splotches on his torso and peeked into his nappy.

"Mild case," Martha said to a nurse. The nurse held her hands out and took Eddie from Jessima.

"What now?" Jessima said, watching where Eddie was being taken like a hawk.

"You wait or you go and come back later," Martha said impatiently. "Either way, you get out of our way. We are understaffed and the babies keep coming. This is the most severe outbreak of baby dysentery I've ever seen."

"What are the other mothers doing?" Jessima asked.

"Most have to go back to work," Martha said, waving Jessima to one side so she could attend the mother and screaming baby behind the queen. "You need to move on now."

"I will help," Jessima said.

Martha raised an eyebrow. "It's messy work."

Jessima nodded.

Martha turned and caught a nearby nurse's attention. "Penny, this one will help you. Tell her what she needs to do."

Penny frantically beckoned Jessima to her.

"We need to keep their nappies clean. They are filling them constantly. Other nurses will be around to give them water and others are administering the right medicine. These babies are our responsibility," Penny indicated an area of the ward, with cots containing four babies each, "they have severe cases. I suggest you roll up your sleeves or they'll get covered in you-know-what."

Jessima did as told as Penny continued.

"Fresh cloth for nappies is over there. Take the dirty nappies and put them in that cart. The washer women are trying their hardest to keep up, but the clean cloth is running low. Martha will tell us what to do when the nappies run out. Right, you start on that side and I'll start here. We work our way into the middle and then out again. If the nappy is clean, leave it. It won't be clean for long."

"I understand," Jessima said, but Penny had already moved to a cot.

The nurse leaned over the first baby. As her deft hands worked to check the contents of the nappy she whispered tenderly to the child, as if it were her own.

Jessima considered her first baby. It screamed and screamed. The purple splotches deeper and darker than on Eddie's skin. A girl. And her nappy was full. Jessima got to work, whispering soothing words in between gagging at the smell.

Later, as Jessima's hands had begun to work methodically as if they had a life of their own and her nostrils had become numb to the smell, she realised two things: her feet were screaming at her and her babies' nappies were not filling so regularly. She looked up at Penny. The nurse smiled at her. Night had settled and Jessima wondered how long she had been there. It felt like minutes.

She took in the ward. The line of mothers was no more and the franticness of earlier had subsided with nurses pausing and looking around at one another. The babies, although still grumbling, were not as vocal.

"We've made it this far, ladies," Martha announced across the ward. "But we're not done yet. These babies are stable but still need constant care. Some of the mild cases might be able to go home in the morning. Not one babe has succumbed to the illness. Well done. I'm proud of you all. We can do anything if we work together."

The nurses clapped and cheered and Jessima joined in. Her mind then turned to Eddie.

"Whereabouts are the mild cases?" Jessima asked Penny.

The nurse pointed to an area in the far corner of the ward.

"I'll be back shortly," Jessima said as Penny continued

with her work.

Jessima walked around the cots, looking in each for Eddie. When she spotted him, he was sleeping soundly in a cot with three other babies. The colour had returned to his cheeks and the purple marks were barely visible. She gently stroked his cheek.

"Thank you," Jessima said to the nurse who flitted about the area, checking on all the children there.

"You're welcome. Thank you for helping Penny," the nurse replied. "We appreciate all the help we can get. I think every mother would've stayed if they could've. But most have families and businesses they're supporting."

"Do you know who I am?" Jessima asked.

"No," the nurse replied, confused.

"I'm Queen Jessima. This is King Edward Hugo Cleland."

The nurse gaped then looked down at Eddie. "Well, he's just another babe to me. And you're just another mother kind enough to help us. There's no special treatment here, Martha makes sure of that. She's an inspiration. There's nothing she'll ask another to do that she won't do herself. And she listens to us, really listens."

In between directing staff, Martha beckoned to Jessima from across the ward. "Thank you for your assistance. Now this is under control I must check on my other patients."

"How many patients do you care for?"

"Oh, hundreds," Martha said.

"Hundreds?"

"I run the biggest hospital in the city. I took over the job of three men when they went off to war. I'm exceedingly busy. My women are exceedingly busy, too, all stepping up to take on the men's work."

"It's exceptionally well run, Martha. Thank you."

"Yes, I have an excellent team. I trust them and they trust me. You have to have the right people around you to lead," Martha said. "It's not an easy job, but if I didn't do it, then who would?"

At dawn, Jessima walked home from the hospital with a sleeping Eddie in her arms. The soldiers encircled her but there were few people in the streets. She was exhausted yet elated. She had made a difference, had saved lives. She'd never worked as part of a team before, had never trusted that others would do their tasks and that they trusted her to do her own. It was true what the nurse had said, Martha was an inspiration.

As Jessima entered the fortress courtyard a steward rushed up to her.

"Your Grace, they await you in the breakfast room," the steward said.

"Who awaits me?" Jessima replied. With each step closer to her bed, her mind slowed in anticipation of sleep.

"The monthly breakfast meeting with Ernie and his administrators. You wanted to attend, your Grace," the steward said.

"Yes, of course," Jessima replied. "Lead the way."

Half awake, Jessima followed the steward into the breakfast room. She was so tired she barely registered who was there, mostly elderly men though, she noted. The chattering of voices quietened as she sat in her usual position.

"Ah, Queen Jessima, we didn't know King Edward would be joining us," Prince Charles said.

He laughed and a number of the men snickered with him. The few women gathered did not.

Jessima frowned. It hadn't even occurred to her not to bring Eddie. She bit the inside of her cheek to try to wake herself up and adjusted the baby in her arms so she could sit up straight. "King Edward is unwell and is recovering. It is best that he remains with me. Let us start the meeting, we have much to discuss."

Ernie spoke then about the city's roads and the ones that were in need of repair and a discussion began with those sat around the table. The droning voices and Eddie's soft snuffles cushioned her like a lullaby.

"Queen Jessima," a voice said gently in her ear.

Jessima woke with a jolt to see Lord Chattergoon's face.

"Apologies, where were we?" Jessima said quickly, realising with frustration that she had fallen asleep.

"The meeting was adjourned," Chattergoon replied moving out of her line of vision, "everyone has left."

Jessima stared around the empty table, seeing the plates of half eaten food and empty teacups. The room was deserted. "Why wasn't I woken?" Jessima said.

Lord Chattergoon didn't reply. It was obvious. Ernie hadn't wanted her there in the first place, neither had the administrators. Not one of them believed she would bring anything valuable to the meeting, so they had left her asleep during the proceedings. She was angry at herself for having failed once again to be a queen.

"If I may, your Grace," Chattergoon said.

Jessima gestured for him to continue.

"In my experience, to rule you don't need to make every decision. Often it is valuable to leave some decisions to those who excel at making them. That enables a leader to consider matters of greater importance."

Jessima blinked at Chattergoon, no words coming to her lips in response. He bowed and took his leave.

Exhausted, Jessima sent away the historian who had come to teach her regular lesson. She checked on Eddie. He was fast asleep, with a peaceful countenance that showed none of the previous day's distress.

She mused, focusing on the valuable lessons from Martha's hospital. The people had no desire to worship her at grand, formal events, had no need for an arrogant, aloof queen as she had been in Fertilian. She connected with them when she was one of them.

And did she need to know all the administrative intricacies, as she had believed? *To rule you don't need to make every decision,* Chattergoon had said. *Consider matters of greater importance.*

A brisk knock on the door made Jessima snap into a Peqkian warrior's defensive stance, fists balled, ready to deflect or attack. A move Ramya had shown her in Riaow and one that Jessima had laughingly practised with her friend, not ever thinking she would use it. But, instead of jumping like a startled bird, she had reacted instinctively to a potential threat.

"Come," she said, relaxing, and a steward promptly entered.

"Prince Ernest and Lord Chattergoon require your presence urgently in the courtyard," the steward said.

Jessima gave brief orders to Eddie's nurses and followed the steward down the stairs to the courtyard. She made her way to where the two men stood. Betsy was sat on Ernie's feet.

Chattergoon bowed to her. Ernie dipped his head in greeting.

"What is this all about, Lord Chattergoon?" Ernie said while leaning forward to tickle his dog's ears.

"Queen Jessima, Prince Ernest, my man has arrived from the tunnel. We have people from Cleland City arriving."

"People?" Ernie said springing upright.

"Many people. We need to attend them immediately," the lord replied.

Ernie looked at Jessima. "You go and rest, my dear, you're surely still exhausted after this morning's... exertions. I'll go with Lord Chattergoon."

"No. I'm coming," Jessima said.

Ernie shook his head. "Is that wise, my dear, we don't know who..."

Jessima started towards the gate. "I am the Queen Regent of Fertilian, and people from Cleland City are *my* people, *my* responsibility."

Jessima had not been back to the Lian tunnel opening since she had arrived almost three months before. When she had reached Lian the place had been quiet and orderly. The contrast when she came upon the tunnel late that morning was absolute. There were people everywhere, with more spewing forth from the exit.

The crowd was noisy, weeping for joy that they had made it. They babbled amongst themselves, unsure where to go or what to do next. Some clung to the guards who attempted to keep order. Many begged for water and food. Most were women and children. The few men with them were either elderly, injured, or incapable of fighting as a soldier.

Unable to get close to the entrance through the swelling mass of people, Jessima, Ernie, Chattergoon, a handful of Ernie's attendants and ten soldiers paused on the edges of the throng.

"Protect the Queen," Chattergoon ordered the soldiers. "Stay alert, there could be Thorne men hidden among the crowd." The soldiers formed a protective circle around Jessima.

"Where are we going to house so many?" Ernie pondered, staring at all those in front of him. "And still they come." He picked up Betsy and held her firmly under his arm. Jessima knew the little dog would soon get lost among all the legs.

"First, we should get them food and water, Ernie, that journey is horrific and they are likely feeling disorientated and exhausted," Jessima said.

She headed to the tunnel entrance, her soldiers encouraging people to move out of her way. Chattergoon edged in beside her. She could hear Ernie giving orders to his attendants in her wake.

Slowly, as the crowd's eyes adjusted to the daylight, and seeing past the crumpled attire, the dirty, day-old functional breeches, they recognised Jessima. Shouts of, "The Queen!" erupted. Eventually the crowd's fervour stilled as all attention turned, expectantly, to Jessima.

She had never given an unscripted speech. The last time she had spoken in public was at the marketplace, and no one, apart from a drunk, had listened to her. Now, they latched onto her every movement, rapt.

Be a Queen, Jessima. Be their Queen. I can do this. I killed a man. I can talk to my people.

"Residents of Cleland City, welcome to Lian. We are bringing water and food for you. We will find you shelter. Please be patient," Jessima announced.

Murmurs of understanding rippled through the crowd.

Jessima turned to a woman who stood near her. She was covered in a layer of dust and tightly clasped the hands of two young children. They stood numb, blinking and silent.

"Madam," Jessima said, "we will organise shelter for you and your family, and are fetching water for your children even now. Please, can you tell me what has happened?"

Through the grime, the woman blushed at being addressed by the queen. She bowed and then said with a raspy, parched voice, "My Queen, the Thorne army has overrun Cleland City, all surviving Cleland soldiers retreated to hold the castle. We left when we could through the tunnels, and many escaped into the countryside. But some poor souls were left behind."

The woman shook her head, a tear etching a line through the dirt on her cheek. "The Thorne soldiers chased us through the tunnels for a while, picking off those at the back but then left us be. We have lost some along the way, taking wrong turns in the maze of tunnels or succumbing to hunger and exhaustion."

She wiped the tear from her face, before she continued, "There was one man who led us true."

The woman looked around and then pointed to the tunnel entrance, at a figure still helping people out. He was tall, cloaked and his hood was up. A scarf was wrapped around his neck and face, exposing only his eyes. Under the cloak, he was dressed in breeches and boots. He had a sword strapped to his back and over that, a pack similar to what Chattergoon had worn when he had led them through the tunnels.

Jessima noticed Chattergoon's eyes narrow. "Who is this man?" she asked him.

"There are few who know the tunnels, and most are here. We shall find out."

Chattergoon strode towards the entrance, the crowd parting like a wave to let him through.

"Thank you," Jessima said to the woman and followed behind the lord.

"You there," Chattergoon said to the figure, drawing his sword. "Show yourself."

The man, focused on his task of assisting the last few people out of the tunnel, looked up. Noticing the drawn sword, he slowly pulled back his hood and scarf, exposing a young face. He was perhaps twelve or thirteen years of age. Those in the crowd nearest the boy gasped.

"Philip?" Chattergoon said, sheathing his sword.

"Father," the boy replied and then ran to him. They embraced.

"I told you to stay at the estate," Chattergoon chided while kissing his son's head. "What were you doing in the city? What about your siblings? Your mother?"

Jessima cleared her throat and Chattergoon's back straightened. The lord extracted himself from the boy's embrace, turning to Jessima.

"Your Grace, this is my eldest son, Philip."

Philip bowed low and kept his eyes down until Jessima spoke, "Philip, you are very brave leading these people to safety. Please, answer your father's questions, and then I have some of my own for you."

"Yes, your Grace," Philip said standing back up to full height. He looked to his father and a grin spread across his features. In a rush, he said, "Joanne and I snuck into the city as everyone was fleeing to see the Thorne army for ourselves."

Chattergoon tutted. "You both disobeyed my order. Your mother must be desperately worried."

Philip shifted uncomfortably on his feet. "Um, well, it was Mother's idea. We knew you would want to know what had happened."

Chattergoon's lips twitched into a small smile.

"Joanne?" Jessima asked.

"My eldest daughter," Chattergoon said.

Pausing to see if Jessima had any further questions, Philip continued in his rapid manner. "The city was evacuating, the remaining soldiers from the Cleland army retreated to hold Cleland Castle, and the Thornes entered the city sooner than we had anticipated. We did it fair and square, Father. We drew straws. Joanne led many of the townspeople out into the countryside and was then to return to the estate. And I led the rest here through the tunnels to find you."

Chattergoon nodded. "And the triplets?"

"Fine. Stayed home to look after the estate with Mother. They all send their love," Philip said.

"You have five children?" Jessima exclaimed.

Chattergoon nodded. "I am blessed with two girls and three boys."

"Your wife must have her hands full," Jessima said.

Chattergoon's shoulders tensed and Jessima realised she had been too familiar with the lord. He had never once spoken about his family to her.

Philip, sensing his father's discomfort, and clearly not shy about being familiar, said, "Your Grace, our mother is expecting number six. She's the famous tunnel runner, Kerrin Smith, otherwise known as the Scorpion Hunter, have you heard of her?"

Jessima's brows furrowed as she tried to recall if she'd heard that name. Smith was a commoner surname, and no women were permitted to be tunnel runners... officially.

Before Jessima could probe for more information about Chattergoon's wife, the lord deftly changed the subject. "Ernest's orderlies are here to tend to these people's needs. Your Grace, shall we return to somewhere more private for you to ask your questions of my son."

Jessima, suddenly aware that hundreds of people were watching them and listening to their conversation, agreed and turned back in the direction of the fortress, giving words of comfort to the crowd as she passed.

Ernie was in his element, busy ordering people about, but paused when Jessima approached.

She recalled Chattergoon's words from earlier that morning. "Prince Ernest, please do everything in your power to care and find shelter for these people. You excel at this, I do not. I trust you to manage this as you see fit."

Ernie nodded and waved Jessima and the Chattergoons on. "Leave this to me, my dear. Take my carriage back, it has just arrived with more of my attendants."

As they climbed into the carriage Jessima could hear Philip Chattergoon.

"So I told him, the stubborn old man, that the tunnel we needed was the second on the left. But he didn't listen, insisted it was the third on the left because that was the way in his time when he was a runner under Lord Horace Chattergoon, and off he went that way. Of course, plenty of people followed him, trusting in an old man before a young man. I was putting on my *man voice*," Philip said the last two words in a deeper tone, "because you said no one trusts a boy, so off they all went and I carried on with all those you saw, and guess who made it? And guess who got lost in the tunnels? I feel bad for all those who followed the old man. They'll never make it out alive.

"Of course, I wanted to tell him that I was Lord Andrew Chattergoon and the Scorpion Hunter's son, no less, and that a lot had changed since Grandpa's time, but like you said, always be discreet, never give up your identity if it's not required…"

Chattergoon held up a palm to silence his son as Jessima settled herself into the carriage and it rumbled back towards Ernie's fortress.

Chattergoon eased himself onto the seat opposite her as Philip perched next to him, gawping at Jessima. The boy near burst with excitement and couldn't stifle the wide-eyed grin on his face.

Not able to contain himself any longer, Philip said, "Oh, but you are prettier in real life, Queen Jessima."

Chattergoon snapped, "Hold your tongue in front of the Queen, Lip."

Philip hunched into himself and dropped his eyes at his father's scolding. His smile dramatically turned upside down.

"My apologies, your Grace," Philip said sheepishly.

"Apology accepted." Jessima smiled broadly and Philip looked up, his face brightening.

"You are very kind, your Grace. We don't call him Lip for nothing." Chattergoon glanced at his son with a warning to keep his mouth shut, that next time the listener might not be so lenient.

"Philip, do you know if the Cleland soldiers held the castle?" Jessima asked.

Philip sat very close to his father, their arms and legs touching. It was clear they wanted to embrace tightly but were remaining proper in the presence of their Queen. Philip glanced up at Chattergoon who nodded.

Philip turned to Jessima. "When we left, the Cleland army still held the castle. The Thorne army was relentless in its attack of the city, it will find a way to take the castle, I'm certain. Joanne and I got close, they had made camp in Three Acres, Father, and we snuck up onto that lookout ridge you showed us. Joanne remembered the way, you know the—"

"Stick to the point, Lip, and answer Queen Jessima," Chattergoon cut in.

"Yes, sorry. Well we got close and there was no sign of

King Hugo. Rumour is he died on the battlefield."

"We have heard," Jessima said.

"But they have Prince Toby as a prisoner," Philip said.

Jessima gasped and her hand flew to cover her mouth.

"Are you sure?" Chattergoon said.

Seeing the distress the news had brought Jessima, Philip nodded vigorously. "Absolutely. He didn't look too good. Beaten and chained. But it was definitely him. Joanne saw him first, and you know how she has his painting up in her bedroom, she's besotted with him."

Jessima retreated into a trance. Chattergoon and his son continued to talk about the Thorne army size, weapons, cavalry but Jessima could not follow.

A flutter began in her stomach and made its way up her chest and into her mouth. She thought she might be sick. She gazed out the window to see how far they were from the fortress and picked at a loose thread on her dress. She was anxious to get back to her son, Toby's son.

18

AMMAD
ಛೇ

Ammad lounged on the terrace of his mother's craterside villa. He'd trained all morning with Samark, washed, had a massage, eaten and was now relaxing.

Naturally, he was exceeding at his training. That morning, the lowly scum had him sparring with a street fighter who wielded two swords. The skill was in speed, not weapons, in anticipating your opponent's next move and reacting before he made it.

A few days previously, Samark had mentioned there was a way to throw a knife with his teeth. Ammad demanded to be taught the skill, but the man insisted it was too soon. Ammad threatened a severe punishment, something about lopping off both Samark's legs, and he relented.

He brought out his throwing knives, which were fastened to a strapping that went around his upper thigh. Samark swiftly pulled on the strapping with his teeth and tightened it. He then demonstrated how to stand on one leg, raise the thigh of the other and pull the knives out with his teeth. He then flung them, with a vicious snap of his head, into a hanging piece of wood that was used as a target.

Samark threw all eight with such precision that Ammad hated the man. And then determined he would learn this skill immediately. However, on his first attempt, he had sliced his tongue, requiring a couple of stitches from a healer. After, Jakira had insisted knife throwing be learnt with dull knives, so a commission to have these made had gone out to a blacksmith. They had been training against swords since, while the blades were made.

Jakira glided out to the terrace, holding Artaz's hand.

"I have appointments. Spend some time with your little brother," she announced and led the brat towards him.

Ammad sighed. Since that old bastard, his father, had wrenched away his title of Crown Prince two months ago, his mother had been intensely scheming. She was livid at Mastiq, seeing his actions as a cutting betrayal, and Ammad knew not to interfere. Jakira's mind worked faster than perhaps five of his own. At the very least, he knew she would restore Ammad to Crown Prince.

He let her get on with it, focusing all his attention on becoming the best fighter with no arms in the city. He would be better than Samark; he couldn't allow that Affarah clan member to claim that title.

Artaz scrambled onto the floor cushions and pulled out some toys from his pocket. Jakira watched him indulgently. She had fallen in love with the Peqkian child and foisted him onto Ammad every now and then as if he was a real brother. Ammad knew better than to argue with his mother so suffered the brat's presence, ignoring him and calling for slaves if the child needed anything or started to cry.

Artaz, for the most part, was quiet, content to play on his own, happy to simply be around others. Since the boy had arrived, Jakira had showered him with affection and Artaz was smitten with her too, calling her Mama. She had organised wisemen to teach him the ways of Drome, and cooed to him constantly.

Jakira kissed Artaz on both cheeks and spoke some

tender words to him. The child nodded and smiled up at her.

"Where's my kiss, Mama? Have you forgotten your eldest son?" Ammad stuck one cheek forward.

She pinched it. "You are no longer a baby." But then softened and cupped it gently before sweeping back into the villa and towards whatever appointment she had organised.

Artaz was chattering away holding his two favourite wooden figurines from Peqkya. A cat and a bird. He always bashed them together as if they were fighting. Ammad watched him languidly.

"I'm like that bird," he said to the child, "I want to smash the cats. One cat in particular. One with hair like yours."

"Violya," the child mumbled. "She like me."

Ammad shrugged. *I don't need to know the red-haired hisspit's name, only that she will die by my hands soon. No, not hands, legs most likely. Get her in a thigh grip and squeeze, squeeze, until her eyes turn the colour of her hair and pop from her skull.*

Artaz placed the bird on a cushion and slammed the cat down onto it. The figurine flew up and landed with a thud against Ammad's tall glass of honeyed lime juice. Ammad had learnt to pick up the glass with his teeth to drink. It fell off the low table and smashed on the stone tiles of the terrace.

"Naughty boy," Ammad tutted, amused by Artaz's look of horror. "That's Mama's favourite cut glass. She'll be very unhappy with you. You'll get beaten and sent away."

Artaz's eyes widened as he looked at the glass smashed to smithereens. Tears began to well.

Ammad, aware that his feet were planted in the midst of this sea of shards, sat upright. He was about to shout for a slave to clear up the debris but Artaz had rallied himself.

Instead of crying, the boy pointed his finger at the pile of cracked glass, scrunched up his face and seemed to be concentrating, his body shaking with the effort.

A chunk of glass twitched. Another trembled. Ammad shook his head, blinked and stared hard at the floor.

The glass pieces jumped in the air, like a giant had thumped the tiles. They fell to the floor and remained still. Ammad took a long breath. *Has someone slipped me some poppy?*

The pieces skittered across the tiles like tinkling bugs, pulled from all directions to the spot where Artaz was pointing.

Slowly, piece by piece, the glass rebuilt itself. The tiniest slivers slotted into place until it was fully made.

Artaz quickly picked the glass up and placed it on the table, looking around to make sure no one else had seen.

"Better now," he said and then lifted a slice of lime off the tiles and dropped it carefully in the glass. He sat back on the cushion, looking sheepish with his hands clasped between his knees.

"What the fuck…" Ammad managed, staring at the perfectly whole glass on the table.

"Sorry…" Artaz grizzled. "For spilling your drink." He sniffled and his eyes went glassy.

Ammad didn't want tears from the boy. He needed to know more, to see more.

The bird figurine, after Artaz had knocked Ammad's drink off the table, had landed next to his foot. He picked it up with his toes, leaned back and swung his leg round, dropping the figurine in Artaz's hand.

"You forgot your bird," Ammad said in the sweetest voice he could muster.

Artaz grinned and picked the figurine up, found the cat tucked down the side of the cushion and offered both to Ammad.

Ammad swivelled on his cushion so that both feet faced the boy, picked up a figurine in each set of toes and, to Artaz's delight, bashed them together. Ammad mimicked the boy's laughter and grinned, lifting his legs up and then soaring the figurines down. Artaz clapped and grabbed at the toys. Ammad pulled them away at the last minute and the boy laughed some more.

What else can you do?

Ammad allowed Artaz to pull the figurines from his toes. The boy clutched them to his chest in happiness. Ammad squirmed his feet under each of the boy's armpits and wriggled his toes. The boy erupted in peals of laughter.

What else can I train you to do?

Ammad played with the boy for hours, it was excruciatingly dull and the Peqkian brat showed no signs of his *ability* again. Ammad wasn't sure what to call it, but that seemed apt for now. *I need to gain his trust, his devotion. If he has some kind of power, I want him to do my bidding.*

The boy tired and lolled awkwardly belly-down across Ammad's lap. His bony hips dug in Ammad's flesh.

"Best friends," the boy said and sighed contentedly. "Me and you, best friends."

A large spider scurried across the tiles and paused close to Ammad's foot.

Artaz pointed at it and scrunched up his forehead as if racking his little mind for some titbit of pointless information. He formed the word, "Spi… spi… spider!"

Ammad – eager to test his speed after hours of Samark hollering "faster, faster" at him – stamped on the creature before it could scuttle off.

Artaz gasped and sat up, elbowing Ammad in the gut in his haste.

"No," the boy whined.

The corners of his mouth turned down and he sniffled. Once again, his eyes glistened with welling tears.

Ammad gritted his teeth, holding back the curses he longed to roar in the child's face. He hated the brat's squalling, but struck with an idea, he lifted his foot and nodded to the bloody squish.

He imitated his mother's honeyed voice. "I know, why don't you make it whole again, like you did with that glass?

Can you do that? Won't that be fun!"

Artaz gazed forlornly at the dead spider.

"Why don't you try," Ammad encouraged. "I know you're sleepy, I promise you can have a long nap after. Doesn't that sound wonderful?"

Artaz blinked at Ammad and drew a deep breath. He pointed at the spider. Nothing happened.

He slumped back and huffed, blinking away tears.

"Try again," Ammad said, a harder, impatient edge to his voice.

Artaz noticed the change in tone. He stared at the spider.

Ammad, too, stared at the spider.

After a moment of stillness, the creature began to rebuild. Broken legs clicked back together, chunks of body slotted into place, blood and innards sucked back into the abdomen from where it had squirted.

Artaz tapped Ammad's shin. "Foot up."

Ammad lifted his foot and the tiniest bit of spider peeled off the sole of his foot and drifted back towards the remade creature. It dropped into position and the spider dashed towards a crack between tiles.

Artaz beamed. Ammad copied the boy's smile with a wide, toothy grin of his own. He touched his forehead to that of the child's in approval.

"You are a very clever boy. Does Mama know you can do that?" Ammad's voice was sugar again.

Artaz shook his head.

"Do you know what these are called?" Ammad touched his nose to the top of one of the boy's arms.

"Arms," Artaz said with a smile.

Ammad nodded. "Your brother Ammad, your best friend, has no arms. He'd like arms, because then he could play even more with his little brother, his best friend."

Ammad nuzzled the top of his head into the crook of Artaz's neck. The boy held Ammad's cheek with a slightly damp hand and rubbed his ear on Ammad's hair.

***

A week later Jakira summoned a meeting at the villa. She had been busy organising, bribing, and scheming around the city. Every waking moment, Ammad had either spent alone with Artaz, or training with Samark.

It was late at night, cooler, and cushions had been organised in a circle around low tables and shisha pipes.

The ex-Minister of War drew a long pull of the pipe nearest him and it gurgled. He let out the tobacco smoke in a long smooth plume from between his lips. Ammad wasn't sure why Whaled was at this meeting, considering him the enemy, but the hairy man had also been stripped of his position and used as a scapegoat. Ammad imagined he was pissed off, and therefore easy to manipulate.

Selmi, Ammad's younger brother, sat rigid with a grimace. Ammad couldn't recall the last time he had spoken to Sel. Must've been before the Peqkian invasion. They were civil to each other, nodding if they passed in the hallway, but the sixteen-year-old had shed his happy, cheerful demeanour and had become serious and brooding. Sel shot furtive glances at Whaled. The older man clearly made him nervous.

Aunty Riv was also there, wearing far too many jewels and gaudy clothing. The Peqkian had grown fatter, not just in girth, but also in wealth since devoting all her attention to her trade operations in Drome.

Jakira gestured for the slaves, who were pouring wine and keeping the table stocked with food, to leave. Medi closed the door after them and then came and sat on a cushion next to Ammad. *Slaves have no place at the table.* He glared at Medi then looked imploringly at his mother. She glared back.

Ammad didn't dare challenge her. He shifted his body away from Medi to show his disapproval. The Head Slave didn't seem to care.

"Medi went to the ceremony today. Tell us," Jakira said.

"Mastiq announced his eldest official son, Hallid, as Crown Prince," Medi replied.

"Fat Hallid?" Ammad blurted.

Jakira had schemed for years to have Hallid, the rightful heir of Mastiq's one official wife, to be replaced by Ammad as Crown Prince.

"He's been cleaned up, lost some weight and looked healthy. But was clearly still drunk," Medi said.

Jakira sneered. "Anything said about Ammad?"

"Yes. Mastiq announced that Ammad had sustained severe, permanent injuries and that he requires ongoing care and attention. He said that the Crown Prince position was too much for Ammad to cope with now and that Ammad had readily relinquished it to a better abled man," Medi said.

Jakira slapped her palm on the table.

"Drunk Hallid a better abled man than me?" Ammad scoffed.

Aunty Riv tutted.

Jakira stood and slowly walked around the outside of the cushions. "Family, friends, new loves." She placed a hand on Whaled's shoulder, and he placed his hand over hers briefly.

Ammad gagged, Selmi's eyes nearly popped out of his skull, Medi's stolid expression was unchangeable and Riv interrupted Jakira to cackle her throaty laugh and say, "I knew it!"

Is Mama using Whaled or is she truly in love? He couldn't tell. His mother was the best actress in the desert. Better than those who were actually paid to perform stories of Drome's history to the rich clans in their opulent villas. His mother must be using Whaled. She used everyone. And how could anyone – especially the most beautiful woman in Drome – find that hairy beast attractive?

Jakira continued to walk and talk and all gathered followed her movements. "Our Ruler Mastiq believes he is the most powerful person in Drome," she said. "The royal

Wakrime family believe they will always rule. But this is false. They have been allowed to believe this by the one who *is* the most powerful in this city. That one has perpetuated those lies to continue to build their influence and dominance. To coerce and bribe and do what is necessary to get the Qacirr holy families and the Tamadeen noble families to bend under their will."

Jakira paused and scanned her gaze around those seated. "Know this. The most powerful person in the city is me."

Ammad grinned, Riv clapped her hands, Selmi retreated into himself and Whaled beamed proudly. Medi had no reaction; he likely already knew this detail. He'd been her head slave since she'd arrived at the palace at fourteen.

His mother settled elegantly on a cushion. "It no longer benefits me to keep Mastiq in power. And, if it no longer benefits me, it no longer benefits the city, or the country. It does, however, benefit me to keep the Wakrime family in power, but not the side of the family Mastiq so treasures. No. The Wakrime blood runs through my sons, and it will be my eldest who will rule."

Ammad's chest swelled and his hump prickled with excitement.

"Once we have established Ammad in position as the rightful ruler, we have unfinished business to take care of. We must smash Peqkya. And once that little pussy cat is tamed, my son Selmi shall rule that mountain nation. And, as has always been my desire, we take back ancient Vaasar from the thieving Ferts once and for all."

Jakira slapped her palm on the low table. "My sons will bask in the glory of the people and be known forever as the brothers who reversed history, who made Drome whole again after thousands of years."

Selmi squirmed on his cushion. He bit his lips in an obvious attempt to keep in what threatened to come out. His face reddened and the words erupted.

"Mama," he blurted, "the corruption of those in rule must change, slaves must be freed, wealth distributed fairly amongst all and our false religion wiped from the world. Will Ammad do this? Will you do this? Or will we carry on as we always have in this filthy inequality?"

"Flesh of my flesh," Jakira said patiently, "the way of things is the way of things. The change will be that Ammad rules. That *our* family rules. Do you want to lose your wealth and live on the streets instead of in this villa? Give up your racing camels so that slaves can have them? You speak of all being equal but that has never worked, nor will it. There are the strong, there are the weak. We are the strong, and I intend to keep us that way."

Selmi rose to his feet. "I do not want to rule Peqkya! I do not want violence," he shouted. He stomped from the room, slamming the door behind him.

Jakira rose a palm to reassure those around the table. "I shall deal with him. He is still young and this is merely a phase. Whatever wiseman has fed him this nonsense will be minus his head by the morning."

Whaled fingered his hairy nostrils. "Removing Mastiq from rule does not pose a problem. But Peqkya does. Our army was decimated. The warriors are remarkable. We need better weapons, training, and men before we can consider returning to the mountains."

"We have the experience now. You know the land, you know the city of Riaow. You have seen them fight. And we have Riv here to help us."

"I have Toya recruiting spies even now," Riv said.

"But we are not strong enough," Whaled insisted. "Fighting with swords against the hisspit warriors is pointless, they are exceptionally skilled. We need some other kind of weapons—"

"We have a weapon," Ammad said. He popped a chunk of watermelon in his mouth using his freshly-slave-cleaned toes and relished the fact that all in the room hung on his next words. "Medi," he said eventually, "fetch

Artaz."

Medi flicked his eyes to Jakira.

"The boy is asleep," she said.

"Believe me, Mama, this is worth waking him for."

Jakira considered him a moment and then nodded to Medi. The Head Slave went to the door and shouted at the house slaves who waited in the hallway then returned to his cushion.

Jakira didn't take her eyes from Ammad, an expression on her face that read: 'This better be good'. Ammad smirked back. It would be good. Very, very good.

A few moments later the Peqkian boy was led into the room.

The slave left him and closed the door. The boy's head was low, and he rubbed at his eyes wearily.

"Come here, little brother," Ammad said.

Artaz drifted towards the voice and crawled onto the cushions to sit on Ammad's knee, his back against Ammad's chest.

"Well?" Jakira said.

"Time to show Mama what you can do." Ammad leaned close to whisper instructions in Artaz's ear. The little boy nodded and pointed at a juicy watermelon that hadn't as yet been chopped.

It wobbled on the low table. Rocked from side to side and lifted into the air.

Riv gasped, but his mother, Medi and Whaled watched keenly, unconsciously leaning closer to get a better understanding of the flying fruit.

It exploded. Pink chunks, pips and green skin flew everywhere. Jakira, Whaled, Riv and Medi ducked and raised their arms as bits of the fruit pelted them.

Ammad laughed.

"Ammad," Jakira warned, wiping sloppy pink flesh from her lap.

Ammad whispered in Artaz's ear and grinned.

Whaled's shisha pipe floated upwards, over the hairy

man's head and slammed against the wall behind him. It smashed to bits, the hot coals burning holes in the carpet and the acrid smell of tobacco water permeating the room.

"Stop this evil," Whaled shouted as he splashed a jug of water over the coals with a sizzle.

Ammad continued to whisper and Artaz pointed at the large Peqkian woman.

"Oh my!" Riv exclaimed.

Artaz's face screwed and his arm shook as he channelled all his effort into the task. Riv hovered off her cushions. She screamed and attempted to move but was locked in place.

Artaz directed her floating form towards the open window.

"That's enough, Ammad," Jakira said sharply as Riv shrieked.

Ammad laughed and directed Artaz.

The boy brought the Peqkian woman back down to her cushion, depositing her there gently.

"He has The Sight! Peqkian magic, like our great Stone Prophetess Sybilya," Riv exclaimed. She cupped her fat cheeks with her hands, staring at the boy. Then she turned to Jakira. "The Sight," Riv repeated.

Artaz yawned and rested his head in the crook of Ammad's neck.

Ammad gave the boy's forehead a kiss. "Well done, best friend," he cooed in the boy's ear.

Then he winked at Jakira. "He is our weapon, Mama. I will train him. His magic will destroy Peqkya. His magic will help us take over the world."

Jakira looked lovingly at the sleepy child.

"Show Mama what we do to cats," Ammad said.

For a few moments nothing happened. Then a scrawny street cat flew in through the window and floated above the centre of the table. It mewed and hissed but its body was locked in place.

Jakira recoiled from the animal, cats were a rare sight in

Drome. They were intensely hated by the Dromedars.

"Now," Ammad said.

The cat's neck snapped, and it went limp. Riv inhaled sharply and shook her head. Artaz didn't flinch.

"I will train him, Mama. I *have* been training him," Ammad said. "You cannot ignore the power he could wield for us. He'll do anything for you, for me. And you know it."

Jakira's face hardened.

"If he is to be adopted into this family, if he is to be my little brother, truly, then he needs to be treated like a Wakrime. You had me trained to be a weapon. Now we do the same for Artaz."

Jakira's jaw clenched. She nodded.

"And that's not all." Ammad jerked his shoulder and the boy opened his eyes. "Little brother, best friend, one more thing before you go back to bed, pull my tunic off. Let's show Mama what else we've been working on."

Earlier that evening, Ammad had deliberately chosen one of his old tunics which still had long loose-flowing sleeves. Artaz pulled it off over Ammad's head exposing his finely muscled torso. Leaner and more honed than it had ever been, thanks to Samark's training.

But it wasn't his divine body that he wanted to show off.

He flapped the two stumps that had sprouted where his old arms used to be. They were both about half the length of his previous arms. Tiny fingers were emerging at the end. There was no definition in them, they looked weak, but once they had grown to full length, Ammad would soon build up the muscle.

"Mama," Ammad said to the stunned room, "he certainly is a special boy."

19

TOBY

ᝄᝅ

Prince Toby Cleland of Fertilian sat on a donkey next to False Queen Charlotte, as her guest. His hands were trussed to the donkey's saddle and a tight gag dug into the sides of his mouth. The old bat wanted to boast, and Toby was all ears.

Captain Denya was off laying siege to Cleland Castle. Charlotte's son Arthur, who Toby was yet to meet, was with the turncoat Peqkian, as was his twin sister Mary's husband, Lord Clement Pullman. Mary was holed up in some appropriated city townhouse out of the way. She was forever in poor health and, according to Charlotte, ever so dull.

So, it fell to Toby to listen to the old bat's incessant drivel. He'd answered back one too many times over the past few months and had been relieved of the privilege of conversation with a soiled rag stuffed between his teeth.

Next to Toby, an invisible Charlotte sat atop her old Flame horse. They waited on a section of the first wall with a perfect view of Cleland Castle. The castle's drawbridge remained resolutely up. There, just out of reach of the Cleland archers on the castle walls, Captain Denya's warriors directed the Thorne soldiers.

This section of the first wall had been cleared of dead

Cleland soldiers, but blood still stained the stone. It pained Toby to see.

It had been three months since the Thorne army had taken the city with little resistance, a few weeks after his charming picnic at Forty Marshes. Most of the residents had fled, either through the tunnels to Lian, or into the countryside. The Cleland soldiers who remained in the city had retreated to the impregnable castle and had held positions on the second outer wall and the first inner wall, which surrounded the castle.

Toby had been forced to watch as a *guest* of the gloating old hag as Denya had effortlessly taken the outer wall, and then, the following day, the inner wall. Scores of Cleland soldiers had fallen in the bloodbath before the survivors retreated to the castle. Toby knew the castle was impenetrable. Surrounded by a wide, deep moat with only the one drawbridge in and out, and on top of a steep hill. He'd also thought the castle walls were unassailable... but he had to have hope.

He had prayed for Denya to attack as swiftly as she had the two walls, and then be cut down by the archers and castle defenders. But Denya was calculating and she took her time. For weeks Toby had watched her manoeuvres with interest alongside Charlotte.

The space between the castle and the first wall was filled with now-deserted houses and stores, as well as the Batten Fields. These fields had been positioned just so to allow the royal family to watch matches from the comfort of a viewing platform at the castle, and out of reach of the archers and tossed missiles.

While Denya had been plotting, she had allowed the Thorne army to play batten on the pitches. It turned out that a couple of players from the Rotchurch City and Edester City batten teams had survived the fighting at Yettle Valley. Toby had been baffled, recalling Denya's words that male soldiers were "undisciplined and lazy". What was she doing allowing the men to relax?

But then, as the roaring crowd, laughter and happy cheering became deafening, he understood. It would unnerve those holding the castle. They would be forced to watch this casual display of cheerfulness. It announced: the Thorne army are not worried about this siege.

He had been even more surprised to see that these games had been followed by a Peqkian tourney of sorts with feats of arms on foot and horseback. But it soon became clear that this was training for the warriors – and yet another way to frighten the Cleland troops in the castle. The most impressive display saw Peqkian warriors on Fertilian purebred horses. Faster and larger than the stocky Peqkian ponies, the warriors were practising mounted warfare and testing their new horses to the limits.

The day after the batten games, Denya had put the army to work. The chop and hammering of wood started up. For weeks, it had been the only sound, and then a clang and clink of ironwork, until a huge wooden fence had emerged on the edge of the batten fields, twice as tall as a man and with an overhanging roof. On the side nearest the castle and on the roof that stretched away from it, the wood had a covering of iron. A huge shield.

Toby watched with horror as Denya had unveiled this iron and wood contraption. She had waited until the wind was just right, lit wet-wood fires on the bank of the moat, out of reach of the castle archers who lined the wall. These smouldering fires blew smoke into the castle, blinding the archers. When the smoke cleared, the fence was in place on the edge of the moat, carried there by hundreds of soldiers who lifted the wooden poles that stuck out from the inside, under the cover of the iron-clad roof.

She had it placed opposite the weakest part of the castle walls and nowhere near the drawbridge. Where the castle wall, through the natural lay of the land when it had been built, was not only slightly lower, but was also thinner. Fewer archers could stand along the top of this section of the wall. From the outside, this section of the wall looked precisely the same as any other, but Denya knew it was the weakest section, because she had been inside the castle and had studied it. Toby cursed the day he had vouched for her on Hugo's war council. If he hadn't trusted her, she would never have entered the castle, never had leave to roam around it at will.

When the smoke cleared, the Cleland archers had loosed arrows. Some penetrated the iron shield, but most bounced off, or landed and skittered on the roof which sheltered the soldiers beneath. Toby had wondered what possible advantage this fence had, until he saw what the sneaky cat captain had done next.

Rocks, stones, tree trunks, sticks, grass, earth and other debris was brought forward. The soldiers holding the fence lifted it and held it over the moat whilst the debris was dumped in the moat and packed down so it could be stepped on. They built this up high enough so that when the fence was dropped, it was perhaps an arm's length away from the bank, and an arm's length nearer to the wall.

This had gone on for weeks, as Denya slowly built a bridge across the moat to attack at the weakest section. The Cleland defenders poured flaming tar on the contraption, but it still stood. They heaved heavy rocks and dropped them on the fence, which dented it but did not stop its advance. They found long poles and attempted to push it over, but it stood firm.

And today was the day. It was time to attack the castle.

"That's one of four, you know," Charlotte said proudly beside him. "Denya will attack the wall in four places. The weakest parts. She calculated how much the water would rise in the moat and where it was likely to breach and has dug an overflow channel so that it will not flood the bridges."

Damn. The cat had it all worked out. From his position, he could only see the one fence shield nearest the drawbridge.

In the distance Denya whistled and a series of whistles replied from her warriors. He heard shouts from the Cleland soldiers at the castle and saw movement along the walls.

"Here we go," the old hag said with gaiety as thick as syrup.

Toby watched as the soldiers holding the huge shield in place, retreated a few steps and then shifted its position so that it was at an angle to the wall. In the slip of space underneath, soldiers then brought ladders against the wall. Soldiers swarmed up the ladders, accompanied by Peqkian warriors who climbed the wall using nothing but their fingers searching out gaps in the old, crumbling mortar between the stones.

As this was happening, large catapults were rolled into place. Peqkian warriors climbed into the bucket as the payload. With a series of shouts, Peqkian archers took aim and loosed arrows at a small group of archers stood on the wall. Their aim was impeccable. As the Cleland soldiers fell, the catapult was launched. Peqkian warriors flew gracefully through the air, landing on the castle walls where moments earlier archers had stood. They drew their weapons and charged. Toby knew few Cleland soldiers would withstand their attack.

"Well, I think we know how this will end," Charlotte said and laughed.

Toby choked into his gag and looked away, the pain unbearable.

"More wine," Arthur Thorne snapped at a servant. "And more roast frog!"

They sat around King Hugo's grand dining table in the ceremonial dining hall celebrating breaking the siege of Cleland Castle. The great wall hanging of the Cleland coat of arms and all the Cleland family portraits that had lined the walls had been pulled down, stuffed into the fireplace and now smouldered and crackled in the grate. A servant had hastily draped the Thorne coat of arms cloth hanging over a few chairs, not yet having time to affix it to the wall.

Charlotte sat at the head of the table, where Hugo had once sat, gloating. She had nursed the same glass of wine the entire night, and her cheeks were flushed. Toby, who had been brought in to sit at the bottom of the table, still trussed up and gagged, realised that there was one person who bragged more than Charlotte. Her son, Arthur.

Arthur was a large man of around forty years, he sat to his mother's right, in the chair Queen Jessima used to take. He wore a huge white fur robe, which Toby recognised as once belonging to Benjamin Thorne. Arthur was tall and thick-limbed, similar to his father in stature, but not much else. Arthur had dull blue-grey eyes, rather than the piercing blue of Benjamin's. The youngest Thorne twin had no beard and long, wavy reddish-blond hair that touched his shoulders. His skin was well-oiled and everything about him appeared clean and tended, from his trimmed eyebrows to his overshined boots. A peacock.

Opposite him sat his twin sister, Mary. She was a small, thin woman. Plain, unlike her mother, and not wearing well. She had deep lines in her forehead and around her eyes. Her pale cheeks were sunken and her frizzy, unkempt hair was almost entirely grey. In contrast to her twin, she had an uncared-for look about her. Poor health clung to her clothes as it did to her body. She hadn't eaten anything; it seemed her husband ate for her. He was as large as she was small.

Next came Mary's weak and sickly son, James. He had a shawl around his shoulders and held his mother's hand. Although a teenager, he was half the size of Mary.

Lord Clement Pullman sat next to his son. With ruddy complexion, round cheeks and a shiny bald head, you'd be mistaken for thinking that Clement was a jovial man. He wasn't. A deep furrow line marred his forehead from years of scowling. There was a danger about him that overshadowed Arthur and came close to that of the

Peqkian.

Next to Arthur, sat his mirror-image son Jeremy. A strapping lad in his twenties. And then came Denya. Across the table, Clement refused to look at her. The warrior's intimidating presence made both Arthur and Clement nervous, Toby noted. But not sickly James, who cuddled into his mother, or Jeremy, who carried a dazed look, as if lost in some daydream.

Toby sat four seats down from Denya, close enough that she could do violence if necessary, far enough away for his prisoner's stench not to upset the diners.

Although, he soon realised, Arthur's stench overrode his. Arthur was highly perfumed, to the point that whenever he moved, to raise his glass or stab at a bit of meat, his spicy scent wafted down to assault Toby's nostrils.

A servant topped up Arthur's wine glass and he splashed it into the air. "We did it," he bellowed, "we smashed the Clelands and avenged Father." He leaned forward to take in Toby, "You hear that Cleland? The Thornes are back in power. Why aren't you celebrating?"

Arthur scraped his chair back violently and loped towards Toby, a jug of wine in hand. Standing behind Toby, Arthur grabbed a handful of Toby's hair and ripped back his head. He poured the wine over Toby's nose and mouth, laughing.

Toby choked, struggling for air through the wine-sodden gag. He jerked his head, the wine sloshing everywhere.

Arthur's eyes glistened with malice, a grin on his face. "This was your brother's finest wine. He must've been saving it for a special occasion, such as this one."

"Stop teasing our guest of honour, Artie," Charlotte scolded as if Arthur was still a child.

Arthur's body tensed and his lips pursed. He let go of Toby's hair, thumped the jug on the table with a bang and returned to his seat, his eyes trained on Toby.

Toby was thankful that at least he could now smell wine and not Arthur. A dribble had also reached his gullet and warmed his insides. *I am forever grateful for small mercies.*

Jeremy jerked in his seat, as if waking from a deep sleep and looked up the table. "Now that Lucrecia is gone, when will I marry Grace Iddenkinge?"

These were the first words Jeremy had spoken during the dinner and Toby understood that although Jeremy looked just like his father, although twenty years younger, he did not share Arthur's intellect.

"We don't talk about your first wife, Jeremy, remember?" Arthur said, his tone was kindly but firm.

"Yes, yes, sorry, father, I keep forgetting. It's just she died so suddenly, almost as if she'd been murdered."

"In fact, it's best if you keep your mouth shut altogether," Charlotte said in the same tone as Arthur.

But Toby had heard. They'd killed off the boy's first wife to make way for him to marry Hugo's granddaughter.

"The Iddenkinges are staying out of town for the time being, we don't want any reminder of the Clelands at this time. Remember? Grace's mother is Matilda Cleland," Arthur said patiently.

Jeremy gazed at a space just in front of his face, as if mesmerising fluffy clouds on a blue day floated behind his eyes. Charlotte shot a look at Arthur, who rolled his eyes.

Then Jeremy jolted again and looked at his father and grandmother. "Will I be expected to, you know, do it with her? To make babies?"

Clement shifted awkwardly on his seat.

"Jeremy, what did Grandmother just say?" Arthur said.

The dimwit considered this a moment. "To keep my mouth shut?"

"Exactly," Arthur said.

Jeremy nodded and fell into his open-eyed trance again.

All paused to see if Jeremy would speak once more. When he didn't, Clement piped up. "Now we are here, we need to discuss the coronation," he said, his palms flat on the table.

He had drunk sweetened lemon water all night and hadn't touched the wine. He had, however, touched the food. A great deal of it.

"Oh, Clem, dear, you really are so terribly efficient," Charlotte mocked. "Can we not have one night to celebrate before getting down to business?"

Ignoring her remonstration, Clement continued, "I believe we should organise the coronation swiftly. Mary should be declared Queen before the week is out."

Arthur banged his fist on the table and laughed. "Mother, I think it is time we tell them, don't you? This farce has gone on far too long."

"Farce?" Clement said, an undercurrent of danger rippling across his ruddy cheeks.

Mary's red-rimmed eyes widened.

Charlotte sighed.

"I'm going to be crowned King," Arthur declared.

"Mary is the eldest. It was agreed. We merge our armies and Mary becomes Queen. We all know my men and my alliances were far greater than your measly army, Arthur." Clement turned to Charlotte. "We made an agreement, Charlotte. Mary will be Queen."

Arthur laughed again. "Nonsense."

Charlotte clicked her fingers and Arthur's mirth dried up in his throat. She focused her attention on her daughter who visibly wilted in her chair. "Mary, my darling, there has been a change of plan. Your brother Arthur will be King. He's more suited to the task, not least because he is a man."

"Absolutely not," Clement shouted on his wife's behalf.

Charlotte ignored him and continued to speak to Mary, who clutched her sickly son. "It was the only way, my dear, to get you to stop being so stubborn. Divided, neither you nor Arthur stood any chance of regaining the throne. Together you have succeeded, for your dear Daddy. And

Daddy would roll in his grave if he thought his daughter would succeed him when his son was still alive."

"Without me you would never have made contact with Iddenkinge and Princess Matilda! Mary will be the Queen and I will be King. If not, I will rally my men, my allies and turn against you. You know we far outnumber Arthur's men and these," Clement gestured at Denya and spat the word, "Peqkians."

Denya didn't react, just continued eating. She was the only one now still enjoying the feast laid out before them.

"Are you threatening me?" Charlotte asked, still looking at Mary. The thin woman squirmed miserably.

"Are you breaking your word?" Clement countered, standing. He put his hand on Mary's shoulder, breaking Charlotte's spell. The thin woman stood, gathering up her son James.

"Mary will be crowned; I shall see to it." Clement clasped a large hand around Mary's childlike arm and marched her and his son out of the room.

"Did they really not know?" Arthur laughed.

"Shut up, Artie," Charlotte said. "You handled that like an utter buffoon. What did I tell you? Hmm? What?"

Arthur's chin dipped and he mumbled, "That you would break the news to them."

"Precisely! And I would've done it delicately and there would be no damn threats." Charlotte steepled her fingers together.

"Can I go to bed now, Grandmother?" Jeremy said.

"Yes," Charlotte snapped.

The simpleton kissed his father on the cheek, then his grandmother and floated out of the hall.

A few moments passed in silence.

Charlotte stood. "I need to think. Denya, would you care to join me."

Denya followed the older woman out of the dining hall.

As Charlotte passed the soldiers at the door, she said, "Take our guest back to his cell."

The soldiers watched her leave and then came around the table to collect Toby.

"Stop," Arthur said. "Take him and a large barrel of the finest wine in the Cleland cellar up to my room."

The soldiers shrugged, and heaved Toby off his chair.

"Oh, and make sure he is bent over the barrel, would you. Face down."

The soldiers glanced at each other but nodded to do their master's bidding. Toby fought against them, snorting through his gag, shaking his head.

Toby smelled Arthur's arrival before he heard him shuffle around the room. Toby was tied over the barrel in what had been a guest bedroom. The soldiers, unsure where to position Toby had put him next to the table, moving a few chairs out of the way. If Toby looked up, he could see the bed. His rump was towards the door.

"It really takes it out of a man, all this war," Arthur said. He perched on the edge of the bed where Toby could see him and pulled off his boots. "And having a legend for a father, really puts so much pressure on a man."

He unbuttoned his shirt. "I need my release. And I have no blasted wife here to satisfy me – all four so *inconveniently* dying – and my usual bed slaves were both left in Rotchurch City, Mother insisting I shouldn't be distracted by those boys, as she calls them."

The shirt came off and Arthur stood, untying the cord on his breeches. Toby struggled, but the soldiers had tied him up tight.

Arthur swanned around him, leaving a thick cloud of cologne in his wake. With a dagger, Arthur sliced through Toby's rag of a shirt, running a finger down Toby's back, and then sliced away Toby's breeches, exposing his bare flesh.

The bastard squeezed Toby's buttock.

"No," Toby spat through the gag, "no, no, no."

Arthur ran a damp cloth slowly from between Toby's

shoulder blades to his bollocks. Arthur dabbed and wiped Toby's body as he spoke.

"My first lover was a friend of father's, Lord Sebille Salter. Much older than me, I was only fourteen. Father would've been furious if he'd ever found out. It's caused no end of trouble with wives along the way. Dear Sebille told me I stunk, insisted I wash and apply fragrance before he came near me."

Arthur grabbed Toby's hips. "Well, my friend, you stunk. So, now I've washed and perfumed you, I can come near you."

Toby squirmed and snorted, snot running from his nose, tears streaming from his eyes. His face burned as he strained against his bindings.

You will die, Toby screamed against his gag as Arthur grunted, taking his pleasure. *I will kill you.*

20

VIOLYA

ॐ

V waited for the absolute still of sleeping warriors. When Monya's gentle snoring began she slipped silently out of bed in precisely the right way to stop it creaking or moving and waking her bunk mate.

V knew precisely how to move, how much pressure to exert, how quickly to lift off the straw mattress. She had learnt how when Emmya was still sleeping above her and V used to sneak off into the bamboo forest to harm herself in her teenage years. Back then, she'd been wracked with crippling self-doubt and fervently denied her magic. Releasing blood was the only way to tamp down the magic's frustration. This had been her bunk since she had left the pen and started training as a warrior.

She dressed in silence, purposely placing her clothes the night before in a specific place and in a specific order so that she could swiftly put them on in the black of the dormitory. Once clothed, she crept past the warrior on duty, and out the back door. On this occasion though she didn't turn towards the bamboo forest. Keeping to the shadows, she silently jogged towards the wooded area outside the Melokai's enclosure.

She edged through the woods and towards a makeshift den. A shallow burrow had been dug out of the earth and covered with fallen branches; the entrance hidden. She crouched low and crawled through the opening.

Darrio and Sarry were curled up asleep. Darrio's eye opened and he watched V crawl into the hollow space.

V moulded herself around the wolves, her face in the back of Darrio's neck. She breathed in his scent and gently placed a hand on Sarry's back leg and stroked her soft fur. Sarry stirred in her sleep and sighed deeply.

"Sleep well, my love," Darrio whispered.

She nuzzled her face into his fur and closed her eyes.

After Sybilya's death, the gaping hollow in her chest had consumed her. Had consumed every Peqkian. V had retreated into herself, hardly speaking, wandering in a daze. Weeks had passed in this state.

Darrio and Sarry had been offered rooms in the guest quarters. They had refused, preferring to make a den for themselves outside. They had scouted the small wooded area and made their den in the heavy snow. They had remained there for weeks, Sarry adjusting herself to the loss of Sybilya.

When V's grief had started to lift, she understood her heart ached for others. She needed to be close to her soulmatch and her child. It was not the appropriate time to declare her relationship to them to her people, so she'd snuck out and found their den.

She'd first gone to Darrio and Sarry two weeks before. Each night since she slept for a few hours curled up with her family, then before first light, tiptoed back into the warrior barracks. And each night she found peace in their presence.

***

Two Peqkians and two wolves ran through their daylight dances in the training ground. They did so silently, more slowly than usual. The mood in the city was still sombre and subdued after Sybilya's passing. But after almost two months, the city was gradually coming back to life. But the great loss still pervaded everyone's thoughts and movements.

The freak winter weather felt wholly appropriate. The most persistent snowfall V had ever known had covered Riaow in a deep layer up to V's shoulder. It had snowed all day, every day for months. The white blanket wrapped the people in a suffocating embrace. The loss of the Stone Prophetess was crippling, and so too was the snow.

Every morning they cleared the training ground of snow, and every day they trained. There was little else to do, they had to wait out the weather. Months ago, Lizya had sent spies to Drome and to Fertilian, but neither had returned. Either the snow held them up or they had been caught. V hoped it was the former.

And she hadn't heard anything yet from Fin and Robya's expedition to Troglo with Gwrlain.

Patient, be patient.

Lizya was overseeing the training of the young peons who had been saved from the culling and allowed to pass into peonhood. There was just under a thousand of them, and the Head Warrior had set up a dedicated camp and training ground outside of the city. Their progress was slow, but they were eager to learn; relieved to still be alive, relieved to have some purpose.

V ached with the desire to do something, to take action. The priority had been to reassess and reinforce Peqkya's borders, which Lizya had capably managed. *And now… and now we wait for the snow to clear, for our women to return so we can strategize. We are as frozen as the weather.*

"Hand-to-hand combat practice today," V said to Monya and Sarry after they completed their final posture.

"The snow is easing," Darrio mused as he sauntered off to one side. He watched the trio carefully and followed the moves but in his own time, his leg injury inhibiting his movement.

V demonstrated an attack move on Monya and then helped the young warrior and Sarry to perfect their stance and movements.

"Here, like this," Monya said to Sarry.

She bent the wolf's elbow into the correct position.

"Thanks," Sarry said.

Then Monya whispered something to Sarry and they both giggled, losing concentration.

"Warriors," V said, "focus."

They continued to practise the move, but Monya bit her lip and Sarry stifled her mirth. She couldn't hold it much longer and she snorted. Monya burst into a fit of laughter and Sarry joined her.

"Sorry, V," Monya mumbled but they couldn't stop.

V should discipline them but let it go. She was pleased Sarry was making a friend. Monya was fifteen and Sarry, in her wolf years, was almost a teenager now.

Darrio rolled his eye at V and she smiled. As Sarry and Monya laughed themselves dry, V watched as the Jute Captain, Brinjinqa, trained with his fighters on the other side of the grounds. They were formed up in a tight pack, moving rapidly as one in quick sequences that V couldn't follow. Next to the Jutes, Captain Laurya led a group of novices in a battle simulation.

"You two, go and report to Captain Laurya, you can train with her for the rest of the day," V said and pointed towards the warrior. "Monya, I'll be right here."

The pair nodded but didn't move as Lizya's grey clevercat skittered to a halt before V.

"The warriorsssss you ssssent to check on the sssstone army have returned. They are coming up from the peon camp now."

Daya and six warriors came on ponies towards the courtyard where V waited with the wolves, Monya and Brin. Lizya ran on foot beside them. At the gates, Daya dismounted, handed her pony's rein to another warrior and gave orders. The warriors trotted away towards the barrack's stables. Daya and Lizya jogged towards V.

Lizya gave V a brief nod and then bent forward, resting

her elbows on her knees. She panted with exertion, fighting to control her breathing. She puffed, "Go on… Daya… don't mind me."

"Well, you did insist on running next to our ponies." Daya rolled her eyes and grinned at V. They embraced and slapped each other's backs.

V thumped her fist to her chest and Daya returned the gesture. "What news, Daya?"

"The stone army is alive and rampaging," Daya said, without preamble. "They became unrooted, more animated on the day our great Sybilya passed from this world."

"Zhaq," V swore.

Daya continued, "The two opposing sides have come together as one force, we estimate eight thousand stone men."

"*Zhaq.*"

"There are also ponies and tigers. They are on the move. At first, they ambled about in random directions, but then came together in a pack. They do not seem to have any purpose other than destruction. They marched, flattening great swathes of land and destroying six settlements. They've ripped numerous flocks of sheep and their shepherds to shreds, and pulled to pieces a herd of ponies.

We watched as they came to the place where the North West Road meets the West Way. V, they turned east onto the West Way, heading straight for Riaow. They'll devastate the town of Qipaz first."

The skies opened and fat rain fell, a blessed relief from snow. All with hoods raised them, but as the rain picked up the plopping noise became deafening. V ushered them towards the covered entrance of the Melokai's buildings.

"Ways to bring them down?" Lizya asked. She was now stood upright, hands on her hips.

"We engaged a stoney straggler. He had only one leg, and was hopping behind the others, following at quite a distance. They all seem of the same mindset. But there does not appear to be a leader that we could determine. We shot the straggler with an arrow, engaged with swords, tackled bodily. I broke my zhaq arm." Daya pulled aside her cloak with a grimace to show V her sling and clenched her mouth in annoyance.

She continued, "The cockface would not go down. It is a lump of stone. We had an advantage as the zhaq stoney had one leg, so we managed to tip him over, but it kept fighting back, kept trying to get up to follow the rest, or dragging itself along the ground. He had two swords, which were also stone and had fused to his hands. The stone swords are blunt, but they hurt when they connect. He was swinging them around endlessly. He did not seem to tire. These stonies don't sleep, eat, shit.

"We managed to tie the arms and leave it trussed up, but the stone cockface broke free of the rope – simply ripping it apart. Their strength is…" Daya shook her head, at a loss for words. "It took all seven of us to take down a one-legger. It would take more warriors to bring down a two-legged stoney and bind it with stronger rope. But how to kill it?" The warrior shook her head. "We'd need hammers, but to catch and smash eight thousand stonies?" She whistled and grimaced.

"Why have they merged as one? They were two opposing armies, why not smash each other to smithereens?" the Head Warrior asked.

Sarry, in a quiet voice with perfect Shella, said, "They have been looking at each other for one thousand years. Their anger lies with who did this to them, and no longer with each other. They have shared the same fate and now they share an enemy. Us."

All considered her. Sarry spoke the truth and they all knew it. It was as if Sybilya had spoken. V swelled with pride for her daughter.

"Do you see how to kill them?" Daya asked the young wolf.

Sarry shook her head.

Lizya scratched her cheek, calculating. "In total we have near seven thousand warriors, mostly novices. Three thousand of those are away from Riaow, dotted around the country protecting our borders. We have one hundred skilled Jutes. There are also one thousand untrained peons, who would be near to useless right now, still young and weak. We'd need to keep at least two thousand warriors here to protect the city, so that leaves us with two thousand against eight thousand stone men."

Daya shook her head. "It would be a suicide mission. Zhaq knows how many warriors would be needed to take down one of the stone tigers."

Brin raised his three-fingered hand, to get their attention. "If I may, we have V's magic," he said with a bow towards V.

V nodded. "We do. But I don't know if my magic alone could defeat the stone army."

It could! came the reply in her mind as her magic swirled in her veins. *We can defeat anything!*

"Not alone, my dear, with our help," Brin said with a grin and twirled his vial in his fingers.

V dipped her head at him and considered for a moment. "We have an enemy within our borders rampaging through our country. We have enemies outside our borders. We must deal first with this internal threat or Peqkya will crumble. We must prevent the stone army from reaching the town of Qipaz, there are thousands who live there."

Those around her indicated their agreement.

"We will take our two thousand warriors and one hundred Jutes. And we will take two hundred traitorous peons and one hundred Dromedars. It'll have to be enough."

"You think the prisoners will fight for us?" Lizya said.

"I'll give them a choice," V replied.

In Riaow's only prison, two hundred peons and the one hundred captured cammer soldiers crammed together in the small cells. They were fed and watered, but there was no comfort. The air was thick with sweat, vomit, piss and shit.

The peon rebellion leader, a steel worker with huge biceps, was dragged from a cell and held by two warriors in front of V. He glared at her, a snarl on his face. All the prisoners had fallen silent, listening.

In a clear voice that carried along the cells, V said, "You succeeded, Lamaz, or Steely as I hear you are known."

Steely's brow tightened, confused.

"The practice of culling useless peens at fifteen has been ended."

"Lies," Steely growled in a deep voice. "Just kill us all 'n' 'ave done with it."

"Peons have a better life now than before your rebellion. There are now three reasons why peons still exist – to pleasure women, to make babies and, now, to fight for Peqkya. We are at war. We have internal and external threats. Peons who fail the usefulness tests will not be culled. They will enter a peon division of the army. Will be trained as warriors and army helpers. Every peen born in Peqkya now has a purpose."

A murmur rippled through the cells. V held up her red palms and said in Steely's mind, *I tell you the truth.*

Steely's eyes widened. His face softened and he nodded.

"You and your traitorous peons should be punished. Tortured and put on public display to suffer a slow, excruciating death as a warning to other peons not to rebel."

Steely slumped between the two warriors. "We're ready," he said quietly, head down.

There were whimpers and cries from the peons in the cells. They had been waiting months for this.

"Peqkya is at war, every Peqkian, be it woman or peon is in the same danger. I am giving you and your traitorous peons a choice. Fight or die.

"If you choose to fight, you will be trained to wield a sword, shoot a bow and fight hand-to-hand. You will fight alongside Peqkian warriors and our allies against our enemies. Some of you might die. As some of my warriors and allies might die. As I might die. When all our enemies are defeated and Peqkya is safe once again, those of you who survive will be given a choice. Return to your old life and profession or remain in the Peqkian army. Progression and success are based on merit, so prove yourselves to me, to Head Warrior Lizya, to your captains. We'll be watching.

"Those who choose to die, I will ask the women of Riaow what they think your sentence should be. I do not imagine it will be kind."

Steely chewed at the corner of his mouth.

"You have until this time tomorrow to consider. Those who want to fight, will be trained. Those who don't will be left in the cells awaiting their sentence. Know this, any peon who disobeys a woman will die. That custom has not changed." V indicated for him to be returned to the cells.

She walked to the other side of the prison where the cammers huddled silently in their cells. Chaz had sent a translator who spoke the Drome language to translate for Lizya and her warriors.

In perfect Dromedari, V said, "Soldiers from Drome. Your rulers committed an atrocity by invading our country, and you were left behind. We have tended to your injuries, fed you and treated you leniently. Be thankful you are still alive.

"Peqkya has a battle looming. I now give you a choice. Fight with us against our foe, and once they are defeated those of you who survive will be returned to Drome. There will be no opportunity to flee, there will be no opportunity to hide from the battle.

"Those who choose not to fight with us will die here in the city. The sentence will be decided upon by the women of Riaow. Many of whom want you flayed, tortured and made an example of."

A cammer dragged himself along the floor to the bars, he was missing half of one leg and his foot from the other. "What if we cannot fight?"

"Those who cannot fight will serve Peqkya in other ways, giving food to your cammer comrades, or tending to the injured. You will be judged on your usefulness."

"If we fight, we will die anyway…" a cammer grumbled from deep in the cells.

V wasn't certain that anyone would survive the stone army, Peqkian, Jute or Dromedar, but she didn't voice her fears.

A hand flew out from one of the cells and V scrutinised its owner. Stood alone, the other cell occupants keeping a respectful distance. *The leader of this little group.*

The Dromedar pulled back a hood and wrenched down the grimy scarf covering the face. Fingers fiddled with something behind the ears and under the neck, and then peeled away the beard, dropping the hairy mask on the floor. The other soldiers in the cell gasped and then groused:

"A woman."

"It's a fucking woman!"

"We followed a woman. No wonder we got caught."

The Dromedar female soldier stood near the bars looking at V, the men crept closer shaking fists, spitting and pointing. She glared at them and raised her own fist and they backed away. She turned back to V.

She was clearly a skilled fighter. Her body was lean and muscular, her shoulders broad and hips narrow – a physique similar to the males around her. But, unlike most of the soldiers whose humps were large and misshapen, her hump was small and round, barely poking out of the split in her shirt. Her dark-brown hair fell to her shoulders in greasy waves, similar in style to the Dromedar males. Her face was hard, scarred and lined, with alert eyes, a small nose and thin lips. She had clearly seen some action and was perhaps thirty years in age. By keeping her face hidden with the beard-mask, wrapped with the scarf and altering her speaking voice, she could easily pass for a Dromedar male.

V studied her for a while. The cammer army was all male, she was an anomaly.

The woman said, "I pretended to be male to join the army. I also allowed myself and these men to be captured so I could remain in Peqkya when the rest of the army was driven out or destroyed."

The men growled and grunted angrily at this news, spitting towards her.

V felt a pang in the bottom of her belly. Sybilya had told her to listen to her instinct. *She speaks the truth,* her gut told her. V indicated for the prisoner to continue.

"What I have to say is not for their ears." The woman gestured towards the cammer men in her cell.

V whistled to the warriors guarding the cells and one came forward with the key to the barred gate.

Two warriors stood either side of the prisoner, securing an arm each and their daggers pointed at her throat. V sat in the council room, Lizya positioned between V and the prisoner with her arms folded. She looked casual, but V knew she would move quicker than any of them if the cammer woman attempted to attack or escape. Monya stood behind V and a further six warriors waited outside the door.

The scholar sat opposite the Head Warrior, translating V's Dromedari into Shella.

"Sit." V gestured for the warriors to allow the prisoner to sit on a stool at the far end of the table.

The Dromedar woman sat and placed her trussed hands on the table. She wasn't worried by the warriors holding their weapons to her neck. She held herself with the confidence of one who knows how to fight. She kept her eyes on V and was not intimidated.

"What's your name?" V said.

"Nameeri," the prisoner answered and dipped her chin.

"Nameeri, tell us your story."

"I am a spy," she said simply, "for a clan in Drome who opposes the ruler and the ruling elite. We are called the Khumarah. Our kind has been persecuted for thousands of years. My mission was to infiltrate the army, to witness the invasion, to report back on the Drome army's strengths and weaknesses, tactics, numbers killed and so on. But I realised when I was here, that the enemy of my enemy is my friend. So, I allowed myself, and the little group that followed me, to be captured, for the chance to speak with the Melokai of Peqkya."

Lizya rolled her shoulder as the translator repeated Nameeri's words. Then she raised an eyebrow at V.

"Go on," V said.

"The Khumarah have a different way of thinking about the world than the ruling clans. We live secretly outside the Parchad city crater wall and in pockets throughout the desert. A number of us are skilled assassins, and have been ridding the city of its corrupt leaders. But we are few, and they are many.

"My partner is the leader of the Khumarah. His name is Ibin. He was reluctant to send me, of course, but after him, I am the most skilled fighter in the clan. He needed someone he could trust to stay alive and return. I know everything there is to know about Drome, Parchad, the rulers. I am willing to share that knowledge with you, should you require it. I ask in return that you help my clan to overthrow the Wakrime clan, to usher in a new rule led by the Khumarah."

V waited for the translator to finish.

The Head Warrior scratched at her cheek. "Drome invaded our country and we will take revenge on the

Wakrime clan. But how do we know that your clan, the Khumarah, will not turn against us?"

Nameeri waited for the translator before she replied, "I will fight for you as you fight for me. You asked the Dromedar soldiers to fight for you. I will. And I will fight with honour."

"A test of her allegiance," Lizya said in Shella to V.

In Shella, V said to the warriors who held Nameeri, "Take her to a cell of her own, treat her well until we have need of her, however she is still a prisoner. Get Chaz to send a language scholar to teach her Shella."

Nameeri was marched away. V dismissed the translator and asked for Monya to wait outside. When it was just the two of them in the council room, Lizya said, "You don't trust her?"

"My instinct tells me that she is telling the truth. But I do not want her to know too much about us. Not yet anyway. First, we must rid Peqkya of the stone army, then we take revenge on Drome."

"And then we deal with the zhaq Trogrs and Denya's dishonourable betrayal in Fertilian," Lizya said and laughed. "I can see now why you picked me as Head Warrior, you're going to need all the help you can get."

V clapped a hand on her friend's shoulder. "We'd better get on with it then."

21

JESSIMA

ॐ

Jessima ignored Prince Ernest's continued fretting at her visiting the displaced Cleland City residents and went out into the city. She was eager to see the woman with two children that she had spoken to at the tunnel exit. Ernie had no idea where that family had been housed, so Jessima wandered the streets and visited family after family.

Two months had passed since the evacuees had arrived, and while there was little room in the city for the Lianites themselves, they had generously given up space in their tiny homes. Ernie had organised the materials to make up shelters on flat rooftops or along the edges of the fields. Any unused space in warehouses had been turned into hostels and the food stores opened to ensure sustenance for all.

Jessima walked slowly through the city, pausing frequently to speak with Lianites and those displaced from Fertilian proper. She was trailed by a handful of stewards and soldiers, Jessima finding the presence of too many cumbersome and unnecessarily intimidating to her people.

They made their way west towards the harbour and down a narrow alleyway close to the fish market. Her steward raised a fist to knock on the door of a small house chosen at random. But before her knuckles touched wood, the door opened and two women bustled out.

"Oh," said one as she frowned at those stood in the street before her house.

The other's eyes widened. "Queen Jessima!"

Three children squirmed behind the two women with one older child attempting to herd the other two.

"We met at the tunnel," Jessima said with a smile, recognising the woman. "We spoke."

"That we did, your Grace," the woman replied with a curtsy. "I'm Fiona, and this is Annette."

The first woman nodded curtly.

"Annette has graciously opened her home to us. My eldest is looking after his sister and Annette's son while we go to work. In return for her generosity, I'm helping her with her job," Fiona said.

"We're late," Annette said, impatiently.

"This is Queen Jessima!" Fiona replied.

Annette shrugged. "Queen Jessima, we're late for work. I won't get paid if we don't get there soon."

"Please, don't let me keep you," Jessima said and stood to one side. She gestured for the women to continue. Annette and Fiona stepped past her and her entourage and the door was closed behind them by one of the children.

Jessima fell in beside the two women. "Where do you work, Annette?"

"At the fish market," Annette replied.

"May I come and help you?" Jessima said.

Annette gave her an incredulous look, then continued to pay attention to the winding alleyway.

"It's messy work," Fiona said, "very messy, your Grace."

Jessima recalled the dirty nappies she had changed at the hospital. "I can manage. And I'm dressed suitably." Jessima had taken to wearing practical clothes, similar to how Fiona and Annette were dressed – she had no time or desire to wear the queenly frippery anymore.

"Best leave that lot out here," Annette said as they reached the back of a large warehouse near the docks. "Not much space in there."

Jessima nodded to her entourage, who acknowledged the order.

"This way, then," Annette said and ushered Fiona and Jessima through a large door.

A frenzy of sights, sounds and smells hit Jessima as if she'd walked headfirst into a wall. She hadn't yet visited the bustling fish market, and the stinking warehouse was bursting at the seams with people and things dredged up from the ocean. Peculiar-looking sea creatures were slumped on great slabs of rock and carved up by fisher-women with huge knives. There were pots of fish still wriggling and crates of crabs climbing over one another.

Annette and Fiona stopped at a beat-up wooden table. Annette covered it with a stained sheet that she had been carrying and then strode off. Fiona rolled up her sleeves and indicated for Jessima to do the same. Fiona reached under the table and pulled out three aprons. She gave one to Jessima.

Annette returned moments later with a sturdy woman wheeling a barrow full of still-twitching fish, each as long as Jessima's arm. The woman positioned the wheelbarrow near to the table and then left.

Annette pulled out two huge knives from under the table and handed one to Fiona. Annette indicated for Jessima to stand on the opposite side of the table so that she faced the two women.

"We'll chop, you can put the chunks in that box there," Annette said and gestured to an empty box at the end of the table.

She grabbed a fish and slapped it on the table in front of Fiona. Then she put a second one in front of her with a moist thud. She raised her knife and paused abruptly as if she'd just remembered something. "Don't get your hands in the way, Queen Jessima. These knives will take off a finger in a heartbeat. Wait until we've finished."

Jessima placed her hands under her armpits. Annette and Fiona brought up their knives and chopped. Fish blood and guts sprayed up and hit Jessima in the face. Once she would've gagged but she was no longer squeamish. Her mind flicked back to the assassin's blood all over her hands. She watched the gory proceedings as each woman hacked their fish with a steely resolve.

"Now," Annette said to Jessima as she and Fiona paused.

Jessima selected a lump of slimy fish and placed it in the box. In that same moment the two women had picked up two more fish and were waiting to flop them on the table.

"Quicker," Annette snapped.

Jessima upped her pace, scooping chunks with her arms to clear the table.

The two fish were slapped down and the process started again. After a couple of runs, the three women eased into a rhythm. Annette, satisfied that the fish were being cut up quick enough, relaxed.

"Fiona's a fast learner," Annette told Jessima. "She's been such a help."

Fiona smiled before bringing down her knife with a sharp crack to remove her fish's head from its body.

"With our men gone, we've had to pick up all the work," Annette continued, "as well as care for the children. It's been hard."

"Both our husbands are in Fertilian proper, fighting the Thornes," Fiona said. "We wonder sometimes if they've met and if they'd be friends, laughing and joking with one another."

Annette nodded sadly and raised an arm to wipe her brow on the front of her shoulder, avoiding the fish slime that covered her arms.

"It's the not knowing," Fiona said. "You know that your husband, King Hugo, rest in peace, died. We don't.

Will they come back to us? Will we ever see them again? It's torture."

Annette paused in her chopping to look at Jessima. "When will we go to their aid, my Queen? What is the plan to get our men home to Lian? To get people like Fiona back to their men and their homes in Cleland City?"

The two women looked at Jessima expectantly. Blood and fish-muck covered their aprons and up to their shoulders. Jessima studied her dirty hands. What could she do to save their men? To save her man, Toby? She was a queen, their queen, but she felt utterly powerless.

"I do not have an answer," Jessima replied.

Annette huffed and clenched her jaw. She ferociously chopped her next fish, each blow told of her anger.

A feeling of helplessness washed over Jessima. She'd made progress with the people, was certain that their respect for her was growing every time she was seen on the streets, every time she visited a home or spent time at a place of work. She was becoming their Queen, earning their favour. But always the same desire – to aid those in Fertilian. Jessima was as desperate as these women to help, but how?

After, Jessima made her way to the biggest church in Lian. Perhaps God would help her find an answer.

She slid unnoticed into a bench at the back of the church as Head Cleric Prince Charles lectured from the pulpit. The congregation listened avidly as he sermonised, but the words washed over Jessima.

As the congregation filed out, Jessima remained seated, head lowered. The bench creaked beside her.

"Queen Jessima, this is a surprise," Prince Charles said.

"I am here for God's counsel."

Charles nodded. "Speak then, and I will listen."

Jessima eyed Prince Charles warily. She knew he wouldn't understand. But then, he was the mouthpiece of God, and she believed He was on her side, for if He wasn't, then who was? She exhaled and decided to speak her mind.

"The people are angry, they want to help their men in Fertilian, they feel impotent here in Lian. I am their Queen, they look to me to do something. But what can I do? How can I fight back? How can I lead in the way they want?"

Charles frowned. He smoothed his lavish purple robe and fingered the great pendant that hung around his neck. He pursed his lips as if an internal struggle raged behind them. Jessima cursed herself for opening up to him, braced herself for the torrent of abuse that would spew forth.

Finally, he spoke. "You have done much to earn their respect, Queen Jessima. You have spoken at length with the people and listened to their troubles. You have become one of them and not a detached royal. I admire you for that, God admires you for that."

Jessima started, surprised by the prince's unexpected praise.

"You have listened to your true self and stuck to your path," he continued. "My mother was the same. She refused to be bound by conventions and struck out on her own. If it hadn't been for her, Hugo would never have retaken the throne from that pretender, Ben Thorne. Truly, I did not think you had it in you, but it seems you have a kindling of the same fire as Olivia Cleland. History may yet repeat itself. Look inside your heart. An answer will present itself." Prince Charles stood and the bench wobbled. "I must prepare for evening prayer."

"Thank you," Jessima said. Her fingers twitched and she picked at her nails before swallowing back the awkwardness, the fear of admitting past faults, and reached for his hand. "I need good people around me. People I can trust. I know we have not always seen eye to eye, but I would like you to re-join my counsel."

The cleric studied her. She sat up tall and raised her chin under his intent gaze. She was the queen, and he knew there was now a line he could not cross. She wouldn't be controlled.

Charles gave her a curt nod. "Certainly, Queen Jessima." He removed his hand from hers and walked towards the pulpit, his footsteps echoing in the church.

"Your Grace," her steward said behind her. "I'm sorry to disturb your prayer, but Lord Chattergoon is here with a messenger from Fertilian."

A few moments later the messenger cried, "Dear God!" and fell to his knees. He clutched his hands over his face.

"Pull yourself together in front of the queen," Lord Chattergoon said and hauled the man to his feet. "Speak your message."

The man sobbed, the noise reverberating through the empty church. "Yes, sir." He stared at the majestic pulpit and then turned to Jessima. She had slid from her bench and the three of them stood in the church aisle.

The messenger used the edge of his tunnel-grubby hand to dash the wetness from his face. "Cleland Castle has fallen. Fertilian has fallen. The Thornes have declared the country theirs. Cleland rule is over. What's left of our army is scattered – in hiding, imprisoned or forced into hard labour. All… all is lost. So many dead…" the man's voice quivered. "Lian is next. They want it all. And with that Peqkian turncoat on their side, they'll take it."

Jessima's heart slammed against her ribs with the force of Annette's knife. She took a deep breath and stood up straighter.

"This city is vulnerable, they are coming," the messenger said. He looked up at Chattergoon, "They all died, they all died so I could get here to you. They sacrificed their lives to distract the guards so I could slip into the tunnels…"

Jessima turned away as Chattergoon spoke with the distraught messenger who rambled about the deaths of people he and Chattergoon had known.

She'd been foolish to think the Cleland army could

hold out. That they would cling on to the castle until…. until what? For sixteen years until Eddie was old enough to fight back?

The Thornes were coming for them, would never leave them alive. They'd end the Cleland bloodline once and for all to secure their place on the throne.

"My dear, I know you're terribly frightened. But you've been wallowing in this church for far too long. I've already made an announcement at the main square that Fertilian proper has fallen to the Thornes," Ernie said.

"I need to *do* something," Jessima replied. Although she'd been thinking for hours, her thoughts were still as frayed as the sleeve she'd been picking at.

Ernie ushered her to a waiting carriage. "To the sea," he said to the driver. "You need some fresh air, my dear."

The carriage trundled through the deserted streets. All the residents were inside, privately digesting the bitter news.

Ernie spoke incessantly. "Here's what we'll do. We'll strengthen our defences, stockpile food and collapse the tunnel entrance. We'll make it as hard as possible for the Thornes. We'll put up a damn good fight before they step foot in this city. I'll put out the orders tomorrow. There are nine thousand residents here now, the majority are women and children. We'll rally around and get the defences built up swiftly. We'll be ready for when they come."

Ernie paused but Jessima didn't respond.

"We'll send you and Eddie off in a ship to the Sarenky Islands," he continued, "get you out of the city. Granted you might never return, but you'd be safe there. No Thorne has ever ruled over Lian before, they won't know how to man a ship and we certainly won't tell them. There will be some deaths, no doubt, but if we can negotiate with the Thornes, we might save some of the commoners' necks. Perhaps more of us can retreat to the Sarenky

Islands. I'll need to speak to my expert on such matters to check the capacity of our ships and the islands."

The carriage turned down an alleyway that led to the sea, then turned north. Jessima gazed out across the vast expanse of ocean, in awe of the moon's reflection glittering on the surface.

"Stop," she said.

The driver brought the carriage to a halt. Ernie's mouth also stopped. Fat rain tapped tentatively on the roof of the carriage and pattered on the rocks beside them.

Soon, heavy rain sploshed on the surface of the sea and the wind that followed behind the swollen clouds stirred up the waves. Although these crashed against the shore, the water looked inviting. *Ramya…*

She climbed out of the carriage.

"My dear, what in all Fertilian are you doing?" Ernie said to her back.

She stepped down past the rocks and onto the pebble beach. The rain slapped her face and stung her cheeks as she pulled off her cloak and dropped it on the pebbles.

"Jessima!" Ernie's voice shouted from behind her.

She continued towards the breaking waves yanking her overshirt free and then stepped out of her skirt. At the water's edge, she sat on the pebbles and undid her boots, heaving them from her feet.

Dressed only in her undergarments, Jessima waded into the ocean. The cool water nipped at her ankles, her knees, her thighs. She held her breath and sunk under.

Move, Jessima, move. She surfaced and swam as fast as she could.

Heart beating loud in her ears, Jessima allowed herself to simply float and experienced a profound sense of stillness in the water.

She shivered and looked towards the shore. *Perhaps I should go in…* But her mind screamed, *move! Keep moving forward. Don't stay still, don't go back.*

She swam harder. Her body was stronger now than it

had been when she bathed with Ramya in Inaly Lake. The daylight dances had changed her figure. Ramya had been so muscular, a tiger. Jessima was a scrawny alley cat by comparison. But alley cats have sharp claws.

I fought off an assassin. I killed a man. She had battled passionately to save Eddie, her loved one. It had been her duty, her responsibility as his mother to save him. She had wanted to be there, had wanted the man dead.

And she wanted to be there for Fertilian. It was her duty, her responsibility to fight for her country and all those in it. Not just for Toby, not just for her own selfish desires to see Eddie as King. For everyone.

I'm not sitting back and waiting for the Thornes to attack Lian. Fertilian is my child. I will fight for her. I will kill for her. I will do everything in my power to save her.

She swam toward the shore.

Who is there to help them? Georgina's question rang in her mind as she waded out of the sea. *Who?*

This time the answer was immediate.

I am.

***

The following morning Jessima knocked on the door to Lord Chattergoon's modest rooms. The lord welcomed her in, and she took the chair opposite a sofa Philip Chattergoon perched on, his father stood to one side.

Jessima got straight to the point. "Lord Chattergoon, we must retake Cleland City. We must reclaim Fertilian from the Thornes. Our people need our help, there is no one else."

Philip's gaze flitted from his father to the Queen and back, rubbing his hands together excitedly.

"And we must rescue Prince Toby," Jessima continued.

"The Cleland army was crushed, and we have no army here in Lian," Lord Chattergoon said.

"We will build an army," Jessima replied. "It will be an army of thousands. And I will find a way to send a messenger to the Peqkians for assistance. After all, it is their wayward captain who lost this battle for us."

"Thousands?" Chattergoon asked. "The only men in Lian are grandfathers, boys or unable to fight."

"Not men. An army of women, like the Peqkian warriors. There are thousands of women in Lian."

"And who will lead this army?"

"I will. I am the Queen Regent of Fertilian."

"And King Edward?" Chattergoon asked.

"Will remain safely in Lian with his uncles and sister."

"You'll leave him?"

"To protect him, I must." Jessima shifted on the sofa. This decision had been the hardest to make. But it was done, and she was not turning back. "When he is older, he will understand. I will free all our people from Thorne persecution. And Eddie will have a country to rule when he turns sixteen. He will know I had the courage to fight back."

Chattergoon paused before he replied, "If you do succeed in raising this army of women, they have no idea how to fight."

"I remember the Peqkian daylight dances," Jessima said. "I will teach them this and those drills I recall Denya practising with Prince Toby and his soldiers on our return from Peqkya. I will attempt to teach the soldiers. There must be a way."

"You can show them how to fight, Father, like you taught us," Philip blurted. "Oh, if only Mother were here, she loves sparring with us, she's a great teacher. I think she's actually a better fighter than you—"

Chattergoon held up a hand to quieten his son.

"Well, that settles it then," Jessima said. "You can teach us."

"Father, you've never trained an entire army before! Mother will be so jealous."

"Yes, your Grace," Chattergoon said over his son's words. "It would be my pleasure."

***

The marketplace was heaving. Jessima had made sure that knowledge of her speech was spread across the city days before it happened. She was ready.

She stepped up onto the stage assisted by two handmaids. They fussed about her, smoothing her skirts and preening her elaborate hair style. Jessima smiled at the crowd. She'd been getting ready for hours and this was her moment.

Thousands of faces glared up at her. There was no booing or jeering, just an undercurrent of hushed muttering. Women stood with arms crossed, impatiently waiting for her to speak.

The handmaids finished their primping and left the stage.

Jessima stepped forward. "Ladies of Lian. I know you are all busy women, so I'll keep this short. Our men are in Fertilian. For some of us, our homes are in Fertilian. I plan to get them back."

A confused murmur spread across the crowd. The women closest to Jessima frowned up at her.

Jessima ripped at her skirts. The audience gasped. She tugged and stepped out of them. She kicked them to one side of the stage. Then she tugged at her bodice, snatching it off. She held it up to her face and vigorously wiped off the bone powder and cheek stain. Satisfied of her clean face she flung the cloth away.

She stood before thousands in men's clothing. Functional breeches and a shirt, similar to those Lord Chattergoon wore. Around her waist was a sword belt, the pommel gleaming above its sheath. A dagger hung from the other side of the belt.

This smaller blade she pulled out slowly. The women stood fascinated, silent, all attention on Jessima.

"A friend once told me that all this hair would get in the way of a warrior," Jessima said. With her free hand she started pulling at her hair, yanking out clips and netting until it tumbled down and fell to her waist. "So, it is going!"

Jessima gathered her hair and pulled it across her shoulder. She held it tight with one hand as she sawed at it with the dagger. Once through the mass of blonde she discarded the locks on the stage.

"If I am to be a warrior, if I am to be as deadly and as disciplined as the Peqkians then I need to dress to fight!"

A cheer rose across the crowd. Jessima sheathed her dagger and took a step nearer the women, close to the edge of the stage.

"Our men are in Fertilian! Our homes are in Fertilian! I plan to get them back!" Jessima looked over the crowd. "What kind of a queen would I be to snuggle with my baby in safety while our country suffers? What kind of a queen would I be to allow my son to grow up in luxury while your sons, my people's sons, are suffering in Fertilian? What kind of a queen ignores the plight of our men, our families, our country? Who sits here safe and sound and allows their slaughter to continue?"

Jessima pulled her sword and pointed it to the sky. "Not this queen! No! I will fight back. We will fight back. The time for hiding is over. The time for retribution is now. We are strong, we are brave, we are determined. We will fight for our loved ones, we will kill. And we will embrace death should it come to us. Our women's army will be formidable! *You* will be formidable! They will underestimate us, and it will be their undoing. We will be their sorrow. There are nine thousand of us living in Lian and we can raise a host of thousands. We will march on those bastard Thornes in Fertilian to fight for our men, for our country, for our King!"

The crowd roared.

"Are you with me?" Jessima shouted and pumped her sword in the air.

The crowd roared louder.

She lowered her sword. "A woman here in this marketplace once told me that you needed a leader who gives a shit. Well, I give a shit! I have listened to you and I have heard."

Jessima walked towards the side of the stage. "We start training tomorrow. Here. Sunrise."

She left the stage to cheering and stomping feet.

22

DARRIO

Darrio watched V. She rode on a horse next to the Head Warrior Lizya, and no matter how hard he tried, he couldn't keep his eye off her. Even though she hadn't done much other than face forward, occasionally talking to Lizya or cocking her head to listen as they passed trickling streams, he found her mesmerising.

Behind V came five hundred warriors on ponies and then behind them, Darrio and Sarry on foot. Behind the wolves came the half-height, blue-haired, pink-skinned Jute fighters, fronted by their leader, Brinjinqa. The strangest little creatures Darrio thought he'd ever seen, apart from perhaps V's pet that had twigs sticking out of its body. And these Jute creatures rode on giant beetles. Beetles! He'd once had to eat the little kind when prey had been scarce one bleak winter.

After the Jutes came a further one thousand five hundred warriors on foot. They were interspersed between the two hundred 'traitorous peons', as the Peqkian warriors referred to them, and prisoners from the desert country of Drome – strange, hump-backed 'cammers'. Behind them, animals known as donkeys laden with supplies; then Peqkian males – the omegas of the pack – who tended to the animals, set up and pulled down the camp every night and organised distribution of the food.

A huge pack, and unwieldly. Not agile like the wolves. They couldn't go hunt, or sleep anywhere, and had to carry food and shelter. Progress was sluggish, they went as fast as the slowest animal. And the weighed-down donkeys moved slower than a wolf after filling its belly.

It had taken them one moon cycle to traverse the West Way and reach Qipaz. They'd passed through the town, V giving orders that if she sent the command, they needed to evacuate. And they were now a one-week march outside of the settlement, and, as he'd been informed by V, were close to the oncoming stone army.

Each night, as they'd made camp, Darrio had attempted to get V on her own. Although he was certain she knew what he was trying to do, she did not allow it. She was polite and courteous to Darrio and Sarry, in the same way she treated her betas, Brinjinqa – and her own warriors – but never intimate, not in front of this giant pack. She was the alpha, and had her position to maintain. He understood.

In Riaow, whenever she could, V had come to sleep with him and Sarry in their makeshift den. But they hadn't really spoken. A few whispers, so as not to wake Sarry. His daughter barely stirred as V had crept in and out again a few hours later. He wasn't even certain if Sarry knew V had even been there. Father and daughter hadn't spoken of it. Apart from those snatched moments of silent intimacy, Darrio and V hadn't had any time alone together. Sarry, even less so with her mother.

He watched V dismount and give the reins to another warrior, who travelled on foot. The warrior nodded at an instruction from the Melokai and climbed up on the horse. V watched as her army progressed past her, and then fell in step with Darrio and Sarry. Both wolves pulled up to walk on two feet next to her. Darrio was just shorter than V, but Sarry loomed over them both. Taller now than her mother by a head and shoulders.

For a while, they walked together in silence. They followed the trail west along the side of a valley, wide enough for the three of them. V gazed out over the lush forest with a peaceful smile on her face, seeming to draw energy from the swishing of branches and the squishy green moss that covered the path here and there.

Perhaps V will tell Sarry she is her mother. Darrio had kept quiet on the matter, honouring V's silence until he could talk to her about it.

"Tell me, Sarrya," V said, "how did you convince the tigers not to kill you?"

Sarry rolled her lips back into a grin. Every time V addressed Sarry, Darrio observed his daughter's entire body straightened, her fur ruffled, and her eyes brightened.

"Well, my brother Harro was caught on the wrong side of the river when the tigers pushed us back to the north bank," Sarry replied in fluent Shella. "It was a vicious fight, and the tigers were taunting him on the bank in view of us wolves on the other side. Pappy was about to jump back into the river to save Harro, but I can do this big roar-growl so I did it then and drew their attention. Then I swam across and spoke to them in their language – it just came out – and they agreed to let Harro go and take me in his place."

"That was very brave of you," V said.

Sarry gave a little shrug. "I guess…"

"And Darrio wanted to save Harro?"

"Of course!" Although Sarry knew he could understand Shella but poorly speak it, she switched to the wolf language to ensure her father understood, "Pappy do anything for his pups."

Darrio huffed in reply.

V, who was walking between them, glanced at Darrio. "So, what happened then?"

"Well, the tigers led me away from the bank and towards Otiss. That big brute stared at me for a long time, and I honestly thought I was about to be eaten, but then he said, 'Sybilya tells me that you are the one she seeks'. And that was that, I wasn't dinner, I was an ally."

"Have you tested your physical magic?" V said.

"I can speak and understand different languages, and I have a sense of what is to come and who to trust, but I do not know if I have any ability, I… I haven't tried to do anything. I don't know what to do."

V nodded and seemed to consider something. After a while, she said quietly, "My magic bristles in my blood. I can feel it, hear it. I do not know what it is capable of. Perhaps we can learn together?"

Sarry wagged her tail and her ears wiggled. "Yes, yes I would like that."

V's hand twitched at her side and she reached it out to touch Sarry, but a whistle from the front drew her attention.

Lizya had halted the army and everyone behind paused. She whistled again and V jogged forward, turning to the wolves, "Come with me." Then shouted, "Brinjinqa, I require your presence."

The two wolves and the Jute captain followed behind V, the warriors parting to let them through. At the head of the army, Lizya stood waiting a few paces away from the rest. Darrio immediately understood why they had stopped. Sarry let out a startled bark.

They had come around the side of the valley on the West Way and in front of them the road meandered down the slope towards flatter ground. From that position they could see the path of destruction wrought by the stone army. The forest was flattened, trees ripped from the ground and trampled into bark, dead animals were scattered amongst the endless wood fragments. Trodden bodies of Peqkians were strewn about and their settlements annihilated.

It was as if Great Mother Wolf had stomped an unfathomably massive paw down and crushed all underneath it. To either side of the road, the destruction spread for thousands of paces, only curtailed by an impassable mountain cliff or overhang.

And there in front of that devastation was its cause. The stone army.

A slow-moving mass of stone. Individual stone soldiers and animals were hard to pick out. The grinding, fractured sound of their movement and the crunching of trampled vegetation drifted up to where they stood.

"Zhaq," V swore under her breath.

"They move slowly, but steadily, bent on their rampage, no matter what lies in their path," Lizya said as they heard the crack of wood and then saw a tree along the path fall, the stone men crushing it underfoot. "We are a mere day away from them."

V stared for a long time at the route the West Way took that led down from their position to where the stone army progressed. Eventually she spoke. "We make camp there, and we meet them on that flat ground where the road levels out. We can get into an attack position and I suspect, when there is space, the stonies will spread into a line."

Snow-capped mountains loomed in the distance. The Melioks, as the Peqkians called them.

Their great pack was in position, the alpha had given her directions. They waited for the stone army to come into view. It was early morning, and the mist rolled across the flat ground.

They were close now, the sound of stone grinding and creaking made Darrio's teeth chatter and each high-pitched scuff drove a ragged claw through his skull. His eyelid twitched. The stone men were rocks come alive.

Although, the Jutes and their beetles are still stranger.

The cammer prisoners made up the first line, the peon traitors next. V was in front with Lizya, and several of her warriors were interspersed between the cammers and peons. These omegas had been roped loosely together in small groups to prevent escape attempts. At the last minute, V had given them heavy hammers and clubs. A few had attempted to turn these on the Peqkian warriors and run away and they were met with a swift end. Those remaining stood ready to fight.

V had ordered Brinjinqa and his Jutes to stay in the rear, along with the wolves. Sarry watched keenly, listened to all her mother said and commanded. His daughter's fur quivered with eagerness to join the fight.

And when the mist cleared and he glimpsed the first line of stone men, mounted on stone tigers and ponies, he was glad they were at the back.

In front, V raised a hand and dropped it. Two groups of mounted warriors shot forward, galloping to each end of the line of stone soldiers. They turned inward as they reached the stone men, galloping parallel to the front line in single file. The warriors held the end of long spears and smacked the pointed heads along the stone men's faces as they passed.

At the same time, the warriors, peons and cammers yelled, clapped, whooped, and stomped their feet.

Sarry inhaled and Darrio braced himself as she let out her huge roaring howl.

Slowly, the stone men became more animated. Realised the threat. Sensed the opportunity for more carnage.

With no hunt ceremony or plan of attack, the front few lines of stonies charged. V gave the order to meet them.

Darrio winced as the two sides clashed. The stone men swung their stone arms, their weapons fused onto the ends and rammed their way through the peons and cammers. The omegas pulled up the slack ropes tied around their waists, held them taut and ran forward in an attempt to trip the stone soldiers. Those stonies that fell were then set upon with clubs and hammers. The clang of each blow ringing throughout the plain.

The Peqkian warriors were armed with great hammers, balls on chains, and clubs. They drove forward. V swung and slammed with a ball on a chain. She skilfully dodged and swept aside stone man after stone man.

"Look at V," Sarry exclaimed, but Darrio had never stopped.

The stonies kept coming and Brinjinqa shouted in his language at his fighters.

"Here they come," Sarry snarled.

She pricked her ears, bared her fangs and dropped to all fours, ready to spring.

Darrio braced himself to attack. He growled as a stone soldier broke free of the peons and lumbered towards them.

Sarry leapt at the stone soldier's chest, claws out. Darrio skirted behind the thing and slammed his shoulder into one of its legs, biting at an ankle and forcing the foot off the ground. The stone man teetered and Darrio ducked out of the way as it toppled to the ground with a thump, dust and stone flying from under it.

Sarry jumped on it and scratched at its face. Her claws scraped along the stone and the noise made Darrio's skin shiver. He clamped his jaws around the ankle and shook his head back and forth attempting to snap off the foot.

A stone hand fastened around Sarry's back leg and tugged. Sarry yelped in surprise as she was flung to the side. Still holding Sarry, the thing righted itself, pushing up with its other hand. Darrio jumped to Sarry's aid, snapping his mouth around the wrist of the hand that held his daughter.

Sarry whined and wriggled, attempting to free her leg.

In the corner of his eye, Darrio saw a bright red flash and heard crashing stone. He had no time to look up as the stone man grabbed his front leg and hauled him away from Sarry.

Darrio yipped at the sudden movement.

The stone man, still sat on his backside, with legs out in front, stretched his arms wide, and with a force like an avalanche brought Darrio and Sarry together in a vicious clap.

Father and daughter smashed together with a bone-shuddering jolt. Sarry yelped as their skulls connected and Darrio yowled as his injured leg hit his daughter's hip bone.

The stone man wrenched them apart to whack them together a second time. Their bones would be pulverised between stone hands, their necks would snap as easily as a rabbit's in a wolf's maw. He wanted to see his daughter one last time but was held in the wrong direction. He cursed his one eye on the wrong side of his head.

A bright red flash blasted into the stone man's torso. The stone shattered into the tiniest pieces. The head rolled away, and both arms dropped, hands releasing Darrio's leg and that of his daughter. Both crumpled in a tangled mess of stone limbs.

Sarry found her paws and heaved Darrio up by the scruff of his neck.

V stood there, a line of blasted stone men behind her. She threw a blast from her outstretched hands that destroyed the thing's head into pebbles.

The warrior reached out her arms and pulled Sarry and Darrio into a tight embrace. He could feel her heart pounding. Then she released them.

V pointed towards the steep slope of the valley, "Go!"

She charged back into the throng, whistling and shouting orders.

Darrio and Sarry made for the slope, dodging stone men and fights. It was covered in scree and they scrambled up. A stone man attempted to follow but slid on the loose slate, making no progress.

V blasted a path for her army to retreat up the scree, methodically reducing stone man after stone man to rubble. The cammers and peons had been decimated, perhaps half their numbers remained. The Peqkian warriors had fared better, swinging balls on chains to smash the stone men, but there were too many of the stone creatures. The majority of the stone army were yet to reach the flat ground, and hadn't even charged. The stone soldiers continued forward at their steady pace, trampling over the limbs of fallen comrades, oblivious to the stonies still fighting.

Soon, only V was left on the plain, blasting the stone men one by one as they advanced on her and she backed up the scree.

Darrio saw her stumble and he bounded down and latched his teeth onto her belt. He guided her backwards as she faced the stone men.

She was breathing heavily but kept firing the red blasts from her hands. Her warriors came forward and picked off the stone men to either side, five warriors to one. Tripping them over with ropes and then smashing their heads with huge hammers.

When none remained at the edges of the scree, V's legs gave out and she collapsed. Darrio crouched behind her and she landed on her rump but then fell against him. Her head lolled back and came to rest on his shoulders.

Sarry was next to him, and she sniffed at V, checking her body for injuries.

Darrio looked over the flatland, at the bodies of warriors, Jute fighters, peons and cammers. At piles of rubble, stone limbs and mangled rock heads. And he watched as the rest of the stone army passed them like a slow-moving stream, not even aware of their presence.

They pushed onwards to Qipaz.

"There are too many," V mumbled. "Too many."

"Too many to fight like this," Darrio replied. "Must be another way."

V's eyes closed and Sarry licked the sweat off her mother's face.

23

VIOLYA

ೞ

V studied the wearied faces. She contemplated her red palms for a moment before standing and walking away from the campfire. After hours of springtime drizzle the clear night was a refreshing change. No one followed. She heard Darrio sniff the air behind her. She had purposely walked into the wind, her scent blowing into his face. She knew he would not worry if he could hold her smell.

She needed to be alone. They had waited, powerless, on the scree as the stone army passed. Then they'd pummelled any fallen, but still conscious, stone men to smithereens and burned their dead from the battle. Peqkian, Jute and Dromedar together.

"Not yet, V," Lizya had said, as V had insisted they follow the stonies. "You need to rest. We all need to rest."

V knew her friend, her Head Warrior, was right. "I have failed them." V swept her hand to indicate the pyre of corpses that smouldered in the centre of vegetation razed to the ground.

Lizya had put a hand on her shoulder. "This is an enemy we've never had to face before. We will defeat them."

V had nodded, blinking away the emotion and

swallowing down the disappointment in herself.

They had made camp right there on the flat ground, close to the scree slope that had been their saviour, and filled their bellies, too exhausted to speak. Brin was devastated at the first losses to his small Jute company. He sat silently with his people away from the others. They were in mourning, the Jutes' cheery, raucous demeanour had been replaced with low murmurs and heavy faces.

Darrio and Sarry stayed near her, but she didn't talk to them. Barely spoke to anyone. Just bit on the inside of her mouth until it was raw and bleeding. *My job is to protect my people, and I have failed. The stonies march on Qipaz.*

The only thing that seemed happy was her magic. With hunger quenched from the battle, it was still and content. It hummed through her blood. Tired from use, but a cheerful kind of fatigue.

V found a small clearing away from the camp. There were a few trees still standing, having survived the obliteration of the stone men's march. She stepped over the remains of a giant lizard, trampled by heavy feet. A pain chimed in her heart. She had always wanted to see one of the rare creatures. And now she had, and it was dead. Crushed by an enemy that she had no idea how to destroy.

There must be a way. Think. She sat on a stump wishing she had Emmo there to fuss and soothe her. But her pet was back in Riaow with Joz. V looked at her scarlet palms and concentrated inwards.

What else can I do? V asked the magic.

Whatever you want, it said dreamily.

V focused on the ground in front of her and willed for a campfire to appear. Nothing happened.

I cannot do whatever I want.

You are not doing it right! Brute force is one thing, but this is more complex magic. It's easy to ball up energy and throw it at an opponent. This is not so coarse. It is finer, intricate. With many delicate strands to be woven and connected just so. Practise.

Focusing her attention on one point, V tried again. She felt the magic well up from every part of her body and release through her hands. She aimed them at the ground.

A pathetic flicker appeared, then died out.

The magic sighed impatiently. *Practise.*

V tried again. A flame sparked to life in mid-air, then fizzled away. Again and again V focused, until night became dawn and she had a campfire crackling in front of her. But there was no heat and she shivered. She'd only managed to create an illusion, not a real fire. Almost as soon as she had begun, the clear night had clouded over and a heavy rain had fallen, dousing the real flames she'd attempted.

So, a pretend fire had to do, and she felt like a fraud, disappointed in her magic.

She stood and strode through the fictitious fire. The illusion dissolved immediately, and wisps floated on the wind. As she neared the camp, a horse whickered angrily and V's right foot slid on some mud.

As she righted herself, a memory flashed in her mind of Fin's horse falling, falling. And then was gone.

"They are pushing onward," Lizya said as V reached the camp. "I'll send messengers now to Qipaz and the settlements along the West Way with the order to abandon everything. More lives and livelihoods will be destroyed."

"Please call forward your two fastest messengers," V said.

Lizya shouted orders and soon two messengers arrived. They thumped their fists to their chests.

V returned the gesture. "Go to Mlaw and tell the leaders there to abandon the village but leave as many buckets and barrels of water for us as they can spare. Tell them not to touch the sinkhole pulley system and to gather and leave any strong rope for us. Also, ask for the village's scholar, Urya to wait for us and for the village's warrior Parzya to keep her safe until we arrive. We have need of her," V said. "Take the fastest Fert horses."

The messengers thumped their fists to their chests, and jogged away to do V's bidding.

"Mlaw?" Lizya said. "That's in the opposite direction. That's at the end of the North West Road."

"I have an idea," V said.

***

V crouched low in the rainforest; a view of the sinkhole stretched before her. In the distance, across the gaping split in the ground, she could see the Jute village that had welcomed her and the Peqkian trading party so many months ago now. Mlaw's old warrior Parzya and the young scholar Urya were crouched next to her, positioned on a hill outside the now-abandoned village.

V surveyed their surroundings. It was raining steadily and the animals and birds in the rainforest hooted, squawked and cried to one another. But not one Peqkian, Wolf, Jute or Dromedar could be heard amongst the din. And, like the forest inhabitants, not one of V's army could be seen.

Any moment now.

They had descended from the mountain path ahead of the stone army by a day. Mlaw had been evacuated, all residents and livestock safely located thousands of paces away. Lizya's scouts had come back and forth watching and reporting on the stone army's progress. They were heading straight for Mlaw and hadn't deviated from their route.

It hadn't been easy to turn them around, but they'd done it. V had blasted the backs of the last few lines of stone men, so one by one they started to turn. Her army had split into three. The first group, consisting of any slower members such as the injured and animals, continued onward to Mlaw. The second and third groups were agile and fast. One group rested far ahead while the other kept just in front of the stonies, allowing them to get almost within touching distance, acting as bait. Then they switched.

She'd allowed the stone army to believe they were chasing her and her women, nipping at their heels as they'd chased the Drome army out of Peqkya. The stonies, yearning to obliterate and massacre, pursued them all along the North West Road and over the Melioks. It had taken weeks, but they were right on time.

Rustling announced the stone army's arrival. The canopy shook and the sound of cracking trunks, the crunching and battering of wooden huts and the grinding of stone on stone amplified, drowning out the rainforest noises.

Urya rammed her hands into her ears and Parzya gritted her teeth.

V watched as the stone army fanned out and pressed forward until she could see them at the edge of the forest, before the open ground that led to the sinkhole. To either side of the clearing was dense rainforest.

A deafening, roaring howl went up from Sarry. The signal.

V focused all her attention on the sinkhole. Willing her magic to come alive in her veins, to do her bidding. A red glow emanated from her hands and she heard Urya gasp.

Across the sinkhole, a wave of Jutes came from the edge of the forest, acking, waving spears, banging drums, stomping feet.

The front line of stone men, interspersed with horses and huge tigers, sensing carnage, picked up their pace and charged.

They lumbered straight over the lip of the sinkhole and fell down, down, down. They made no sound as they dropped into oblivion. They windmilled arms and grasped at air for some kind of purchase, but the blackness devoured them.

The second line, seeing their comrades plummet, paused, but the momentum of those behind, and the slick, slippery mud on the ground carried them forward and pushed them over and into that great chasm. Like a thick soup they poured over the edge and into the deep.

The stone soldiers hesitated, uncomprehending. They looked at the noisy Jutes and seeing no obstacle in their path, only grassland, continued forward.

They fell in droves, until the momentum began to stall as the stone men thinned out, with the last stragglers coming from the mountain pass. Lizya blew her horn and the warriors, peons and Dromedars came running from their hiding places in the rainforest.

They positioned themselves either side of the stone men, pulling up heavy rope buried in the mud. Grabbing each end, the warriors brought the rope behind the backs of the stone men and pushed them forward towards the sinkhole. The stonies, all still facing forward, attempted to resist, to turn, but were forced forward and into those in front, who slipped and plunged into the earth's cavernous maw.

V's army had laid ropes a few paces apart all along the grassland. As one of V's group came close to the edge, they dropped the rope and moved away. A second group pulled up another rope behind the stone men to force them forward.

Thousands upon thousands fell into the sinkhole. But those who came behind slowly understood what was happening and didn't charge forward. They spread out to the sides to engage the warriors, Jutes and Dromedars. Soon, no more stone soldiers came from the direction of the village. All that remained were in this clearing. V estimated that out of the initial eight thousand stonies, two thousand remained, a similar number to her army.

The warriors fought in disciplined groups, having learnt from the last battle the stone men's weaknesses. They worked together to tackle one stone man at a time. Tangling legs with rope or tripping the stonies onto their backs and then smashing skulls with hammers. Swords and daggers were useless, as were arrows.

Nameeri led the Dromedars, she shouted orders in the

Drome language. After the first battle, the Dromedars realised they were more likely to survive if they worked together and listened to the woman. They grouped close together and barrelled forward to push a stoney to the ground. Once there, Steely and his peon troop would smash their heads with clubs or go for their eyes with other bits of rock and stone. Once blinded the stone men floundered, flinging arms around but directionless.

V's magic faltered as she watched her army fight. The illusion of a great, flat, grassy plain that she had created over the sinkhole flickered and then fizzled to nothing.

"Stay here," she ordered Parzya and Urya, and then ran down the hill, winding through the damp forest and out into the clearing.

Steely and ten of his men were attempting to take down a stone tiger. The thing was twice the size of Strongcat Otiss and lashed out viciously with heavy stone paws. One swipe knocked Steely backwards and he landed in the sludge and skidded towards the sinkhole. He desperately grabbed out at mud attempting to stop his momentum, but it was useless. He slipped over the edge.

V leapt forward and landed on her belly, grabbing his forearm before he fell. She held him, grit her teeth and yanked. Steely's other hand grasped at the lip of the sinkhole but only found mud. The rain had softened the earth, and before the stone army had arrived V and her warriors had wet the entire length along the edge and churned it into mud.

She reached to her magic and commanded it to lift him. Steely became as light as a feather, the earth solidifying under her body. She pulled him up and swung him behind her.

"Why'd you save me?" he mumbled, dazed.

"You're a warrior. Warriors don't let other warriors die. It is our code."

Steely grunted.

V left the peon and stormed into the battle. She blasted

stone men with balls of energy, smashing them to tiny shards.

She angered at the niggle in her mind from her magic.

I'm tired, it moaned.

I thought you could do anything! I thought we *could do anything.*

We can! But not all at once.

V ignored the complaints and continued, relentless. She blasted stone man after stone man, but more kept coming at her. She roared her defiance. Beside her, warriors, peons and Dromedars fought. She saw a flash of Jutes moving in unison out of the corner of her eye.

There must only be stragglers left. She had ordered the Jutes and the wolves to only fight when there were a few hundred stonies remaining. When the battle had turned in their favour.

She paused to take in the clearing.

As she did a giant stone tiger leapt forward, sweeping her up in its huge mouth and taking her with it over the edge of the sinkhole.

V heard shouts from warriors, yells from peons and Sarry's bone-shaking, roaring howl as she fell.

The stone tiger had clamped its jaws around her waist. She summoned all her magic into her fists and punched both down, pulverising the thing's face. It let go and fell under her.

The light was rapidly fading as they fell deeper.

Fly. V ordered her magic.

She kept falling. Fear scraped under her skin.

Fly!

We've not practised flying… her magic argued.

Fly!

She jerked to a stop and hung suspended in the void. Her body rotated, head upright. She looked down to see the tiger falling, becoming a tiny dot in the black. She looked up and moved in that direction, slowly, then gathering speed until she could see faces peering over the edge.

She shot up past them and warriors cheered, shouted and pumped fists in the air. V glided up and over them, lowering herself onto the ground a few paces from the edge.

Her legs wobbled and warriors, peons and Dromedars were at her side, keeping her upright. She looked out over the clearing. Lizya, Nameeri and Brin were leading the fight against the last remaining stone men, each commanding their people. Darrio was with them.

V took a step towards where the battle still raged but stumbled. Her magic was spent, and she crumpled to the mud.

"Go," she ordered those around her. "Leave me. End this!" She pointed at the battle and they ran towards the fight.

Sarry came bounding up to her.

V pushed herself to her knees and Sarry placed two paws around her neck and licked her face.

"Sarry, go and help your father. I… can't… but you can."

Sarry snuffled at V, put her nose high in the air to catch her father's scent and raced in that direction.

V fell backwards, used the last of her energy to turn her head and watch the battle. She was surrounded by blasted pieces of stone limbs and bodies; a stone hand was by her foot. There were dead warriors, dead Dromedars and peons. *Too many.*

Hands gently lifted her head and placed it back down on knees. The young scholar Urya knelt behind V, as Parzya ran past them towards Lizya. Urya held her cloak out to shield V's face from the rain as V watched the last of the stone men brought down. She couldn't move, could barely breathe. Forced her eyelids to remain open.

She attempted to say something to Urya but it came out in a slur. V's eyes slammed shut. No matter how hard she tried she could not open them again. She had lost all control of her body and her mind felt as thick as honey.

"There are ten stone men left," Urya said shyly, "Lizya and her warriors are tackling them. Old Parzya is there. I've never seen her fight, she's still so strong. The Dromedars and peons are hauling broken stone men towards the sinkhole and then pushing them over. One wolf is helping. But one is injured. The Jutes are roaming the clearing ending any stone men that still live by swarming over them and bashing them with rocks."

V emitted a faint groan.

"I cannot imagine the devastation they would've wrought on Qipaz… or on the capital…"

Urya continued to talk, but V heard no more.

24

JESSIMA

ೲ

J essima watched as Chattergoon demonstrated the move slowly on the stage in the main square. Next to him, his son Philip mirrored his father perfectly.

She stood below the lord, amongst her people. Behind her were five thousand women – her army – all following the same movement.

Jessima clasped her wooden practice sword in her hand, swinging it in an arc and jabbing as Chattergoon had done. The women behind her used sticks or lengths of iron, whatever they could get their hands on that was similar in length to a sword. Some women had made their own practice swords, others had nothing, but practised anyway.

Dotted amongst them and further to the back, were Chattergoon's men and her soldiers, who followed the lord's actions so that the women who couldn't see the stage could copy the poses. Today was sword practice, tomorrow would be archery. They trained for five hours each day.

Two months ago, the day after her rousing speech in the marketplace, the training had been attended by a mere handful of women. But Jessima hadn't lost hope when she'd seen.

She'd recalled the nurse's words about Martha — "there's nothing she'll ask another to do that she won't do herself" — and determined to show the Lianites that their queen would train with them. She had demonstrated the daylight dances to the women who were there, thankful for their presence, and then had stepped down among them to follow Chattergoon's demonstrations.

Most of the women in the marketplace hadn't joined in, instead they had watched her. *The queen meant what she said — she's actually learning to fight, no less!*

Word must have spread across the city because the next day at sunrise there were double the number at practice, and on it grew until the entire square was full.

Ernie had fretted that the city would fail to function with so many women not doing their jobs for five hours every day. Jessima reminded him he was an exceptional overseer, and tasked him with finding a way. And that he did. He'd galvanised the Lianites and put measures in place so the city continued to run smoothly.

In the distance, a constant clanging drifted up on the smoke from the forges. The blacksmiths were busy making weapons and armour. The little pocket quarter, now pointless with no men in Lian and no more orders from Fertilian, had been repurposed as the smithy district. The forges were powered by women and the older men who hadn't gone to war, or by those who had made it through the tunnels from Fertilian.

Lian had become a war factory. As well as the weapons, basic clothing was being produced for the female soldiers including breeches and hardy boots. A hugely productive carpentry industry had sprung up making bows and arrows. Ernie had also organised huge warehouses where food rations were being stockpiled, including preserved meat and salted fish as well as ale and wine.

"We are going to do something different today," Chattergoon announced. "We are going to practise fighting together in lines."

Jessima stood and wiped the perspiration from her face. It was only spring, but it was as hot in Lian as high summer in the Fertilian mainland. The women nearest to Jessima shrugged to each other and murmured. They had practised fighting in pairs, against an opponent, learning to defend and attack. But this was new.

"If we want to win this fight," Chattergoon said, "we need to work together in tight, disciplined formations. Line up in rows facing me."

The women all shuffled into place and Jessima moved with them, at the head of one line.

"Now all face in the direction of the sea," Chattergoon demanded and he jumped off the stage.

He indicated for the first two lines to move closer together, so that one woman stood directly behind another. He indicated for the second two lines to do the same and so on until there were pairs of lines across the marketplace.

"Watch me!" Chattergoon returned to the stage and gathered his sword and a shield. "Women on the front line will have shields, we're in the process of making them. For now, imagine you have them until we have some ready to train with."

He beckoned to one of his men who positioned himself behind Chattergoon. The lord bent sideways and put his left shoulder into the shield, ducked his head below the rim and stood in a split stance, left foot forward and right back.

The soldier came up close behind Chattergoon, placed one hand on the lord's right shoulder, raised his sword, held it over the shield and pointed down. Philip ran in front of his father and pretended to be the enemy with his sword up, and the soldier pretended to thrust his sword into Philip over the top of the shield. The boy mimed being struck, clutched his arm and then flung himself to the stage writhing and yelping in agony.

"He got me, he got me," Philip shrieked.

The women laughed and clapped at the boy's performance.

Chattergoon's head popped up from behind his shield. "Lip, get up."

Philip stood, bowed to the crowd, which elicited a second appreciative round of applause from those gathered.

"Right, get into position," Chattergoon ordered. "Those in front pretend you are ducking behind a shield, you are using it for cover and, eventually, to push forward. We'll learn that tomorrow."

Jessima turned her body and crouched, bringing her left foot forward and planting her right. The woman behind, placed her hand on Jessima's shoulder.

"Queen Jessima," the woman said, "we meet again in decidedly different circumstances."

Jessima glanced up. It was the noble woman who had spoken at Jessima's failed feast all those months ago. She smiled. "Lady Fletchling."

"I look forward to dining with you on the long journey to Fertilian," Lady Fletchling said, "that is, if the offer is still open?"

"It most certainly is," Jessima replied, "although we'll be dining on saltfish and ale rather than the finest fare that Lian has to offer."

"I am certain it will taste just as delicious after a long day's march," Lady Fletchling said. "And what a feast we'll have when we have liberated Fertilian from the Thornes and brought our men home."

She squeezed Jessima's shoulder as Chattergoon's voice boomed from the stage.

Later that day, after Jessima had fed Eddie, she sent a request for her councillors to join her in Ernie's library, which had become her war room.

She'd had maps brought in of Fertilian and Cleland City, as well as all available drawings of Cleland Castle and its walls. She'd sat in many of King Hugo's war planning sessions and knew what was needed, as well as taken advice from those in her war council.

Lord Chattergoon had proved invaluable in their strategizing.

"My father, Lord Horace Chattergoon, helped to plan King Hugo's attack on the false King Benjamin Thorne, while serving the false King as his tunnels advisor," Chattergoon had told her. "I sat in on every one of those secret meetings until I was sent to Lian to deliver the message to King Hugo that we were ready."

"We replicate that plan," Jessima had replied. "It was a success, after all."

"We use it as the foundation. I know more now than I did then. About the tunnels, the city, and the surrounding area, than ever my father did," Chattergoon had replied.

King Hugo had taken back Fertilian from the false King and reclaimed Cleland City with four thousand men. She had five thousand women. But now the Thorne twins, Benjamin's errant children, had many thousands of soldiers and one thousand Peqkian warriors. She would need to do things differently.

Chattergoon was announced and he moved to stand in his usual position next to the window, hands clasped behind his back. "Your Grace," he said as he entered.

"Lord Chattergoon," Jessima replied.

She had attempted informality, had called him Andrew but it had made the man visibly uncomfortable, so she had refrained. She had also attempted small talk, but again, it had been met with a stony face. He had either ignored her or replied with one-word answers. She also asked him to sit every time they met, and every time he remained standing.

The two princes entered next. Ernie was followed by Betsy who yapped at his feet and then jumped on his lap as he took a chair. Prince Charles arranged his religious garments and then sat, running a hand through his thick hair.

Jessima welcomed her council and cut straight to it. "Lord Chattergoon, when will we be ready?"

"The women's army has come a long way, but it is hard to say," Chattergoon replied.

"Weeks? Months?" Jessima pushed.

"More like years," Chattergoon replied in his blunt manner that Jessima had come to appreciate, although his answer made her baulk.

He continued, "The male Thorne soldiers our women will be up against have trained for many years, they are blooded, experienced fighters. And you know the exceptional skills of the Peqkian warriors. We have to give our soldiers the best chance."

"We both know we don't have years. We have weeks, perhaps a month or two. We must strike back before the Thorne twins get too comfortable on the throne. Every day we delay we risk the death of thousands of our men and the entrenchment of the Thorne rule."

Chattergoon's face remained inscrutable. "The women are quick learners, determined and focused. If we can up the daily training, practice drills and formations with weapons then we can be ready in three to four months. Our plan relies heavily on the element of surprise."

Jessima tapped a finger on the map of Fertilian spread out on the table. "And we won't be alone. King Hugo is sure to still have allies. The Cleland royal family will still have people to call upon to assist them. We just need to find a way to tell them we are coming. And we need to get a message out to the Peqkians, I know it is impossible from here. We can only hope they have already had news of their wayward Captain Denya and are inclined to support our cause. Can we send a man through the tunnels? Can he sneak into Cleland City somehow through the gates?"

Chattergoon shook his head. "Not a man, a boy."

"A boy?" Prince Charles scoffed.

"My son," Chattergoon said.

"Can we not send one of your men? It is worrisome that the fate of this attack rests on one child's shoulders," Prince Charles said.

"He is the only one who knows the way. I am not prepared to divulge the directions to another," Chattergoon said.

"Preposterous," Prince Charles said.

"I trust Lord Chattergoon and his actions implicitly, Prince Charles. If he wants to keep this information secret, then it shall be kept secret," Jessima said. She indicated to Chattergoon to carry on.

The lord ordered one of the soldiers positioned outside the door to fetch Philip. In the moments that followed, all in the room were quiet. Only Betsy's light snoring could be heard. Once, Jessima would've filled the space with chatter, with questions, with small talk, entertained as she had been taught to do. But now, she was comfortable with the silence. She deliberated the strategy and looked over the maps again.

Philip came bounding into the room and bowed to Jessima. "Your Grace," he said.

She favoured him with a smile. He bowed smartly to the two princes before rushing to hug his father.

Chattergoon embraced the boy and a flicker of fondness passed over his countenance before he stood him at arm's length.

"Philip, we must take an important message back to your mother. Only you know the way," Chattergoon said.

Philip gaped at his father. For once, Chattergoon's son had no words.

Jessima took the boy's hands, and his astonished face turned towards her. She looked up at him, still unbelieving at this child's towering height. "It is an honourable task. I know this is a dangerous mission, Philip. Those tunnels are frightening, and you will be on your own..."

Before she could finish, Philip grinned. "Frightening?

I'm not scared of the tunnels; I've been running around down there since I can remember. And besides, there's no big scorpions left anymore, Mother saw to that. My sister Joanne has made the run in fifteen days, that's the family record, isn't it, Father? Well, your Grace, I plan to do it quicker."

"I see," Jessima said with wonder and released his hands.

"And Joanne said she'd stopped to see Great Uncle Jarack because he's settled in that village now that he's so old, but I don't believe her. Do you believe her, Father?"

"Great Uncle who?" Jessima said but Chattergoon cleared his throat over her words.

He said, "Tell your mother about everything that has happened here. But only her. Tell her we will be at the estate in four to five months' time. Tell her we need help to recapture Cleland City and to send a messenger to the new Melokai of Peqkya for assistance. Your mother will know what to do."

Philip rubbed his hands together with glee and bumped playfully into his father, tapping at Chattergoon's chest. "How old were you when you carried that important message for Grandpa? Eighteen? Pah, *so* old. I'm only twelve. Joanne will be so jealous!"

"Don't antagonise your sister, Lip," Chattergoon said and quickly ruffled the boy's hair, before dropping his hands again and easing back into his reserved presence. "Philip will leave tomorrow, if you are in agreement, your Grace."

"Agreed," Jessima said.

"It is all very well sending messages to allies," Prince Charles said. "But there is one thing that we have not discussed, which I feel is somewhat critical." He ran a hand through his hair. "Namely, how do we get this army to the mainland? I imagine the tunnel entrance in Cleland City will be heavily guarded and they will simply gut us as we attempt to leave. Plus, can five thousand soldiers traipse through the tunnels? That would be a logistical nightmare, would it not?"

"There must be another way from here to Fertilian," Jessima said. "Perhaps over ground through the Drome desert?"

"Then we will be gutted by the Drome army, instead," Prince Charles replied. "The Dromedars do not take kindly to us traipsing over their land. One or two of us could get away with it but not an entire army."

Jessima refused to be deterred. "Even so, we have no other way to get to Fertilian."

Philip burst out, "You could go the secret overland route, Father!"

Chattergoon's face stiffened momentarily. Philip shrunk into himself and chewed his lip, not daring to catch his father's eye.

"What secret route?" Jessima asked.

"There is a third way, but it is dangerous to traverse," Chattergoon said.

"But you and Mother have done it," Philip blurted, "more than once! And with a whole train of animals, including that Flame—"

"That's enough, Philip! You're excused." Chattergoon pointed to the door. The gangly boy loped from the room.

"Wait," Jessima said.

The boy turned to look at her, a forlorn expression plastered across his face.

"Thank you," she said, and the boy's cheeks burned. Then he beamed.

He grinned at his father and Chattergoon's lips twitched ever so slightly in return. Clearly the pair shared a deep bond.

Would her relationship with Eddie be like this? Would Eddie look upon her with respect and admiration? She prayed that she would survive to see him grow to Philip's age.

When the boy had left the room and closed the door,

Jessima said, "Tell us of this route, Lord."

25

AMMAD

ೞೲ

Jakira's allies were willing and ready. Whaled's men were in place. Ammad's hump tickled with the promise of power.

Our Ruler Mastiq, pathetically devoted to religion, had called a grand ceremony in the Holy Square. High Priest Zeead, Jakira's puppet, had ordered a cleansing of the Drome Ruler.

Jakira and her two sons had not been invited. But here they were, hidden towards the back of the noble families. The Tamadeens milled in front of the stage, surrounded by their slave-guards to keep the poorer Parchaders firmly away.

A dank odour emanated from the crowd. It was scorch season, and the relentless sun hammered down on their heads. All sweated and the dense humidity stifled breathing. Slaves fanned the women, and the men dabbed at their foreheads with cloths in their family colours and decorated with their family crests.

Jakira did not feel the heat. She wore a stunning, bright turmeric-coloured silk gown under her plain tunic. Her skin glowed, and her scent of aniseed and nutmeg wafted about her and cleansed the putrid sweat-stained air. She was calm and oozed confidence. Two and a half months of scheming, bribing, manipulating and negotiating had led to this day.

Although she was hiding, wearing clothes that made her seem as if she belonged to a lowly noble clan, she commanded a presence that made people step out of her way, lower their eyes near her and speak in a respectful tone to their neighbours so as not to disturb or offend her.

Whaled had insisted the trio have armed guards, but Jakira declined.

"A poor Tamadeen family that has fallen from favour does not have money for guards," she had said. "And besides, my sons are accomplished swordsmen and competent in hand-to-hand combat. Nothing will befall me while I am with them."

Selmi was anxious. He hung close to Jakira, always slightly behind her, out of her immediate view. His eyes skirted Ammad's and he purposely looked everywhere but at his mother. He had voiced his concerns, had spouted nonsense about equality one too many times and Jakira had reprimanded him. Ammad wasn't certain what their mother had said or done, or whether Selmi had received a slipper beating, but he'd fallen in line, kept his mouth shut and his views to himself.

For months now Ammad hadn't heard his brother utter a single word. He was rarely in the villa, sneaking out when Jakira wasn't there. Where he went, Ammad had no clue. And, frankly, didn't care. He hoped his brother was off carousing with whores, but knew it was more likely the dullard was in some wiseman's library salivating over dusty tomes.

The crowd squeezed closer together as Parchaders poured in from the lanes and alleyways that led off the Holy Square. The heathen scum loved a cleansing, especially of a ruler who had soared in popularity for many scorch seasons but, following the failed invasion of Peqkya, tipped over into the most loathed person in all Drome. The poorer Affarah peasants gathered around the edges, taking up position wherever a space presented itself with no concern for others' personal space.

Ammad was jostled and elbowed. People stomped on his foot and knocked into him. His temper flared and he longed to shrug off his sweat-damp cloak, kick out and headbutt back, fling a few of his throwing knives in the foreheads of some peasants. Selmi, too, was being hustled, but he swayed and absorbed every bump, as if being buffeted by the wind atop the crater wall. Jakira, however, stood perfectly unmolested. The crowd flowed unconsciously around her, surging forward but leaving a small serene orb around the woman.

"This reminds me of a time when I was younger," Jakira said, more to herself than to either of her sons. "When I witnessed the assassination of Our Ruler Shaan in this square."

"You saw grandfather die?" Ammad said; his mother had never mentioned that before and he had a fleeting interest in learning more about her past. Then it passed.

She said nothing more, gesturing instead towards the stage.

A huge glass tank was centre-stage. Holy men had been filling it with buckets of congealed blood gathered from the temple, and other unsanctioned places. It was now full, and the musicians were taking up position at the side of the stage.

A lone drummer began proceedings, soon to be joined by more drummers and ouds. Bellydancers writhed onto the stage, their ankles and wrists tinkled with the bells tied there.

A line of temple enforcers – the holy heavies – filed onto the stage behind the dancers and lined up along the back edge. Each was dressed in their ceremonial robes, complete with daggers hanging from belts. Temple enforcers did the High Priest's bidding, and while considered holy, were essentially just brutes who guarded the Qacirr holy clans' interests.

Official members of the Wakrime family stepped onto the stage, met with an odd mingling of boos and cheers as if the mob couldn't decide if they were happy or enraged at the royal family.

The music quickened and the bellydancers sashayed to either side of the stage and ululated in a high-pitched tone.

High Priest Zeead stepped onto the stage. Dressed in his finery, he waddled forward with his strangely oversized bottom. His head was shaved in a line from ear to ear over the top of his head. This hair butchery was believed to bring him closer to God. Ammad believed it made him look like an idiot. The remainder of his knee-length hair was split into two. Each section had been braided, woven with gold thread and adorned with small bells. The braids had then been twisted and pinned into an intricate mass that hung in an ugly bulk around the man's shoulders. He wore a red robe, patterned with elaborate shapes stitched in gold and white thread.

Zeead waved to the crowd and a rumble of voices – predominantly positive, Ammad felt – replied from the mob.

The music reached a frenetic pace and cut out. A single drumroll sounded. Our Ruler Mastiq, trailed by his elite guard, made his entrance. The roar that greeted him was decidedly hostile.

Ammad counted ten Cuttarrs. They stood to either side of the stage, fanning out as the bellydancers swanned down the steps and out of sight. As well as this group of cutthroats, a further fifteen loitered off-stage, just out of sight.

They stood in the exact formation Whaled had said they would. The ex-Minister of War had overseen Mastiq's security for almost twenty scorch seasons, until he was unceremoniously sacked. The hairy beast had trained many of the cutthroats who now surrounded the ruler on stage. Whaled was still highly respected amongst the elite guard, Mastiq's decision to fire him had been met with ill feeling.

Now, thanks to Jakira's assistance, many of the cutthroats were in Whaled's pocket. Ultimately controlled by his mother. Most of these Cuttarrs were in on the plan, but not all. Ammad was always surprised when he heard there were still some honest men in Drome who could not be bought.

Jakira, through the ex-Minister, had negotiated with the Head Cuttarr, a friend of Whaled's. He would select men to protect Mastiq who were willing to turn a blind eye to whatever befell their charge. Understandably, they wouldn't want to interfere in any way with God's will at the holy ceremony.

Mastiq was adorned in a golden robe, that, although handmade by the best tailors in the city, still stretched across his massive pot belly. His shoulder-length hair, now mostly grey, had been freshly dyed with henna and had a reddish-purple tone. He shuffled forward next to High Priest Zeead and in front of the glass tank. Mastiq moved awkwardly, chin down and head rigid, to keep his monstrosity of a headdress balanced on his head.

He looked out across the crowd and raised his arms. "My people, for twenty scorch seasons I have served you. And in twenty scorch seasons God has never once demanded my blood. But He is unhappy with my servitude. I am forever His faithful servant. I serve Him today by shedding blood as He has demanded."

The crowd hollered and cheered at each utterance of the word 'blood'. That was the only reason they were here.

Our Ruler Mastiq, dipped his head to High Priest Zeead in deference.

The holiest of holies dipped his head in return and then turned to the crowd. He gave the religious gesture, touching his hands to his heart and then up to the sky and sweeping them out to the crowd. "I share God's love with you."

The horde faithfully returned the sign of God, each replying with a mumble of "I receive it from you with thanks."

"Our Ruler Mastiq has ruled Drome for many, glorious, happy scorch seasons. We should celebrate his achievements, his love of his people and his eternal kindness," High Priest Zeead said in his high-pitched voice.

Mastiq beamed with pride as the members of his family who stood on stage clapped their approval.

"We should all celebrate this man, rejoice in his presence, thank God for creating Mastiq and giving him to us," Zeead continued.

Ammad grew impatient with the praise and studied the crowd. Although Zeead had an odd voice, he held the multitude captive. A hush had settled over the square and all eyes were firmly on the priest.

Zeead paused. He took a step away from Mastiq and leaned towards the crowd. His demeanour changed, and his tone matched it. He pointed an accusatory finger at Mastiq, emphasising each word with a stab of anger.

"But *he* has lost his way. This man has erred from the path demanded by God. He has failed God. God is angry about the failure in Peqkya. God is angry that those mountain heathens still run amok, unabated. Our Ruler must shed blood to appease Him. He demands blood! He demands this man be cleansed to redress that failure, to prove his worth to the Almighty," Zeead yelled.

Mastiq's knees wobbled and he raised the back of his hand to his forehead. Advisor Farack ran to steady him.

"It is time for Our Ruler Mastiq to be cleansed, to prove that he is worthy of God's blessing, to atone for his weaknesses."

A slave and a holy man rushed forward. The slave carefully removed Mastiq's monstrous headdress and the holy man took Mastiq's arm and guided him up the steps on one side of the glass tank. The High Priest turned with a sweep of his robe and waddled up the opposite stairs.

Both men stepped into the pool of blood. It sloshed

around their thighs. Zeead, with a warm smile, indicated for Mastiq to kneel. Tenderly Zeead put his hand on the back of Mastiq's head.

"God, see this man! See how he cleanses for your forgiveness! Forgive him of his sins," Zeead yelled and pulled a ceremonial knife from a pocket of his robe.

As if resisting a great counterforce, Mastiq held out his shaking arms, obviously not relishing this moment. The ruler glanced away and cowered from what he knew would happen next.

Zeead grabbed one of Mastiq's wrists and slashed it brutally with his knife. Mastiq squealed in pain. The crowd squealed in delight. Zeead hacked at the other wrist. Mastiq panted and blustered as he held his arms as steady as he could manage. The priest watched as Mastiq's blood flowed into the tank.

"Our Ruler Mastiq sheds blood for God, he bathes in blood for God," Zeead announced as he thrust Mastiq's head forward and under the surface of the congealed blood.

Selmi muttered, "such camel shit," and shook his head.

Mastiq didn't struggle. Not at first, anyway. The crowd held their breath along with Mastiq. Ammad held his too and counted.

Just as Ammad thought his lungs might burst and he let out his breath, Mastiq began to writhe. He pushed his head up against Zeead's heavy hand, thrashed his arms on the front and sides of the tank with deep thumps, and kicked out backwards. Zeead stared up to the sky, as if communing with God, his arms solid in their task of keeping Mastiq's head beneath the surface.

Blood splashed over the sides of the tank. Muffled groans and grunts emanated from behind the glass.

His father's death throes were a joy to behold. Ammad grinned gleefully. Jakira truly was a genius. No one would suspect her of orchestrating this holy ceremony to murder the ruler.

People around him gasped and held palms to their cheeks. One woman fainted. She fell in a slump among her neighbours, who ignored her, too engrossed by the spectacle on stage.

"Are you sated?" Zeead screamed upwards. "Are you sated?"

Zeead convulsed and let go of Mastiq's head. He raised his arms to the sky and shuddered.

Mastiq's body floated in the tank. It was obvious to all that he wasn't going to sit up again. The Wakrime family gathered on stage sobbed and wailed. Advisor Farack, horrified, attempted to scale the steps but was held back by a brute of a temple enforcer.

Zeead's body convulsed again and he shook out his arms. He lowered his head to stare at the crowd.

"He is not sated," the High Priest yelled. "He is not sated!"

Whispers rippled across the crowd. Mastiq was dead, who would be next?

"He demands more blood," Zeead screeched.

The High Priest turned to face the Wakrime family, and he made a show of pointing at each in turn as if his hand was guided by another force.

"You!" Zeead finally shouted, his roving finger coming to a halt at the new Crown Prince, Hallid.

"No," screamed Mastiq's official wife, Hallid's mother.

Advisor Farack, attempting to wriggle free of the temple enforcer's grip, shouted, "Cuttarrs! This is lunacy. Our Ruler is dead. Hallid is Our Ruler, protect him."

Hallid didn't move. His eyes, normally dulled with drunkenness, were alert and frightened. He shook his head at High Priest Zeead and refused to move.

A temple enforcer shoved Hallid toward the tank. He resisted, attempting to run from the stage, but was surrounded by enforcers. He dropped to his knees, his plan to be an unmovable dead weight.

"I will not cleanse! I am the ruler now, and I will not

cleanse," Hallid shouted. "I order this ceremony halted. I order you to take your hands from the flesh of a royal!"

"God does not hear your petty orders," Zeead said. "He wants your blood."

The enforcers hefted Hallid, held his body aloft as he thrashed and twisted. Shifting Mastiq out of the way, they deposited him in the tank of blood.

They held him in place as Zeead grabbed Hallid's wrist and held it high for the crowd to see as he eagerly sliced it with his knife. He did the same with the other wrist. Hallid sobbed and screamed.

"Crown Prince Hallid sheds blood for God, he bathes in blood for God," Zeead yelled and submerged Hallid's face down in the tank next to the dead body of his father.

The mob was enraptured. For a second time, all held their breath. Unlike his father, though, Hallid struggled from the start, providing exceptional entertainment with sploshing blood flying everywhere. The temple enforcers held him under, staring up to Zeead in awe and apparently waiting for direction.

Once again, Zeead did his convulsing and "Are you sated?" performance. And, as before, when it was clear Hallid had stilled and horribly drowned, Zeead yelled, "He is not sated!"

The spectators stirred, too stunned to do anything other than gape and murmur under their breath.

Mastiq's family gathered on the stage included uncles, brothers, nephews, cousins, as well as his official wife and various favourite concubines. Mastiq had twenty-three known children, and only the favoured adults graced the stage. Along with the Wakrime family entourage, stood Mastiq's loyal advisors, including Farack, and those Tamadeen nobles Mastiq considered his close friends. This one-hundred strong group huddled together. Some made attempts to exit the stage, but to no avail.

The entourage was gathered up by temple enforcers. The women cried and the men attempted to break free.

The bemused crowd watched High Priest Zeead, impatient for his next words.

"He demands more blood," Zeead hollered and indicated the entourage.

Each of the holy heavies drew a gleaming dagger. As handsomely bribed to do, the Cuttarrs didn't so much as twitch a finger as temple enforcers slashed throats, pierced hearts, stabbed guts. The Wakrime entourage fell one by one, bellowing for rescue. Their blood spattered the boards of the stage, gushed through the gaps between planks to douse the sand that lay underneath.

Ammad whooped, he couldn't help himself. The theatre of carnage playing out in front of him was spectacular. Jakira cuffed his ear with a sharp glare.

Only the important members of Mastiq's extended family were on stage and had been massacred. But Ammad knew his mother despised loose ends. Although he wasn't privy to all the details of her scheme, he expected Jakira's heavies to be slaughtering those Wakrimes who had remained in their homes.

Zeead came to the front of the stage and slumped heavily. Holy men fussed about him, fanning him and holding a cup of water to his lips. They helped him to his feet.

Clinging onto a holy man as if exhausted, Zeead looked out towards the dumfounded audience.

"He is sated," Zeead said in a relieved, quiet voice. "He is satisfied."

Holy men clapped and cheered, "Praise God!" they yelled. Swept up in the moment, the onlookers applauded too. It started as a tentative hum but exploded into a deafening cacophony.

Zeead smiled and waved, lapping up the attention. After a while, as the applaud wilted, Zeead held up a palm for silence. The spectators obeyed.

"He has chosen His ruler. A man worthy of our adoration, a man worthy of fulfilling God's will. God has told me, the holiest of holies in all of Drome, of His demands, and we will obey. God has spoken."

Zeead brought his hand to his brow and looked out across the crowd as if searching for God's chosen man.

"Ammad el Wakrime. Where are you Ammad? God has told me you are here."

Jakira gave him a look that seemed to say, *don't fuck this up*, as she stepped to the side, the crowd parting around her. It allowed a small space to form around Ammad in the densely packed crowd.

Then a light shone down on him, and he smiled.

"High Priest Zeead, I am here," he replied.

The crowd edged away from him and he basked in their gawking attention.

"Come here, my child, for you are God's chosen one," Zeead announced from the stage. He beckoned Ammad forward.

It was a slow walk Ammad took toward the stage, and the hushed crowd split into two forming a tunnel for him to strut down. A constant bright light shone on him from carefully angled mirrors. Jakira had ordered Medi to position himself and others in high places around the Holy Square and to discreetly reflect light from the mirrors.

A temple enforcer came to meet Ammad and respectfully escorted him onto the stage to stand next to Zeead.

"Ammad el Wakrime, God has chosen you to rule Drome. He has chosen you to enforce His will in this world. What do you say? Do you accept God's will?" the High Priest squawked in his high-pitched voice.

"Holiest of holies, High Priest Zeead, I am humbled to be God's instrument in this land. I will honour His demands and execute His will. I will not fail Him," Ammad replied with a small bow.

"But he has no arms," an anonymous voice shouted from the crowd.

If Ammad had identified the heckler, he would've split

their tongue in ten places. How he wanted to sneer, but softened his face instead. He had to keep up the humbled act. Jakira had schooled him on his part. "People love a show," she had said, "we'll give them a show." He was giving this scum the performance of a lifetime. *Mama will be proud.*

And, he thought, channelling all his loathing and venom towards the owner of the voice, *my arms are growing back.*

Zeead turned in the direction of the voice. In a vicious tone, he shouted, "He has given his arms for God. Fighting God's holy war in Peqkya. Mastiq did not even go to war, he luxuriated here in his palace. And I doubt that intoxicated, oblivious Hallid – his nominated Crown Prince – even knew there was a war happening. What have each of you given to God? Hmm? What? Nothing, I imagine. Nothing!"

The audience, suitably chided, piped down.

"As the voice of God, I declare the new ruler of Drome: Our Ruler Ammad el Wakrime. May God see him and bless him." Zeead clapped Ammad on the back a little too fervently.

Ammad glared at him momentarily before smiling broadly once again. It was at this point he should've been waving to his loyal subjects. A few weeks and he'd be able to do that again.

The holy men on the stage cheered. A few strategically placed slaves in the audience cheered. Unable to resist the exuberance, the mob joined in.

Ammad smiled and nodded, smiled and nodded. *I am the Ruler of Drome. Finally. If my cock worked, I'd fuck a hundred, no, a* thousand, *women. Starting with the choicest meat from Mastiq's harem.* Infuriatingly that thought didn't even raise a twitch in his dead groin.

Zeead flapped his arms for silence. "Until Our Ruler Ammad takes an official wife and bears a son, his God-approved second-in-command, his Crown Prince, shall be his brother, Selmi el Wakrime."

The spectators, never having heard of Selmi before, but spurred on by Jakira's clapping slaves, applauded too. They looked around confused, as if Selmi would be spotlighted and identified within the mob.

The High Priest stepped back and gestured to Ammad to take centre stage. Ammad was only too happy to oblige.

"People of Drome, God's people, *my* people, I am honoured to bask in God's blessing," Ammad announced in a clear, steady voice. *Don't shout*, Jakira had instructed, *simply elevate your voice so that it carries, it is much more powerful.*

"I am honoured to be God's chosen one to rule over Drome. I will do as He demands, I will not fail Him as my father and brother did. I will not fail you, Dromedars," Ammad continued.

The spectators appreciated his words, whooping and applauding. The musicians even banged their drums in approval, no doubt paid in advance by Jakira.

Swept up in the magnificence of the moment, Ammad went off script. "Each ruler commissions his own headdress and mine will be the most elegant, the most opulent and the most expensive of any ruler before me. It will be breathtakingly spectacular, cast in gold, jewels and fine fabric. I will unveil it to you in spectacular ceremony, my people."

The spectators continued to clap, but a confused hum passed from one onlooker to the next. *I know something that will get them going,* he thought.

Ammad strolled up the stairs to the tank, now full of dead Wakrimes. He indicated the two bodies with his foot.

"These monstrosities failed our God and failed us. We will not mourn them. There will be no forty days and forty nights mourning as is custom when a ruler dies. No! And there will be no lavish burial either. No! They do not deserve it. Instead I, personally, will ride out into the dunes and will dump Mastiq's body in the desert, unmarked and unmourned. There he will rot and be forgotten," Ammad declared to what he thought would be deafening ovation.

Instead he heard Jakira hissing at him from the side of the stage. She jerked her head in a gesture that Ammad understood to mean, *get the fuck off the stage you dumb calfling*.

Confusion and then annoyance swept around the spectators. Only the clapping slaves continued with an uncomfortable jubilance. Ammad looked out across the swamp of frowning, unhappy faces.

"My people, God's people. I will come before you again soon," Ammad said and promptly exited the stage towards his mother.

In the litter that bore Jakira, Selmi and Ammad back to the palace, Jakira sat next to Ammad. She put her hand around his neck and touched her forehead to his. For the briefest moment, Ammad thought she was pleased with him.

She dug her sharp fingernails into his flesh.

"Ow," Ammad moaned.

Selmi contemplated his knees.

"You stupid boy," his mother hissed, "don't ever speak out of turn again, do you understand? The people don't give a piece of camel dung about Mastiq's death. They do, however care about the forty days mourning period, where, by tradition, they are not required to work. And they care about the burial, where, by tradition, they are freely given plentiful wine and food for four days."

"How was I supposed to know that?" Ammad shrugged and pursed his lips.

"This is why you don't say anything unless I tell you to!"

Jakira's fingernails dug deeper and Ammad fancied he could hear a pop when one pierced his skin. Blood dribbled down the back of his neck.

"You have no idea how to sweeten the people, how to make them love you," Jakira said.

"Nope, I have no idea," Ammad agreed and sweetly kissed Jakira on the cheek. "Will there be a feast at the palace when we arrive, Mama? I'm starving. And I want a wash and an oiling down. Being around so much street scum leaves a slimy film on the skin, can't you feel it?"

Jakira shoved his neck before removing her hand. "Do exactly as I tell you, do you understand, flesh of my flesh?"

Ammad farted, much to Jakira's disgust. Selmi held his forearm up to cover his nose. "Ahhhhh, that's better," Ammad said. "I've been holding that in for hours. Mama, I'm now the all-powerful Ruler of Drome, I can do whatever the fuck I like. You are my advisor. I'll listen to your counsel, but I won't always follow it."

Jakira whipped off her slipper and slapped Ammad viciously, climbing on top of him for a better aim. The litter wobbled as the slaves carrying it attempted to readjust their balance without toppling over.

"I understand, Mama, I understand!" Ammad grovelled, cowering from the blows.

***

Whaled and Jakira sat on plush floor cushions in the palace's opulent courtyard. Water tinkled from fountains and raised pools reflected the night sky. The courtyard overlooked the crater's great lake and the palace gardens. Behind them the palace glittered and twinkled as candles and torches could be seen through the huge floor-to-ceiling stained glass window in the grand hallway. A massive glass chandelier hung from the centre of that room, complemented by smaller chandeliers in each corner.

More slaves than Ammad could be bothered to count stood in a semi-circle around the sunken seating area, leaving the view to the garden open. They fanned large palm fronds in an attempt to move the scorching heat around the occupants. Each slave was slick with sweat and had cloth stuffed into their ears under an elegant cap. Jakira had ordered the slaves to wear this new item of clothing to prevent eavesdropping, but also to look the part. Jakira didn't want the palace slaves to look untidy.

It was one week after the assassination and she had made numerous other changes at the palace. Including removing all staff, sycophants and slaves who had been loyal to Mastiq or had become too powerful. She had established Medi as the head of the household and bestowed Mastiq's old quarters on Ammad.

She'd taken full control of the governance of Drome, too, to Ammad's great relief. She had picked his advisors and appointed numerous administrators; had organised various official ceremonies which Ammad simply had to reside over and say a few appropriate words in a few appropriate places.

Ammad was too busy training with Samark, bulking up his growing arms and riding his new camel. He was also obsessed with turning Artaz into a weapon. He diligently created elaborate drills for the boy, which progressively grew in difficulty and duration, but at the same time ensuring the child enjoyed himself. Ammad knew Artaz needed to unconditionally love his big brother and unquestioningly do his bidding. If the brat was going to wield destruction on Peqkya then he was going to need to be strong, loyal, and compliant.

Tonight, though, Ammad had been ordered from his sundown session to attend his mother and her pretend-lover. Selmi had also received a summons.

Both brothers stood before their mother. Ammad wiped his brow, with the small hand of his left arm, now long enough to reach. Selmi shifted his feet awkwardly. His hands were stained with ink and he clutched a book, as if disturbed from some utterly dull study session.

Jakira flicked a wrist to indicate they could sit. Ammad plonked down on a cushion and sprawled his legs wide to allow any breeze possible to cool his testicles. Selmi remained standing, clearly impatient to leave.

"Ammad, flesh of my flesh, you must take a wife and produce an heir, and fast," Jakira said with no preamble. "A spectacular royal wedding will please the people, to appease them after you cancelled Mastiq's mourning period."

"Yes, Mama," Ammad said.

Jakira sipped her wine and placed a hand on the hairy beast's knee. Now reinstated to his previous position as Minister of War. Ammad's nose wrinkled.

"Whaled and I have agreed that you will marry his daughter Razanne," Jakira said.

Ammad frowned. The hairy beast's daughter. *I hope her moustache is not as dark as her father's.*

"No!" Selmi yelled with more vehemence and passion than Ammad had ever seen spew from his brother.

Selmi stood with his fists clenched and his face raging.

Relishing his brother's distress, Ammad said, "Gladly, Mama, but I've never met her, I do hope she's not as ugly as her father."

Whaled snorted at him, then shouted to a slave, "Fetch Razanne."

"No," Selmi said again, taking a step towards Jakira. "Mama, you can't."

Jakira's tone turned icy. "This has nothing to do with you, flesh of my flesh. It is a good match."

Razanne entered. She wore a simple dress and had the same stained-ink hands as Selmi.

"Father," she said and immediately walked to stand next to Selmi. A bit too close.

Selmi looked at her with affection and she smiled up at him. The flesh of their arms brushed together.

Ammad gawped. She was beautiful. He wondered if Whaled was truly her father. As he looked harder, a twinge of familiarity pricked at the outer corner of his mind. She had similar golden-brown eyes to Jakira, and long, lush brown hair. But the resemblance to his mother wasn't it...

I have seen that high-born brow, those eyes before. At the Hand of God sculpture outside the city's crater wall when I returned from the Urakbai village pillage. Was that really Selmi who I saw? And was he with this beauty? Why?

"Razanne, my love, my world, my precious, the time has come for you to marry," Whaled said, in a loving fatherly tone that made Ammad's stomach lurch.

Razanne beamed, her eyes dazzling with pure joy. She took hold of Selmi's hand, touched her lips to his knuckles and held it against her chest with a deep sigh. She didn't notice Selmi's pained grimace.

Whaled's brow furrowed at his daughter's gesture. His tone darkened. "You are to marry Our Ruler Ammad."

A small groan escaped from the beauty's mouth. She clutched Sel, nuzzling her face into his neck. Sel placed his arms around her to keep her steady.

"Razanne," Whaled growled. "Come here, now."

"But, Father," she pleaded, turning her face to look at him but keeping her ear against Sel's torso, "I am in love with Selmi. I want to marry Selmi!"

"You have no say in the matter," Whaled thundered. "You are to become Our Ruler's official wife – a great honour – and you will produce a male heir to the throne. He will be the next ruler."

It was Selmi's turn to plead. "Mama," he said, "I beg you to reconsider. Razanne and I have been in love for many scorch seasons, ever since we shared the same classes with wiseman Alli. The one you so cruelly beheaded."

Jakira sprung from her cushion like a snake striking prey, and slapped Selmi fiercely. "I do not care about love! This is duty. Ammad and Razanne will wed next month. Medi, take Selmi to his rooms and lock him in there."

The hulking head slave, who had been hidden in the shadows, approached Selmi and gently prised him from Razanne. He placed a hand on Selmi's shoulder and steered him away. Selmi continued to hold Razanne's hand until just their fingertips touched.

The beauty watched Selmi's retreat and fell to her knees. She wept bitterly, slapped at the tiles and pulled at her hair.

Before his little brother was out of earshot, Ammad clapped and said, "I can't wait to bed this beauty and produce a palaceful of heirs! We'll fuck for forty days and forty nights."

Razanne shrieked. Ammad watched with glee as Selmi's entire body tightened and then slumped. Medi shoved his brother out the door.

26

VIOLYA

V floated in the cool water of Inaly Lake. The sun was shining, and the city was warming up.

Five weeks had passed since the stone army battle. She couldn't remember the aftermath, had spent much of the journey home and the following weeks flitting in and out of consciousness. That morning she'd woken early in a strange bed with Emmo snuggled against her side. It had taken her a while to realise she was in the Melokai apartment in Riaow. She'd last been in these rooms with Gwrlain clutching the dead bodies of Melokai Ramya and the baby Terya.

It had been scrubbed clean, aired, made fit for the new Melokai. Although V had specifically said she'd sleep in the barracks, she knew her councillors had made the best choice by bringing her here to recuperate. Her presence in the barracks would've caused unrest and worry.

This room had belonged to Melokai Ramya, and Melokai Naranya before her. And every Melokai before that. It was where she was supposed to be.

She had flung open the shutters to a bright day, changed, left Emmo tucked up in the sheets and jogged to the shore of Inaly Lake with Monya and the clevercat Amya. The warrior had been sleeping on a small cot

311

outside V's room, just like V herself had done when she had guarded Melokai Ramya. The difference being that Amya was sprawled across Monya's chest, purring. Ramya's clevercat Bevya had always curled up in a corner, her back to V.

"Come on," V said, "I want to go for a swim."

Monya had jumped up and stared at V, not hiding her surprise. V was lucid for the first time in weeks. Amya stretched out her back and mewed sleepily.

As they jogged to the lake, V noticed with pride that all traces of the Drome invasion had now been scrubbed clean from the Riaow streets. There were Riat women up early going about their business, bustling and directing peons with livestock and produce for the market, unaware that an army of rampaging stone soldiers bent on destruction had been heading straight for their doorsteps.

"Tell me what happened. I do not remember much," V said to Monya as they found the path to the lake.

"We finished the last of the stone men and sent every last one over the edge and into the sinkhole. Every piece of stone that had once belonged to a stoney was gathered up and flung over the side. We burnt our dead and gave thanks for their lives. Then we helped the Mlaw scholar, Urya, set up the pulley system once again with the Jute village on the other side and Brin was hoisted across to carry the message of thanks to the villagers who had drawn the attention of the stone men. He also sent messages back to their Potenqis about those Jute fighters who had died."

"How many dead?"

"Five hundred and seventeen Peqkian warriors, twenty-two Jutes, forty-eight peons and sixty-seven Dromedars. Six hundred and fifty-four all told."

V nodded sadly. "And the wolves?"

"Both survived. Sarry took a stone fist to her ribs, but she's healing up well. We've been training together."

Amya found a shady tree to lounge under as V and Monya had run through their daylight dances, stripped off and waded into the cool water. Monya now waited on the shore, drying off and giving V some space.

V angled herself to face the Mount of Pines. The charred hill was desolate, empty. Sybilya's presence truly gone. The statue sat in the middle of the scorched circle where Sybilya's magic had turned the prophetess to stone.

We stopped them, Stone Prophetess. Be at peace.

Sybilya's magic had cursed her. But V's magic exhausted her, took an immense toll on her body.

But you flew! Her magic replied indignantly. *I raised you up and out of that great chasm in the ground.*

Yes, and I almost killed myself with the effort.

V swam back to the shore where Monya and Amya met her as she emerged from the water.

"Amya, call my councillors to a meeting."

A few hours later V sat in the council room, Emmo curled up and snoring in her lap.

Joz had embraced her and kissed her cheek when she'd entered the room, Brin had grinned his big filed-teeth grin and Lizya had slapped her on the back. The other councillors were more reserved, welcoming her back and taking their seats.

"Food is being distributed, no one is without shelter or nourishment," Joz was saying enthusiastically. "Peqkya is learning to be self-sufficient again. The foodstuffs we had previously imported from Fertilian, Drome and Troglo are no longer coming into the country. So, in return, the exports we traded with these countries are being redirected to our own people. The carpet and cloth trade has suffered, as has the lotions and potions trade, but the women who run these trades have been offered new posts in the redistribution of previous exports and peons have been reallocated to farming and food production."

"You've been busy," V said with a smile.

"Oh, you know me, V, I love a challenge." The Head Trader clapped her hands together.

V looked to her councillors. "What can we do to help those who have suffered from the destruction wrought by the stone army?"

"We've sent a delegation of scholar, trader, speaker, teller, mother and warrior to assess the damage and plan what to do next," Head Scholar Chaz said. "We will rehome those who are displaced and find new work for those who have lost their livelihoods."

V nodded her approval.

The shy Mother of Mothers, Naomya, raised her hand and tentatively said, "My Melokai... ah... V. We have conducted a thorough count of all our children following the invasion and have updated our practices to account for the additional peens that will pass into peonhood. This has thrown up an... ah... discrepancy." Naomya wrung her hands nervously.

"Go on," V encouraged.

"There is one peen missing."

A shiver tickled down V's spine as she remembered Sybilya's words: *I saw a vision of my death. My time would end when the three discovered their magic. That time has come. The third has awakened. A peen. You must save him from corruption, V... hurry... hurry.*

At the time, these words had not made sense to V. But her instinct told her this was the third.

"Did this peen show any signs of being different, of having The Sight?" V said.

Naomya nodded vigorously. "Yes, Mother Samya said he had a physiological oddity. He was born with both male and female sex organs but as he grew, he was presenting more as male, so they treated him as such. He was tested at birth initially for The Sight but showed no signs. However, he was due for another test."

"What is his name?" V asked.

"Artaz," Naomya replied.

"How old is he?"

"Four years."

"*Is?*" Head Speaker Zecky said, tapping her pencil against the table. She was pregnant, her seventh child, a small bump swelling against her tunic. "Why do you think he's alive? If he's not in the pen then he's likely dead."

"I don't think he is," V said. "Before she left our world, Sybilya spoke of a third awakening, a peen. I think it is this child, and we need to find him."

Zecky flicked her thick braids out of her face and scribbled on her parchment. "I'll get a message out to the people to search for a missing peen. Check outbuildings and so on. We'll find him, V."

V beckoned for Amya and gave her a message. Monya opened the door, and the ginger clevercat ran from the room.

"We defeated an internal threat, but at a great cost. We must give our warriors a proper send off in the city to mark their passing," V said.

"Agreed," Zecky said. "I'll organise it. Five hundred and seventeen gave their lives, I believe?"

"No, six hundred and fifty-four. Warriors, Jutes, peons and Dromedars."

"You mean to honour peons? And *Dromedars?* The invaders?" Zecky sputtered.

"Six hundred and fifty-four gave their lives to protect Peqkya, to protect you and every Peqkian. That is how many shall be honoured."

Zecky hissed through clenched teeth and scratched a note.

"That is a kind gesture, V," Brin said with a small bow. "We are honoured to mark the passing of our dead with those who fought with us."

"The peons who fought and survived the stone men are now camped with the peon novices," Lizya said. "I promoted the leader, Steely, to captain, and he's now training the younger ones."

"You promoted the leader of the peon rebellion to a captain?" Zecky spat. She shook her head in disgust.

"He is now passionate about Peqkya, about protecting his country," Lizya said, her voice like steel. "He is also loyal to V, his Melokai. The peon fighters will be a formidable force. We need the numbers, Zecky, or will you take on every one of our enemies on your own, hmm?"

Zecky huffed and shifted on her stool, fanning her face with a sheet of parchment.

Amya meowed from outside the door, scratching her claws down the wood.

"Monya, please show in Darrio and Sarry," V said.

The wolves padded into the room, looking around them and sniffing. Sarry nudged Monya playfully on the arm with her nose as she passed. Monya kept a straight face.

Head Teller Omya steepled her fingers and Chaz watched the wolves intently, as if noting down in his mind every detail. Until now, V had kept them apart from her council. Like the Dromedars, their presence in the city was tolerated but not welcome. Many were still angry at the wolf war, still prejudiced against the wolves after years of conditioning.

V gestured for the wolves to sit. They shunned the stools and sat on hindlegs, head and shoulders looking over the table.

"These wolves have fought bravely with us. They have proved their friendship and I formally accept them as our allies. Peqkians and wolves are no longer enemies."

Joz clapped excitedly and Lizya slapped Darrio on the back.

Sarry stared at V, as the Melokai continued. "Sybilya chose to mark this wolf, to communicate with this wolf. She has The Sight. Sarry is to be welcomed and honoured in Peqkya."

Sarry glanced at Monya but the young warrior remained impassive.

"We will open up the south Trequ Valley to the wolves," V said. "Together Peqkians and wolves will live in peace. That land once belonged to the wolves and Melokai Tatya took it from them. The wolves attempted to take it back to great loss of life on both sides. The wolves have shown themselves to be true to their word. They want peace between our kinds. And I want peace too."

"Well, that is a remarkable decision, V," the Head Scholar said.

"She's been sat on her arse for a few weeks, plenty of time to think, eh, V?" Lizya said.

V smiled. "I've made another decision."

Lizya whistled in mock astonishment as V gestured to Monya. The young warrior opened the door to let in the Dromedar woman, Nameeri. Zecky hissed and Naomya gasped, clasping a hand over her mouth.

"Nameeri, take a seat," V said.

The Dromedar woman positioned herself next to Omya, who recoiled with an expression of utter repulsion.

The Head Teller had been silent for the entire meeting, but now she snapped, "You bring not one, but two enemies into our council room? Where we rule our great country. It is a disgrace. What was Sybilya thinking when she chose you?"

"That V would be a damn fine Melokai," Lizya said, thumping a large fist on the table. "The wolves and this woman fought bravely for us. Show them some respect."

Naomya jumped. Omya, however, did not startle and sneered at Nameeri.

"Omya, I understand your concerns," V said. "I am a warrior first and the Melokai second. My warrior training tells me to recognise enemies, to be alert for the worst in everyone. But my instinct tells me the wolves and the Dromedars will be strong allies. They will play a part in the protection of Peqkya. And as a Melokai, the safety of this country, our people and our way of life is my priority. Sybilya trusted me, I ask that you trust me."

Omya glared at her for a few heartbeats and then dipped her head. "Forgive me, my Melokai."

V raised a palm and smiled. "Nothing to forgive. We are each entitled to our opinion."

Joz reached out to Omya, put an arm around her shoulder and squeezed the woman into her chest. Omya grimaced at the physical contact but Joz beamed.

"We're all in this together," she said sweetly.

Omya melted slightly. "Hmm."

"That we are," Lizya said. "Anyway, back to Nameeri here, or we'll be hugging each other all day."

Joz released Omya and turned back eagerly to give her full attention to V.

"Nameeri disguised herself as a man to enter our country as a soldier, to spy for her clan. This clan opposes the ruling elite in Drome," V said. "She has been learning Shella, so that she can tell you her story, and so that you can ask of her your questions. Nameeri," V gestured for the Dromedar woman to speak.

Nameeri dipped her head in thanks. In accented Shella she said, "My clan is the Khumarah. We once had magic. The ruling royal clan, the Wakrimes, and the other clans Qacirr holy, Tamadeen noble, Affarah peasants, Yuurnan desert villagers and Eqmadeh nomads do not have magic.

"It was the Khumarahs who founded Vaasar. They were destroyed when the *Ferts*," Nameeri spat the word and scowled, "invaded and claimed that city as their own. The Khumarah who remained in the desert and on the outskirts of Parchad have been persecuted for thousands of years. The powerful Wakrime, Qacirr and Tamadeen clans have always feared our kind. They murdered us, wiped us out.

"We hide in plain sight in the crater and we gather in the slums outside the crater wall. Many Khumarah are now slaves," she shook her head sadly. "There are perhaps a few thousand of us left. A handful of our kind still have traces of magic, and we practise our religion in secret. In Drome there is one god, one bloodthirsty, vicious god. Religion is corrupt. Belief is engineered to keep the majority Affarah peasants in their place, and to make the Qacirrs money, and in turn to fund the Wakrime royal clan and keep them in power."

Nameeri took a deep breath. "I ask for Peqkya's aid to help my clan overthrow the Wakrimes."

The councillors, rapt with the Dromedar's speech, broke their stillness at this entreaty. They shuffled on stools, shot astonished looks to one another and muttered.

"The zhaq Wakrimes," Lizya sneered.

Zecky tapped her pencil to her lips. "And what would the Khumarah clan do if you were to gain control of Drome?"

"We would abolish slavery, abolish the corrupt religion and customs, distribute the wealth fairly. There are starving people in Drome, there needn't be. There is water and food for all. The Wakrime family waste water on plants and gardens at the palace. Water that is so desperately needed by the poor inside and outside the city."

The Head Speaker waited to see if another councillor would speak, when none did, she said, "How do you plan to keep control when there are only a few thousand of you?"

"We have friends in high places. In the Wakrime clan. We have secret supporters who would assist our cause."

Omya squinted at Nameeri, nose wrinkled. "And once the Khumarah are in power? What then? Another invasion?"

"We do not believe in war, in needless death. We would trade peacefully with Peqkya. We want you as an ally. This atrocity, this invasion was a disgrace. This is your land and your people. We do not want to take that from you. We want to restore Drome to glory, to equality, to humanity."

"I understand we have plans to punish the Drome rulers for the *atrocity*," Omya retorted. "What should we care about who takes control in the aftermath? They will not dare to step foot in Peqkya again."

Sarry gently scratched her claws on the table and all looked at her.

In perfect Shella, she said, "We need Drome on our side. Without them we cannot defeat our bigger foe."

"Our *bigger* foe?" the shy Mother of Mothers, Naomya, asked with alarm.

"From the east," Sarry replied. "It is coming for us all. It does not distinguish between borders, between Peqkians, wolves, Dromedars, Jutes."

A ripple of unease spread across the room from her daughter's pronouncement. The councillors shot uneasy glances at one another.

"Sybilya's prophecy," Chaz said, and his white patch flushed red with worry.

"Our enemies to the east are the Ferts," Nameeri said, confused.

"It is not the Ferts," Sarry said. "Fertilian will be your ally, to face what *is* coming."

Nameeri hissed at the idea. Drome had never forgiven its neighbouring country for stealing Vaasar.

"We face something powerful coming from further east than Fertilian," V said. "Our world has larger problems than deposing your corrupt ruling clans. If we assist you, then you will readily assist us when the time comes. That means you fight alongside Fertilian."

Nameeri pursed her lips. The Dromedar woman met V's eye and then respectfully lowered her head. "You have my word, V. I have the ear of the head of the Khumarah clan. We do not take your assistance lightly. If you choose to help us in our cause, we will honour any terms you care to make."

V smiled in acknowledgement.

"Yes." Lizya thumped a fist on the table. "It's time to go to Parchad."

"You're not going, Lizya. You'll be staying here to keep Peqkya safe," V said.

"Zhaq. Can I give up the Head Warrior thing for a

while? Go on a break?" Lizya said to shocked tuts from some of the older councillors.

V laughed. "Absolutely not."

Lizya gave an exaggerated huff. "I'll make a plan with Nameeri and send our finest warriors."

"I'll be going," V said.

The room bristled as councillors shifted on their stools and mumbled.

"You are the Melokai, your place is in Peqkya," Zecky voiced their concerns. "It is too dangerous, we cannot risk losing you."

"I go to Parchad."

This time there was no argument from her council.

Peqkya needed Drome on their side, this had turned from a revenge attack for the invasion into a strategic move. She had warriors to lead the mission successfully, but she would finish the worm.

The Crown Prince Ammad was hers.

***

V took a long, deep breath and sunk back on the mossy earth. Emmo scampered off her shoulder to snuffle through the undergrowth.

Bamboos swayed in the gentle breeze and a calm settled over her. The spongy moss was damp, the morning dew not yet evaporated. The earth's moisture touched her skin, soaked through her leathers and tickled at her neck. It made her feel more alive, more connected.

She would leave tomorrow for Parchad after days of preparation, and this was her only chance to spend some time alone with her daughter.

Beside her, Sarry sniffed at the earth. She padded on all fours in a circle, nose to the ground, before slumping down in a curl. Her front paws touched V's thigh and her nose brushed V's hip.

"Another was here," Sarry said.

"My friend, Emmya," V replied and a pain stabbed at her chest.

Sarry huffed. "She is no longer with us. I hear it in your voice."

"Her death was the fault of the cammer prince, the same who murdered Melokai Ramya and her baby." V's heart banged in her ears.

Sarry didn't reply. The mood tightened.

V loosened her jaw and unclenched her palms, patting the clumps of moss that she had just pulled up back into the earth. *I'm not here to dwell on that anger.* She listened to the cats' faint purring. They had followed V and Sarry out of the city, had settled in amongst the bamboos. They kept their distance and remained out of sight.

"Let's talk about our magic," V said.

Sarry's head shot up eagerly. "How does it feel to you? How do you know how to use it?"

"It bristles in my blood. A fizz, a tickle. It feels to me like another being, an *other* inside of me. When I use it, it's either instinctive, or else I have to focus hard to summon it, to make it do my bidding."

"It is within you," Sarry said.

"Yes. Although I don't feel it all the time. I cannot hear it now. My magic sleeps."

"But if you summoned it, it would come."

V nodded. "I do not know what I'm capable of and that makes me cautious to use it."

"Why?"

"In case it overcomes me and I hurt friends and not just foes. In case I destroy the things, places, people that I love."

Sarry's ears twitched. "My magic tells me truths. I cannot tell you the future or what might happen, but it's a feeling I have. There's nothing physical I can do."

"Shall we practise?" V's fingers scrabbled in the moss and came upon a small twig. V turned on her side so she was facing the wolf and placed the twig between them. "Can you lift that?"

Sarry's gaze turned to the twig and her head cocked to

one side. A few moments passed. The twig remained stationary. Sarry looked to V.

V looked at the twig. *Lift.*

Her magic rolled up and down her body, as if waking up, like a cat stretching out after sleep.

I could pull up every bamboo from the earth and toss them into the sky!

Lift the twig. That is all.

V brought the twig up and tapped Sarry on the head, between her ears.

Sarry swatted at the twig, rolling on her back and kicking up all her paws. V brought the twig down to tap Sarry's belly and Sarry swiped at it playfully before snapping her powerful jaws around it.

The wolf rotated onto her front and with a paw holding the twig down on one side, she chewed at the other end, the wood splintering.

V laughed as her daughter chewed happily. "Your magic will break out. I'm sure of it. I think you have a greater power in you than simply knowing the truth."

Sarry snorted as she continued to gnaw and V stroked her cream fur. The wolf did not seem to notice, still occupied with chomping on the wood.

I should tell the council, my people. I am proud of my daughter, but it is too soon. They have had to deal with so much, so many changes. They are adapting, but could this news tip them into rebellion? Her instinct told her it wasn't time. For now, she would keep the secret.

V's hand flew off Sarry as the wolf spat out the splintered twig and leapt to all fours. She shook her head and snarled at the bamboos. Her ears were pinned back and her entire body shivered, her fur rippling. Her orange eyes turned to V.

"Pappy and I must return to Zwullfr. I… I saw something. I cannot un-see it. We must return." The wolf took off at a run towards the city.

V found her feet, grabbed her caterpillar and sprinted

after Sarry, the cats yowling as they followed.

27

GWRLAIN

ॐ

"Why did you lie to Melokai Ramya?" Robya said, wringing her hands.

So, here it was. After months of conversations, the shy scholar had finally plucked up the courage to ask.

Gwrlain sighed. They'd been talking about the moon and stars. Her voice had been calm and her breathing relaxed. But now, his senses told him that she chewed at the side of her mouth and held her breath. She sat wrapped in a cloak on her makeshift bed outside the cave entrance and in front of a small fire. She liked to sleep out of the cave on clear, warmer nights, to set up her little bed and write her journals, full of that day's discoveries. One of Fin's warriors was stationed inside the cave, a little way off to give the scholar some privacy.

Fin had sent a clevercat messenger back to Riaow, but months later, there had still been no reply. So, the Peqkians waited. Fin and her warriors trained and continued their disciplined lives, vigilantly watching over the five women and their Trogr lovers in Peqklo. Two more women were pregnant, their linked males singing to their bellies each morning in their desperate hope for a daughter. The peons continued to take their turns with

325

Lulac, and Robya doggedly quizzed Gwrlain to eke out every scrap of new knowledge she could.

She had practically followed Gwrlain around for the past five months learning about the Trogrs, about their capital Lauago, and their customs.

At first, Gwrlain found her insistent questioning frustrating, preferring to be in the thick of the sprawling Trogrs in Lauago singing his lament for his lost loved ones. But soon Robya's eager curiosity became a distraction, and then… enjoyable. He found he liked to talk about his people and their history. He had done so with Ramya, but he'd only had limited Shella and could not find the right words in his basic vocabulary.

The scholar spoke to him fluently in the Troglo language. Ramya, his love, hadn't found the time to learn, although she had always promised she would.

On clear nights, like that night, he sat out with Robya under the stars and talked for hours. Until now, however, she had stayed well clear of the topic of Ramya and Terya, and how he came to be in Peqkya in the first place.

Robya shifted awkwardly in the silence that hung following her question. He heard her heart rate quicken and could smell her unease as her sweat glands oozed.

He had never told Ramya the truth and would never be able to. That knowledge ate at his soul.

Trogrs did not keep secrets from one another. It was impossible. They could sense lies with subtle changes in the body, increased sweating, a rise in the pressure of the blood, a quickening of breath. These humans were too reliant on their eyes to notice such things.

He sighed. Robya's breathing quickened, in anticipation or apprehension he couldn't be certain.

"I was sent to Peqkya to link with a female and mate with her. To produce a female child. The Trogr species is dying. We have one purpose, and one purpose alone. Daughters. A link is so strong, so instant and unyielding that the hope was my linked female would convince more

Peqkian women to return with me to Troglo in the hope they, too, would find males they love."

"Why were you sent?" Robya asked.

"I was the last male Trogr to have produced a female child."

"So, you'd had a baby before Terya? I thought Trogrs only matched with one female?"

"They do. But when the female numbers reached a critical level, the females agreed to open their wombs to all in the hope of pregnancy and a daughter. At first, females were paired with a male for a longer duration of time, not how you see my mother and sister today. I mated with a female who was linked to another, and we produced a female baby. She was the first female child in many tens of years. But both mother and baby died not long after the birth. I was the last male to have produced a female. It was deemed likely I would father a girl again and so I was sent out from the caves."

"Why tell Ramya that you'd been banished?"

"We knew from trading that Peqkians were a nation of strong women and hardened warriors. We created an elaborate lie to gain the Peqkians' sympathy and trust. I could not simply walk into Peqkya and tell you I wanted sturdy females with healthy wombs to breed with."

Robya's pencil scratched something on her parchment sheet and he heard her shuffle her papers.

He continued, "I saw how Ramya dealt with other nations, how the Fert messengers asking for her help were sent back to their country. I witnessed the war with the wolves first-hand. I couldn't risk her sending me away. Even though we were linked, Ramya would've always put her nation and her people first if she believed I was a threat."

The noise of Robya's scribblings greeted his confession, and her silence spurred him on to speak.

"I loved her. But I also love my people. I cannot allow them to die. I stuck to the lie we had created, and I bided my time. I told my people to be patient, that Ramya was with child and that I would ask her for ways to join our people when it was the right time. But then the Dromedars…"

Gwrlain's breath hitched in his throat as the roar of his devastation overwhelmed him.

"As you know, all we care about is daughters to continue our kind."

"You told your people to be patient? How?"

"I sent and received swifts with messages."

Robya whistled and jotted something on her parchment. "Well, if Ramya had heard all that then you'd be in some serious shit," she mumbled, barely audible.

Gwrlain tensed. He knew it to be the truth. "Would she have forgiven me?"

"You knew her better than I. Would she?"

Gwrlain's heartbeat throbbed in his ears.

Robya's papers shuffled once again and then stopped. "Who is Bance?" she said, deftly changing the direction of the conversation to check off all her facts and spare Gwrlain his pain.

"Bance was once my sister's link. He died many years ago."

"So Bance didn't save your life by dropping you near the Peqkian border, as you stated?" Robya said.

"No."

Robya blew out heavy breath through her teeth. "How do I know you're not lying now?"

"You don't," Gwrlain replied. "But know this, I hate myself for lying to Ramya. It will always haunt me."

"Why didn't you do your death-rattle on the Dromedars? To save Ramya and Terya?"

"Because my death-rattle would've killed Dromedar and Peqkian alike. It does not distinguish. The only beings it does not touch are the Trogrs. I made a terrible mistake by not killing the scar-faced man. I thought I'd done enough but he stabbed Ramya in the leg. That was her undoing and it was my fault.”

The memory of Ramya stumbling with Terya tied to her back flashed in his mind. Their blood mixing as they died.

“You don’t want to take revenge on the Dromedars?” Robya asked.

“No. Would revenge produce daughters? We are not interested in power, or land, or money or revenge. All these trifles the Peqkians care about mean nothing to Trogrs. Survival and reproduction are what we are obsessed with. We have no desire for bloodshed or want to know what is happening in the countries outside our caves. We are not concerned by unimportant squabbles, by warring over what small piece of land we can take from another race. I have proof the Peqkians and the Trogrs can breed and produce healthy daughters. This is our future.”

Robya placed down her parchment and wrapped her cloak tighter around her shoulders. She looked up. “How do you know there is a moon and stars when you can’t see them?”

“Our vibrations travel straight up, there are no obstacles in the way. A long time later we hear the faintest echo in return.”

“So you can sense birds high up in the sky?”

Before Gwrlain could reply, the warrior stationed inside the cave entrance shouted, “Robya, Gwrlain, you are needed urgently in Peqklo! It’s Freya.”

***

“A girl,” Robya announced as she held Freya’s squalling daughter in the air. The scholar was no medic but knew enough about childbirth to act as midwife.

Freya’s linked Trogr took the baby from Robya and started to sing, to craft her name-song. The four Peqkian women fussed around Freya. Fin and her warriors stood guard, keeping back the Trogrs that crowded the small cavern. Gruack and Lulac had been carried at the head of a procession from Lauago to Peqklo to preside over the birth. And even Gwrlain's ancient father Daneil had made the journey.

During the birthing, a chant of "Let it be female" had drowned out Freya's screams. Now, every Trogr in the place quietened, listening to the baby's name-song being so lovingly shaped in verse by her father.

When he was done, Gwrlain joined his voice to the many Trogrs there to sing the baby's name-song. As they sung, the baby quietened, feeling this song in the depth of her little soul for the first time and knowing it expressed her very essence. The linked male handed the baby back to Freya and it suckled on her breast.

She smelled so much like Terya.

"She has pearlescent grey skin, a mix of her mother's black and father's white. She has pink eyes and a fine silky down covers her body. She looks strong and healthy. What I'm told Terya looked like, the first child born of a Peqkian and Trogr," Robya said aloud, no doubt to remember for her journals.

When the name-song had been repeated three times, Gruack cleared her throat. "We shall all love this child. This daughter of Troglo and Peqkya will be raised and loved by every one of us. We will teach her to sing. We will teach her our ways and when it is time, she will choose her partner, we will not force a Trogr male on her. That must be her choice, if she does not find a male to link with then she will be free to find a Peqkian male to love. And through her, our race will continue," Gruack paused. "I am growing old. My pregnancy has failed. I fear it was the last."

Gwrlain hung his head, as did the other Trogrs. He joined his voice to a desperate wail from each Trogr, that filled the cavern.

"This is sad, but Lulac, my dearest daughter, our Living Goddess is pregnant. And two more Peqkians are with child. Let us hope for daughters, my sons."

"Let it be female," each Trogr chanted.

Lulac patted her belly. "I cannot be certain until I give birth, but I think it might be from peon seed."

Fin grimaced at Robya's translation, but the Trogrs sung joyously.

Gwrlain stepped away from Peqklo and made his way back to the Peqkian clothes he had dropped at the entrance to Lauago all those months ago. They remained precisely where he'd left them, untouched, but now layered in dust and cave dirt.

He crouched and picked through them until he found a pocket which contained what he was looking for. He unscrewed the cap of the small glass bottle and inhaled deeply. The smell knocked him off balance and he fell against the rocky tunnel wall. He howled in pain at the memory the smell induced.

When his voice was hoarse and he could wail no longer, he stood and returned to Peqklo.

The cavern had quietened, with Trogrs dispersing back to Lauago. His parents and sister had been carried back to their rock.

Freya reclined in the centre of the cavern, holding her daughter to her chest. Her linked male crouched beside them singing a sweet song to soothe the baby.

"Here," Gwrlain said in Shella and handed the glass bottle to Freya.

She took it and studied it before looking up at Gwrlain for an explanation.

"Ramya used to smooth this lotion on our daughter Terya's skin. It has a beautiful scent."

Freya smiled in thanks.

He made his way through the tunnels and out of the cave entrance. He sang Terya's name-song with all his might into the night sky.

The vibrations and sounds of footsteps alerted him to Robya's presence. She came to stand by him and listened to his song.

When he had finished, she said, "You lied. And that is

despicable, and incomprehensible. But I believe you loved Ramya."

Gwrlain raised a hand to his heart. His skin flushed pink as the emotion rose to the surface.

"And she loved you back, Gwrlain. That was obvious to all. I'm certain she would've forgiven you."

28

TOBY

πє

Toby bounced on his bollocks on the bare back of a donkey. He was tied to it and led by Arthur Thorne on a stallion. Toby hadn't spoken a word for what felt like an eternity, but he'd still been gagged for this occasion. He watched silently and waited for the moment.

Four months had passed since the Thornes had taken Cleland Castle, but a King or Queen of Fertilian had still not been crowned. Lord Clement Pullman had done precisely what he had threatened and kicked up a fuss. And, being on friendly terms with Lord John Iddenkinge, Clement had managed to delay the wedding between Lord Iddenkinge's daughter, Grace, and Jeremy Thorne. Much to Charlotte's extreme irritation.

After months of negotiating, Charlotte had yielded and agreed that Mary would be crowned Queen and, by marriage, Clement would be King. Arthur had bowed to his mother's demands. Clement had declared a hunt in celebration and here they were in the forest outside of the city.

Clement was surrounded by his men, all watchful and suspicious. His son James had remained in the castle with Mary, too sick to leave his bed. Arthur had brought a handful of Thorne men, including his simpleton son,

Jeremy. Lord John Iddenkinge, now too elderly to participate in vigorous hunts, had declined the invitation.

It was the first time in months that Toby had left the castle, being shuffled between Arthur's bed chambers and the dining hall. He breathed in the fresh air and observed carefully.

"What the hell is that, Thorne?" Clement had said as they gathered on the outskirts of the city.

"My pet," Arthur replied, patting Toby's knee. "I'm breaking him in."

The Thorne men, all except Jeremy, had laughed but Clement had pursed his lips and his men had stayed silent. It wasn't honourable to openly abuse your high-ranking prisoners. Toby stared at his trussed hands and remained passive.

And at that they'd set off into the forest. Toby bouncing painfully on the back of his donkey.

He watched as Arthur deferred to Clement and flattered him shamelessly. It was clearly an act, but Clement, wary at first, began to lap it up. The Thorne men were equally polite to their Pullman counterparts. Soon, the ale and conversation flowed and laughter peppered the air as the men relaxed.

"Will you have a drink, Clem?" Arthur asked loudly and held out his wine flask.

"Haven't touched the stuff in years," Clement replied.

"But you'll soon be King! I think that calls for a drink," Arthur insisted.

Clement, bolstered by his men's good spirits, grabbed the flask and downed the contents. He burped, dashed his wrist across his lips and laughed.

Arthur and his men laughed with him. Clement gestured for another flask. He gulped it down to more cheers and merriment.

"I think I saw a boar!" Jeremy piped up suddenly. "It went that way." He pointed his pigstick spear deeper into the forest.

"Come on, lads," Clement hollered, inebriated, and kicked his horse in the direction Jeremy had pointed. The group followed.

The tree canopy thickened and blocked the bright spring sunshine. In the gloom the party searched the undergrowth and stuck their spears in randomly. The group stretched out and Arthur fell to the back, leading as he was a slow donkey. Clement was up ahead and the Thorne and Pullman men had mingled.

"Are you sure you saw a boar, Jeremy?" Arthur shouted.

His son woke from his dreamworld at the sound of his father's voice. He looked behind him. "There it is!"

And at that moment, Toby knew. *Murderous bastards.* This is why he suffered Arthur's torture. To learn. He shook in his saddle, mmm-ed through his gag, anything to try and get Clement's attention.

Arthur ensured no one was paying them any notice and delivered a swift, powerful punch to Toby's face. Stunned, he quietened.

As if on cue, a huge boar with great tusks charged from thick undergrowth. The men all pulled their pigstick spears. But as if staged, the Thorne men were on the inside of the Pullman men and moved their horses to either side of the path the boar was headed. This forced the Pullman men out of the way too.

Although the Thorne men feigned stabbing with their spears, they deliberately missed. But in the commotion, the Pullman men didn't notice, all eager to get pigsticking themselves.

The boar, thus directed, charged straight at Clement Pullman. He readied his horse and attempted to sidestep the boar, ready with his spear to stick the thing. The group followed in the boar's wake, spears up and ready.

Clement stabbed at the boar as it charged him, landing a precise hit. The boar, mad with rage, turned and charged into the fray. The nearest men piled in. Jeremy hung back and Toby watched as Arthur half-heartedly spurred on his horse.

Arthur reached his son and sniffed dramatically.

Jeremy jerked and shouted into the scrap, "Someone brave needs to get off their horse and stick that boar once and for all!"

Clement took the bait. He raised his hand.

Toby shook off his daze and shouted incoherent warnings at Clement through his gag and tried to break his hands free.

"Shut your pet up, would you, Thorne," Clement slurred.

Arthur obliged with a second punch for all to see. Toby's head rung and one eye swelled to a slit.

The ruddy-cheeked lord slid from his horse and lurched toward the rear end of the boar while his men and a number of the Thorne men kept the front end of the beast occupied.

But a Thorne man nearest to Clement poked the hog viciously, when he should've let it be so Clement could get close to stab it from behind.

The boar whirled and saw Clement. It charged.

Toby sat at Arthur's feet under the table. Arthur had fastened a dog collar around his neck and held the leash in his hand. The Thorne twin jerked at the lead and Toby came forward to rest his chin on Arthur's knee. Toby knew this game now. Arthur held some meat between his fingers and Toby gently took it using his teeth. Arthur caressed his head.

Toby ate the meat, played the game. He needed to keep his strength up for when he slaughtered the man. His time would come.

"You do treat your pets despicably, Artie," Charlotte said with a tut.

Arthur laughed and tore off another piece of pork. He threw it on the ground a few paces away from Toby.

"Fetch."

This was new. Arthur released the leash so he just held the end. Toby didn't move. He was not about to pick up food from the floor. Arthur beckoned to a nearby guard who kicked Toby's ribs. Toby flinched but stifled a yelp. He wouldn't give the bastard the satisfaction of hearing his pain.

"Fetch," Arthur repeated.

Toby edged forward on hands and knees and went to pick up the meat with his bound hands.

Arthur jerked at the leash and Toby's head whipped back. "Bad boy, pick it up with your teeth."

Toby glared at Arthur. The bastard winked at him. Toby swallowed his pride and picked up the meat from the dusty floor with his teeth.

"Good boy, bring it to daddy."

Toby crawled back to Arthur's knee and spat the meat in his outstretched hand. Arthur once again threw it.

"Fetch," he said.

"Oh, Artie. Enough," Charlotte said.

But Toby obediently went and picked up the meat and brought it back to Arthur.

"Eat it," Arthur said. He enjoyed this torture.

His time will come, Toby thought as he chewed and swallowed the gritty meat. *I need the strength.*

Arthur's attention turned from Toby as the door to the hall swung open and his twin stumbled in. Mary was dressed in black. A fine gauze veil over her face.

"How can you eat?" Mary wailed as she reached the table and clutched the back of her usual chair to steady herself. "At a time like this? We should be in mourning. My husband died this morning. I am a widow! My child is without a father."

"I'm wearing black," Charlotte said. "And we are enjoying the fruits of the hunt."

"The boar that killed Clem. How can you eat it?"

"Why not, it's excellent," Arthur said as he stuffed a

hunk of meat into his mouth. The juices dribbled down his chin before he dashed them away with a pristinely clean napkin.

Mary pointed a shaking finger at the stuffed carcass on the table. "My husband is dead because of that pig!"

"Well, dear, he shouldn't have got in the way," Charlotte said and looked at Denya.

The Peqkian warrior was oblivious to Mary's whimpering, and continued to eat heartily. Although Toby knew the warrior would have a handle on the situation and be ready to spring to action should the need occur.

"Get in the way? Get in the way!" Mary's voice increased, the pitch a squeal. "Clem was an experienced huntsman. The boar…" Mary braced herself, standing up straight. Her knuckles went white as her cheeks flushed red. "It is said that the boar was goaded to charge Clem by one of Arthur's men. One of its tusks pierced Clem through the heart. You…" Mary jabbed a finger at her mother. "You planned this."

"Nonsense," Charlotte dismissed the accusation with a brief wave of the hand. "Clem was drunk, it was an unfortunate accident." She popped a hunk of pork in her mouth.

"You… you *murdered* him!"

Charlotte slowly put her knife and fork down and fixed her daughter with a glare that made the woman cower. "Shut up, Mary. What a lot of nonsense is spewing from your mouth. Sit and eat. You are a widow now. You need to stay strong for James. To help advise your brother when he becomes King."

"What?" Mary whispered, and then held herself taller, faced her mother. "No, I am Queen. Clem made an agreement with you. *I am Queen!*"

"Dear, you have no King now. He's dead. Sadly killed by a charging boar on this morning's hunt, if you recall. Arthur will be King. The coronation will take place in three days. I'd like you to arrange the flowers, my dear, to take your mind off poor, dead Clement."

Mary slumped to the ground. Toby dipped his head to watch her under the table. She sobbed and clutched at her face, distraught.

Spit fell from Mary's mouth as she muttered, "My mother and brother have just murdered my husband. Oh, my dear Clem. We were played for fools."

"Dremond," Charlotte shouted to an old servant who hovered outside the door. The thin old man – who must've been in the service of the Thornes for an eternity – entered, with hands clasped in front of him. "Take Mary to her rooms and ensure she is made comfortable. She is mourning her husband and needs time to gather her wits."

Dremond came forward and lifted Mary from the floor and ushered her out into the hallway as she bawled and muttered.

The three around the table continued to eat in silence. Arthur fed Toby scraps of meat and the odd vegetable. Toby ate. He played along. And he knew what would come later in Arthur's bedroom and fought back the vomit that rose up his throat.

Your time will come, bastard. I'll make you suffer for every violation of my body.

***

Toby was tied to a chair. Arthur's guards had come in earlier to bind his hands and legs and stuff a rag in his mouth. Toby didn't fight them. He conserved his strength.

He had been placed near the window, out of the way, as hand servants fussed around Arthur. He was being preened for his coronation in every manner possible. The hand servants trimmed his hair, on his head, face and also pubic area. They shaved the rest of his body and then massaged oils and lotions into his skin. One clipped his toenails, another his fingernails. Another still worked on his face. Beetroot stain was pinched into his cheeks, black charcoal mixed with water carefully painted onto his eyebrows and lashes. He sat naked as the servants groomed him, eyes closed and a serene smile plastered on his lips.

The False Queen was announced as 'Queen Mother'. Charlotte strode in with her Peqkian warrior bodyguards. Not Denya. The Peqkian captain, Toby assumed, was busy securing the castle courtyard where the coronation would take place in mere hours.

"How is it that I am ready, and you are not?" Charlotte chided. A servant moved a chair and positioned it for her in front of Arthur. She didn't recoil at his nakedness.

"I must be well-anointed and well-appointed for this day," Arthur said. "It's the most important of my life, Mother. I will be King."

"Indeed, I have not forgotten." Charlotte pursed her lips in a motherly smile and rolled her eyes. "And how much longer will you be? We have important guests to greet."

Arthur waved at a servant to reply.

"We have the scenting to do," the servant said without looking at the old hag.

"Ah, my favourite part," Arthur sighed.

There was a kerfuffle at the doorway and the old servant, Dremond, burst in, with two Peqkian warriors and two Pullman guards.

Dremond simply looked at Charlotte and she frowned. "What is it?" she asked.

The old servant shook his head sadly. "My Queen, it is Mary and your grandson James. Mistress, they have died."

Arthur sat upright and shooed away the servants. They waited, poised to powder and primp.

"Died?" Charlotte said. "How have my daughter and grandson *died*?"

Dremond spoke, his old voice still strong and unwavering. "Just moments ago, she and James jumped from the window of their chamber in the tower. I saw them fall as I entered the room. She held James' hand, whispered to him the entire time."

Charlotte brought a hand to her mouth as her eyes brimmed with tears. They did not fall, however, unlike her daughter and grandson. Charlotte's face hardened. She indicated the guards, "Can you confirm this?"

A Peqkian warrior stepped forward. "Yes. We checked their bodies where they fell, both dead. A warrior on watch saw them come to the window and jump. They took their own lives."

Arthur leaned forward and touched his mother's knee. "I didn't think she'd have that in her," he said.

Charlotte blinked, straightened her back. "Can they be seen from the castle courtyard?"

"No, they are on the other side of the wall," the warrior replied.

"Leave them where they are. We will deal with them later. Prepare for the coronation." Dremond, the guards and warriors filtered out of the room. "Well?" Charlotte glared at Arthur's servants. "What are you waiting for? Get the King ready."

The servants buzzed around Arthur once again. He watched his mother closely.

Charlotte thumped a fist on the arm of her chair. "I loved that girl, I did. How could she do this? How could she steal attention from you on your big day?" She leaned forward and cupped Arthur's cheek. "Well, I still have you, my sweetling, and that is all that matters. You will be King. You will take the throne in honour of your father, my beloved Benjamin. Fertilian is yours."

Toby watched the coronation from a balcony overlooking the courtyard. It brimmed with nobility. No common folk, Toby noticed. They had likely been killed during the siege or fled the city before the Thornes arrived. He didn't think that Arthur would be the kind of King who cared for his people anyway.

As Arthur had left his chamber in all his finery, he'd ordered his guards to move Toby, still bound in the chair and gagged, to the balcony to watch.

Toby had seen the royal party file in, the other guests already stationed in their places. He surveyed the crowd and saw his treacherous niece Matilda, Hugo's eldest daughter, next to her elderly husband Lord John Iddenkinge. The old man was straight-backed and firm, denying his advancing years. Their daughter Grace stood behind. And next to her stood her betrothed – Arthur Thorne's son Jeremy.

Toby wanted to hurl abuse at Matilda for her betrayal, for her stupidity in trusting the Thornes. Instead he grumbled and snorted through the gag. She did not look up; she couldn't hear him cursing her. No one could see or hear him.

Arthur gave a speech, but Toby couldn't hear it. The roar of the crowd marked when it started and then again, when it ended. The new False King and his party left towards the great hall to feast and celebrate. The courtyard slowly emptied. Those invited to the feast headed that way, those dismissed proceeded towards the main castle gate and stables.

Toby remained on the balcony, forgotten. The sun reached its pinnacle and then dipped, the sky darkened and it rained apples and pears. Toby's entire body ached in its bonds. As the rain splashed on his cheeks, he fought against the urge to weep. Sounds of the revelry drifted up towards him from the windows of the great hall. Music and singing, laughter and women's squeals.

Late into the night, three guards came to collect Toby. He shivered uncontrollably. They placed him in front of a freshly stoked fire in Arthur's chambers. A servant came in with gruel and bread. One of the guards pulled down his gag so that the servant could feed him. Toby devoured the hot meal. He had not eaten since the day before.

Two more servants entered the chamber and under the watchful eye of the guards, helped Toby to piss and shit and then washed and preened him. They dressed him in fresh clothes and he was tied once again to the chair.

Thus prepared, Toby was left once again. He dozed, but the bindings and unnatural position of his arms tied behind his back made his bones scream.

Hours passed before Arthur returned from his party. He was singing and stumbled into furniture.

He walked into the back of Toby's chair and – to Toby's insane relief – caught it before it tipped forward and into the fire. Arthur dragged the chair around to face him and ran a finger down Toby's smoothly shaven cheek.

"Hello, beautiful," Arthur slurred.

The beery fumes on his breath clawed at Toby's eyes.

"Do you like my crown?" Arthur swayed as he brought his fingers up to touch the gold band around his head. It was inlaid with precious stones and fat pearls from the Sarenky sea.

"I'm King! And I want to celebrate by fucking you, my pretty little pet. A Cleland, no less. My enemy once, the Clelands, but look at you. Your family has been reduced to rubble. We'll take Lian next and go after Hugo's bitch and his brothers. I won't leave one Cleland alive. I've renamed this place Thorne City and this is now Thorne Castle. I'm going to scrub your filthy name off the face of this country. But not you, you're my good little boy." Arthur pulled down Toby's gag and brought his lips to Toby's mouth.

Toby clenched his lips firmly closed as Arthur slobbered on his mouth and probed with his tongue.

Arthur's mood changed, anger crept into his demeanour and Toby realised something. *I need to keep him merry, and stupid.* Repulsed, Toby opened his mouth. Kissed the bastard back.

Arthur softened immediately. "You want it, don't you? You've resisted me but now I'm the King, I'm the most powerful man in all Fertilian and you want it."

Toby grimaced but forced himself to nod.

"Well, come on then, eager boy." Arthur stood and

thrust his erect penis in Toby's face.

Toby thanked God the bastard still had his breeches on.

Arthur dropped to his knees and nuzzled his face in Toby's crotch whilst fumbling to untie Toby's ankles from the chair. Once released, he stood behind Toby and rubbed his hands up and down Toby's chest whilst kissing and licking at Toby's neck.

Then he did the thing that Toby had hoped for. The drunken bastard undid Toby's hands. He pulled Toby up to standing and slowly pulled off his shirt.

"Go and wait for me on the bed," Arthur demanded as he undid his sword belt, and pulled off his clothes.

Toby registered where the sword belt fell as he pulled off his breeches, climbed onto the bed and waited on all fours, his feet hooked over the side, his rump facing Arthur.

"I'm the King, the King, the King," Arthur sung as he squared his bare body into position behind Toby, grabbing Toby's hips and pulling them back.

Toby's foot edged its way between Arthur's thighs and just as Arthur went to thrust, Toby rammed his heel up into the bastard's bollocks.

Arthur yelped, and clutched his testicles. Toby swung around and cupped a hand over Arthur's mouth and head-butted Arthur in the forehead. Arthur crumpled onto the bed. Toby shoved him aside to reach for the sword.

A firm hand pulled him back onto the bed as Arthur swung a punch with the other. It connected with Toby's jaw. If the man had been sober, that punch would've knocked Toby off his feet. Instead it dazed him and allowed Arthur to grapple him to the bed.

Arthur's hands went for Toby's neck. Toby coughed and spluttered as his breath was cut short. He mirrored the move and tightened his own hands around Arthur's neck. Both men's faces went red, eyes bulged, lips turned blue. They tossed and rolled on the bed.

Toby knew that at his full strength he would be well matched with Arthur. But he was weak from months of little food and no exercise. Arthur was a large man, strong and solid. But the alcohol had dulled his speed, his decisions.

Arthur rolled on top of Toby, crushing Toby's chest with his bulk. He squeezed Toby's neck harder. Toby choked and stars began to sparkle in his vision. He gasped for air. His grip on Arthur's neck slackened. Arthur grinned.

Toby jabbed his fingers into the man's windpipe and with his other hand punched the bastard in the ear. Arthur toppled to one side but kept his grip firm. Toby pushed his thumbs into the man's eyes and Arthur moved his hands to swat at Toby. Toby pressed deeper, harder until one eye burst. Arthur yelled out in pain and wrenched his head away bringing a hand up to his bloody eye.

Toby pummelled the man's head again and again until Arthur was near to unconscious. Toby sprung from the bed, grabbed the sword belt and pulled free the sword.

Guards banged on the door. "King Arthur! King Arthur!" The grunts of both men whilst grappling had no doubt sounded like coitus. But that yell had been different.

"Guards," Arthur garbled as he slid down the side of the bed to the floor, still cupping his blinded eye. "Guards!"

The door, that Arthur had barred from the inside, banged and buckled as the guards put their shoulders to it.

Toby had little time. He plunged the sword through Arthur's chest. The man gurgled, looked down at the hilt protruding from his chest and up at Toby whose hand still held it.

Toby pulled the sword out and then thrust a second time in the bastard's gut. "King Arthur Thorne, the shortest reign ever recorded in history. One day and not even a night. And… killed by a *Cleland*, no less." Toby spat at the dying man as the doors swung open and two guards fell on top of each other in the momentum.

Toby twisted the sword for good measure then ran for the window as the guards gained their feet.

"Murderer," the guards shouted at Toby's back.

He put his hands on the windowsill and pulled up his rump, swinging his legs up and over so he sat there with his legs dangling out the window. As the guards reached him, he slipped down out of their grasp.

"He jumped! The bastard jumped," one guard shouted. He peered out of the window and looked down.

"He'll be dead then," came the other guard's reply. "No one would survive that drop, Mary and the boy splattered everywhere. His bastard body will have to be scraped off the flagstones."

Toby flattened himself against the cold stone wall under the window and waited for the guard to stick his head back in.

There was a small ledge there, as Toby knew there would be. And just above him there was a small hole in the castle wall, protected from the elements – and from prying eyes – by the lip of the windowsill.

The wind whipped at his skin. He was naked. Not ideal.

Toby turned carefully so that his belly pressed against the wall. The hole was just above his head and he reached his hands up, found purchase and hauled himself headfirst into it. There was just enough room to fit Toby's shoulders, and with some deft manoeuvring, he heaved his body inside.

The downward slope took over and Toby slid, face-first through the smooth tunnel. The chute spat him out in a flat section as tall as a man and wide enough for two to walk abreast. The floor at this section was flat, but Toby knew in a few paces there was a steady descent, and then steps. Many, many steps.

He knew this secret tunnel well. He just hoped the Thornes did not. King Edward Cleland had told his children and heirs, one of whom, Olivia, had passed the information about the network of secret tunnels to her five sons. Toby hoped the knowledge, passed down through generations of Clelands had avoided the Thornes. He blessed his mother for having the foresight to educate her sons, even though at that time they lived in Lian and nowhere near Cleland Castle.

Toby's entire body ached. It hurt to swallow. He stumbled downward in the utter darkness, hand trailing the wall. It was uneven rock here. Not polished stone as in the chute he had just tumbled from. It nicked at his hand.

He stumbled on the first step and took the first five on his rump before he righted himself. Down and down he stepped, the circular stairway never-ending. A dizzy feeling swept over him, but he dared not pause.

In his disorientation, he ran straight into the door, slamming against it with his shoulder. He'd reached the bottom of the stairs. This doorway would lead him out into the city beyond the first castle wall. Then he'd need to get past the second, outer, wall, through a secret tunnel he hoped still existed.

First, though, he needed some damn clothes.

He felt in the darkness for the door's handle and gave it a huge yank. It groaned and creaked impossibly loud. The hinges hadn't been oiled since the Thornes had arrived. That meant that they did not know about it. This both pleased him and worried him. The noise would alert suspicion in any nearby guards.

He gave the door a second pull and it squalled like a flock of seagulls as it opened a sliver. Toby edged through the gap, not wanting to risk the noise a third time.

He scanned around him. Dark shadows clung to the wall, the sun was rising on the other side of the castle. It was silent. The city streets in front of him were still. Most of the residents having fled. In one of those deserted houses he'd find something to wear.

He took a deep breath and set off.

But two hands grabbed his arms and he was wrenched

backwards. Out of the shadows came the owners. Two lithe Peqkian warriors emerged before him.

"Fuck," Toby shouted. "Fuck, fuck, fuckedy fuck!"

He writhed under their grip. One of the warriors simply shook her head. He knew it was no use. He couldn't beat a Peqkian at full strength, let alone two when he was weak.

With the utmost efficiency, one of the warriors thumped his head in a very precise spot with the hilt of her dagger and he passed out.

Toby woke to the sound of wailing. He was back in the bastard's bed chamber, lying on his side with his hands and feet bound, the cold stone tiles stinging his bare skin.

Slowly, he looked around.

The sword rested on the carpet in a bloody pool, and False Queen Charlotte kneeled next to Arthur's body and rocked back and forward, hugging her son's head to her breast. She kissed it in between wails. "My boy, my dear boy. You cannot be gone. You cannot. You are King."

Denya kicked Toby in the gut and he groaned. "He's awake."

"Torture him, Denya, pull his skin from his muscles, his muscles from his bones, his organs from his body," Charlotte hissed. "I want him a bloody pulp before we drag him through the streets from the back of a horse."

The Peqkian captain yanked Toby up to his knees by his hair and punched him in the ear for good measure. Pain blossomed across his skull, but he knew it would get worse.

Charlotte wailed and watched. "Torture him!"

Still holding his hair, the captain delivered a brutal punch to Toby's mouth. His front teeth shattered, and he spat out the shards. His nose and mouth clogged with blood.

"We need him alive. He is a good bargaining piece." Denya let go of Toby's hair and pushed him back to the ground.

"Kill him," Charlotte screamed at the warrior. "Kill him as he's killed my child!"

Denya didn't move.

"Kill him, Denya!"

"No."

"Denya," Charlotte bellowed, glaring at the Peqkian. "Do as I say, or I shall be very displeased with you!"

Denya's nostrils flared but she didn't reply.

Toby laughed. Blood, spit and tooth flew from his mouth and down his chin. "Now this is a lover's squabble that should be a delight to watch. The old hag versus the treacherous turncoat."

The Peqkian captain stamped on the side of his head. It smacked into the flagstone with a crack.

29

VIOLYA
ೞ

V, the captains Laurya and Daya, the youngblood Monya plus six more skilled warriors travelled with Nameeri from Riaow to the edges of the Meliok mountains on the South Road. They rode Fert horses and led pack animals with food and barrels of water.

At the Melioks they met three hardened border warriors. One took their horses, and the other two guided them and the pack animals up into the Melioks, along a secret path that took them west. It was risky to take the South Road down into Drome, the usual trade route. And it was also risky to use the newly formed earthquake path. Both were likely being watched by Dromedars and, possibly, the Ferts. Although V suspected their gaze was directed inward with the present Thorne turmoil.

They trekked west for four days, the bright summer sun beating down although there was still snow on the ground. Nameeri struggled with the lack of air at the high elevation, wheezing to keep up. When she fainted, the warrior Daya, her broken arm now healed, heaved the Dromedar over her shoulder and carried the cammer until she came to.

Eventually they came to a border camp. High in the Melioks it afforded an incredible view down the mountains, across the flat wastelands and to the edge of the desert. They could see anyone coming or going for thousands of paces in either direction.

They rested the night, refilled their barrels and strapped them to their backs, leaving the pack animals. They descended slowly along a little-used path, clambering across jagged rock and boulders, clinging to the side of the mountain using their fingertips, dropping down to ledges that the warrior guide assured them were there.

They waited where the mountains jutted into the flatlands until the still of night, said goodbye to their guide and then ran across the exposed flatlands and into the dunes. No one lived in the strip of land between mountain and dune. Nothing could grow in the dry, dusty earth and there was no shelter and little water.

Once in the desert, surrounded by high dunes almost as large as the mountains they had just left behind, Nameeri took the lead.

She scrutinised the sky for a very long time, then looked at the dunes, then the mountains and then back to the sky. V and her warriors waited patiently, stood in formation, poised for danger.

"Make camp," she said eventually. "The sun is almost up and I navigate using the stars. The dunes shift and change with the wind, but I know precisely where we are. It's also cooler to travel at night."

They passed an uncomfortably hot day under makeshift tents.

When it was V's time to guard the camp in the blazing sun, she sweated more than she believed possible. Every pore wept and her clothes became sodden.

Nameeri came to stand with V. The cammer wasn't sweating. "We are on the outskirts of the desert so it'll only get hotter," she said with a smile. "Peqkya was cold. Always a crisp breeze, a sharp cool sting on the skin. But in Drome, there is always the warm caress, the stifling, suffocating touch of heat. You can never escape it." With a smile, she said, "I'm home."

As the sun set, they packed up camp, shouldered their bags and barrels of water and ran after Nameeri. She set a quick pace, gliding through the dunes effortlessly. V and her warriors struggled behind her. Unused to the moving sand beneath their feet, unsteady as the ground slid and shifted with every step. They ran in single file, placing their feet in the holes left by the person in front.

"Come on," Nameeri said as she waited for them to catch up. "We're not far away now. We should reach New Urakbai by dawn."

"Let's go," V said and made to run down the dune. She'd found a rhythm to running in the sand and wanted to perfect it.

"Wait," Nameeri said and slammed her hand into V's chest.

V went for her sword, but Nameeri pointed to the sand in front of V's feet, where she would've stepped.

All froze.

A small circle shifted and filtered, the gritty powder sifting away to reveal a curled-up snake. The snake's body waved from side to side, the sand pouring away. The snake's head became visible and it was looking straight at V. Its forked tongue flicked in and out, tasting the air.

A few steps behind, V heard a warrior slowly pull her sword.

Nameeri lunged, grabbed the snake's head and flung it down the dune. It slithered away from them. She brushed the sand off her hands. "That's not a poisonous one. If it had been a striped sidewinder, you'd have been fucked."

V raised her eyebrows.

"Follow in my footsteps. It's safer." Nameeri set off again at a run.

"Zhaq," Laurya said and sheathed her sword. She clapped V on the back as she ran past her, carefully stepping in Nameeri's path. "Let's hope we don't meet a striped sidewinder then, eh?"

As dawn broke Nameeri directed them to pause in the scant shade at the foot of a tall dune. She scaled the sides, dropped to her belly and shuffled up to the peak, peering down.

Hands flew up from the other side of the dune, grabbed Nameeri's tunic and wrenched her over the top. She yelped as her figure disappeared from sight.

V dropped her pack, unshouldered her barrel, pulled her sword and ran up the dune to where Nameeri had been moments before. Nine warriors followed her.

Near the top of the dune, V slowed and brought her sword forward, edging slowly so that she could see over the lip.

Nameeri was on her feet, suffering the embraces and kisses of an old Dromedar man. He jabbered at her in Dromedari, clutching her cheeks with his hands.

Nameeri pulled her face from the man's grasp. "This is Jarack," Nameeri said. "We're here."

She jerked her head in the direction of a small, ramshackle village with tents and huts, centred around what looked to be a makeshift well. There were sheltered pens for livestock and camels.

Jarack turned to face V and she saw he wasn't just old, he was *ancient*. His craggy face had deep lines and wrinkles, the skin of his hands thin and papery.

"Welcome," he said heartily in Dromedari. "We heard you coming. Your friends, Nameeri, are noisy with all their drinking. Slurp, slurp, slurp." He chuckled and beckoned V forward.

"Jarack," V said in his language as she sheathed her sword and approached him.

He grabbed her face, pulling it down towards his own. Monya leapt forward, a dagger at the old man's neck.

"He won't hurt her," Nameeri said in her accented Shella. "He can see people's futures."

V raised a hand and Monya lowered her dagger, remaining close and alert.

Jarack stared intently into V's eyes, and she stared back. They were a rich brown but with a glassy sheen that betrayed his age. His crinkled face frowned, and his eyes widened.

"You have magic," he said. "Stronger than I've ever seen before." He scrutinised her face, her hair, her chin, turning her head this way and that. "You use it wisely." He beamed at her with a gap-toothed smile and released her face. "Come, let's get out of the sun."

They collected their dropped packs and settled in the largest tent in the village whilst Nameeri went to find another villager. Jarack had spicy goat stew and rice brought for them and V gifted him a barrel of water.

"You Peqkians must be sloshing on the inside the amount you drink," he laughed. "This barrel will last my entire village, including animals, an entire scorch season." He found a cup, filled it with a dribble of water and took a sip.

He smacked his crinkly lips together. "This is the purest water I have ever tasted."

"Straight from the mountains of Peqkya," V said.

"Now, tell me, young red-haired warrior. Where is the rest of your army? I count only ten and Nameeri tells me you plan to overthrow the Wakrimes."

"We will overthrow the Wakrimes. We only need ten."

Jarack took another small sip and leaned in close to V, even though her warriors could not understand their Dromedari conversation. "You don't need ten. You only need you." Then he sat back and patted his belly, sniffing at the last drop of water in his cup before swallowing it.

"I have magic. I am Khumarah. It was once stronger, but now all I can do is keep living. My magic keeps me alive when others around me die from their age." He sighed heavily. "Poor old Samma had reached a ripe old age, completely naturally. He was of the Yuurnan clan and a great friend of mine. We didn't always see eye to eye, of course, but he didn't deserve the end he got. He should've died from old age, but that bastard Crown Prince slaughtered him and his village. I was a wanderer, but I'm too old now to move very far. I founded New Urakbai here in the same place, in Samma's honour."

"Why did the Crown Prince slaughter this village?" V asked.

"Well, it is unclear. But I believe he was looking for those who help the Ferts."

"There are Dromedars here who help the Ferts?"

"Oh yes." Jarack leaned close to V again. "And I am one of them. I've traded for many years with Ferts. They give us water and food. Among other things… They have kept me and my people alive. More than the Wakrimes in their crater have ever done. That clan care only for themselves. They've never cared about those they rule."

Jarack leaned back and sighed, his wrinkled eyes glassing over. "Samma and his village paid the price for my dealings with the Ferts. For that, I am deeply sorry."

V reached out and placed a gentle hand on the old Dromedar's arm. It was a gesture she would never have thought to do in Peqkya. Peons were not to be comforted. But this old male was special, V could sense it. Ancient and wise. Jarack smiled his gummy grin at her. Then he tapped the side of his nose.

"Don't tell Nameeri," he whispered with a small wink. "The Khumarahs are a good clan, mostly, but many are still bitter about Vaasar, the hatred of the Ferts runs deep."

"Mostly?"

"There's been a few rotten leaders. Ones who have become consumed by power and greed and their own gain. But the leader now, Ibin, cares for his people. Has no interest in personal glory."

A warrior positioned outside the tent whistled to indicate people approaching and a few moments later the flap of the tent flew open and Nameeri stepped inside followed by a small, young Dromedar male.

She dipped her head to V and found a space to squat.

The male crouched behind her.

"This is Ackbah," Nameeri said.

Ackbah's eyes stayed resolutely on his hands, which were clasped between his knees.

"Ackbah has been waiting here for me. He never lost faith that I'd return." Nameeri grinned at the male and squeezed his shoulder. V noticed Ackbah squirmed awkwardly, his eyes looking everywhere but at Nameeri.

"Ackbah is a special calfling," Jarack said. "We've enjoyed his company."

Ackbah squirmed under the attention, flinging his hand up to his face and scratching at the wispy beard that peppered his cheeks.

"He's been busy trading with nearby villages and wandering nomads to gather twelve fast camels for us," Nameeri said.

"How did you know to gather this number?" V asked.

Ackbah jabbed a finger at Jarack.

The crinkled face of the chief lit up. "I had an inkling that twelve camels were needed. My magic has been dormant many years, but every now and then it still talks to me. I'm happy to hear it again."

"Does it tell you anything else?" V asked.

"I had a vision that a black and red cat from the mountains sneaked into the crater and changed Drome forever."

***

Late the following evening, after the Peqkians had rested, the villagers loitered in the red-grey twilight gawping as Ackbah distributed raggedy clothing to the Peqkians. His movements were shifty, his eyes downcast and his body turned away from the Peqkians. He had the same manner with the Dromedars and V understood it was his way. Her warriors watched him, as they watched everyone, for any sign of a threat.

Once all ten of them had their outfits, Nameeri demonstrated how to wear them. The Peqkians gave their heavy fur cloaks to the nearest villagers who handled them with curiosity, never having seen animal hide with such thick fur before.

V put on the baggy trousers and long-sleeved tunic over the top of her leather vest and shorts, hiding her short sword that hung around her waist and the daggers strapped to her arms. V and her warriors all followed Nameeri's directions on how to wrap the tattered sand-coloured cloth around their heads in the style of the Eqmadeh nomad clan so that only their eyes were on show. Some of the female villagers came forward to help tie the knots, tuck in the folds and stuff rags to look like back humps.

With their cloaks up, it looked as if the little bit of black skin on show between their eyes was simply in shadow.

Jarack ushered forward a few males who bound the Peqkians' hands with long strips of thin cloth to cover the leather vambraces that poked from beneath the tunic sleeves. They expertly wound it around the palms so that only the tips of their fingers were on show.

"The feet are a problem," Nameeri said as she looked on at V's leather boots. "Eqmadeh clan members cannot afford shoes of any kind and mostly go barefoot, but your bare feet reveal your origin."

In the end, it was decided that the Peqkians keep their boots but wrap rags on top, as if protecting their feet from the scorching sun. This was a practice occasionally adhered to by the clan, and it was felt to be adequate.

As such, though, V's feet were the hottest part of her body.

They took their leave of Jarack and the villagers. Ten Peqkians and two Dromedars set off into the black desert on fast camels. Nameeri navigated using the stars.

The Peqkians bounced as the camels picked up speed. Nameeri led the way, riding smoothly, her body moving in perfect unison with the camel. Ackbah brought up the rear with Laurya.

The camels had been strung with small bells and charms and as they ran, the clanking and tinkling shattered the stillness of the night. Ackbah sang and beat out a rhythm on one of the barrels his camel carried. Ahead, Nameeri ululated and sang, clicking her fingers. When V had asked about the bells before they set out, Nameeri had told her that the noise keeps the desert spirits away. V had accepted the strange custom without much thought. But now she was in the desert, she understood.

The silence and utter stillness were oppressive. The vast emptiness, coupled with the sweltering heat, was like being underwater. The pressure of it closed in around her, touched and swarmed every tiny part of her, stuffed up her ears, swarmed up her nostrils. V focused her attention on the jingling of the bells.

Soon, Laurya chanted a famous Peqkian rhyme, usually performed to drums. V and the other warriors joined in, clapping their hands to the beat. The chanting seemed to push back the crushing air, that threatened to stifle them.

The camels ran faster than V had imagined, kicking up dust and fine sand into a thick cloud. At dawn, Nameeri slowed and looked for a suitable place to stop for the day, leading them toward the side of a tall dune.

The camel plodded and the slight breeze V had enjoyed at top speed evaporated into nothing faster than water. V's legs hung limply either side of the shaggy hump of the beast. She wriggled her damp toes and the sweaty leather of her boots squelched. A tang like sour milk wafted up to assault her nostrils.

"Nameeri," she said, to take her mind off her stewing feet, "tell me of Ibin."

"He came to the Khumarah after defecting from the ruler's personal guard, the Cuttarrs. He was injured when the Khumarahs assassinated Shaan, Mastiq's father. Ibin had believed that he was of the high-class Tamadeen clan, but it turns out he was a slave. He'd been brought up as the son of glass merchant Haibal Khilad, only to be given to the cutthroats at ten. His false father then cruelly cut him off from the family Ibin thought was his own.

"We thought Ibin was a spy at first. The leader at the time told him he must prove himself with an assassination. Ibin went out one night and killed the entire Khilad family in their beds. Men, women, children. They were spread across four villas in different parts of the city, each with guard-slaves and high walls. He arrived back without a scratch or a drop of blood on him, but with a child who he'd found in a cage. In Drome, it is an embarrassment to have a child who is not the same as all the others, and families keep them locked away. Especially in the Tamadeen clan. Ibin had taken pity on the boy and brought him back."

Nameeri looked over her shoulder.

V followed her gaze. "Ackbah?"

Nameeri nodded. "Ibin became famous for that hit. Four villas in one night, an entire family wiped out and all at the hands of a lone Khumarah assassin. But it's not something he's proud of. In fact, he hates himself for it. He'd been driven by revenge. He raised Ackbah as his own. Gave him a life he never would've had. Eventually Ibin became the clan leader. He's been nominated year after year by the people for the past fourteen years."

Nameeri pulled her camel to a stop. "We'll rest here."

They dismounted and erected a rickety shelter to keep off the worst of the blistering daytime sun.

V helped Nameeri and Ackbah tend to the camels.

"These are incredible creatures," V said as she helped to unburden the beasts with Nameeri. "They run so fast."

"Ha, they'd run faster if they didn't have all this strapped to them." Nameeri tapped a barrel of Peqkian water.

She and Ackbah barely drank any, using their humps to store fluid. By comparison, it seemed for every drop swallowed by the Dromedars, the Peqkians consumed an entire lake.

Once the camels were settled under the shade, V allocated watch and attempted to sleep.

***

V had never been so hot. Her breath came in shallow gasps, every scorching inhale was a bitter, syrupy fog that snatched at the air in her lungs rather than refilled them.

After three weeks of fast riding, Jhabia Ridge was now behind them and their small procession walked. It was painfully slow. They had left the fast camels on the far side of the rocky ridge with Ackbah. A camel train was expected to head either into the city or in a different direction to where their destination lay and would draw too much attention. Ackbah would keep the camels hidden and Nameeri would send someone to relieve him when she reached the camp. They had taken their last long drink of water and left everything behind other than their weapons.

They climbed up and over the jutting rock and, as the sun set, they continued towards Parchad on foot. They walked in a line, to seem as if they were the poorest wandering nomads from the Eqmadeh clan, not even able to keep a camel. "No one pays any attention whatsoever to poor Eqmadehs," Nameeri had said. "Don't look anyone in the eyes. And don't walk so upright, walk with a stoop. Eqmadehs aren't usually this tall. Try to blend in."

As V dragged her feet through the dunes towards the capital of Drome, she could feel the fine sand between her toes. It had bullied its way through the rags, through every crack and crevice in the leather and settled in her boots. The sweat had turned it to a gritty paste and she felt as if it was now working its way into every pore in her skin. *If I was to be cut in half now, sand would pour out.*

The twinkling lights of the crater city grew closer. Around her was black desert, nothingness, and this beacon of civilisation shone bright in the centre.

As they picked up a well-trodden trail, V noted the

slums on her right, tucked up against the outside of the crater wall. Weary travellers streamed out of the desert from different directions to pick up this road. Some on foot, many on lumbering camels that formed long caravans carrying supplies.

Nameeri stopped to allow V to catch up. "The Khumarah area is just there. But we head past it and towards the Hand of God sculpture to pay our respects. It would be suspicious if we didn't. Every traveller gives thanks for their survival and for their safe return before they continue on to wherever they are going. Do precisely what I do."

V turned to the nearest warrior to her, the youngblood Monya, and whispered the order, who in turn passed it to the warrior closest to her and so on down the line. V could understand and speak Dromedari but her warriors could not, and she could not risk anyone hearing them speak Shella.

V and her warriors kept their heads down, shuffling forward behind Nameeri. They blended in with almost every other traveller on foot trickling in from the dunes. Exhausted, thirsty, dirty and relieved to be there.

The huge sand sculpture was as high as the crater wall, depicting a hand reaching up and out of the sand at the wrist and into the sky towards God. It loomed large at the start of the road over the crater wall and into the city. It stood in a small area on its own, but stalls, tents and camel pens had been erected nearby to cater for those travellers who had money to spend.

Nameeri hustled her way through the milling crowd that gathered at the foot of the sculpture and then took out her small knife and pricked her little finger, allowing a droplet of blood to fall into the sand. V and her warriors copied her movements. They carefully moved their arms to ensure the long sleeves and hand wrappings revealed nothing of their skin.

Blood offerings? A strange custom, V's magic tutted as her blood dripped from her finger. *A waste.*

"Walk in small groups, we cannot follow in procession in the slums. Stay behind me, but not too close," Nameeri whispered to V as she trudged back the way they had just come and towards the entrance of the slums. V signalled to indicate for two of her warriors to go with Nameeri, and for the others to split into small groups.

V allowed Nameeri's group to get a little way ahead before following with Daya and Monya. The youngblood warrior was trying her hardest to keep her head down but kept looking around her in wonder at all the strange sights, before dipping her head low again.

They entered the slums. A maze of tents, wooden shacks, sleeping mats and runnels overflowing with a stinking slime of excrement, offal and discarded rags. V took in her surroundings, identified landmarks that would help her navigate her way out again if required. They were heading parallel to the crater wall, away from the sculpture and deeper into the chaotic slums. V knew there would be districts and neighbourhoods and, for the residents, main thoroughfares. She noted everything.

The same tinkling bells and charms adorned the tents and added their jingling to the cacophony of children screaming, adults nattering and goats' bleating. V had always considered the Riaow markets to be boisterous, but the noise of this place was ear-splitting. There were so many people crammed together, living on top of one another that it was almost as oppressive as the desert's utter emptiness.

Nameeri took passageway after passageway, V counting twenty-two turns. Then Nameeri took a hard left towards the crater wall. There was a noticeable change. These tents and shacks were quieter. There were no children running and screaming, no tinkling charms, fewer candles burning.

They want to hear who is coming. V searched for the watchers she knew would be there but couldn't discern any. The shadows didn't stir, gave no hint of a lookout.

After years of oppression, these people excel at hiding.

V turned the corner and Nameeri and her group was gone. V slowed her pace to evaluate. They stood on a single-file scrap of land between huts that twisted and turned and disappeared around a shack. Monya and Daya stood close to V in a defensive formation.

A hiss came from an unadorned tent a few paces away. Nameeri was crouched in the entrance, holding back the flap. She beckoned to V.

The red-haired warrior entered.

Her warriors already inside the tent were crouched, hands on weapons, ready to fight. V crouched in front of them as Monya and Daya filed in and took their positions behind her. There was no one else in the tent apart from them. It was bare inside with sand on the floor. Nameeri could stand upright, but V and her warriors were too tall.

Soon, the last of V's warriors arrived. V whistled and three remained outside, taking up positions around the tent.

Nameeri turned towards V. "They will know we are here and someone will come soon. This is a meeting tent for the leaders of my people. It's used late at night when the rest of the slums sleep, but it's early. Your warriors should come inside."

V shook her head and whistled. The three warriors stationed outside whistled to each other. Then one whistled their report to those inside. *All clear.*

"Do you not trust me?" Nameeri asked, affronted.

"I trust you," V replied, "I do not trust those I have not yet met. A lot of time has passed between you leaving here and your return. Desires move on, ambitions change."

A whistle from outside. *One approaches. Unknown, unarmed.*

Daya pulled the flap aside and eyed the male. He had his hands in the air. He had the stance of a fighting man, holding himself with discipline. Daya looked him up and down and then moved aside to allow him to enter. He bent his head and stepped in.

"Nameeri," the male said and embraced the woman. She pushed him away with a smile and gestured towards V.

"This is Melokai Violya of Peqkya," Nameeri said. "And this is Ibin el Khumarah, chosen leader of the Khumarah clan."

"I am honoured, Melokai Violya," Ibin said and dropped to one knee.

"And these are my esteemed warriors," V said.

Ibin acknowledged them with a dip of his chin. "Truly, we are honoured by your presence and that of your warriors, Melokai Violya."

"Call me V."

Water and food were brought and after V and her warriors had rested, V agreed to walk with Ibin and Nameeri towards the crater wall. Laurya, Daya and Monya followed behind at a distance.

It was late evening now and the temperature had dropped, although it was still stifling. The moon was bright in the sky and it dimly lit the way.

"Let us get some air, and find a quiet place to speak," Ibin had said and had led the way through the snaking paths of the slums towards the crater wall.

Up they had climbed and now the three stood on a ledge with a fierce hot wind battering them, as if angry they stood in its way. It wasn't refreshing. It blasted the dusty heat into V's face, making her eyes sting, but it was a welcome change from the dead heat in the desert. She longed for the brisk, cool wind of the Meliok mountains.

The three warriors stationed themselves around the ledge, keeping a watch on the surroundings. Immediately beneath them were the slums and in the distance the great black expanse of sand.

Ibin sat and placed a glass bulb in front of him. He nicked a match along the rock and lit a candle, dropping it in the glass.

"To protect from the wind," he said.

"That is a Peqkian invention," V said and indicated the match. "Made in Riaow."

Ibin nodded. "We are running thin here in Drome since the invasion. No more trade. They are now hard to come by. No Drome chemist has been able to recreate it. There is much from Peqkya that Drome is missing now."

V swelled with pride at the skills of her people. The three sat in a circle around the candle.

"Much has changed since you have been away, my love." Ibin took Nameeri's hand in his own and kissed her knuckle before dropping it. "We have a new ruler."

Nameeri's body jerked, her eyebrows knotted, and she cocked her head at Ibin in astonishment.

"Our Ruler Mastiq and the majority of his family, including his harem and many children, were assassinated," Ibin said.

Nameeri's hand flew to her mouth. "The Khumarah?"

"No, it was not our doing, although it has always been our wish. The Crown Prince Ammad returned from war without his arms. Mastiq stripped him of his title and was to grant it to Hallid."

V's body remained impassive to the mention of the worm cammer. Internally, she roiled.

Ibin proceeded to tell them of Jakira's scheming, the slaughter at the cleansing ceremony in the Holy Square, and the announcement of Ammad as Ruler of Drome and Selmi as Crown Prince.

Nameeri whistled through her teeth. "And what of our *friend?*"

"He has completely turned to our side and embraces our cause. He wishes for the corruption to end and the true religion to re-emerge. He is keener now than ever and pushes us to act."

"Friend?" V asked.

"We have an ally on the inside. He has Khumarah

blood. He has always favoured our philosophies, our religion, our culture, ever since he was a boy. He supplies us with exceedingly useful information on this new royal family. Information that will inform our plans to overthrow their rule."

"So, why have you waited?" V asked.

"We have fighters, it's true, but we do not have great numbers, and many aren't highly skilled. They need to eat, to provide water for their family. Most work. Fighting is not all they know or do."

"Ibin, one Peqkian warrior is worth many, many of our men. I have never seen such impeccable fighting. And, V, well…" Nameeri said.

As she told Ibin of V's magic, V checked the positions of her three warriors, feeling uncomfortable at being singled out.

"You have a plan?" V said.

"We have," the leader of the Khumarah said.

"Tell me."

30

VIOLYA

V ambled through the city, adjusting her hood, stooping to conceal her towering height.

The hood had been blown off as they followed the road over the crater wall. At the top, the severe wind had reminded her of the gale atop the Chaos Cliffs in Majute. But as they descended into the crater hole the wind dropped off and the thick heat rose up from the hot sand. An acrid sweat stench from thousands of residents hung heavy in the clotted air.

V's scarf covered all but her eyes. Her ragged cloak covered her weapons and her hands and feet were bound with tattered strips of cloth. The only skin on show was that on the tips of her fingers.

They had to travel at this time from the outside slums, over the crater wall and towards the palace because this was when Jakira held her weekly meeting with her closest allies. Ibin had not been worried. "Hide in plain sight," he had said. And now V understood why.

It was the busiest time, as the sun was setting and the heat cooled, a few hours before people went to sleep for the night in whatever shack or dusty piece of ground they called home.

The cramped streets were heaving. Most people had

their heads down and were going about their business oblivious to those around them. The wealthy were either carried on covered litters heaved by slaves or strolled on foot, followed by a slave holding a palm frond over their heads to shade them from the last of the sun's rays.

The poor Affarah peasants who lived in the city wore skull caps, the poorer still had bare heads with scorched scalps and hairlines and the tops of their ears blistering. Some had barely any clothes on their backs at all, and most had bare feet. These poor were skin and bones, begging for water and food, or rifling around in the dirt for scraps. Peqkya had always ensured its people were clothed, fed and watered, and V planned to uphold that custom during her reign. *A ruler who allows their people to starve is despicable.*

The slaves were noticeable for their shaved heads, wrist cuffs and identical rough-hewn sleeveless and collarless tunics that fell to the knees with two front pockets. They went about their business in the same way as all the other Parchaders. Some of the slaves had chains around their ankles or between their wrist cuffs, lashed together and being led by their sellers or owners.

There were scores of wandering Eqmadeh nomads with scarves wrapped around their heads and only eyes on show. Although V and her warriors still had cloth wrapped around their hands and feet, which the Eqmadehs didn't. But nobody seemed to notice, and Ibin assured her that if they did, they wouldn't do anything about it.

V and her warriors ignored the elbows, the pushing and shoving, the people stomping on their feet. The noise in the crater was double that out in the slums. It made V's ears ring. She had once thought Riaow a busy city, but it paled in comparison to Parchad.

"No one moves quickly in this heat," Ibin had said. "To do so will draw unnecessary attention."

So, V sauntered. It was not her usual pace or gait. She kept the agreed distance away from the Khumarah Assassin ahead of her and he kept the same distance behind the Peqkian warrior in front of him. The group stretched out in a long line, each looking like a lone individual in a throng of Parchaders. Ibin, Nameeri and eight of the Khumarah clan's best fighters had joined V and her nine warriors. They ambled towards the palace.

Ibin had sent assassins to the villas of the High Priest Zeead and his family. Another larger group was headed to the Peqkian traitor Rivya's craterside villa. Although Melokai Ramya's treacherous Head Trader would be at the palace with Jakira, her equally treacherous assistant Toya would not. She was a Peqkian and knew how to fight. V insisted the Khumarahs allocated four assassins just for her.

Two further groups were dispatched to visit the villas of notable and powerful families, and allies of Jakira, in the Tamadeen and Qacirr clans. All targets had been watched closely for many months. Their daily habits and routines remembered, the flaws in their villa's security identified and their guards' strengths and weaknesses noted.

The Khumarah leader was confident in his plan to enter the palace. Even still, V had insisted she scout the place. Ibin trusted in the loyalty of his 'friend'. But much rested on the actions of this friend. So, disguised as beggars, V had sat on a street corner with Ibin and watched the palace guards come and go. They had walked slowly around the walls to spot overhanging trees that could be climbed; guard posts that could easily and swiftly be breached; and which guards would require immobilising.

Ibin had once been a Cuttarr. The posts and drills and the breaks and shift changes had not changed in the twenty years since he had left. Lazy and undisciplined, thought V. But for their purposes, the lax protection of the Drome royal family was a boon.

V turned into a dark and deserted, dead-end alleyway between two villas and opposite a quiet part of the palace wall at the far end of the gardens, a spot little visited by those who lived within its walls. The alleyway was used to dump rubbish and it stank. But it made a good gathering place for the ten Peqkians and ten Khumarah assassins.

The friend had suggested this place. Had found it and used it to sneak out of the palace for many months without being discovered. Ibin confirmed there were no palace guards stationed nearby, that the Cuttarrs patrolled the area infrequently. This friend had sent another contact to meet them on the other side of the wall. A childhood playmate and low-born son of a cook, according to Ibin. His name was Baghadd, and over the years, had delivered many messages. Ibin trusted him.

They waited silently in the alleyway for all in the line to arrive. V could sense the nervousness of the Khumarah clan fighters. They fidgeted, checked their weapons, puffed out cheeks and glanced at each other and at the Peqkians. Her warriors stood ready. Neither eager nor afraid. Waiting for the order. V knew why the Khumarahs had not attacked before her arrival. They had the desire, but not the skill.

The last man in the line turned into the alleyway and Ibin crept out and towards the palace walls, to await the signal from Baghadd. Nameeri edged out to watch him. There were few passersby in this part of town; the wealthy all tucked up in their villas. But it still paid to be cautious.

V gestured to her warriors and all removed the rags from around their boots and hands, and discarded them in the alleyway.

"It's time," Nameeri said to V.

V ducked and darted to where Ibin was standing by the wall. She found gaps in the stone and scaled the wall effortlessly. Her warriors followed, like a swarm of ants climbing up and over. At the top V swung her legs over, assessed her landing place and dropped silently. Her warriors landed next to her.

A cloaked figure waited a few paces away. Baghadd. The male's back was to them, his gaze towards the palace.

Ibin passed her and went to the figure, reaching out a hand to squeeze a shoulder. Baghadd turned and they embraced.

V shed her ragged clothing and pulled the scarf from her face. It would hinder her fighting and was no longer necessary. Her warriors did the same. They stood in their Peqkian warrior garb for the first time since leaving their country and the Khumarah assassins gawked at the weapons on show and their strong bodies. The Dromedar women were mostly soft and curvaceous. Nameeri, with her small, tough figure was unusual. V and her warriors looked formidable, and she knew it would give courage to the Khumarah fighters.

V was here for one purpose, and she would fulfil it. The Khumarahs had found them a way in. The Peqkians would do the rest.

Ibin pointed her out to the cloaked figure and Baghadd bowed his head in her direction, then took off at a run towards the palace. Ibin followed, then V and her women. Nameeri and the Khumarah assassins brought up the rear.

Baghadd followed a moon-lit path through the well-tended gardens and around the side of a huge lake towards the palace. All the walkways were covered with cloth to keep the scorching sun off those taking a stroll in the garden. All this cloth could clothe every one of their people. There would be no half-naked people sunburned and blistering if it was repurposed.

But it was the fields of crops growing next to the lake that disgusted V more. Most of it was going to rot whilst outside of the palace walls people were starving and dying of thirstation. Here, there was abundant food and water going to waste.

Baghadd's arms came up and he stopped, gesturing ahead and to the left. He held two fingers in the air. V gestured to Laurya who sprinted in the direction he had indicated. As she passed, she pulled both daggers from her belt. She turned off the path to the guard station, lithe like a cat.

A few moments passed. The raucous sounds of the city drifted in from over the wall. Laurya appeared on the path a few paces ahead and beckoned them forward.

Baghadd moved on and slowed as he stared at the two guards piled one on top of the other behind Laurya. She hadn't made a sound.

They filed past, Laurya slipping in behind V in formation once again.

Five more times did Baghadd point out guards, and five more times did V's warriors swiftly and silently dispatch them.

V watched Baghadd for any sign of betrayal or second thoughts. The cook's son did not once turn around to look at those he led. Her magic was still. It did not sense any danger or false intention. Baghadd was bent on the task to get them into the palace and lead them to the room Jakira, Ammad and their cronies were sat in.

As they neared the palace, Baghadd indicated for them to wait in the shadows as he approached the four guards stationed at the door.

"Who goes there? Show yourself," one of the guard's said.

V used the distraction to send four of her warriors forward. They crept in the shadows and approached the guards from the side whilst their eyes were turned to the cloaked figure who slowly walked towards them with arms lifted.

The guards drew their swords as Peqkians emerged to slit their throats. Each warrior caught their victim as blood gushed and eased their bodies onto the ground.

And with that, they were inside.

The palace was quiet. So much empty space compared to the squash outside. Baghadd led them across a grand hall, the height of two storeys. An intricate coloured-glass window stretched from floor to ceiling. There was glass everywhere, small baubles and trinkets on shelves around the edges, glass mosaics on the walls. A huge glass ornament hung from the ceiling; twinkling in the moonlight shining through the window. On the floor was a huge Peqkian-made carpet, and on top more plush rugs. The hall was not lit, perhaps only used for ceremonial occasions, perhaps never used at all.

They went up some stairs and through a convoluted route Baghadd had told Ibin he had scouted and used many times. It was free from slaves, palace inhabitants, guards. But when they neared the place Jakira and now-ruler Ammad resided, the Cuttarrs and guards would massively increase.

Baghadd held his hand out to them indicating they should pause and gently tapped on a door. It opened immediately and out stepped a male resplendent in fine clothes. He nodded to Ibin and whispered to Baghadd.

"Go to the kitchen and find your mother. Get out of the palace. Hide in the gardens. I'll come for you when this is over. Stay safe."

Baghadd cradled the male's head and gently rested his forehead against it, then hurried back the way they had come.

The male came slowly towards V. Her magic was still.

"I have told this to Ibin, but I will repeat it again to you. There is an innocent in the room. Ammad's wife. She sits to his left. No harm must come to her. That is a condition of my assistance."

The male had a familiar face but was young. Perhaps only fifteen. He was slender with serious eyes and a small nose and back hump. He carried no weapons.

"We will not harm this innocent," V said.

The male nodded, turned and continued onwards. As he approached the bottom of some more stairs, his shoulders heaved as he steadied himself with a deep breath.

From the top of the stairs came bright light, and voices of men. This was the hallway to the room they sought. It was at the back of the palace, directly over the kitchens.

Although hotter than other rooms in the palace, Ibin's intelligence had indicated Jakira had purposely chosen this room for her weekly meetings. The clatter from the busy kitchen below drowned out any eavesdroppers. And it was a long way from the slave quarters, in a part of the palace rarely frequented.

The male walked up and entered the hallway.

"Ah, here he is," said one voice.

"That was a long piss," said another.

"A piss turned into something more, my friends," the male replied, as V and her women crept up the stairs.

"A shit?"

"No, no, lads! I took a quick turn by the royal harem, there are those in there that would suck my cock whilst their master is occupied."

The soldiers laughed.

"Which one? The new one with the green eyes? It's said she's the child of some Fert whore and cammer father."

"Not her, the top heavy one. Gather around and I'll tell you of her tits. They are as big as watermelons," the male said.

V could hear the guards shuffling into position, each with their backs to the stairwell. This was V's signal, and she and her warriors swarmed into the hallway.

The six soldiers fell without a sound as V and her women overwhelmed them, apart from one who let out a whelp as he took a sword through the neck. All in the hallway froze.

The male stared at the door the soldiers had been guarding. Within was V's quarry. They needed to keep this attack silent so as not to alert those in the room to their approach.

A male voice shouted from inside, "What goes on out there?"

The male nodded to V then he moved forward and opened the door, entering the room. "It's me, Medi. I was joking with the men."

"Since when do *you* joke with the men?" a haughty male voice said. "You're the dullest creature alive."

"You took your time," a female snapped.

Then V stepped in.

31

VIOLYA

◑❧◐

V assessed the room in the same time it took for the occupants to fathom her presence. All were sat where the male had told Ibin they would be.

A few things happened at once. The male moved to the younger woman sat on Ammad's left. Ibin and Nameeri flowed in the room behind V, followed by Laurya, Daya and Monya. All five with their swords drawn. V's remaining women and the Khumarahs waited in the hallway for the soldiers and Cuttarrs who were bound to come.

The woman who had spoken moments earlier, shrieked. *Jakira.* She sat opposite V at the far side of the room under a slit of a window. A position of highest authority, according to Ibin, to catch the little breeze that flowed in. She considered herself higher than the ruler.

To Jakira's right, was the hairy beast of a cammer V had seen before at the battle in Riaow, the Minister of War, Whaled. Then a space where the male should be sitting, then the traitor Peqkian Rivya. Jakira's head slave, Medi, sat with his back to the door. To Jakira's left was the murderous worm, and now Drome ruler, Ammad.

The cammers sat on floor cushions around a low table covered with platters of food and brass tea sets. The room

376

was smoky, filled with a sweet fragrant tobacco that bubbled from hookah pipes smoked by Whaled and Rivya.

"Selmi! You have betrayed us," Jakira shouted and screamed again, clutching at her dress over her heart. "You have betrayed your family. You have betrayed your mother. Oh, flesh of my flesh, what have you done?"

"You…" Ammad gasped, "the red-haired warrior…" He slowly rose from his cushion, eyes narrowed on V.

"Deserter!" Whaled pointed at Ibin.

The Minister of War shoved over his hookah pipe as he sprung to his feet, pulling a dagger from his belt and flinging it with precision at V's chest.

She watched it as if time had stilled, plucked it out of the air, catching the hilt as it spun, and tossed it back at Whaled. He ducked to his left and yanked Jakira to the floor.

Medi, the head slave, was up. He pulled his sword and pivoted with a growl to engage the first behind him. Nameeri met his attack. Ibin jumped onto the low table, ran to the far side of the room and met Whaled's sword as the hairy cammer stood in front of the screaming Jakira. She was not fighting, as the male, Selmi, had said. Jakira did not know how to.

V could hear the patter of feet along the hallway and the clash and clang of swords outside the door. Laurya ran to Riv, who had grown even fatter and sprawled on the floor attempting to right herself like a tortoise on its back. Monya shadowed Nameeri and Daya moved towards Ibin.

This would've gone quicker with just V's women. But both Dromedars had insisted they fight their enemies. It was pride, V knew, rather than practicality. V's orders to Daya and Monya was to allow the fight, but to step in if Nameeri or Ibin needed assistance.

V's eyes locked with Ammad's and a rush of vengeance swept through her.

She drew her sword and pointed it at him.

Blast him to smithereens! Her magic insisted. *Peel his skin from his body!*

V ignored it. She curbed her emotion. She would do what she should have done months ago. End him swiftly and precisely, as a Peqkian warrior was trained to do.

She jumped on the table to get closer. Ammad planted his feet as if he might fight. This was either valiant or stupid. He had no arms, she had seen to that.

She brought her sword back ready to thrust.

As she did, she saw out of the corner of her eye Ibin stab Whaled in the gut. The hairy cammer staggered, one of Daya's daggers protruding from his neck. Jakira's screams intensified as her lover fell, his head landing by her feet. Blood sprayed from his wound onto her legs.

Nameeri cheered behind her as Medi was taken down.

V heard Laurya: "You are a traitor of Peqkya! For that, you die."

The ex-Head Trader begged for mercy. The mumbling ended as Laurya slit the woman's throat.

V jabbed her sword at Ammad. She would skewer this murderer through the heart and have done with him.

But his sword came up to meet hers, blocked it and curled under to slice her torso. She ducked back, so the tip sliced through her leather vest and scratched a line across her taught stomach. She stumbled off the table onto the ground next to Rivya.

As V's blood oozed out, her magic came to life. It fizzed in her veins, pumped into every cell of her being, boomed in her ears.

Ammad leapt the low table and was on her. She blocked his stabs, dodged his swings. Regained her footing and then returned with thrusts and stabs. He had a new arm. As he fought, the long sleeve of his tunic flew back to reveal a fully formed limb. Muscular. Perfect fingers held the sword. He had impeccable balance, and she glimpsed a second new arm.

He was fighting skilfully, using his legs to kick at V in between blocks and parries.

"How?" V said in Dromedari and nodded at Ammad's arms.

He laughed. And laughed and laughed.

"Finish him, V," Laurya shouted. She was stood next to the body of Rivya.

V shook off her curiosity as a cat shakes off water and swung at Ammad. Her movement was so fast he could not block it or duck out of the way. She buried her sword to the hilt through his torso.

He choked and gurgled, stumbled back and sprawled on the low table, clutching his wound. The silver platters and tea sets clattered to the floor.

"No," Jakira yelled and a ball of fire exploded in V's chest, knocking her off her feet and slamming her into the wall.

Drowsily V watched as Jakira spun her hands in a circle to create a fiery sphere and then she cast it at Laurya who had moved to engage. Laurya was blast back.

"She has magic," Nameeri yelled as she came forward with Monya.

"She's always had an ability. She's Khumarah," Ibin replied as he stepped up, Daya next to him.

"That's right, *Ibin*," Jakira spat his name. "But I've been practising in secret since I last saw you."

"What happened to you?" Ibin said.

"I was tired of being owned by another. I decided I would own everyone instead."

One by one Jakira spun and threw the fiery orbs, knocking back each of her attackers, singeing their clothes and skin. Each were stunned. Then Jakira turned to Selmi, who stood protectively in front of Ammad's wife and the woman Selmi wanted unharmed, Razanne, who was backed into the corner.

"There are no words for what you have done here." Jakira spun her hands, building a ball of fire.

"Enough," V bellowed and found her feet. Her magic responded, exploding from her outstretched hands.

The lightning bolt of white light sliced into Jakira just under the ribs. She clutched her spilling innards and crumpled on the low table. Her face frozen in the shock of dying.

But she didn't slump on Ammad. The worm had rolled off the table and, lying on the floor, thrust up with his sword, his goal to slice through V's thigh. But Laurya had seen. Still winded from Jakira's blast, the warrior threw out her sword arm, knocking Ammad's strike so that it missed V's inner leg by a hair's breadth.

"This is your end, murderer," V said.

She moved to thrust her sword through the worm's skull, to finally slake her revenge.

"No!" A deafening, high-pitched yell rattled through the room and stilled her hand with its power. She looked up to see all eyes turned to the doorway.

There stood a small Peqkian boy, no more than four years old. Tears streamed down his face. Behind him, out in the hallway, V could see a tangled mess of bloody limbs. Peqkians, Khumarah and Cuttarrs, all dead.

"Mama?" the boy said and stared at the body of Jakira on the low table. He took a tentative step forward and his foot caught on the body of the head slave. He looked down. "Medi?"

They watched as the child stepped carefully over Medi and came closer to the low table. *He has an aura and red hair, like mine.*

Nameeri raised her sword, but Monya held her back and shook her head. They waited for V's orders.

The child looked to his side and gasped as he saw Ammad's bloodied form. "Brother," he murmured and his little back heaved with sobs.

Ammad reached out a shaky hand to the boy. "Come here, come to me."

"Who is this Peqkian child?" Laurya whispered to V.
The third.

Sybilya had said, "The third has awakened. A peen. You must save him from corruption..."

Had he been corrupted? Was V in time to save him?

"Artaz," Selmi said gently and came forward, with arms spread. "Little brother, come to me."

"He did this," Ammad burbled, wrestling to stay alive with blood oozing from the wound in his torso, and indicated Selmi. Then he beckoned. "Help me."

The child, Artaz, glared at Selmi and pursed his lips. With a flick of Artaz's wrist Selmi's arms stuck to his side and, frozen, Artaz lifted him into the air.

"No, Artaz, it's me, your brother, don't do this..." Selmi said, still with the gentle tone.

Artaz moved his hand in an arc and pointed at the window. Selmi shot out the window as if thrown. His yell dwindled as he travelled further away.

Razanne screamed and went to run to the doorway, Daya grabbed her and hissed, then placed a finger on her lips. The girl shrunk down at the warrior's feet, fear in her eyes, but silent.

Artaz gingerly stepped closer to Jakira. He leaned over her body, careful not to touch her exposed guts and put his arms around her neck. He sobbed into her chest. "Mama, Mama."

V raised her hand to get all those in the room's attention. She held her finger to her lips. Silence, so as not to disturb the child. She gestured to Laurya, and then pointed to the window. Laurya silently ran from the room to find Selmi. V pointed at Monya and then indicated Ibin, Nameeri and Razanne and jerked a flat hand. Get them out of here and far away. She indicated to Daya and spun a finger in the air and then jerked her flat hand again. Round up any innocents nearby and get them far away.

Both her warriors nodded and did as she bid.

Ibin resisted, "V—" he started before Monya's palm plugged his mouth.

The youngblood turned her head slowly from side to side. There was no argument. He obeyed immediately.

Within moments, it was just V, four bloody corpses, the half-dead worm and the sobbing Peqkian child in the room.

His bawling subsided. V stepped closer and crouched down. She rested her hands, red palms up on her knees.

"Artaz," she said in Shella, "you are a Peqkian, like me."

The boy raised his head and sniffed as the snot flowed from his nostrils.

"We are the same, you and I. We are touched by magic." She wriggled her fingers slowly to draw his attention. He looked down at her red palms. She slowly brought a hand to her hair and he followed the movement with his eyes.

"See, we have the same hair," V said and smiled.

Artaz wiped his nose, starting at the tip of his finger along to his elbow. A snail's trail of snot smeared his forearm. His tears had stopped and he looked at V with fascination.

"We need you back in Peqkya. Back at home," V said.

Artaz's eyebrows screwed together. "This is my home." He looked down at Jakira's lifeless face and his hands bunched into little fists. He thumped them on Jakira's bare collarbone. He took a deep breath and closed his eyes.

A spark crackled from his fists and latched on to Jakira's flesh. His face contorted and his body tensed as he concentrated.

He has so much power, can you feel it? V's magic said in awe.

Jakira's little finger moved. Her leg twitched. Horrified, V watched as an eyelid flickered. *He is bringing the woman back to life!*

"Stop," V said, in a gentle tone that belied her dismay. She touched Artaz's shoulder. "She is no longer with us."

His eyes sprung open and he glared at V. In a voice that sounded like a fully grown adult, he snarled, "You! You killed her. I saw!"

He turned from Jakira's body and faced V. As he

stepped forward, V stood and took a step back, holding out her palms submissively.

"Artaz, you are Peqkian, like me. Let us be friends."

"I hate you," Artaz yelled. He brought up both hands to attack.

32

VIOLYA

ᘓᘔᘐᘑ

Artaz jerked his hands and a flash of jagged light flew at V.

She crossed her arms in front of her and blocked it with a shield of red that shimmered before her from head to foot.

The boy looked confused as the bolt flew off to one side and blasted a hole in the wall through to the next room.

This is the magic he must've used to kill my warriors and the Khumarahs in the hallway. It had been effortless, instinctive. He had mastered his magic, had tested his strength, trusted completely in his abilities. *He is far more advanced than I am.*

The child is stronger than you, it's true. V's magic replied, *but you are not weak.*

He attempted a second time. The bolt of light bounced off her shield and upwards into the ceiling. Rubble and dust dropped on their heads and Artaz ducked, alarmed.

V's shield protected her from the brunt of the debris.

As the dust settled, with a thought her shield evaporated. She walked towards the child, lying under rubble. His eyes slowly opened. A look of shock upon his face.

Destroy him!

No, he's only a child.

His magic has turned to evil!

No. He has been corrupted by these Dromedars. He can be saved. I will save him. Sybilya said we need him.

Her magic was angry. V shut out its chatter. She kneeled by the child and brushed off the debris that littered his chest.

"Artaz, you have much power. I want to help you to use it for good."

"My brother is helping me; my brother is training me."

Ammad groaned. "Artaz, do not listen to the hisspit. Kill her."

"Artaz," V said, "that is not your brother. Ammad is an evil man."

The boy flicked his attention between Ammad and V. She braced herself for an attack. Brought magic to her fingertips.

"I grew back his arms," Artaz said with a whimper. He sat up and sniffled. He hugged his body and rocked from side to side as the tears started again.

"Just imagine all the good you can do in the world. You are a chosen one, you belong in Peqkya where you were born." V gently placed a hand on his knee and, for a moment, his body softened.

"Kill her!" Ammad shouted.

The boy looked up and swung a fist into V's chest. The force was so incredible that it lifted her off her feet and smashed her through the wall and into the next room.

She was stunned at his power. For the first time in many years she was frightened. A deep, blooming pain spread from her chest. She could feel the dampness of blood seeping through her leather.

Artaz froze her body in place as he came running after her, throwing blast after blast at her chest. He spun her off her feet so she hung horizontal and then pulled down the ceiling on her body. He lifted her through the rubble and threw her ragdoll body against the floor. Up and down repeatedly.

Fight back! Her magic said urgently as V's body was pummelled.

I cannot kill him, he's only a child! We need him.

Then he will kill you.

V yelled in frustration as Artaz slammed her so hard that she smashed through the floor and into the kitchen below. She fell on pots and pans, platters and tea sets. Slaves screamed and ran through the pillars that stood in place of a back wall, ripping down the fine gauze that was tied between pillars to get out into the garden.

Artaz jumped from the hole above and controlled his fall. He floated down to stand at her side. His eyes twinkled as he spotted a wall rack lined with knives. They flew from their resting places and at V, pricking her skin all over.

Enough! The knives halted mid-strike.

Artaz steadied his feet as he willed all his might into forcing them down as V channelled everything she had into pushing them away.

The knives hovered mid-air, wobbling. The handles distorted and the blades bent with the extreme force exerted on them. They exploded apart, shards and splinters flying in all directions.

Artaz's hold on V ended as he brought his arms up to protect his face. V sat up and didn't cower from the sharp pieces flying at her. She used this momentary distraction to throw a lightning bolt at Artaz.

It smashed into the boy and knocked him off his feet. But he absorbed the blow. The aura around him expanded and strengthened. He spit the energy back out as a scorching blast of white light. It boomed louder than anything V had heard before and the building around them imploded.

V was buried under rubble. She threw it off her with ease.

Artaz grinned as he waited for her to emerge, he stood

on the fallen stone and masonry, arms outstretched to the night sky. V could hear screaming and shouting. One side of the palace was destroyed and the half that remained creaked and groaned.

The boy pinched his fingers together and pulled them slowly apart. V's body jerked and her arms flew out to the sides. Half of her flesh and innards wanted to go left, the other right. The pain in her chest intensified as her body was stretched.

She gritted her teeth and launched herself at the boy. As she reached him, she clasped her arms around him. She drew on every drop of magic in her blood, commanding it to explode.

A huge explosion of energy flowed through her body and into his. The night sky lit up with a bright white, as building rubble, earth and trees all blasted apart. It propelled the pair high into the air, and as they fell, V clutched the stunned boy.

"Artaz," she said in his mind, *"you and I are the same. We have magic. We are one. Great Sybilya told me about you."*

She willed all the goodness, all the joyful energy of the Stone Prophetess into Artaz. She projected an image of Sybilya sitting in her hut, surrounded by cats and replicated the great lady's soothing purr that reverberated through their bodies.

Artaz pummelled her with his fists, wriggled in her embrace but she wouldn't let him go.

"No," he moaned.

She flooded him with visions of the stunning snowy mountains, the delicious crisp air, lush green vegetation and majestic tall trees.

"No, no, no... stop it!" Artaz yelled. "My home is here!"

'Do you not remember Riaow? That is your home.' She brought to their minds the city, with its colourful dome-shaped huts and circular streets, it's green spaces and bustling quarters. She shared memories of the rustling of

the bamboo forest, the smell of pine on the breeze, Inaly Lake on a clear day when the ripples glittered in the sunshine.

A memory flashed in V's mind – of the boy splashing on the shore with his pen-mates, his laughter rung out in her mind; his happiness apparent. He recalled his pen-mother rubbing him dry with a cloth while singing and V perceived a feeling of contentment wash over him.

"Mother Samya…" His body softened, then tensed as a memory of a great loss filled him. "The stone lady stopped loving me. Jakira loved me."

"No, the Stone Prophetess' love, her presence, left us all." V allowed her pain of Sybilya's passing to flow into Artaz.

"You too?"

"Every Peqkian. But we have magic like she did, and it hit us harder." V showed him Sarrya. And the wolf's desperate sadness at Sybilya's loss. "You are not alone, Artaz. We understand."

He shared a fear-tinged recollection with her: of being taken from his pen, a frightening man stuffing him into his cloak and forcing him to drink a disgusting liquid. And then he woke in a strange place with strange people. Artaz had been terrified.

"You were stolen, Artaz, but you can return," V said.

When they neared the ground, Artaz used his magic to stand them upright. He clung onto V in a desperate embrace. He reached into a pocket and pulled out two grubby wooden figurines, of a bird and a cat. He clutched them against his chest before looking up at her with understanding in his large, blue eyes.

"You… you are my sister. Peqkya is my home. That's where I belong."

"Yes. I'm going to take you home." V stroked the boy's red hair. She would save him from corruption, would show him how to use his magic for good.

He smiled. And she sensed he was at peace, felt as if he

could finally belong. His energy bristled with excitement to return to the mountains.

His head jerked and then a second time. His eyes went wide and he stared at V in desperation as the light drained from them.

A third thud jolted his head. He slumped against her. Three throwing knives were lodged in his crown.

V's eyes snapped up. Ammad slumped against a still-standing wall, behind it was a staircase. One arm clung to the wall to keep him upright. The other was wrapped around his torso, to stem the flow of blood from the wound she'd inflicted earlier.

With his teeth he pulled a fourth throwing knife from a holder on his forearm and flung it at V. She dodged it easily. She gently lowered Artaz's body and stormed towards Ammad.

"He was a child!"

Ammad snarled. "No, he was a weapon. And if I can't wield him, then you can't either."

V reached for her blades, noted that her sword and daggers were gone. She thrust the last of her exhausted magic into her hands and grabbed Ammad's new arms. She wrenched them from his body with a wet crunch.

Ammad shrieked.

She flung his limbs into the rubble.

Ammad flopped to the ground, writhed like the worm he was. Although she desired to rip him to shreds, to torture him for all the pain he had inflicted, all the deaths he had caused, she crouched and snapped his neck. Efficiently, as a warrior was trained to do.

V's eyes flicked open as she felt a pressure on her shoulder. Although every part of her felt bruised, she reached for her sword.

"It's over," Laurya said, removing her hand from V. "We've cut the boy into seven pieces as per mage custom, to make sure his body won't be abused or used for evil."

V closed her eyelids slowly in thanks. In times past, long-dead mages had been unearthed by people looking to harvest the magic in their skeletons. Artaz deserved to rest in peace after such a short, tumultuous life. She'd come so close to saving him. Her heart ached.

"We will bury each piece one hundred paces away from the next, and one hundred hands down in the earth. No place will be marked," the warrior continued. "Toya is dead, all targets are dead. We have identified the bodies. However, there is one missing. Jakira. We could not find her remains, but we're certain she's dead, buried under the rubble."

V blinked again and parted her lips

"Selmi lives," Laurya said, guessing V's question. "A tree broke his fall. Broke a few bones and a couple of ribs too. But he'll survive."

V attempted to move, to sit up but couldn't. Her magic was silent. *Gone? Spent?*

"You're badly injured, you've lost a lot of blood and used a lot of magic. Ibin has gone to fetch healers. Be still," Laurya said.

***

"I will go," V said and dragged her legs off the bed and rested her feet on the tiled floor.

The Dromedar healer wrung his hands and shook his head, attempting to push her back onto the bed. She swatted him away.

Monya came forward to help V stand.

"You are not yet strong enough," Ibin said. "I cannot allow it."

In an instant, Daya's dagger was placed against his throat. "Do not dare to tell the Melokai what she can and cannot do."

Ibin took a sharp intake of breath as Nameeri's hand twitched towards her sword and Laurya made ready to throw a dagger at the Dromedar woman.

V gestured for her warriors to stand down.

"I will go," she repeated and all in the room nodded.

She raised herself up with a hand on Monya's shoulder. Laurya fastened V's sword belt around her waist and tied a dagger to each of her biceps. She had spent three weeks in that bed in a wing of the palace still standing, tended to by Dromedar healers. She had slept for the entire first week, according to Monya.

Laurya had overseen the ceremonial burning of the Peqkian warriors slain by Artaz. They had built the pyre outside V's room. She was too weak to stand to look from the window but the smoke of their bodies filled her room and as she breathed it in, she said her goodbyes to her women. Honoured them in death as they had honoured her in life.

V's legs wobbled and her balance took a while to centre. A pain throbbed in her chest from Artaz's blast that she knew would never go away. A constant reminder of that boy's power, that if she'd left it unchecked, he could've destroyed the world.

He had nearly killed her. Her magic was silent, had not stirred since the fight.

The familiar weight of her weapons bolstered V's strength. "Lead the way," she said to Ibin.

Ibin headed their small procession from the palace towards the Holy Square. Laurya walked behind him, followed by Monya and V. Behind came Daya and Nameeri.

The streets were crowded, but all parted for the Peqkians. They cheered and ululated. News had spread of how the Crown Prince Selmi had eliminated his family to claim the throne for himself. Another coup, so soon after the last one. But this one was different, for Selmi wanted change. He had done much already, including distributing all the surplus food from the palace gardens to those who had none.

Selmi was for the people, wanted to help the poor and abolish corruption. He was also now a sworn ally of

Peqkya.

The procession stood to the side of the stage. A great fanfare announced Selmi's arrival and the crowd cheered as he stepped onto the stage. One leg was in a cast, he sported a black eye and grazes as well as bandages on his hands and forehead. Ibin and Nameeri followed him. Khumarahs and Cuttarrs – ever loyal to the ruler, whoever that might be – flanked Selmi.

Ibin beckoned for V to come up on the stage too, but she refused and remained to the side with her women. This moment was for Selmi and the Khumarahs, she had no inclination to draw any attention away from their glory. And besides, there was always the chance he might call on her to make a speech, and she hated speaking to a crowd.

Drums pounded to a crescendo as Selmi waved to the crowd.

He walked to the middle of the stage and the drummers stopped.

"People of Drome, I am to become your ruler. There will be no ceremony or pomp. I have commissioned no expensive headdress or fine clothes. I want none of that frivolity that has marred the rulers before me. Mine will be an austere rule, but a happy one. Why? Because the funds previously frittered away on luxuries and idle pleasures will be used to nourish every one of my people. You will never go thirsty again!"

A cheer went up from the crowd.

"Wealth will be redistributed amongst all of you. There will be no rich and poor divide, no wealthy Tamadeen clan with too much food to eat and too much land to live on and no Affarah clan with no food or water, and barely a scrap of sand to sleep on.

"Every person will have a house for them and their families. Any unoccupied villas will be redistributed to those in need, no more wealthy families with second, third or fourth homes for their men's concubines or to hide away irritating in-laws."

A loud groan rippled across the crowd from the wealthy men. It blended with chuckles and clapping from the poorer people.

"And there will be no more slavery. I hereby announce that any family that still keeps slaves by this time tomorrow will be punished. Every slave is to keep their jobs should they wish, but is to be paid fairly for their service and has the option to leave whenever they please. Every chain, every slave bond in Drome is to be broken today. The slave quarter will be razed to the ground, and huts to house Drome's good people will be built in its place."

More whoops and cheers.

"My blood is Khumarah as well as Wakrime, but the Khumarah beliefs are more civil, more humane. I am relinquishing my Wakrime lineage and embracing my Khumarah heritage. And so shall you. Magic was feared by the Wakrimes and other clans as they had none. Those with a magic ability will no longer be persecuted but celebrated. Our history has long feared the Khumarahs but not anymore."

Selmi beckoned to a Cuttarr waiting off-stage. A few moments later, a naked man was dragged up onto the stage. He was hunched over, eyes downcast, and his hands covered his genitals. He had skinny arms but an abnormally large bottom. He had a shaved strip across his head from ear to ear. The rest of his hair was sectioned into braids that had been lopped off close to his chin.

"And the Holy Temple, for so long the home of corrupt religion will be opened to all gods. The bloodthirsty god that we have been forced to worship for centuries is no more! No more blood-giving, no more slaughter. Every Qacirr holy man and holy family is hereby stripped of their titles and wealth."

Selmi lifted the arm of the naked man on stage with him. "Including this man, Zeead, once the High Priest." Selmi pointed at the Holy Temple across the square and heads turned towards it. "And all those corrupt men."

At that moment, the Holy Temple's main doors opened and holy men stumbled out. They were naked. Only the shaved scalp indicating who they once were. Their long braids had been cut.

"Each of these men and their families will now need to work to earn their living. They will never luxuriate in others' donations again."

Selmi shoved Zeead toward the edge of the stage and as he waddled down the steps and into the crowd, he shouted in a high-pitched voice, "You will suffer for this. God will smite you down!"

The naked men from the temple followed Zeead's lead and scampered away into the crowds and dispersed down side streets. The crowd jeered and slapped the men on their bare flesh as they edged their way past.

"We will embrace the old ways of ancient Vaasar. People worshiped whichever god they chose. You are free to worship your personal god of choice. I will revere and celebrate all! The Holy Temple is open to all no matter your choice or even if you have no god at all. It will be a place for love, contemplation, rejuvenation. A place for happiness and not fear."

Selmi walked toward the edge of the stage and gestured to a mother holding a baby near the front. The mother lifted up the child and Selmi gently took it and held it in his arms.

"For too long our children have been neglected. For too long only the privileged few were given an education. No more. My great grandfather was Tufik the Teacher. He set up schools and systems to teach all Khumarah children. These schools will be expanded and open to all. Every child born will be taught their numbers and letters."

Selmi kissed the baby's head and held the bundle in the air to raucous clapping and cheering. He carefully handed the child back to its mother.

"But do not think I am only for the poor. There is a

cruel custom that takes sons from mothers. The Wakrime custom to take the first-born son of a Tamadeen family for the Cuttarr guard is herein abolished. Men from any clan can sign up to join. They will be given a fair wage and opportunities. Those of you Cuttarrs who wish to leave, can. I will hold no judgement."

Women cried out with joy and V heard weeping as relieved Tamadeen mothers clung to their male children. The Cuttarr guards who stood on stage shuffled and glanced at one another. But none moved.

Unsure of the sincerity of Selmi's declaration. Wise to be cautious. He has promised a lot in this one speech, V thought.

"Now, to love." Selmi held out his hand. Razanne stepped on to the stage and took his hand and he kissed her passionately. "This woman was forced into marriage with my brother. But that marriage was never consummated. Razanne is pure and whole. We are in love, have been in love for many years. She will become my wife. You are all invited to our union."

He paused to allow the crowd to quieten.

"Razanne will be my only wife. I will not take any more, I will not have a harem of concubines. I will devote my life to her, as she devotes her life to me."

Razanne beamed and waved at the crowd.

Selmi continued, "Until Razanne and I are blessed with sons, and until they come of age, I name Ibin el Khumarah as my Crown Prince."

Ibin stepped forward and bowed deeply as Nameeri and the crowd in front of her clapped.

But not all were happy. V scanned the crowd and saw many frowning and with arms crossed. They were dressed in fine clothes and V knew them to be of the wealthy clans, now suddenly stripped of their human and material possessions.

Selmi has much to do to keep control.

"He has grand visions for this place," Laurya whispered behind V.

Daya replied, "That's if this place lasts much longer. Nameeri tells me that each year there is less and less rain, and more and more people."

Selmi continued, "I am turning over good land in the palace grounds to growing more crops for you, my people, so that no one goes hungry again. And we will build huts in the slums, real homes…"

V didn't hear the last of Selmi's words as a vision raced in front of her eyes.

Finya, sword drawn and teeth bared.

She swayed. Daya caught her and kept her from falling. Laurya and Monya moved closer.

V steadied herself. She indicated for her warriors to make a circle. They leaned into one another and touched their foreheads.

"My women, my warriors. We must leave here. We go to Troglo."

***

Ibin had granted them four of his fastest camels, a young guide on an equally fast camel and a pack-camel to carry water and supplies. The group had run through the desert, V surprised and thrilled at the speed of the camels and the distance they could travel.

The guide was ambitious and eager to impress. He took them on a route across a line of gigantic, sweeping dunes avoided by travellers for its dangerous slopes that, if approached from the wrong angle, could suck a camel and its rider down into sandy depths never to be seen again.

The shortcut took a week off their journey. "Why go around," the guide had said with a glint in his eye, "when you can go through."

They had left him and the camels where the sand met the dusty, scrub-dotted plains, the forbidding Meliok mountains looming in the distance. No-woman's land. They shouldered the remaining supplies in backpacks and crossed the flat strip of inhabitable wasteland on foot. They ran for days until they reached the start of South

Road, the well-trodden traders' path that meandered up into the mountains. It was an easier ascent for animals, and those not used to traversing inhospitable mountain trails.

As they neared the mountains and began to climb, Peqkian border warriors stepped out to meet them. They had crossed into Peqkya. These women had watched them approach across the desolate flatlands, there was nowhere to hide. The spiked grasses and hardy shrubs grew to ankle height and no more.

At a specific time of year, devastating westerly winds ripped through the area, and anything not low to the ground was torn up and blown off in the direction of the Sarenky Sea. The windy season was not far off, and V and her women had fought to keep their footing against the sudden, violent gusts that slammed into them from haphazard directions.

Once their group had been identified, the border warriors thumped their fists to their chests at the Melokai's return. V sent a fast messenger on ahead of them to Riaow as the remaining warriors made V and her companions comfortable in their camp. They ate, rested overnight and gave thanks for the cleaner, cooler air.

V, Monya, Laurya and Daya left the following morning on fresh ponies. They followed the South Road, climbing up over the mountains before descending into their heart. Peqkya.

The sight of home filled V with the right kind of warmth. The oppressive, suffocating heat of Drome a distant memory. This inner heat spread like a balm to all the places in her body that revenge had left empty. One year had passed since the Drome army had invaded her country, since Melokai Ramya had been so brutally slayed. Twelve moons since she had learnt of Emmya's death, of Gogo's murder.

I killed the murderer. I killed Ammad. I taught Drome a lesson they won't forget in a hurry and have installed a new leader with no ambition to enslave my country.

She had taken her revenge. The worm had not escaped her fury. And now, as the grip of retribution lifted and dissolved, she found her mind opened to the possibilities of rule, to the responsibilities of being Melokai. The shock of Sybilya choosing her had settled. She had a country to protect, to serve, to nurture. And suddenly, she felt up to the task.

But as the ponies galloped through the country, past small herds of sheep, through thickly forested valleys and rocky plains, one thought dominated the rest, cut through the urgent need to reach Troglo.

She was excited to see the wolves again. Her wolves. Darrio and Sarrya.

She had almost died, had witnessed the death of a child, and it had put things into perspective. Her confidence in rule had grown and she had mastered her magic. It was time for the Peqkian people to broaden their outlook, to accept and welcome other races from ally neighbours. Melokai Ramya had led the way with her Trogr lover.

V would take Darrio as her official soulmatch, declare Sarry her child. It was time to embrace the family she had left behind. Her sense of duty to her people was stronger than ever, but so was her heart.

Love is love, no matter what. It is time.

33

DARRIO

After days of running and clambering up and over the small Meliok mountains, Darrio picked up the scent of home in his nostrils. A wash of wolf odours flooded his senses after many moons away and he stood on two legs and howled in delight.

Sarry nudged his ankle and growled low in warning. She slunk next to him, cautious and alert, and not so happy to be back in Zwullfr.

He dropped to all fours. "What, daughter?"

"No welcome here," she said and crept forward.

He frowned and followed her. She had been sullen the entire journey, cagey about why they had to return, tense. As they had neared, her mood had soured as his had lightened. Darrio did not share her reluctance to return. With every step closer his excitement swelled in his chest. *I'll see my sons once again. My Warrio and Harro.*

They reached the south bank of the Great River. Scars from the recent battle with the Peqkians and their tigers still marred the landscape. Flattened areas of forest with churned-up mud, discarded rags, blood splatters and stains, deep scratches and gouges in the tree bark. There were also dead wolves rotting, their bodies left where they fell to feed the earth and all Great Mother Wolf's children.

The Peqkians burnt their dead, a custom he still did not understand.

It was quiet here. Darrio had expected to see Peqkians patrolling their border, and perhaps a wolf or two on this side of the river, but there was no one. *They aren't expecting us and all is peaceful, this is a good sign.* He tried to convince himself, but deep down, his bowels twinged. *Something is not right.*

Sarry studied the northern shore and Darrio tracked it with her. No wolves. He sniffed the air but the wind was in the wrong direction, blowing their scents north.

"Come on, Pappy," Sarry said and plunged into the river and swam for the other side.

Darrio followed his daughter, gasping as the chill water engulfed him and made his bones ache.

They heaved themselves up onto the northern bank. Darrio closed his eyes and shook out his fur, warming himself with the movement and relishing the summer sun on his back.

He opened his eyes as a pack of snarling wolves surrounded him and Sarry. She growled. The male wolves were stood on two legs, clutching pilfered Peqkian spears that were pointed at him and Sarry. The females were on all fours, with no weapons, but just as vicious. He didn't recognise any of them.

"What is this?" Darrio demanded. He flicked his muzzle towards Sarry. "She leader, your great-pack alpha returned."

The circle of wolves edged forward, noses wrinkled and baring their teeth. Darrio and Sarry drew closer together. His hackles quivered in warning.

"Our alpha in den, traitors," one of the female wolves replied.

Baffled, Darrio took a step forward, but Sarry held him back by nudging his paw with her own.

"Take us to alpha," she said and lowered her head, belly and tail to the floor in submission.

"That his order," the female said. She jutted her nose towards the mountains.

Sarry and Darrio skulked in the direction she had indicated. The pack surrounded them and nipped at their lowered tails to keep them together and moving the right way. The wolves emitted intimidating grumbles and snapped their jaws to maintain their dominance.

"Sarry?" Darrio whispered.

"Tried to tell, Pa—" she replied, before her words were cut short by a menacing howl from one of the wolves and a poke with a spear in her side. She yapped and remained silent.

The forest here was familiar as it was the Wulhor-Aean's territory. But they weren't heading towards the pack's old den, or towards the fallen tree, with its huge, gnarly roots pulled up from the earth. They were heading into the mountains, towards Aaowl Peak, Darrio soon realised as they turned onto a well-worn path. The place where the first great pack-meet had occurred, and where Sarry had revealed herself as the first female to stand on two legs.

As they drew closer, wolves came forward to join the pack that surrounded them, all snarling and snapping their jaws aggressively. Darrio's shoulders hunched in submission. He felt as if he was prey that had been hunted and singled out, and was now being herded to its death.

Hundreds of wolves lined the path they took towards Zwullfr's highest and most iconic mountain. Aaowl Peak was shaped like the crescent moon and could be seen from a great distance all around. Darrio and Sarry were directed to the flat clearing under the peak, that was surrounded by boulders. The place where Lurra, the Wulhor-Aaen alpha and Arro's mated female, had once sat to receive the wolves that Darrio had gathered.

"Wait," the female said.

Darrio and Sarry crouched with ears, eyes and tails lowered.

"What this, Sarry?" Darrio whispered.

"Wait, Pappy," she said and jerked her chin towards a large group of hostile wolves.

The wolves slowly parted and there, sat where Lurra once had, was his youngest son. Cowering next to him, with clumps of blood-matted fur dotting his body, was his eldest.

"Harro?" Darrio said and stood to all fours to take a step toward his sons.

The wolves around Darrio growled menacingly and swiped claws at him. Darrio slunk down once again.

"Pa, I leader now," Warrio said.

Warrio jerked his nose and a young wolf was pushed forward from the group. Sarry yapped in surprise. It was her friend, her shadow, Arro and Lurra's son Ricarro. He'd been viciously mauled and was bleeding from innumerable wounds. He collapsed to the earth with an exhausted whimper and didn't move again. His breath laboured and shallow.

"Ricarro?" Sarry said, but there was no answer. Her eyes narrowed and nose wrinkled in anger as she stared at Warrio.

"Those who do not submit are punished," Warrio said.

"Sarry leader, Warrio," Darrio said gently. "Went to negotiate with Peqkians. Now returned."

"Wolf allegiance moved on, Pa. Do not honour Peqkians, do not bow to them. Sarry too quick to submit. Wolves a powerful, ancient race. Wolves bow to no one."

"Fool," Sarry said. "Do not submit to Peqkians. Equals. Partner to face coming threat. Must unite with Peqkians, with other races in known world to fight bigger enemy. We do not fight together? We all lose."

"Lies!" Warrio yelled. "Too quick to give up Lost Lands, to run off to aid them. What bigger enemy? Lies. Enemy is Peqkians. Always been Peqkians and always be Peqkians. Pappy united wolf packs to fight them, not help them."

"Warrio, listen to Sarry," Darrio insisted.

Warrio stood to his full height and Darrio gasped. His son had grown in their absence. Warrio was as tall as Sarry, shoulders now as broad as an elk's antlers. His frame was becoming more human.

"Sarry no longer your strongest pup, Pa," Warrio said and howled.

The wolves gazed up at him in admiration. Darrio's jaw hung open.

Only Sarry wasn't impressed. "Brother, you grow in stature but not in intelligence."

Warrio took three strides towards Sarry and she stood to her full height to meet him. Their crinkled noses touched and they curled back lips to flash fangs at each other.

"No say here now, sister. We unite to fight Peqkians, to reclaim what is ours. To take back the Lost Lands. Peqkya not friend."

The wolves howled in agreement.

"Pups," Darrio said. "Enough."

Sarry flicked her eyes to her father and took a step back from her brother.

"Harro always smart one," Warrio said. "And he my counsel. Harro!"

Darrio's eldest son crept forward, eyes downcast, to cower at Warrio's paws. He was still the same size as Darrio, the size of a normal wolf. Harro had scratches and gashes on his face and body. Some fresh, Darrio noted.

"Sorry, Pappy," Harro mumbled.

Warrio growled and swiped out a huge paw at Harro's muzzle. Harro whimpered.

"Enough, Warrio," Darrio yelled and shot forward to shoulder-barge into Warrio's legs.

But Warrio didn't budge. Darrio was no longer strong enough to topple his son.

In return, Warrio clamped his jaws around Darrio's neck and squeezed them. Darrio felt sharp teeth puncture his skin and he whined in pain.

Then Sarry was on Warrio. She went for his neck and he spat out Darrio to fight back.

Harro picked Darrio up and guided him away from the sparring siblings. A space opened up around Warrio and Sarry as the wolves moved back. They watched the scrap intently, with low grumbles and snapping jaws.

Warrio and Sarry pawed at each other with sharp claws, attempted to lock each other's muzzle. They fell to the ground and tussled, rolling over one another. Before, Sarry had won this game, but not now. Warrio was just as strong.

Sarry's claws connected with Warrio's shoulder and drew blood in four deep gashes. Warrio yowled in anger before snarling.

"Only one can rule," Warrio said. "Me."

Warrio attacked viciously and Sarry whined as his mouth latched onto her neck.

Darrio leapt into the fray, attempted to come between them, to split them up as he had when they were pups brawling.

Warrio shoved at Sarry and she lost her footing. He came at Darrio.

A massive paw swiped down Darrio's chest, cutting open the flesh to his ribcage. Darrio squealed in agony.

"Didn't want this, Pa, but you always stand in the way." Warrio bit down on Darrio's neck, aiming to sever a jugular vein. To kill him as they killed their prey.

Darrio whimpered as Warrio's jaws snapped shut.

"No!" Sarry scrambled up.

She launched herself at Warrio, slamming him to the ground. He took Darrio with him, teeth still locked in Darrio's flesh. Darrio hung limp from Warrio's maw, his body twisted.

Sarry wasted no time, she stood on Warrio's chest and clawed at his muzzle. Warrio's jaw loosened and Darrio eased his neck out of his son's teeth.

Harro was by Darrio's side in an instant, dragging him away from the pair. He licked at his father's wounds and placed a paw over the blood that gushed from Darrio's neck.

Warrio glared at Sarry, eyes full of hatred. He began to get up, but Sarry wouldn't allow it. She took his neck in her jaw and smashed him back to the ground. He writhed and snarled, but she would not let go, her powerful muscles bulging with the effort. She pressed her claws into Warrio's chest.

But Warrio would not submit. He fought on. With strength Darrio did not think his daughter possessed, she stood up to her back legs, keeping her lock on Warrio's neck. She lifted her brother, his legs scrabbling for purchase and then she slammed him back to the ground again.

He huffed as the wind knocked out of his chest. She repeated this move a further three times until Warrio barely moved.

She went to pick Warrio up again, but Darrio said, "Enough, Sarry."

She dropped Warrio's neck and her brother made no attempt to move. She swiped a paw across his nose, and he lowered his eyes in submission.

Sarry glared at the wolves surrounding them, and each dipped their noses to the ground, not able to meet her blazing orange eyes. She took off towards the peak. They watched in awe as she climbed the crescent-shaped peak, using her front claws to find cracks in the rock to heave herself up.

A few moments passed as Sarry disappeared from view. Then a surge of barks announced that she could be seen again. She had scaled Aaowl Peak – a feat no wolf had ever achieved.

At the top, Sarry lifted her nose to the moon and produced her roaring howl. It shook through Darrio, through the wolves gathered under the peak and reverberated throughout the snowy wilderness of Zwullfr.

Sarrya, Darrio's daughter and tamer of tigers, was the leader of the wolves. Now and until she died.

Warrio heard.

They all heard.

***

"He would've killed you," Harro said. "He would've killed Pa. He would've killed all of us."

"I know," Sarry replied.

"He grew big. Power clouded his mind. Was hungry for it. Killed many alpha wolves to take control of packs by force. To rebuild army and attack Peqkya."

Sarry sniffed.

Darrio rested on a bed of moss in the secret thicket where they had once slept as a family, many moons ago. His eyes were closed, but his ears were open. Beside him slept Ricarro, the young wolf's rising ribs the only indication he still lived.

"Warrio turned wolves against you. They angry about deaths of loved ones in war, angry you forgave Peqkya so fast," Harro continued

"They don't understand," Sarry said with a weary tone. "Tried to tell them. Peqkya not enemy. Enemy comes from east."

There was a pause and Darrio heard the two wolves shuffling and padding in circles to get comfortable.

"Will Warrio come back?" Harro asked.

"Yes," Sarry replied.

Warrio had limped into the boulders at Aaowl Peak after Sarry's night-shattering roar. A self-imposed banishment, Darrio supposed. Warrio would sulk alone, to lick his wounds and his damaged pride. No wolf would follow him after they had seen him submit to Sarry.

"I have sense of what to come," Sarry said. "Had vision in Peqkya, knew needed to return to Zwullfr. Told have physical magic too, but yet to break out. Spark may never ignite within me."

"You see what is to come. Why know we ally with Peqkians, not fight them," Harro said.

"Yes. Many still do not believe it. Many only see what in front of them, must open minds, trust what I tell them."

"Why, Sarry?"

"First standing female, speak with tigers, have magic. That is enough."

Harro snorted. "They follow you now without question, saw your strength. None will attempt a challenge."

Sarry's voice wavered. "Knew Warrio would betray us. But not again. He will be great warrior, like mother."

"Mother?" Harro said.

Darrio's eye pinged open.

"Much to tell, brother. Mammy alive. Peqkian."

Darrio spun up to sitting. "You know, daughter?"

"Known for while, Pappy. Forgive you. Harro and Warrio will forgive you too. Would've been hard to explain *that* to wolves." Sarry snorted.

Harro's eyes flitted from his father to his sister. "Tell!"

"Much to tell, brother…"

Darrio drifted into sleep as Sarry told her brother of Violya. Darrio's secret was no longer a dead weight that tugged at him constantly, that rankled his every interaction with his offspring.

He thanked Great Mother Wolf for the blessing that was his pups.

***

Weeks later, after Sarry had received many wolves under the gnarly roots, Darrio woke one night with his daughter urgently nudging at his ribs, but carefully avoiding his healing wound.

"Pappy, we must go east. To Troglo."

Darrio groaned, but he did not question his daughter.

34

GWRLAIN

Captain Finya paced around the edges of the fire where Freya and her linked Trogr cooked their breakfast: bat soup with wild plant leaves and herbs foraged from outside the cave. Gwrlain had to admit, the Peqkians made excellent food.

Gwrlain held Freya's baby. He sang to her and inhaled the familiar scent of her delicate skin.

"It has been nearly a year and still no return message from Riaow," Fin said. Impatience had replaced her anger and every morning she paced and ruminated on their situation. "Our order was to protect the five kidnapped women. Since they want to stay here, so must we. But I was sure V would've told us to return by now. My message was clear. The women are happy here, we've witnessed it first-hand for months. There is no trickery. They don't need our protection."

"Perhaps the clevercat never reached Riaow. It is a treacherous route to traverse. There are bears and other dangerous creatures. Or perhaps V was not there to receive it. Clevercats are trained to only deliver their messages to the intended recipient," Robya said, patiently repeating her sentiment from previous conversations. "It does seem odd that V wouldn't reply."

"What if V is in danger in Riaow and that's why she hasn't replied? What if we should return anyway?" Fin considered.

Freya laughed at something her lover said. But the Trogr quietened her abruptly and placed his hands on the ground.

A jolt of movement bolted up Gwrlain's legs from the rocky ground. A deep-booming rumble reverberated from above. A constant, yet random sound. The other Trogrs in Peqklo had sensed it too and stopped still to listen and feel. Gwrlain inhaled deeply, but they were too far inside the mountain to pick up a distinct smell. It would also be pointless to use his echoes as there were too many obstacles in the way.

A few moments later, as the noise reached the Peqkian's less attuned ears, Fin stopped pacing. Her deliberations dried up in her mouth. She whistled and brought a finger to her lips. Her warriors sprung to action, hushing the Peqkian women in Peqklo. Fin pointed upwards.

"Gwrlain?" she hissed.

Gwrlain gave the baby to Freya and put his hand to the rocky floor.

"We are near the base of the mountain," Gwrlain said, "This feels like a great herd trampling down from the mountain peaks. Coming from the east."

"That does not bode well. Sybilya's prophecy said trouble would come from the *east*," Robya said.

"Freya, move everyone down to Lauago. Robya, stay with them," Fin commanded.

As the inhabitants of Peqklo moved, the captain shouted orders to her five warriors. Four to see the women to safety and return to her, one to take a message to Riaow. The warriors thumped their fists to chests in understanding.

Without hesitation Fin turned and sprinted down the tunnel that led out of the mountain.

Gwrlain ran after her.

Fin squinted as her eyes adjusted from the near-dark to daylight. It was an overcast, grey day with a hard, relentless rain. As they neared the cave opening, they could hear the hum of many voices.

"I do not recognise the language," Gwrlain said, his ears picking up snippets of the drifting chatter.

Fin stayed close to the cave walls, creeping forward in the shadows, ahead of Gwrlain.

The entrance to the cave was unchanged. Gwrlain hummed to sense the trees and vegetation, the valley beyond.

But it was obvious now, the trample of feet was coming down an unknown path overhead. Gwrlain listened to the sound as it got closer to the rock lip that jutted out from the cave entrance.

Fin waited, hidden from sight as the first of the feet found the space outside the opening. She gasped as she saw. Gwrlain's quiet hums sensed the beings.

More and more piled down from the mountain path and amassed before the cave. There was a brief pause before the dark shadows swarmed into the cave opening.

Fin jumped in their way, baring her teeth in a snarl. She raised her sword with both hands, primed to attack. Gwrlain stepped out behind her.

She yelled and charged.

35

VIOLYA

ℭℨ℞ℭ

V ate the chicken and lentil stew ferociously. Stuffing in crispbread and pickles at the same time. Only pausing bites to gulp down some water. Daya, Laurya and Monya shovelled food into their mouths in a similar, ungracious fashion. They had arrived in Riaow at the crack of dawn, half starved, and headed immediately to the mess hall to wake up the cooks.

Lizya debriefed V as she filled her belly.

"Fin sent a warrior with a message, she arrived just before the border messenger turned up to announce your return. Fin's warrior said that there were a great number of unknowns approaching Troglo. It wasn't clear whether they were friend or foe. Fin called for reinforcements. The messenger left for Riaow before she saw the unknowns, Fin wanted her away before engaging to ensure the messenger didn't get swept up in any attack or violence," Lizya said.

V nodded.

"Another messenger hasn't come," Lizya continued. "I decided to wait for you before giving orders. I've been busy building up our army."

Amya, V's big ginger clevercat, jumped on the table in front of V. Clinging to the clevercat's head with all ten of

411

her little berry-red feet was Emmo. Amya dipped her head so the trilling caterpillar could scamper down and launch herself at V. She snuggled up under the Melokai's chin and rubbed her head along V's jawline.

"I'll be leaving you again soon," V said to her pet, as it smothered her with affection.

The clevercat mewed. V indicated for her to speak her message.

"Your counssssellorsss requesssst a meeting, now that you have returned," Amya said.

V swallowed her mouthful. "Tell them that I have no time. I leave again for Troglo in a few hours. I trust in their abilities to govern a little while longer. My priority is the safety of Peqkya."

Amya let out a quick meow to acknowledge the message and jumped off the table, skirting under V's legs to deliver it swiftly.

Lizya raised her eyebrows. "In a few hours?"

"Yes, there's no time to wait," V said and leaned back in her chair, allowing her belly the chance to digest for a moment.

"It'll take longer to mobilise the army."

"No need, I go with a small, elite troop. Daya, Laurya and Monya will come with me. We make a good team and understand each other."

"Four of you? Against a *great number of unknowns*?" Lizya replied. "You know Fin will be pissed that she's requested reinforcements and four warriors show up."

"We'll take the fast Fert horses and arrive there much quicker than if an entire army has to march over the Eastern Melioks. If I need reinforcements, I'll send Monya back."

"Oh wonderful, so then there will be three warriors to reinforce Fin's number. She'll be really pissed."

"V unleashed some crazy magic in Drome," Daya mumbled with her mouth full. "Fin won't give a shit how many warriors she has when V starts throwing fire bolts at the enemy."

"Mmmm hmmm," Lizya replied through pursed lips. Then she clicked her fingers and started giving orders to clevercats and novice warriors waiting nearby.

V spooned a heap of spicy pickles onto a crispbread and crunched down on it. Then loaded up a second.

When Lizya was done delegating tasks, V said, "While all the supplies and horses are prepared for our journey east, I must see the remaining Dromedar soldiers."

"Let's go then, greedy guts," Lizya said and stood.

V followed her out of the mess hall. They mounted ponies and galloped through the streets of Riaow that were just waking up, the two warriors guiding their mounts towards the peon barracks and training grounds outside of the city.

When they arrived, the training ground was busy with peons and Dromedars running through their daylight dances. They remained seated on their ponies as Lizya shouted orders and V watched the peons. She was impressed by their focused discipline. *They will make adequate warriors if they can follow orders.*

The thirty-three Dromedars gathered in front of them. They stood like warriors, at ease but poised for action. Once again, V was impressed.

"Before you speak to them, you might want to wipe that bit of pickle off your chin," Lizya whispered and chuckled as V swiped a hand across her face, dislodging a chunk of pink-stained turnip.

Emmo shot forward, caught it mid-air and munched happily next to V's ear.

"You could've mentioned that before," V said through gritted teeth.

Lizya winked at her.

The Melokai took a breath and turned to face the Dromedars, who looked up at her with neutral faces, their emotions in check.

"Dromedar soldiers. Drome has a new ruler," V said in

Dromedari.

"They know fluent Shella now, by the way. We've been busy training them up," Lizya said in a low voice.

V dipped her head. Impressed for the third time. She continued in the Peqkian language, "Selmi el Wakrime now rules in Drome. Mastiq el Wakrime, Ammad el Wakrime and the majority of the Wakrime family are dead. Selmi has embraced his Khumarah heritage and is now known as Selmi el Khumarah. He has abolished slavery, has opened the palace gardens for farming, has redistributed property amongst the poor. He is an ally of Peqkya."

The Dromedar soldiers blinked at her, betrayed no emotion.

"Ruler Selmi welcomes you back to Drome. You will not be persecuted, and you will be provided with food, clothes and homes. We will escort you to the Drome border, where Ruler Selmi will organise camels so that you can make your way home to Parchad, or any part of the desert from which you come."

Silence greeted her. The Dromedar soldiers remained completely still.

One at the front thumped his fist to his chest.

"Speak," Lizya demanded.

"Melokai Violya, I do not speak for all here, but I do not want to return to Drome," the Dromedar said in heavily accented Shella.

"Why?" V asked.

"Most of us were slaves or from the poor Affarah clan. We had nothing. Here we have water, food, a purpose, a family of sorts. We are valued for our abilities not our bloodlines. Drome may have a new ruler, but if we return, we will still have nothing."

"I understand," V replied.

Selmi had big dreams, but the clan culture went as deep as the deepest grain of sand. It would take many lifetimes to shift those dunes.

"Well?" Lizya shouted across the other Dromedars.

"Do you all wish to stay in Peqkya? Raise your hand."

Every right hand was raised. Lizya looked at V.

V thumped her fist to her chest. "Very well, you can remain in Peqkya as members of the peon army. You will train hard, you will fight hard for Peqkya when called upon. If any of you stray or are unwilling to fight, then a suitable punishment will be meted out upon you."

As one, the soldiers thumped their fists to their chests and shouted, "Melokai Violya!"

"Now, get the zhaq back to your training, desert rats," Lizya shouted and the Dromedars jogged back to join the Peqkian peons in their morning drills.

"I'm impressed," V said to Lizya.

Lizya put an arm around V's shoulders and said, "You're impressed by these pathetic creatures? Come with me, this won't take long."

The Head Warrior urged on her pony and V followed. They cantered back towards the city, but at the outskirts turned north. Soon they arrived at another basic barracks. Lizya guided them in through the gates and stopped, overlooking the training grounds. V came to a halt next to her.

The familiar sounds of clanging swords, grunting and senior warriors shouting commands engulfed V. She looked out on row upon row of women fighting an opponent, practising the techniques and sequence flows directed by a senior warrior.

Wide-eyed V turned to Lizya for explanation.

"These are all your civilians. They volunteered to train as warriors and fight. I had to turn some away, either too young or too old. There were so many that we built these huts and a training ground to accommodate them."

"How many?" V asked.

"Just over one thousand. They've come from Riaow and the surrounding countryside. They want to fight for you, with you, for Peqkya."

***

They travelled fast along the East Way towards the eastern Meliok mountains and Troglo. Four warriors and eight horses. Four horses to ride, four to carry a few, lightweight provisions.

As night fell, they made camp and ate some of the dried meat and fish, pickled vegetables, lentils and flatbreads that Lizya had organised. At the crack of dawn, they packed up the camp and set off on the fresh horses, allowing the ones they had ridden the previous day some measure of respite.

In this way, they covered more ground in a few days than the army would've covered in weeks. They only slowed their pace as they reached the start of the mountains and the well-worn path of the East Way became a rocky trail. This mountain route was for trade, and so took the easiest path around the peaks, suitable for horses, ponies and pack animals to be guided slowly over the uneven terrain.

There was a continual light snowfall as they marched, leading their horses, but the ground was still warm from the summer months and it didn't settle. A few more weeks and the fall would get heavier and they would be navigating through waist-high powder in some parts. If the snows came before they could return to Riaow, they would be stuck on the wrong side of the Melioks for months until the pass cleared again. That was not an option.

V tugged the hood of her fur cloak tighter and picked up her pace. The two horses she led refused to increase their speed and the rope tightened. The Fert horses were built for speed across flat, grassy lands and not for harsh weather. The warriors had wrapped them in fur blankets and every night picked the hard, compacted snow from their hooves. V tugged again and the horses reluctantly obeyed. Behind her, her four warriors increased their speed to keep up.

Along the route were sturdy but simple shelters that had been erected by traders. V and her warriors rested overnight in these when they were available. Otherwise, they found craggy overhangs to set up camp under.

As they descended, they came to the border camp that marked the end of Peqkya. The path continued onwards towards the mountains of Troglo, to the trading point. Once a hive of activity, the trading point was now deserted, following the kidnap of the five women by the Trogrs. All those living and working near the trade point had been found jobs and rehomed elsewhere by V's councillors.

The border warriors made them welcome and that evening they sat around a fire.

"You'll need to continue north up the valley until your first glimpse of Zyr Peq to the north-west," the head border warrior said while warming her hands over the flames, "then, head east. There is a huge cave opening, one which no Peqkian had ever ventured to before Fin and her party. That opening leads to the Troglo capital of Lauago, deep in the guts of the mountains. That's where the Trogr took them, and that, I believe, is where they still are."

The directions matched those spoken by Fin's messenger warrior, back in Riaow.

"And what of the trading point, any Trogr activity?" V asked.

"None whatsoever. No sign of Trogrs since the kidnapping. Warriors went in after the women, there was fighting and many warriors died. The Trogrs fight viciously in their caves. Afterwards, the Trogrs retreated down into the caves and haven't surfaced since – at least not from this cave opening."

***

The following morning, with replenished supplies stuffed in packs carried on their backs, V, Daya, Laurya and Monya set off north at a run. They left the Fert horses behind, the border warrior insisting that the terrain was near impossible for horses and that they would slow V down.

They followed the boulder-strewn, sparsely forested valley between the western Meliok mountain range that marked the border of Peqkya and the higher, bleaker, more dangerous mountain range that the Peqkians had never managed to conquer. Within which, the caves of the country of Troglo twisted and wound, like a labyrinth.

The Peqkians knew of four openings into the caves, one of which was at the trading point. When they spotted the second opening, V and her warriors crept towards it silently, scouting it out for a few hours. There was no activity. The third and fourth were the same. All was still. And V had no sense that they were being watched.

They continued to pick their way through the forest and over the black and white boulders that lined the small river's path. All four looked up often, hunting for the imposing peak of Zyr Peq in the distance.

"I wonder what lies to the east," Monya mused as they jogged through the forest after passing the last known cave opening.

They had picked up speed as the boulders had dwindled into small rocks, then pebbles, then dirt. The four warriors had maintained a companionable silence for most of their journey, but today, the young warrior's curiosity had got the better of her and her lips spilled her thoughts in great torrents.

"I wonder what we'll find when we arrive," Monya continued. "What these unknowns are, what they can tell us, whether they are fierce fighters and formidable enemies. I wonder if they'll put up more of a fight than the unskilled Dromedar soldiers. I wonder—"

"I wonder if I'll fall and wedge a rock in my mouth so I can't wonder anymore," Laurya said in a high-pitched voice that mimicked the novice.

Daya laughed. "I wonder if I'll trip and slice out my tongue so I can't wonder anymore."

Monya tutted at their teasing. "Well, your conversation is so limited and dull that I have to talk to myself."

"Well, your conversation is so—" Daya went to copy Monya's words but V stopped and held up a fist.

Her women fell silent immediately, alert, planting their feet with hands creeping towards weapons.

V pointed through an opening in the forest canopy. There was Zyr Peq. The highest peak in the Meliok mountains. The day was clear and dry, and the view was perfect. Zyr Peq thrust its snowy, brutal peak through a skirt of cloud. V felt a tug in her chest, as if the peak held a string tied around her heart and was pulling her in.

She felt a twinge in her ankles that crawled its way up her body and ended with a shiver across her shoulder blades.

Her magic stirred, for the first time since the fight with Artaz in Drome.

Sleepily, it spoke. *We should pay our respects to the majestic peak.*

V smiled inwardly at the magic bristling in her blood, tickling every fibre of her being.

So you're not gone then.

Where did you think I'd go? You are me, I am you, we are one.

Then, more urgently, *we should go and pay our respects.*

V gazed up at the distant peak. In times past, those with The Sight would go on pilgrimages to the peak. The mountain held great power and rejuvenated those with magic, and honed their abilities.

The mountain tugged at her a second time.

No.

She turned her face away and looked east, ignoring the magic's protestations until they dwindled to silence. Ahead of V was a steep, craggy slope dotted with trees, that stretched up further than V could see. At some point, it joined the Troglo mountains. The formidable peaks were higher than Zyr Peq, standing like angry sentries. All rigid fists and hard scowls. Somewhere up there was the cave opening that V had seen in her vision. Somewhere up there was Fin.

And a great number of unknowns.

Without speaking the four warriors exchanged glances and silently climbed upwards. They reached a sheer rockface and Laurya led the way, hunting hand and foot holds, heaving herself up, clinging to the rock with her fingertips. V, Daya and Monya followed the path she found.

V glanced up to see Laurya's feet disappear over a ledge. V carefully positioned her feet and wedged her hand into a slit in the rock and then flung the other arm over the lip. A hand grabbed it and heaved her up.

V came face to face with Laurya, nodded and then turned to help the warrior pull Daya and Monya up too.

They were on a rock shelf that jutted out from the side of the mountain. To the east was flatter ground, strewn with huge rocks.

Laurya pointed to her ear. *Listen.*

V heard the rumble of voices and the low, constant murmur of activity. Coming from the east, behind the boulders, from the side of the mountain. The cave opening must be here.

V signalled orders, and they silently unshouldered their packs and removed a few layers to ensure their movement was unobstructed to fight. The day was warm, the sun beating down on their backs, but V knew the night would not be so kind to them.

V edged forward and the three warriors followed. They darted from boulder to boulder, keeping out of sight of whatever – or whoever – was in front. The noise bloomed as they neared.

The boulders grew sparser and shrunk in size. The rocks levelled out. The chatter of hundreds of voices intensified.

An army.

The warriors dropped to their bellies and heaved themselves forward using their forearms, each finding a low rock to hide behind.

V snuck her head around the side of her rock to take in the scene.

There was a smooth, flat expanse about half the size of the makeshift training ground where V had seen one thousand civilian women training not long before. Behind it was a huge, circular cave opening, like a mouth in the mountain forming the letter 'o'.

And on that flat expanse: people, people everywhere. Squashed together in front of the cave opening, but none inside the cave.

It was not an army.

V's magic didn't stir.

The people were unarmed, sat huddled together or curled up asleep. Exhausted. Eyes downcast. They were dressed in rags, unsuitable for the cold weather. They appeared to be soaking up the warmth of the sun.

V scanned the bedraggled mass and her eyes found a Peqkian. Not a warrior. She was handing out food from a basket at her hip. Birds' nests. Those who she gave the nests to had barely enough energy to lift them to their mouths. To V's left, two serving peons distributed water from a great pot, handing cups to people, waiting for them to drink, taking the cup back and moving on.

On the perimeter of these people stood three Peqkian warriors. One was positioned fifty paces to V's right. They stood facing inwards, keeping control. Fin wasn't there. And neither were any Trogrs. She knew they shunned sunlight, but she could see none in the shadows of the cave opening either.

Gesturing to her warriors, V stood and walked towards the warrior fifty paces away, holding her hands high.

The warrior heard her approach, turned with sword drawn and whistled to the other warriors around the edges. When she saw it was a Peqkian, she did not lower her sword.

I'm pleased that she is alert, but also sad it has come to this. Ashya's betrayal has taught us not to always trust our own.

"I am Melokai Violya, warrior. Friend," V announced.

The warrior's face uncrumpled into a smile as she recognised V.

"My Melokai." The warrior lowered her sword and thumped fist to chest. She sheathed her sword and shouted, "Melokai Violya. The Melokai is here!"

Laurya, Daya and Monya appeared from the boulders to protect V, daggers drawn and pointed at those hunched on the ground. But the people near to them didn't cower or frighten at the sudden appearance of more Peqkian warriors. They stared blankly, oblivious to the weapons.

"They have seen such horrors. They are resigned to their fates, no longer in charge of their destiny," Daya observed, but she did not withdraw her weapon, scrutinising every move of those near to her for any threat.

"Take me to Captain Finya," V said.

The warrior nodded and stepped over people and children towards the cave entrance. V and her three warriors followed.

V looked closer at those she was stepping over. Humans, smaller than the Peqkians, closer to the height of the Fertilians. Their skin tone was similar to the brown of the Dromedars but with a golden sheen. Their hair was a golden blond and eyes a gilded yellow. A gold sheen touched everything about them. As if kissed by the sun.

There were males and females, but few children. Adults firmly grasped the children that were there, kissing their heads and whispering soothing sounds. The children melted into the arms of their protective guardians with no argument, and were silent and still. Their little eyes bore no childish liveliness, they were dull, unfocused, and full of fear. They'd seen things no child should ever see.

These people wore simple, undyed clothes, most of which were now rags. They had no bundles or possessions with them. Those who were lucky had worn-out sandals clinging to their feet, many had rags wrapped and tied at ankles, a few had bare feet, with their toes raw and blue in colour from the cold. They carried no weapons, either the Peqkians had seized anything dangerous or, as V judged more likely, they had arrived with simply the rags on their backs. These golden people did not look like fighters.

V reached the cave entrance and whistled into the cavern. The whistle echoed and soon Fin came running out of the near-darkness of the tunnel and into the light.

They embraced, thumping each other's backs. Fin acknowledged Laurya, Daya and Monya with a wink and a grin.

"V, this place is crazier than Majute," Fin said and laughed. "The Trogrs are bizarre and then these no-homers showed up. Came piling in from over the mountains glowing like the zhaq sun and practically dying on their feet looking for shelter in the caves. The Trogrs freaked the zhaq out and refused them entry into their caves. We had to herd them together and during the day they sit out there and at night they come into the entrance of the tunnel, but not any further.

"We're trying to work out where they came from and what happened. Robya is learning their language. She's attempting to speak with one who seems to be the nominated leader."

"The kidnapped women?" V asked.

"Oh, yes. They're fine. Safe and happy. One's had a baby. Two are pregnant."

V's eyebrows raised.

"It's a long, weird story. It wasn't rape, it was consensual. These no-homers are a priority right now," Fin said.

"Let's find Robya then," V said.

"This way."

V indicated for Laurya, Daya and Monya to stay put as she followed Fin.

The cave was near empty, but as they went deeper into the darkness, Trogrs lined the walls humming quietly. Not a threat to the Peqkians. But a threat if required, V sensed.

Sentries. Peqkians could pass this point, no-homers could not.

Under the light of a few torches against one wall, Robya sat with Gwrlain and one of the no-homers, an older male. Grey spiked his golden hair and his skin was leathery. He was painfully thin, his craggy face gaunt. He emitted a sunshine glow, giving off more light than the torches.

"V," Robya exclaimed, shooting up from the rock she sat on. They embraced. "Oh, it's so good to see you," the scholar beamed. "I've learnt so much here. The Trogrs are fascinating, truly. And these people…" She gestured to the male, who stood with his head bowed.

Gwrlain had also taken to his feet and towered over the strange sun-kissed male. The white giant sniffed and hummed.

The Trogr nodded to V and spoke in his accented Shella. "Melokai Violya. I will show Lauago to you. But first…" Gwrlain inclined his head at the male.

V gestured for the trio to continue with their discussion and all took their seats again. V crouched to listen.

"We think there was a great battle fought where they come from," Robya explained to V. "They fled their homes, kept going until they reached here. Many thousands died on the journey. These are the few that remain. They are the first beings to ever come east and make it to Peqkya. We've never found a path over the mountains. Melokai Annya tried it five hundred years ago and failed. We've never attempted it since. Remarkable they got this far."

Robya indicated the male. "We could not find a female who would talk. Their language is nothing like any I've heard, I'm working as fast as I can to decipher it."

She turned to the male and using her hands to help communicate her words, said, "What are your people called?"

The male replied with a deluge of noise. He produced

his speech from the back of his throat, using high-pitched clicks and low, beating thumps. Occasionally he'd use different fingers to make popping sounds with his cheek.

The scholar's forehead clenched in bafflement. She held up a palm and then one finger. "Slowly, one word at a time."

The male rambled once again, but this time V held up a palm and he immediately quietened. He flicked his eyes up once to see her red hair and then shrivelled into himself, frightened.

"He says they came from the sky. Consumed everything in their path. His people had no hope," V said as the scholar gaped. "I understand him. I understand all languages."

"Well, I wish I had that skill," Robya said.

"Me also," Gwrlain said.

"What are your people called? How did you come to be here?" V asked the male, in his language of clicks, thumps and pops.

He jolted at hearing his language from her mouth and clutched his hand to his heart.

Stuttering, he replied, "We are the low-plains people of Sema. We travelled across vast wastelands, where nothing grows or lives, where the earth is scorched and barren. We kept going, we could not return to Sema to the devastation and atrocities there. Many died on the journey. But then our feet carried us from the nothingness into life once again. Trees and animals. We climbed, up and up. We had never seen such things before as the rocky towers jutting up from the earth."

He shook his head in wonder.

"They are called mountains," V said, using two clicks and a cheek pop that she thought was most appropriate.

"Mountains," the male formed the word.

"Continue," V said.

"Many more died in the... mountains... when the white chill settled over us."

"Snow."

"Snow? So many new things," the male mumbled and looked at his hands.

"Keep talking," V said.

"It was hard to find a path. We went in circles some days and at other times had to backtrack after hitting a dead end. Eventually we realised we were descending and the... snow... lessened and we could see green forests. Our path led us down in front of this opening. We hadn't eaten in weeks and arrived near to death. We had not seen another human, or near-human since we left Sema. We ran into your people and *these* creatures," the male glanced at Gwrlain, "and gave ourselves over to your mercy or menace. We had nothing left in us for aggression and we don't know how to fight. But we were shown a kindness and for that we are very grateful."

"What are we to do with you now?"

"We are a farming people. Provide us with some land and we will farm for you, produce crops for you, help to feed your people." The male sighed heavily, defeated. "Or do with us what you will. We submit. We cannot return to Sema. We escaped horrific deaths in our country, all I hope is that we haven't walked into the same in this place."

V studied the male. He spoke the truth, she knew, although he could not meet her gaze and kept his head low. Robya twitched in her seat, tapped her pencil to her sheets of parchment and cleared her throat. She stared intently at V, impatient to know what the male spoke.

"Tell me of who attacked Sema," V said.

"They came from the east—" the male started but was cut short by faint howls echoing through the tunnel.

V leapt to her feet and ran for the entrance.

"Wolves," Gwrlain yelled in his language as he followed closely behind V. "We are being attacked. Prepare to fight!"

The Trogr sentries bristled and charged towards the entrance.

"No," V shouted. "They are allies."

"Allies? I witnessed the wolf war, I was there with Ramya," Gwrlain said.

V stopped in the cave entrance as Darrio and Sarry bounded over the lip of the rock and headed towards them, howling. V's heart leapt with joy.

But behind her the hums of the Trogr sentries grew louder.

"Tell them to stand down, Gwrlain."

"You have no authority here, Violya. This is Troglo. You are no longer in Peqkya."

"These two are friends, Gwrlain. Much has changed since Melokai Ramya's war."

The wolves scaled boulders and jumped over the sitting no-homers. They skidded to a halt at V's feet.

Darrio stood to his full height and embraced V, panting in her ear. She could feel his pounding heartbeat through her chest. Sarry stood and threw her arms around them both.

After a few moments of delicious contact, Sarry peeled away but Darrio lingered.

I sensed that you needed us close, so we came, " Sarry said in V's mind.

"V," Darrio managed, his chest still heaving.

His one eye flitted to Gwrlain, who stood a few paces behind them in the shade of the cave entrance. Lines of Trogrs stood behind him. Darrio bared his fangs in a warning growl.

V pressed a palm to Darrio's chest.

Sarry stepped forward and sniffed at the white giant. They were of the same height.

"Gwrlain, this is Sarrya, the leader of the wolves. And this is Darrio, her father," V said in the Troglo language.

Before Gwrlain could reply, Sarry spoke in his guttural language, her accent perfect: "I am honoured to meet you, Gwrlain."

"You have the skill of speaking tongues," Gwrlain

replied.

"Sarry was blessed by the great Sybilya," V said.

"We mean you no harm, Gwrlain. We come now from Zwullfr. The wolves and the Peqkians have formed an alliance. If your people are friends of Peqkya, we are friends of yours."

Gwrlain's attention faltered as a swift swooped down and glanced past the top of V's cloud of red hair, chirruping frantically. Its flight was fitful, appearing disorientated. It headed to Gwrlain. He hummed intensely and then shot out a hand to catch it. He spoke to it. The bird squirmed and chirruped back. He let it go and watched as it flew away with an effort to go straight.

A gust of wind hit those stood at the cave entrance as the swifts that nested in the tunnels, tended to by the Trogrs, flew out and circled randomly above the no-homers in the clearing. They bumped into each other, squawked, continued on.

Gwrlain gestured to V. "A faint call comes from the east. One the birds attempt to resist but it is getting stronger. Those that call are coming here," he said.

"The same as attacked Sema?" V asked, but deep inside, she already knew the answer.

36

GWRLAIN

V watched the swifts' erratic flight, deep in thought. Gwrlain, along with the others, waited for her next order. No one spoke or rushed the warrior. Even the no-homers were quiet.

Eventually V spoke in the Troglo language, "Take me to my women, Gwrlain."

"This way," Gwrlain replied and led her down the tunnel.

The two wolves slotted in behind her, trotting close together, sniffing at the air and growling to one another in their language. He could hear V whistling orders to her women, to Captain Finya. He listened as V repeated what the old male no-homer had told her to the scholar Robya.

Gwrlain could smell the two wolves. A dank, earthy tang. The last he had seen of their kind was when Ramya's army had fought them. They were vicious, ugly creatures. But good for breeding? He wasn't certain just yet. The female had a hint of human about her, but the male did not.

He sensed that the tunnels began to darken and hummed his way. The Peqkians slowed in the darkness, a faint light behind them from the opening and a faint light in front from the Peqklo cavern.

Gwrlain paused at the turn before the cavern. "V, your women are safe and happy. Here they are." He gestured for her to go on ahead of him and she did.

V stood for a long while taking in the scene. The wolves stood behind her, sniffing, continually sniffing. Fin sought out Freya and brought her forward.

They spoke in rapid Shella and Gwrlain's mind wandered. Backwards. Always to the past, to what he had lost. *Ramya*, he thought, *Terya*. The image of the sword through Ramya's chest and out through her back into his baby. His daughter.

V's voice snapped him from his reverie. "Take us to the Living Goddess. Your mother, who was meant to be dead."

Gwrlain could hear no malice in V's voice, sensed no change in her body heat or heartrate. It was a statement of fact. As if she already knew.

They travelled deeper into the caves. His skin drank in the cool, humid air and he felt refreshed after so long near the surface.

V didn't speak behind him. And because she was silent, so was her group. She had become a formidable leader. Respected and honoured. Ramya would be proud of her.

He berated himself. No matter what he thought, his soulmatch was there, always there. But never there. He had misled her, it was true, misled her people. *But there was love, deep love. And surely mistruths could be forgiven for love?*

The wolves' sniffing intensified as they neared Lauago. The noise level increased and the Trogrs' singing drifted down the tunnel.

"This is their capital, Lauago," Robya said.

"The singing is majestic, Gwrlain," V said.

"It is, V, it is." Gwrlain paused to allow the melodies to sweep through his body, waking up all the tiny hairs on his skin, before taking the steps down.

"Why are they not scared of us?" V asked. "Not alarmed at strangers in their city?"

"You are no threat to us," Gwrlain replied. "Each one of us knows how to hum the death-rattle. No being other than a Trogr can survive that."

"You are certain?" V replied.

Gwrlain paused, recalling V's own death-rattle at Ramya's apartment. "Apart from you, perhaps. But could you survive the chorus of every Trogr? Unlikely."

"Let us not find out," V replied, but her body's unseen behaviours told Gwrlain that she was confident that she would survive it.

This Peqkian is very different to the others.

As they reached the central rock where his mother and sister lounged, a long line of male Trogrs stretched off into the distance behind. They dropped gifts at their feet. The three Peqkian males lounged around Lulac, rubbing her legs, massaging her swelling belly and feeding her birds' nests. His mother Gruack sprawled next to his father, her womb now spent.

"The peons?" V said.

"I gifted them to Gwrlain's sister Lulac," Fin replied, sheepishly. "One might have fathered her child."

V nodded.

Fin leaned in close to the Melokai. "I know, not the greatest gift to receive – three scrawny serving peons, but she seems happy."

"More guests," Gruack said drowsily to Gwrlain in the Trogr language. "And what are these furred creatures?"

"Wolves," Gwrlain said.

Gruack hummed and the fur on the wolves fluttered as if in a breeze. They both whimpered and snarled and raised up on to their two back legs with sharp fangs bared. She stopped the hum and listened to its return vibrations, then stuck out her tongue.

"They are similar in kind to us, Gwrlain. You bring more potential mates. I assume they are willing? The continuation of this race will succeed because of you. Bring the male to me. He might be able to revive my dead womb. Let us hope the female links with a Trogr."

"No…" Gwrlain replied but V cut him short.

"They are not for breeding. They are not willing. Touch them and die," V replied fluently.

A faint flush came to Gruack's transparent skin. "You speak our language perfectly. Has a Trogr attempted to match with this one, Gwrlain?"

"We are not for breeding," V repeated, stepping closer to the rock and Gruack's aged face.

Fin and the warriors behind her reacted immediately, hands on their sword hilts, watching V closely.

But V didn't pull her sword. "You and your daughter are the two remaining pure females of the Trogr race. You do not want to die. Touch any of my people without their explicit consent – and the wolves are my people – and you will breathe no more."

Lulac shifted her position to gaze at V as a male Peqkian rubbed her shoulders. Gruack laughed. She took in a deep breath to let out the death-rattle hum.

"Mother," Gwrlain said but knew it to be fruitless. She did precisely what she wanted. She was their Living Goddess after all.

The vibrations from Gruack blasted into the Peqkians and wolves, who were locked in place as their entire bodies juddered.

But V was not affected. She raised her hands, as if catching the vibrations and thrust them back at Gruack.

His mother was lifted off her rock and slammed down upon it. Her death-rattle broke and her grip on the Peqkians and wolves faltered. The female wolf snarled and leapt forward to V.

V placed a gentle hand on the wolf's neck.

Gruack inhaled sharply as her body jerked. She rolled onto her side, stunned. Lauago went silent. The singsong of the Trogrs abruptly halted and all took deep breaths ready to protect their goddess, ready to throw out their vibrations to kill these intruders.

"Mother," Gwrlain said again. "This is the ruler of Peqkya. Violya. She has a unique power. We must *negotiate*."

Gruack's body relaxed. She had no desire to risk the survival of her race on squabbles with other beings. She accepted V's power with little more thought. The tension in the air dissipated and the Trogrs began to sing once again.

"What is it you want, Peqkian ruler?" Gruack asked.

"My women died at the hands of your people, believing their fellow Peqkians had been kidnapped. This is abominable to me."

Gruack made no reply.

"I will forgive your people," V said. "I will forgive the nation of Troglo for these deaths because a bigger threat is coming. One which you will fight alongside us. Yes, a few of my exceptional warriors died. But there will be many hundreds of thousands of deaths if we do not fight together."

Again, Gruack remained silent.

"The no-homers need shelter in your caves until Peqkya can home them," V continued.

"Turn them back where they came from. They don't belong here. The females are weak and sickly. If a Trogr links, then so be it, but it is doubtful the pairing will bear fertile offspring."

"There is war where they came from," V replied. "War that is coming here. Our enemy is coming to this mountain, to these caves."

"*Our* enemy? We have no enemies. It is *your* enemy."

"Your enemy is reproduction. Your species is dying and you fight to survive. Give shelter to the no-homers, help us to fight our enemy and we will help you to fight yours."

Gruack didn't respond.

"You are reliant on your swifts. I witnessed just moments ago the effect on the swifts wrought by this enemy. The birds fought against it, but it will only get stronger. Could you survive with no swifts to produce the food you eat or the bedding you rest upon? Could you survive without them?"

His mother shifted her arm slightly. "We could not," she said slowly.

"Give shelter to the no-homers, help us to fight our enemy and we will help you to fight yours," V repeated.

Gruack considered for a moment. "How?"

"I will grant permission for my women and their children to remain with their Trogr lovers. And for Trogr males to visit Riaow. If any of my women desire one, they can match. Gwrlain and Ramya fell in love and created a female child. Other pairings might produce the same. I understand from Freya that she is happy, she is loved and her daughter is healthy and adored. And she was not forced. Who am I to stand in the way of love?"

Lulac pushed away the peon fussing around her. "I am with child."

Gruack stroked her daughter's face. "Let it be female."

Gwrlain joined his voice to that of nearby Trogrs to intone, "Let it be female."

"Let it be female," Lulac repeated and smoothed her pregnant bump. She slowly turned her attention back to V. "Violya offers us a good deal, Mother."

"If we refuse, then our race will die," Gwrlain said. "If this enemy from the east enters our caves, then we may die. We do not know what they are capable of, whether they will succumb to our defences or override them. V has shown us that we are not unbreakable, for she controlled your power."

Gruack exhaled. A long moment passed before she said, "We will send our males to fight. And when this enemy is defeated, our two peoples will link and reproduce. Trogrs will not be defeated. This is not our end."

The female wolf next to V howled. The sound echoed

around the vast chamber, rising above that of the Trogrs' songs.

"Now," V said, "we prepare for war."

***

They left the following day. V insisted.

"Winter draws closer," she had told Gwrlain. "We can't risk getting stuck in Troglo, on the wrong side of the Meliok mountains, for months waiting for the passes to clear."

So Gwrlain had set off for Riaow with V, her warriors Laurya, Daya and Monya, the scholar Robya and the two wolves. They also brought the Sema male with them, his name Efram, to learn from him on the journey. He was reluctant to leave at first, but had no family left in the group. All had died on the march west from Sema. After a brief discussion with V, conducted in his odd language of mouth-pops and clicks, he soon acquiesced.

No doubt realising, as Gruack had, that he was securing the future of his people by agreeing to help the Peqkians.

Fin remained in Troglo, her warriors keeping control of the no-homers. And when the host of Trogr fighters were ready, she would accompany them to Riaow. Gruack had promised they would be ready before the winter snows, and so following closely behind this delegation.

The Sema no-homers would remain in Troglo until the snows had come and gone. "My councillors need time to prepare for their arrival with homes, jobs and the appropriate communication to the Peqkian people," V had said. "They are not fighters, and will be no use in the army, but they could farm and prepare food, could tend to animals. They will have a purpose and I will ensure they are integrated into Peqkian life."

Gwrlain had simply nodded at her. He had no interest in them, the new Melokai of Peqkya had promised that his kind could attempt to link with Peqkian women, with their strong, fruitful wombs. That was all he cared about, and that was why he agreed to her wishes. It had given him hope that the Trogr race would survive.

On the journey back to Riaow, the young female wolf and the young warrior who had arrived with V established a deep friendship. The pair laughed, trained, sparred, whispered. V often watched them and smiled. They were rarely apart, giggling like well-loved Trogr children tickled and sung to by attentive adults. It pained him to watch, knowing Terya never experienced that joy of friendship.

The male wolf spent his time with his one eye flicking between Sarrya and V. He kept watch over them both and was never far from either. At night, Gwrlain could feel the vibrations and smell the change in air as Darrio crept into V's tent. It was their secret, and he would not reveal it. He understood what it was for a Peqkian to love someone outside of their own. Ramya had broken traditions, had risked her people's disapproval to be with him.

Robya had brought all her notebooks and drawings documenting the life the Peqkian women had with their Trogr soulmatches to share with Head Scholar Chaz. Every day, she continued to scribble notes, as if desperate to record every piece of knowledge she had gleaned for future records.

V helped Robya to learn the Sema language and to communicate with Efram. Together they asked him questions about the enemy that had destroyed the Sema people's lands.

Gwrlain was silent for most of the journey. He observed. He listened intently to the Sema male's story, helped set up camp, assisted with any task when asked. But he barely spoke. Robya's attention was elsewhere, and he found he missed her conversation.

He did, however, sing every evening as the camp retreated to their sleeping places. He sang into the night, yearning for his link and his daughter. He was once again leaving the peace of Lauago and going back to Riaow, a place he didn't think he'd see again. Where they had lived and died.

"He sings for Ramya and Terya. He is still in mourning," Robya had explained to V the first time Gwrlain's melody rang out across the forest, and loud enough for him to overhear her. "He loved them deeply. He will never love again; it is their way."

37

JESSIMA

☙❧

Jessima kissed Eddie's head as he gurgled and fidgeted in Princess Georgina's arms. The Queen of Fertilian knew her son wanted to be set down and given the freedom to crawl as he pleased. At ten months old, his personality was beginning to bloom. He was adventurous with a deep curiosity about the world. He was pulling himself up to standing from a seated position, clinging onto furniture and taking tentative steps. She knew he would be walking soon.

And she would miss it.

She would miss his first birthday too, and possibly every other birthday after that, but she shook that thought away. She had to believe she would see him again, and soon. And if not, then she had to trust that when he was old enough to understand, he would be proud of his mother for fighting back, for leaving him in order to protect him.

"Goodbye, my love." Jessima's voice faltered.

Princess Georgina leaned forward and kissed Jessima's cheek. "You and I have never been close, but I admire your bravery. I pray for your victory. Know that I will do everything in my power to keep my little brother safe."

"Please tell him every day that his mother loves him,"

Jessima whispered.

"I will," Georgina replied. "Now, go and get my Hadley back. And tell him I want to make lots of babies of our own."

Jessima took one last look at Eddie and mounted her pony. It was a squat, sturdy thing, the same as the Peqkians rode. Better for the mountainous paths, she knew.

Chattergoon was already in his saddle, squinting up at the sky and frowning.

Jessima looked back to see Georgina with Eddie balanced on one hip and her other arm wrapped through Ernie's. They watched on sombrely. Prince Charles stood to one side. He fingered his religious pendant and silently spoke prayers for the army's safe journey and triumphant return.

"Let us be off before the clouds break," Jessima said to Chattergoon. "I fear a storm is heading our way."

"As do I, your Grace."

Chattergoon gave the order and the procession started. He led the way, followed by Jessima. Behind her came five thousand armed Lian women, hundreds of donkeys carrying supplies and live goats tethered in a line. They had gathered in the high fields in the northern-most part of the town the previous day. All the soldiers had been kitted out with clothing and boots, weapons and armour. And at dawn, they marched.

Some of the soldiers rode ponies, but most were on foot. Ernest had purchased every Peqkian pony the city owned for the army. But they were scarce in Lian, being largely unneeded except for working the fields. People went everywhere in the crowded city on foot, there being little room for riding horses or using carriages.

Those who weren't off to war lined the streets and cheered for their loved ones who were. Jessima waved to them and smiled at the children. However, the procession wasn't heading in the direction of the tunnels, they were heading west towards the sea.

She urged her pony forward. "Lord Chattergoon, where are we going?"

"The back route, your Grace," he said. She realised he hadn't confirmed where the back route started from in the city.

"How did you come about this overland route, Lord Chattergoon?" Jessima said.

Chattergoon's shoulders tensed. This was another secret he was reluctant to divulge.

The lord shifted in his saddle. "My wife discovered it, your Grace."

"How?" Jessima pressed.

"It is a long story."

"We have plenty of time," Jessima replied. She was bitingly curious but didn't want to scare the man off from talking by appearing too eager.

Instead though, Chattergoon raised up on his stirrups and turned to the army behind. "This way. And hurry up about it. No dawdlers!"

He directed his pony up a small alleyway, heading north towards the Melioks. Lian backed up into the mountains, with buildings perched as high as they could go before a sheer, rocky cliff face forced the boundary. They climbed up and passed the last row of buildings until they met the rock wall.

"Your Grace, there is a view of the sea if you turn your head now." Chattergoon gestured to the west and Jessima looked.

It was a truly stunning sight. The walled city of Lian lay ahead of her, sloping down towards the harbour. In a meandering line was the shore, the waves breaking in a white foamy streak. Beyond, the endless sea. It was a patchy bright blue with darker inky sections under the rain clouds. A dark grey sky hung in the distance, heading in their direction.

"This way," Chattergoon said and nudged his pony towards the edge of the cliff. "Please dismount, your

Grace, we must walk and lead the animals from here."

Jessima dismounted as the order went down the line behind her. Chattergoon led his pony straight into the cliffs, but then turned a sharp left towards the sea, heading towards huge boulders. He picked his way through and Jessima followed.

What appeared to be blocked, had a single-file track. It was barely perceptible, but now Chattergoon was on it, Jessima could see it easily. Hidden from view by the boulders, it snaked along the cliffs that led all the way to the sea. When they had reached the very edge, and close to a sheer drop into the sea below, Chattergoon turned inland and the trail led up, in a north-east direction.

Jessima took a last look at the sea then showed it her back.

The path led them into a deep, dark pine forest that clung to the side of the mountain. They, too, hugged the side as they picked their way along a thin pathway. Through the trees, and down below the cliff, she could see Lian. She flicked her eyes once or twice at the sight but kept her gaze firmly on where she was placing her feet. One false step and she would tumble down the side of the mountain straight back to the city.

"Are you certain we can traverse this path, Lord Chattergoon?" Jessima called ahead.

"No," came the reply.

Not reassuring, but Chattergoon continued onwards.

"I have a destination in mind for our first night's camp. We need to move quickly to get there before night falls."

And with that he picked up the pace.

"I'd like your tent set up here," Chattergoon said.

They had reached a relatively flat plain dotted with huge boulders and bizarre, spiky trees that were shaped, to Jessima's puzzlement, like an upright penis, complete with two bushy testicles at the bottom.

Chattergoon pointed to an area in the centre. "I'll call

over some soldiers."

"Thank you, Lord Chattergoon, but I shall do whatever is necessary," Jessima replied.

"Take your pony over there where I've ordered a stable of sorts set up. Then clear all the small rocks, flatten the ground as much as possible and set up the tent here." Chattergoon drew a line in the sand with the toe of his boot. "I shall set up mine and then come to assist you."

Jessima did as instructed and paid close attention to Chattergoon as he helped her to erect her tent. She would remember what to do for the following night.

She was exhausted. Her legs ached from walking; her hand was chafed from holding the pony's reins for the entire day. The deluge had erupted while they were in the dense pine forest, the canopy sheltering them from the worst of it. But as the forest had slipped away, opening into rocky scrublands, the rain had battered them for hours and all were soaked through. Jessima's historian had volunteered for the army and they had attempted to continue Jessima's lessons as they marched. But the rain had drowned out the woman's words.

Jessima's muscles niggled at her to rest, but Chattergoon was striding back to where the army streamed in to the plain from the narrow path. He shouted orders and pointed out directions.

If he doesn't pause, then neither shall I. I am the Queen of Fertilian, a warrior Queen. Jessima followed behind the lord, listening to his commands, watching and learning.

"Any accidents? Any injured?" He asked occasionally as the weary women trudged in. They shook their heads as they passed.

He stood in that same position for the next few hours, shouting directions and watching every soldier traipse in, every donkey trundle past, to the very last goat. Jessima stood with him. Straight-backed, alert and grateful. She would be seen by these brave female soldiers who had come to fight for her, she wanted them to know that she appreciated every last one of them. If they looked up from their feet, the women gave brief nods or smiled. She was one of them, would fight side by side with them. It not only bolstered their will, it bolstered hers too.

"Hello," Martha said from atop a pony. The medic led a team of healers and donkeys with medical supplies.

"Greetings," Jessima said. "Would you care to join me for some mead and pottage once you are settled?"

"I would very much like that, however I feel I shall have many blisters and cracked heels to soothe this evening," Martha replied as she passed.

"Tomorrow night?" Jessima called to the medic's retreating back.

"I wouldn't miss it," Martha returned from over her shoulder. "Bring the lord, he looks like he could do with a drink or two."

Chattergoon, for his part, completely ignored them, deep in concentration, focused on his task.

"Stay close together," he yelled every now and then, "pack in close and we'll all fit and have a place to rest our heads tonight. Pack in close!"

"Any message?" a soldier asked Chattergoon.

She smiled at Jessima.

"Fiona?" Jessima said. "From the fish market?"

"The very same. Annette is here too. We've left our children with Annette's mother. We both wanted to fight. Annette said you got your hands dirty for us that day at the fish market, so we'll get our hands dirty for you."

Chattergoon beckoned to Fiona and reeled off orders to set up a perimeter guard, to work out watches for the night, to ensure all were accounted for and had somewhere to sleep. Fiona listened intently and then ran off to deliver his orders to the appropriate people.

Soon after, the woman in charge of rations and the head cook came to him to confirm the night's food allocation. He gave specific instructions, down to the number of ladles of stew per bowl. Jessima was reminded of eating precisely seven nuts each day during her journey through the tunnels, and just how much had changed since then. She was now heading back to Fertilian, but not via the tunnels, on a secret route that only one man – and his wife – knew.

Once all the army had arrived and was settled, Chattergoon noticed Jessima. "Your Grace, I will inspect the camp. Go and rest before we eat."

"I shall come with you."

Chattergoon gave her a curt nod and strode off.

She followed.

When she finally pulled the cover over her body, her damp clothes laid out to dry next to a small fire, she found she couldn't sleep. She had passed the point of exhaustion. She closed her eyes and prayed for Eddie and for Toby. And just as her mind began to settle, a thump on the side of her tent woke her up, mere moments later, or so it felt.

"It's dawn, your Grace," came the call from outside.

Jessima sighed. They had another month of this, at least. Marching, barely sleeping, marching. She pulled the covers over her head.

She refused to bring handmaids, would dress and tend to her own needs. She thought of Marcy and Tina, her handmaids from so long ago left in Fertilian at Cleland Castle. She wondered if they still lived. Her mind turned to her family; did they still live? And then to Toby. A prisoner. Would the Thornes treat him with courtesy? Was he still alive? Her heart ached with longing.

I will destroy the Thornes. I will reclaim what has been stolen from us.

She swept her legs out of the covers, stood and dressed in the breeches, shirt and sword belt of a man. Of a soldier. She had no time to dream of handmaids and luxuries. She was a pampered, passive queen no longer; she was the leader of an army that was heading to war. *Every dawn I will wake and lead my women in our daylight dances. We will train before breakfast, eat, and march onward to battle. And I will do that every day until we reach Fertilian.*

And then, once she got there? War. Death. Pain.

But maybe Philip had delivered his message and there would be allies waiting – possibly even the Peqkians – and Toby would still be alive.

Maybe, just maybe, what awaited her was victory.

38

VIOLYA

ೞ

V sat in the council room, her hands resting on the table in front of her. The carved wood mapped out the main Peqkya landmarks. Her caterpillar preened while sat directly atop Riaow.

The councillors reported on the state of the country. They had governed well together, debating on significant issues, taking votes and agreeing the best plan. V listened to their updates.

"I think that is all, my Melokai," Head Scholar Chaz said.

V looked at each of her councillors in turn. The councillors who had served Melokai Ramya: Head Teller Omya, Head Speaker Zecky, Mother of Mothers Naomya, and Chaz. Then she smiled at her appointed councillors, Lizya the Head Warrior and Jozya, now the Head Trader. They waited for her reply.

"Thank you for all you have accomplished," V said. "Peqkya thanks you. As Sybilya once said, 'embrace change, for when it comes you cannot stop it'. You have stepped up to the challenge of advising a new Melokai in times very different from before and adapted to changes in customs that could've ripped our country apart if we'd let them. I am proud of your achievements."

The councillors acknowledged her praise with murmurs, smiles and nods.

"Great Sybilya has passed. We mourn her and we miss her, but we endure. We continue her legacy." V thumped her fist to her chest in remembrance and after a few moments of silence, she continued. "War is coming to Peqkya, to the known lands. And as another of Sybilya's Sayings stated, 'what comes next is based on solid plans and solid action in the present'. So, now, I summon a council of war. We must plan and we must take action."

V spoke to her clevercat Amya and the ginger cat jumped from the table to do her bidding. Within moments serving peons dashed into the room and positioned more stools about the table.

In came V's war council. She watched them all as they took their seats. First in the room was the Jute Captain Brinjinqa. His short, squat pink body spotted with intricate markings and blue spiked hair offering a complete contrast to the translucent-skinned Trogr who followed him. Gwrlain ducked under the doorframe. He hummed quietly to himself as both took their seats.

A pregnant Nameeri followed. She had arrived from Drome as the new ruler Selmi's ambassador while V had been in Troglo. She had perfected her Shella and trained with Lizya whilst they waited for V's return. The Dromedar woman smiled at V as she settled, her back-hump poking through a slit in her tunic.

Then came the two wolves on all fours. They both unfurled to full height on their two back legs. Sarry sat awkwardly on a stool, shifting her weight, not certain where to place her front paws. But Darrio refused the human contraption, flinging it out of the way, and sat on his haunches, his head and shoulders poking above the table.

Finally, in came the tall scholar Robya. She dipped her chin reverently to Head Scholar Chaz and then went immediately to Joz. The Head Trader jumped up and the pair hugged. Joz twittered and fussed about the scholar, in her charming way. Robya smiled shyly. Joz pulled a stool close to her own and insisted the scholar sit beside her. As Robya settled, Joz took the scholar's hand and held it tightly. The friends happy to be reunited after so long apart.

"For one thousand years there has only ever been Peqkians in this room," Head Speaker Zecky grumbled. "Then Melokai Ramya with her Trogr, and now Melokai Violya with, well, *everyone*." She flicked a thick braid from one shoulder to the other and folded her arms tightly in front of her.

Gwrlain leaned his ear closer to Brin, the Jute telling him an anecdote in Shella. Brin's clawed hand rested on the Trogr's shoulder. The white giant sat upright and laughed. A beautiful sound that V hadn't heard since Ramya's passing.

To V's amusement, the two wolves growled to each other about the stools. Sarry complained and her father replied with practical, but ultimately unhelpful, guidance.

V raised her hand and the room quietened.

"Thank you for coming to this war council, my friends. Before our thoughts turn to war, I wish to make an announcement," V said. Her voice faltered and she drew in a deep breath.

"I nearly died in Drome. When you are close to death, you have clarity on certain matters." She glanced at her red palms. "When I was eighteen, Sybilya sent me away from Peqkya for a year. Told me to go north-east, past the Melioks, and to explore. I met someone in that time. And I became pregnant."

Zecky gasped in shock. Joz squealed in excitement. Darrio shifted on his haunches.

"This someone was not a Peqkian."

Zecky groaned and ran a hand over her face in despair. She would need to explain this turn of events to the people in due course.

"And I did not have one child, I had triplets."

"Zhaq," Zecky muttered.

"This someone is here today, as is my child," V said.

She stood and went to Darrio and Sarry. Both wolves stood to their full height.

"Darrio is my soulmatch. Sarrya, the leader of the wolves and blessed by great Sybilya, is my child. They shall be known as such from herein. I will tell the people."

Joz burst out into a vigorous clap, followed by Robya and Brin. Nameeri thumped the table and ululated. Omya pursed her lips tighter and Naomya gawped behind her hand. Zecky swore again and furiously scribbled notes on her sheets of parchment, glancing up now and then to shake her head at Darrio and puff out her cheeks.

"You don't say," Lizya said. "It's pretty obvious, V. Sarrya looks like you."

"And you sneak around at night to see each other," Gwrlain said in his heavy accent.

"I wolf, I sneak. It is my nature," Darrio said, in his equally accented Shella.

The tension in the council room broke as laughter peppered the room.

"You produced offspring?" Chaz said delightedly. "As did Ramya and Gwrlain. Fascinating that our peoples can mix... and beautiful."

V touched her daughter's muzzle. The wolf's orange eyes glowed with happiness. At the same time, V squeezed Darrio's shoulder. He winked at her with his one eye.

She turned to those in the room. "Our custom is that 'No baby will ever know its parents and no parents will ever know their baby. Progression and success are based on merit, not bloodlines'. Sarrya is first and foremost the leader of the wolves, blessed with The Sight. She will be afforded no special treatment because she is my daughter."

V took her seat once again and held up her hand for silence. Now that her long-buried secret was a secret no more, her mind sharpened with purpose, with her duty to her people.

"War is coming to the known lands," V said. "And soon. We must prepare."

A ripple of nods circled the room.

"United we can face this enemy," V continued. "We have the support of Majute in the north-west."

Brin dipped his head.

"We have the support of the wolves in the north-east."

Sarry scratched her claws across the table.

"We have the support of the Trogrs in the east."

Gwrlain hummed just enough for them all to feel it vibrating in their bodies.

"And we have the support of Drome in the south-west."

Nameeri slapped the table.

"But there is one missing," V said.

"Fertilian," Chaz said.

"Why do we need them?" Zecky said. "They fight their own war. Leave them to it."

"They have a weapon we need," Sarry replied.

"What kind of weapon?" the Head Warrior asked.

"I do not know. But my sight tells me we need it," Sarry said. "We can only win when all six countries in our known world come together to fight as one. There is no other way."

Zecky harrumphed. "There's always another way."

"There is no time to debate. We need Fertilian on side," V said.

Zecky folded her arms.

"A few days ago," Lizya said, "a messenger arrived from Fertilian asking for the new Melokai. Refusing to speak her message to anyone else. I think it's time we hear what she has to say, don't you, V?"

The Melokai nodded. "Bring her in, we shall hear her message."

Lizya went to the door, giving orders to the warriors that stood guard there. Sarry shifted on her stool with a low growl, adjusting her tail to get comfortable.

Moments later Lizya brought in the messenger and stood her in a corner far away from V, in case she attempted an assassination or something equally foolish.

She was a mere girl with yellow straw-coloured hair swept back into a messy bun and wearing leather breeches and tunic. She had been relieved of her weapons but had a sword belt and dagger sheath. She also wore the vambraces of a keen archer. She was tall and wiry, pale-skinned. Her body toned from exercise. But her face told of her age.

"Speak messenger, for this is Melokai Violya of Peqkya," Lizya said. The Head Warrior had one hand around the girl's bicep, and the other on the hilt of her dagger.

The girl's eyes widened as she took in V's aura and her bright red cloud of hair. The Fert girl glanced quickly at the others in the room, her amazement only heightening as she saw wolves, a half-sized pink-skinned blue-haired creature, a hump-backed Dromedar and an almost see-through blind giant.

She gathered herself and bowed low to V, as low as Lizya's clutch on her arm would allow.

"Speak," V said.

"My name is Joanne Chattergoon, my father is Lord Andrew Chattergoon and my mother Kerrin is known as the Scorpion Hunter. Lord Andrew Chattergoon is with the true Queen of Fertilian, Jessima Cleland. They are marching from the city state of Lian to Fertilian proper with an army to oppose the false Queen Charlotte Thorne. She and her twins took Fertilian from King Hugo Cleland with the assistance of Captain Denya of Peqkya and her company."

The Head Warrior hissed at the mention of the traitor and Joanne glanced at her, alarmed, before continuing in a rush in her southern Shella accent.

"My father sent my brother through the tunnels to my

mother in Fertilian to tell her they plan to fight. My mother sent me here. She couldn't trust anyone else and she knew she needed to send a female. Mother is gathering allies to Queen Jessima Cleland within Fertilian, but the false Queen watches closely. She's viciously hunting down any Cleland supporters and executing them in front of her captive, Prince Toby Cleland, to teach him a lesson. We need your help. Queen Jessima was friends once with Melokai Ramya and calls for aid."

"What is this lesson Charlotte Thorne is teaching her captive?" V asked.

"Well, Charlotte is angry because her daughter Mary killed herself and her son after Charlotte had Mary's husband killed. And then Charlotte just had her son, Arthur, left. He was crowned King but then Prince Toby valiantly killed him that same night. So now the false Queen Charlotte has taken the throne because she doesn't trust Arthur's eldest son, Jeremy, to do a good job, because rumour has it that he's a simpleton."

"I see," V said. "How old are you, Joanne?"

"Sixteen," Joanne replied quickly.

V paused and watched the girl, who squirmed under the scrutiny.

"Fifteen. Sixteen in two weeks' time."

"She speaks the truth," Sarry said to V in the wolf tongue.

V replied in the same language. "She does."

The girl, worried that she would be dismissed before she had said her piece, blurted, "My father is leading Queen Jessima's army on a secret path into Fertilian. The army is made up of women from Lian because most of the men died in Hugo's campaign and at the siege of Cleland City. There are five thousand soldiers. They are poorly trained but determined. They need your help. Please."

"You are a brave warrior, Joanne Chattergoon," V said.

Joanne's back straightened and a small smile spread across her lips. "I'm not scared of anyone or anything. I know how to fight and survive on my own. I know all the secret routes in to, and out of, Fertilian. My parents taught me," she said and eyed V expectantly.

Emmo trilled and launched herself from the table onto V's chest. V waited for the caterpillar to settle around her neck before replying to the Fert girl, who visibly thrummed with anticipation.

"We will assist Queen Jessima to take back the throne from this Charlotte Thorne and the traitor Denya. We will deliver the country back to Jessima, for she will aid us when the time comes. Charlotte and Denya will not, for they have their own agenda."

Joanne looked as if she wanted to jump on the spot. But Lizya's grip kept her firmly grounded. "Oh, thank you, thank you!" the girl exclaimed.

"Go and train with our warriors, there are many new skills you will learn."

Joanne's grin stretched from cheek to cheek as Lizya deposited her into the hands of the warrior guards in the hallway and closed the door.

"So," Lizya said as she returned to her seat. "We need to go and fix this mess in Fertilian."

V nodded.

"And find this weapon," Lizya continued, "which we'll use to fight our enemy coming from the east."

V nodded again.

"Well, we'd better get planning then," Lizya said with a laugh.

"If I may interrupt," Zecky said. "I appreciate we need the numbers, but I am still concerned about giving the peons knowledge of how to fight. We have spent the past one thousand years weeding that out of them. We all know about the Xayy atrocities."

"I have no intention of taking Peqkya back one thousand years and allowing the peons to repeat the Xayy atrocities. They will fight with us for their country. Not against us," V said.

"And after this war?" Zecky said.

"There may not be an after," Sarry replied.

All looked at the wolf and a chill settled over the room at the proclamation.

Zecky tutted. "There is always an after, my dear."

But Sarry wasn't listening, she gazed out of the window, distracted.

V suppressed a shudder. *There may not be an after.* "Robya, tell us what you have learnt of our enemy from the Sema male," she said to change the subject.

The scholar replied in a timid voice, "It seems they are winged creatures with an incredible power. The Sema male could not articulate, but I think there is some kind of magic ability. They—"

But Robya's commentary stopped dead as Sarry shot up. Her stool flew backwards and clattered on the floor. She leapt to the window.

V moved to her side, closely followed by Darrio and the others in the room.

Sarry pointed skywards.

A huge swarm of birds passed overhead, travelling east. It darkened the sky, the beating of wings and squawking of scores of birds was deafening. The warriors in the training yard below paused to watch the sky as Peqkya emptied of its birds.

Sarry's orange eyes glowed. "They are coming."

ALSO BY ROSALYN KELLY

Want to delve deeper into this world? All my stories are set in The Known World, which centres on the mountain realm of Peqkya and its surrounding neighbours. These countries include Fertilian, Drome, Troglo, Zwullfr and Majute.

NOVELS
In the Heart of the Mountains
Melokai
Violya
Book Three – coming soon

NOVELLAS
The Sand Scuttler
The Fall of Vaasar

SHORT STORIES
Peonhood
The Tunnel Runner
The Clash at Jagged Canyon
Ruby's Return

AUTHOR'S NOTE

Enjoyed what you just read? I would be very grateful if you could take a couple of minutes to leave a review (even if only a few lines) on the book's online sales page at the store you purchased it from. Reviews help other readers to discover the trilogy and your help in spreading the word is hugely appreciated.

VIOLYA is the second instalment of the *In the Heart of the Mountains* trilogy. Book Three is coming soon.

Get a free ebook of THE FALL OF VAASAR here: www.rosalynkelly.co.uk/free-book

This prequel novella is set 2,000 years before MELOKAI (*In the Heart of the Mountains Book One)* and tells of the event that sparked the bitter, bloody feud between the countries of Fertilian and Drome.

Subscribe to my email newsletter to be notified when Book Three is released, and for giveaways, price promotions, free books, free short stories as well as exclusive extra content. You can sign up here: www.rosalynkelly.co.uk/subscribe

Thank you for taking the time to read VIOLYA.

Rosalyn Kelly
November 2019

ABOUT THE AUTHOR

Rosalyn Kelly grew up in the magical New Forest in the south of England and has lived around the country as well as in the Middle East, and travelled all over the world.

She studied English Literature and Language at Oxford Brookes University before embarking on a PR and marketing career.

After ten years telling the stories of international brands and businesses, she decided the time had come to tell her own and quit her job to write. Her debut novel MELOKAI was published in 2017. Her second novel VIOLYA was published in 2019.

The inspiration for her epic fantasy trilogy came when she was trekking in the mountains of Nepal's stunning Annapurna Sanctuary.

When she's not putting her heart and soul into writing book three of the *In the Heart of the Mountains* trilogy, she daydreams about where to travel to next, paints with acrylic, reads voraciously and writes book reviews on her blog.

Keep in touch:
Website www.rosalynkelly.co.uk
Blog www.rosalynkelly.co.uk/blog
Twitter www.twitter.com/rosalynkauthor
Instagram www.instagram.com/rosalynkauthor
Goodreads www.goodreads.com/rosalyn_kelly
Facebook www.facebook.com/rosalynkellyauthor
Pinterest www.pinterest.com/rozkelly

ACKNOWLEDGMENTS

Massive shout-out to my mum, Ann, who reads all my stories and champions all my efforts. She gives me invaluable feedback every time and I'm beyond grateful for her selfless support.

To my dad Brian, for all his encouragement and my sister Kathy, for all her help with my sales descriptions – you both rock!

A gigantic big up to my brave and dedicated beta reader, Becky, who tackled the first draft. And huge appreciation goes out to my editor Amanda J Spedding who totally 'got' where I was coming from and was a joy to work with.

Much love to all my enthusiastic friends and family who continually encourage me and inspire me. The fantasy author community also deserves special mention for being a bunch of brilliant, creative, kind and collaborative folk.

And finally, thank you to my readers. I promise to keep writing and entertaining you for as long as I can!

Rosalyn Kelly
November 2019

APPENDIX 1 – CHARACTERS

PEQKIANS:
Violya (V) – distinguished warrior with magic
Melokai Ramya – ruler of Peqkya, *deceased*
Sybilya – ancient prophetess, known as Stone Prophetess
Chaz – eunuch, Melokai's councillor. Head Scholar
Lizya – distinguished warrior
Emmya – distinguished warrior, *deceased*
Monya – young warrior, looks like Emmya
Zekya (Zecky) – Head Speaker and councillor
Rivya (Riv) – ex-Head Trader and councillor, instigated plot to overthrow Melokai Ramya
Omya – Head Teller and councillor
Jozya (Joz) – assistant trader
Robya – apprentice scholar
Ashya – high ranking warrior, *deceased*
Toya – ex-assistant trader, part of plot to overthrow Melokai Ramya
Naomya – Mother of Mothers and councillor
Steely (Lamaz) – leader of the peon rebellion
Laurya – warrior captain
Finya (Fin) – warrior captain, sent to Troglo
Daya – distinguished warrior
Parzya – warrior at Mlaw village
Urya – young scholar from Mlaw village
Denya – warrior captain leading 1,000 warriors in Fertilian
Terya – Melokai Ramya and Gwrlain's baby, *deceased*
Artaz – Melokai Ramya and Ferraz's child
Mother Samya – leads pen that Artaz was in
Emmo – V's pet caterpillar from Majute
Freya – one of the Peqkian women kidnapped by the Trogrs
Stone army – army of men that Sybilya cursed and turned to stone
Amya – V's clevercat messenger

Marshya – warrior, deserted Captain Denya in Fertilian
Strongcat Otiss – tiger, leader of the 100 Strongcats in Peqkya
Melokai Naranya – ruled before Melokai Ramya
Ferraz – pleasure giver, part of plot to overthrow Melokai Ramya, *deceased*
Hanya (Hanny) – High Courtesan and councillor, *deceased*
Gosya (Gogo) – Head Warrior and councillor, *deceased*
Bevya – Melokai's clevercat messenger, *deceased*
Melokai Annya – ruled in Year 500 and brokered the truce with the Trogrs
Melokai Tatya – ruled in Year 700 and during her reign the last known sighting of a wolf was recorded during the Wolf Expulsion, 300 years previously

WOLVES:
Darrio – wolf, father of three
Harro, Warrio – Darrio's sons, yearlings
Sarrya (Sarry) – Darrio's daughter, yearling, first standing female wolf, leader of the wolves
Arro – alpha male of Wulhor-Aaen wolf pack
Lurra – alpha female of Wulhor-Aaen wolf pack, *deceased*
Ricarro – son of Arro and Lurra, yearling
Zerra – alpha female of Arracht-Aaen
Navrro – beta wolf of Arracht-Aaen, son of Zerra

DROMEDARS:
Our Ruler Mastiq el Wakrime – ruler of Drome. Has 23 known children with 1 official wife and 200 in harem
Crown Prince Ammad el Wakrime – Mastiq's heir. Second eldest son of Mastiq and fifth child
Hallid – eldest son and first child of Mastiq, alcoholic. Mother is Mastiq's official wife
Jakira – mother of Ammad and Selmi, a favoured concubine of Mastiq
Selmi (Sel) – second son of Mastiq and Jakira, brother of Ammad. Sixth son of the ruler, eleventh child

Zeead Medra – High Priest
Whaled – Minister of War
Razanne – Whaled's daughter
Qabull – Ammad's most trusted guard with scar from ear to mouth, *deceased*
Baghadd – friend of Khumarah's palace insider, son of a cook
Samma – old chief in Urakbai village, *deceased*
Medi – Jakira's head slave
Nameeri – Khumarah infiltrator in Drome army
Samark (Street Sam) – Ammad's combat trainer
Gad – Ammad's weapons instructor
Ibin el Khumarah – leader of the Khumarah clan
Advisor Farack – long-term advisor of Mastiq
Our Ruler Shaan – deceased, assassinated. Mastiq's father, Ammad and Selmi's grandfather
Jarack – chief of New Urakbai village
Ackbah – Khumarah clan member, raised by Ibin

FERTS:
King Hugo Cleland – rightful King of Fertilian, he has ruled for 24 years. (Known by his family as Hugo Salmon, Cleland is the royal family name). Eldest son of Princess Olivia and Lord Ernest Salmon
Queen Jessima Cleland (nee Walter) – King Hugo's third wife
King Edward – deceased, murdered by false King Benjamin. Parent of Olivia. Grandparent of King Hugo, Ernest Jnr, Edward, Charles and Toby
Princess Olivia – deceased, natural causes in old age. Mother of five sons: King Hugo, Ernest Jnr, Edward, Charles, Toby.
Lord Ernest Salmon – deceased, assassinated. Husband of Princess Olivia and father of King Hugo, Ernest Jnr, Edward, Charles, Toby.
Prince Ernest Jnr (Ernie) – brother of King Hugo. Second son of Princess Olivia and Lord Ernest Salmon.

Current Lord of Lian

Prince Edward – brother of King Hugo. Third son of Princess Olivia and Lord Ernest Salmon. Presumed dead, lost at sea

Prince Charles – brother of King Hugo. Fourth son of Princess Olivia and Lord Ernest Salmon. Chief Cleric in Lian

Prince Toby – brother of King Hugo. Fifth son of Princess Olivia and Lord Ernest Salmon. Army General

Queen Jayne – deceased, in childbirth. Second wife of King Hugo. Mother of Princess Georgina

Princess Matilda – eldest daughter of King Hugo, mother is King Hugo's first wife, Gracie, deceased. Married to Lord John Iddenkinge. Has two children, Johnny Jnr and Grace

Princess Georgina – second daughter of King Hugo, mother is Queen Jayne. Married to Lord Hadley Smyth

False King Benjamin Thorne – deceased, murdered by King Hugo. Ruled for 15 years until Hugo's rebellion. Took Kingdom by force from King Edward. Married to False Queen Charlotte. Father to twins Arthur and Mary

False Queen Charlotte Thorne – Wife to Benjamin and mother to twins Arthur and Mary

Mary Pullman (nee Thorne) (Miserable Mary) – eldest child of false King Benjamin and false Queen Charlotte, her twin is Arthur. Married to Lord Clement Pullman. Has one child, James. Other three have died in infancy

Arthur Thorne (Awful Arthur) – Only son of false King Benjamin and false Queen Charlotte, his twin is Mary. Widower – has had four wives, all deceased. Has three children, eldest son is Jeremy

Lord Clement Pullman – wealthy lord, married to Mary Thorne

Lord John Iddenkinge – elderly lord, married to Princess Matilda

Jeremy Thorne – Arthur's eldest son, betrothed to Grace Iddenkinge

James Pullman – only child of Lord Clement Pullman and Mary Thorne

Grace Iddenkinge – daughter of Princess Matilda and Lord John Iddenkinge, King Hugo's granddaughter. Betrothed to Jeremy Thorne

Lord Alon Sumner – army general, oversees South East watch on Mary for King Hugo

Lady Cynthia Sumner – Alon's wife

Marcy, Tina – Jessima's handmaids in Cleland Castle

Lord Andrew Chattergoon – oversees the Lian tunnels for King Hugo

Elmgard – hapless soldier turned spy

King Edgar – ruled two thousand years previously, captured Vaasar from Drome which he renamed Lian

Geraldina – Jessima's sister

Lord Sebille Salter – instrumental in Benjamin Thorne's seizure of the throne from Edward Cleland

Kerrin Smith – Lord Chattergoon's wife, known as the Scorpion Hunter, mother of five children (Joanne and Philip), pregnant

Joanne Chattergoon – eldest child and daughter of Lord Andrew Chattergoon and Kerrin Smith

Philip (Lip) Chattergoon – second child and eldest son of Lord Andrew Chattergoon and Kerrin Smith

Edward Hugo Cleland (Eddie) – Jessima's son with Toby, but all think he's Hugo's child

Betsy – Prince Ernest's dog

Martha – medic in Lian

Fiona – displaced Cleland City resident

Annette – Lian resident housing Fiona, works at fish market

Lady Jane Fletchling – noble Lian resident

TROGRS:
Gwrlain – Trogr from cave nation of Troglo
Gruack – Gwrlain's mother
Lulac – Gwrlain's sister

Bance – Gwrlain's friend and lover of Lulac
Daneil – Gwrlain's father
Efram – male from Sema

JUTES:
Brinjinqa (Brin) – Captain of 100 Jute fighters sent with
V
Utuli – Potenqi (ruler) of Majute

APPENDIX 2 – PLACES AND PEOPLES

Peqkya – realm ruled by women, high elevation, surrounded by mountains. People are called Peqkians (referred to as cats, hisspits). Called Xayy before Peqkya. Speak Shella language

Riaow – capital city of Peqkya, residents called Riats

Meliok mountains – circular mountain range that surrounds Peqkya to all sides (the north-east range is called the Small Mountains by the wolves)

Zyr Peq – highest mountain in the Melioks, north-east boundary

Mount of Pines – hill where Sybilya resides

Inaly Lake – vast lake on outskirts of Riaow

Mlaw – village on border with Majute

Qipaz – village in central Peqkya

Sarenky Sea – to the west of Peqkya

Jagged Canyons – to the north of Peqkya

Troglo – cave nation to the east of Peqkya. People are called Trogrs (referred to as cave creatures)

Lauago – capital of Troglo

Peqklo – small settlement in Troglo

Ashen Valley – where the stone army has stood for 1,000 years

Zwullfr mountains and wilderness – wolf territory, vast, remote, mostly snow-covered tundra and dense alpine forest that lies to the north-east of Peqkya, north of the Meliok Mountains

Wulhor-Aaen wolf pack – one of the many packs in the wolf territory

Aaowl Peak – highest and most iconic mountain peak in Zwullfr, shaped like the crescent moon

Wul-Onr Valley – Great River runs through the valley that separates the Zwullfr mountains to the north and the Small mountains (Melioks) to the south. (Called **Trequ Valley** and **Trequ River** by the Peqkians)

Lost Lands – area south of the Great River before the Small (Meliok) mountains

Drome – desert kingdom to the south-west of Peqkya, beyond the Meliok mountains. Shares a border with Fertilian. People known as Dromedars and speak Dromedari (referred to as desert rats, cammers)

Parchad – capital of Drome, situated within a giant crater

Orean – town near to Drome

New Urakbai – village in northern Drome on site of Urakbai

Jhabia Ridge – ridge of rock outside Parchad

Wakrime (royal), **Qacirr** (holy), **Tamadeen** (high status), **Affarah** (majority peasants), **Yuurnan** (desert villagers), **Eqmadeh** (nomads), **Khumarah** (the assassins) – ancient Drome clans

The Cuttarrs (cutthroats) – Drome Ruler Mastiq's elite guard

Fertilian – lowland kingdom to the south-east of Peqkya. People are called Ferts (referred to as southerners, thieves / occupiers). Speak Shella language

Lian – walled harbour city and major port on the Sarenky Sea in the west, linked to Fertilian by underground tunnels (called **Vaasar** by Dromedars)

Cleland City – capital of Fertilian, within King Hugo's lands

Rotchurch City – capital of Arthur Thorne's lands in Fertilian, north-east

Edester City – capital of Mary Thorne's lands in Fertilian, south-east

Yettle valley and Yettle Bottom plains – west of Rotchurch City

Froggerton – settlement far north of Fertilian, near Melioks

Majute – rainforest nation, people are called Jutes (referred to as pygmies, little people) and speak Juutayan

Ujen – capital of Majute

Qaziik, Janugah – ancient Jute tribes s